The Pomegranate Blooms

a novel by

Cindy L. Katri

This book is a work of fiction and, as such, is not intended to represent any real living or deceased person, place or situation. Any resemblance is coincidental. Any exercise training and descriptions are meant purely for entertainment purposes, not for instruction, and in no way will the author be held responsible should someone attempt to engage in the exercises described. Consult a physician and exercise expert before beginning any exercise program.

Cover Art by Josh Nelson, http://nelsonarts.tumblr.com

For the thesaurus with its words of love and confidence, and for everything before and after, I dedicate this book to my most magnificent parents, Lorraine and Sam.

CONTENTS

Acknowledgements

I must, of course, acknowledge my husband and daughters for putting up with my divided attention during the book-making process. As we know, life is short, so thank you for allowing me to grab this essential part.

A huge nod to my nephew Josh Nelson who designed the book cover artwork while keeping up with his architectural studies.

And one more THANK YOU to all my extended family and my friends. Our lives together inspire me—and teach me—on a daily basis.

Chapter 1

October

"HE'S NOT A BAD LOVER," thinks Suzanne as her husband of twenty-two years exercises—what? His abdominals maybe? His gluteus maximus? Anyway, she knows only those two muscles by name, and he exercises something as he grinds on top of her.

"Do you want it faster?" Joe asks, at least trying to satisfy her.

"That's okay," she says, a noncommittal answer that won't give her true thoughts away. If she were being entirely honest, she might have answered with her own question, "Do we *have* to do this?" But she's not being honest, and, in truth, she hasn't been for quite some time.

As Joe continues—he's broken a sweat now and looks like it shouldn't take too long—Suzanne thinks, as she has many times, about how they've ended up in the bedroom, again, on the bed with two distinct sides, his and her dips with a ridge down the middle exposing the nightly separation of the long-married. Spooning couples have no such great divide, do they?

A few more minutes and she can go to sleep.

Anyway, why do they always end up in the bedroom, in the bed? Probably because they start there, with the late night question, "Do you want to have sex?" It doesn't matter that both daughters are away in college, with every room in the house now fair game. With those six words—*do you want to have sex*—how can you end up in any place other than where you've had sex these past more than two decades?

She can tell he's almost done. Good thing, too, because she feels bone-achingly tired and needs sleep now. She has a meeting early tomorrow, and reports due later in the day and a rare evening out with her friends...

* * *

She awakens, the room still dark. A familiar sickening feeling washes over her, and she knows what's next. Sure enough, a moment later she feels the moustache of beaded sweat on her upper lip and the pooled perspiration between her breasts. It's October now, but it might as well be August. She looks first at the clock. The obnoxious, bright green numbers read four in the morning. Then she looks at her husband. He's asleep, snuggled into his sweatshirt and sweatpants. The entire nighttime clothing budget certainly rests on his side of the bed. Her thin tank top and cotton shorts surely didn't set them back too much.

From long experience, she knows she won't fall back to sleep any time soon. She gets up, turns on the standing fan pointed only to her side of the bed, grabs her iPad and climbs back into her spot, pushing her blanket under her legs to prop them up. She takes a deep breath of the fan-blown air, cooling her from the inside out.

She'd rather sleep, what with her long day coming up, but at least the iPad mind-freeing Apps are better than attempting to sleep while consciously thinking about all the things to think about that she doesn't want to think about.

Suzanne lowers the background light of the iPad, but it's still plenty bright to see Joe turn over, his large frame shaking the bed like a rolling boat. He seems to grumble something but quickly returns to his usual stock-still, restful sleep.

Suzanne sighs and begins her game.

Chapter 2

GIRLS NIGHT

"DID YOU WALK HERE?" ASKS Lori, stepping aside to let Suzanne through the front door and into the narrow hallway. Not waiting for her to answer, Lori turns her head and yells towards the back of her house, "Suze is here," then turns again to Suzanne.

"Yes, I walked here. Why do I get the feeling you're going to yell at me?"

"Because I don't want to have to drive you home. Not planning on abstaining tonight. Oh." She calls to the back of the house again. "I'm making Melon Balls. I know it's Melon Liqueur, vodka and orange, but someone's got to tell me the proportions. Look it up if you don't know." Back to Suzanne, "If I'm Melon-Balled, you'll have to find another ride home."

"It's two blocks, Lori. The same feet that brought me here will take me home."

"It'll be late. And dark."

Suzanne slips off her flats, pushes them against the wall next to all the other visiting shoes, and walks towards the back of the house, followed by Lori. On the way, Suzanne catches sight of her own reflection in the mirrored hall. "And I'm forty-nine, not four." Certainly the reflection confirms this. Just when she morphed into her mother's motherly, stomach sagging body, she doesn't know, but now that body partners her every move down the hallway. Not so with Lori. Like Suzanne, she has two children, but the strong genes of her still-shapely seventy year old mother serve Lori well. Suzanne has always hated this mirror. Okay, every mirror, in fact.

Dee, Marilyn and Fran, sitting at the dining room table, look up.

Dee asks, "You're only forty-nine, Suze?"

Suzanne nods.

"We let a baby play Bunco with us?" asks Fran in mock disgust.

As Lori reaches into the credenza and pulls out a large bottle of a shockingly bright green liquid, she lets the ladies know she's only forty-seven. "I think the better question is why Suze and I would bother spending time with you old farts."

Suzanne takes a look around the table. Actually, her friends look nothing like "old farts." They look damn good, in fact. Hard to believe they all have about ten years on her. She wants to ask how they dealt with turning sixty. Better yet, how they dealt with turning *fifty*, but, in truth, she's not about to bring up *that* conversation. She keeps quiet and takes a seat. Besides, she has another eight months until the five-oh. Eight months that will surely feel like eight minutes.

"Suze? You in there, honey?"

Suzanne focuses and sees Lori staring at her. "Sorry, just thinking."

"Well, you're not allowed to think without sharing, you know. That's Rule One of Bunco Girls Night Out."

Suzanne chuckles.

"What's funny?" Lori asks.

"Not funny. You sound like Joe. He has to know everything I'm doing and thinking."

"They all do," says Fran.

"But don't ask them a thing, right? 'Cause if you ask them a question, you get nothing, am I right?" asks Marilyn.

"Best friends need to know everything each other thinks. Husbands definitely don't. So, what were you thinking?" prods relentless Lori.

"You don't want to know."

"I *do* want to know."

"Okay. I was thinking how much faster time goes the older you get."

"You're right. I don't want to know. Next conversation..."

"Faster and faster," says Dee, staying on *this* conversation. "Ever watch a television show and then, in the series finale, they show the future of all the characters, speeding through the years so you see everything to the bitter end?"

"You think it's bad at fifty," pipes up Marilyn.

"Not fifty yet, be-otch," interrupts Lori.

Marilyn continues, "Whatever, Sunshine. Dee's right. The years will just get faster."

Fran adds, "One day it's New Year's and the next it's Thanksgiving."

Suzanne certainly did not mean to start all this. She looks forward to these nights as a necessary super-mini vacation from her real existence, as necessary as the escapist television shows she relies on as her usual alternative to a good stiff drink. "Changing the subject..."

"Thank you, since you started it," says Lori.

Suzanne gives her friend a look but continues. "Did

any of you see our favorite dancing show this week?"

The mood lifts immediately. Simultaneously, Dee and Lori say, "Yes," and then also sigh in unison.

Marilyn shakes her head. "Not yet, but it's DVR'd. Was it good?"

"O.M.G. He... was... spectacular!" Lori takes her seat, as though the thought of this man makes her weak kneed. "That Salsa. Holy shit."

"Who was, what Salsa?" asks Fran, confused.

"You don't watch it?" asks a disbelieving Dee.

"Watch what?"

Suzanne happily provides details. "'He' is Rafael, a Latin god: hulking, muscle rippling, washboard abs, and the sweetest personality."

Marilyn snorts on the last point.

"Hey, none of that. I agree with Suze," says Lori. "He really seems like he's a good guy. A good guy with the cutest accent—and lots more."

Suzanne turns to Dee and Lori, since they had seen the show. "Did you see the very beginning of the dance, when he grabbed his partner—what's-her-name—and he gave that smile? Total control, flirting with the audience—that was..."

"She's going to have an orgasm just talking about it," comments Lori.

"Let me tell you," Suzanne continues, not really disputing Lori's remark, "the way he handled that woman, his partner, whatever her name is—so much power, so sure of himself, and his eyes, never leaving hers. Hmm."

"You always go for those big, foreign guys," says Lori. "Joe's tall. Not foreign, though."

Joe *is* tall, at least most people think so. To Suzanne, he doesn't seem so tall any more.

"So you married him for his height?" asks Fran.

Suzanne would rather stay on the Rafael conversation, but she answers Fran's question. "I don't know about marrying him, but *maybe* that's why I agreed to date him." After a string of failed first dates, her grandmother had insisted upon the set-up with her grandmother's friend's nephew's son. The only thing her grandmother knew about him, besides him being over six feet, was that, according to her, he was a financier. "You like a tall man, don't you?" her grandmother had asked. A tall financier—certainly worth a look. What he turned out to be was a just over six-foot-one gawky, inexperienced man in a Finance department of an IT consulting company. They dated for four years until, one evening, when they were watching television together at her parents' house—where she still lived at the time— her father marched into the room, turned off the television, turned to the couple and asked, "So, when are you two getting married?" Joe was—still is—a kind soul, a good man at his core. A good core with a very difficult shell, but that was discovered after they married, as usually happens.

Suzanne relates the story—most of it—to the ladies.

"That's how you got engaged? How romantic," says Lori. "It brings a tear to my eye."

"Yes, well, that's Joe."

Dee complains that if she wanted this boring old married couple talk, she could have stayed home, and the ladies get down to their Bunco playing. They have a small group tonight—usually three more join—and since four is the magic number in Bunco, they take turns not playing. Suzanne sits out first but not for long, because the simple, dice-rolling game goes quickly. The simplicity also makes it easy to drink as they play, and they all—except for designated driver Dee—enjoy the

Melon Balls.

An hour later, they take a break to have some dessert prepared by their host.

"Is this the real stuff, Lori, or some of your fake shit again?" asks Marilyn. "Do I need to have the garbage pail ready?"

"Be daring. Taste it, and you tell me," answers Lori, a gleam of humor in her eye.

The chocolate cheesecake actually tastes great, but when Suzanne sees that Lori takes a slice, she figures she knows the truth. Turns out she's right. It's a trimmed down version of the classic original, with lots of hidden pureed, high fiber strawberries, but with flavors that good, who cares? Suzanne and the other ladies all take second helpings.

"Oh, Dee, can you give Suze a ride maybe? She walked here."

"And I told you I'll walk home, too. Got to work off the drinks and dessert."

Fran puts in her two cents. "Don't you pass that crazy Cybil's house, walking home from here?" Like both Suzanne and Lori, Fran had grown up in town, and everyone who grew up here, then or now, knows crazy Cybil. Many generations of walkers have avoided both her and her house.

"I think I can handle it."

"I seriously almost didn't buy this house," says Lori, "just because it's so close to hers."

"What are you, seven?"

"The real question, Suze, is how old *she* is. She seemed ancient when we were kids."

"When I was a kid, too. Ancient and creepy," adds Fran.

"Everyone seems old when you're a kid."

"Well, she can't be that old. She's still walking."

A while later, sober Dee packs a tipsy duo into her car, making sure Suzanne doesn't want the ride as well. Suzanne rolls her eyes, says thanks again to all for a fun evening, and sets off on her "long journey home." She hears the last of the car doors slam and looks up to wave goodbye to the back of Dee's silver sedan. The lights from the car soon fade, and Suzanne realizes the moonless night sky and a missing streetlight bulb have made for a startlingly dark street. She pulls her cell phone out and uses it as a flashlight, trying to resist the urge to regret the ride not taken.

Three doors down from Lori's house, the thought does enter her mind to cross to the other side of the street, avoiding Cybil's house completely, but she decides not to give in to the silly paranoia and stays straight on the sidewalk, opening and closing the cell phone to keep it lit. Just as she has almost navigated the width of the driveway, she hears a noise. She hesitates for a fraction of a second but then continues, beyond the driveway and a few steps away from the end of the property. Realizing she has been holding her breath, she starts to let it out when, suddenly, a figure dressed in a white flowing gown appears directly in her path. Taken so completely by surprise, her heart pounding out of her chest and into the top of her head, she thinks, "Run," but then a single word stops her, and she becomes the proverbial deer in headlights.

"Zuzanka," says a high pitched, ethereal voice. Zuzanka. Her name. Not the one by which everyone knows her but her true name, the one her parents had given her.

The wraithlike voice, the willowy, billowing dress with as many wrinkles as the face of the woman wearing it, the black night surrounding the white garb, the pale, iridescent skin seemingly shining out of the darkness, the name no one but her parents has ever used. A moment so beyond this world that Suzanne—Zuzanka—feels almost as if she's crossed into a different realm.

"I knew your mother, you know."

Suzanne somehow finds her own voice. "Hello, Miss Cybil."

"A very kind woman. An old soul, like yourself. You know, I told her so when you were born, that you had been here before... many times." The old woman hesitates, as though expecting a response. Suzanne has none to give, speechless, a little in awe, and irrationally but utterly scared of this ancient woman. After a brief moment, Cybil reaches into the voluminous folds of her gown and pulls out a small box. "I want you to have this," she says in a voice quiet yet filled with great pomp and circumstance. Then in an even softer, more sincere tone, she adds, "For your anniversary." The old woman has crept close to Suzanne, so close Suzanne can see her face clearly despite the darkness. No, not so wrinkled, although the reflection of the material had made it seem so. A smooth face, hiding no fears but telling no secrets. "You have lost your path, dear child. I pray this helps guide your way back. Use it well." The woman presses the box into Suzanne's hands.

Suzanne looks down and, although she knows she should not accept it, she cannot help but pull the top from the box. Inside rests a long silver chain, and attached to that chain she sees a small crescent shaped medallion. It appears filigree-like, but, shrouded in the darkness, she can't tell for sure. What if the old woman, in confusion, has given away something truly valuable? After all, her age must be quite advanced and confusion seems quite likely. She looks up to say a polite and genuine "thanks but no thanks" but finds she stands alone. Well, the woman had appeared without any sound or warning, why shouldn't she depart the same way?

Suzanne decides to bring the necklace to her house, take a closer look at the curious object and then return it to Cybil in the light of the morning. Coincidentally, just at this moment, the streetlamp buzzes and, a fraction of a moment later, shines once again. Since it's still not enough light to get a good look at the gift presented to her, she sticks with the plan and heads for home.

Chapter 3

THE ARGENTINE TANGO

As soon as she steps into the house, Suzanne heads directly for the kitchen with its bright, almost harsh light. She opens the box once more and takes a close, long look. In fact, she can't stop staring at the strange gift bestowed upon her in such an unusual manner. The charm hangs on an unremarkable silver chain, but the medallion itself—an elaborate filigree, just as she had thought—looks like some abstract flower or plant. Rather, half an abstract flower or plant. Did someone snap it in two, or was it designed this way?

When she can finally pull herself away from the necklace, she pours and drinks a tall glass of water to ward off the inevitable Melon Ball headache. Shortly after, with the gift in hand, she makes her way upstairs to her bedroom. She finds Joe asleep in bed, the soft night table light on but certainly not bothering her snoring husband. She readies herself for bed as quietly as she can, although the proverbial herd of elephants wouldn't wake him now.

A short while later, Suzanne takes a sip of water from the bottle she keeps on her night stand then turns off the light and leans her head back on her double pillow. Knowing she needs to fall asleep soon to be alert for her day ahead, she tries to fill her head with thoughts of the evening in order to lull herself into unconsciousness. She chuckles at the thought of her outspoken friends then looks over at her sleeping husband. What a shame, but she looks forward more to a date with those friends than she does to an evening with Joe, with whom she bickers and finds they don't want to do the same things, eat the same foods, or even watch the same movies or television shows. Oh, television. Yes, that's a good thing to think about to try to fall asleep. Rafael Derosa—who wouldn't want to think about him? Yardstick broad, exactly the right tall, an exquisite creature, oozing sexuality. Just the thought of him makes her...

Joe snorts in his sleep, and Suzanne laughs at his timing. She thinks, "Well, maybe I can get lucky in my dreams." She rolls to her side, her back to her husband, not even realizing she still holds the necklace. "To be a young woman in the strong arms of..."

*   *   *

Well, what a weird dream. This place looks vaguely familiar, though. Maybe I've been here before—when I was awake, I guess. Definitely have seen this, but it looks like backstage someplace—the heavy long curtains, the wires. What are those—big theater lights? But when have I ever been backstage any place?

Maybe I should take a little walk around. I kind of feel like an intruder, but, after all, this is *my* dream, so I guess I can intrude wherever I like. Oh, that looks like some kind of scenery. Looks pretty fake up close, with its painted broad strokes and bright colors, but I bet when you see it on the stage it looks much better. And, next, a bank of mirrors which look like make-up stations. I know I don't belong, but I take a seat at one of the high chairs in front of the rectangular mirrors, anyway. Oh my god—who is that? That's not *my* reflection in the mirror! I move my head to the right. Yes, the image follows. How bizarre! I don't think I've ever dreamed about someone who's not me. I move my head again, a slow nod. The image again follows. Well, maybe it is me, just a different me. A young me, except that's not what I looked like, hmm, I'd say maybe twenty-five, thirty years ago. That girl in the mirror, she's a pretty twenty-something, blond, only a single chin, petite nose. And those translucent green eyes. Nice. Maybe I should see what else I've fixed on my body in this dream of mine.

I push back the chair and stand. Wow—the body I've never had. Is that a bra giving that incredible shape? I look down—oh, I'm wearing the cutest soft green dress, an A-line which falls low on top and short on the bottom—and gently tug at the V-neck collar so I can see my boobs. Okay, I have never worn that lacy a bra in my life, and certainly it wouldn't be holding up anything that wasn't holding itself up. I'm liking this body more and more, from the flowing blond tresses to the two inch strappy heels. I take a walk again, now that I know I'm wearing heels I've never been able to handle in real life. It feels so natural. Short dress, high heels. I feel so tall and leggy.

My walk takes me to another area of the stage, and I stop quickly. I thought I was in my own little wonderland, but someone else has joined me. A tall, broad, male someone. He stands with his back to me, but I swear, like this whole backstage area, he looks familiar. He seems to count while moving his hips just the barest bit, side to side. Small movements, like he's practicing a dance mostly in his head, and he turns, head down, concentrating. Even in his minute gestures, I can see he's graceful. And even though I can't see his face, that gnawing feeling of familiarity won't go away. Wait a second, of course I know him! I gasp out loud because, dream or not, it startles me to see Rafael Derosa standing right before me.

Rafael—can you believe it? Rafael!—seems to hear my small, surprised sound and looks directly at me. He is glorious. More glorious, more attractive than on the small screen. A deep chest, brilliantly wide shoulders, thighs almost bursting from his jeans—all in magnificent 3-D. Oh. He definitely looks so much better in person than on my fifty-inch high definition television. Okay, so a dream's not really in person, but it sure feels that way.

He's still looking at me, with his deep brown, puppy dog eyes. Oh, crap, he's walking over to me. He's walking, anyway, and I think it's towards me. There's no one else here, right? I turn my head ever so slightly to the right, straining to see as far around me as possible without seeming to look. Then to the left. No one. Alone with Rafael Derosa. Well, really, I'm alone with my husband, who's sleeping next to me. Wait. Why am I even thinking of that? Rafael Derosa is... about to talk to me.

"Hello."

There, he did it. He spoke. To me.

"Hello?" Why did that come out like a question?

"I am sorry to bother you, but do you think you can help me, just for a moment?"

He wants my help. That accent. So... oh. He wants my help.

"Sure?" A question, again? I'm an idiot.

"I must practice my tango. The Argentine tango. My partner, she had, she must... I'm sorry, my English is not so good."

"No, it's fine," I reassure. And anyway, who cares? "She is not here for now. So you can dance with me the tango?"

"Okay." Okay?! I don't know how to do the Argentine tango! I don't know how to do *any* tango!

He steps closer to me. So close to me. Rafael is standing next to me. He's reaching for me, my hand, and pulls me even closer. I think I'm going to faint. Okay, Suze, just remember you're lying in bed. You can't faint when you're already lying down.

"What is your name?" With his face right next to me, I can feel the tickle of his breath. Before I can answer, he says, "Oh, I know. Shoshanna, no? The makeup girl. Sorry. Woman. Yes?"

"Yes." Well, how could I say no? Shoshanna? Makeup? Okay, why not?

"Okay, then, Shoshanna. We dance." He's holding a small remote, which he clicks, and the beginning strains of a song—how do I know that's the *Assassin's Tango?*—start to play.

We hold still as the music starts, the violin roughly hitting the strings, the firm but gentle stroke of the piano, the guitar's enticing, deliberate notes. The sound fills the entire backstage area. Then, as slowly as the wide vibrato from the violinist's skilled fingers, he runs his leg up from my ankle to my thigh, keeping the rest of his body, and mine, absolutely still. The rough denim almost chafes my skin in a tantalizing sensation. And then he begins to move, intentionally slow but purposeful. My body follows. It feels natural, as though I've been dancing the Argentine Tango, the *Assassin's Tango*, for years. Except the only experience with it, with dance at all, has been watching on television. Watching *him* on television.

With fluid movements, we cross the area back and forth. I don't know how, but I know the dance. Even so, I'm surprised as he flicks his massive leg between mine—so high it momentarily pulls up my short dress. I return the flick, careful not to hit the wrong spot. Even in a dream I don't want to damage Rafael.

Suddenly, his strong arms pick me up, my legs encircle his hips and he twirls the both of us around. I can feel him intimately rub against me. No, I shouldn't think like that. We're just dancing. He sets me down, the piano pounding, and I vaguely register a drum added into the mix. I savor his strong leading movements while over and over he pulls me towards him, slams me into rock hard muscles for only a second and then pushes me away. Delicious, cruel, teasing torture. The music crescendos, the violin saws across the strings and Rafael and I alternate staccato and smooth movements. How am I doing this? And while I pray for the dance to continue—I wouldn't mind for the rest of the night—I can tell the end nears. On the last beat, he yanks me to his chest, and the music stops.

We do not move, except for some winded breathing. Very softly, he says, "You are a wonderful dancer."

I manage to whisper, "Thank you."

"You must have been watching me practice, hmm? To know the dance?"

I don't answer. I don't *have* an answer.

Reluctantly for me—and, by the slow way he moves, I think for him as well—he gently pulls away. Who am I kidding? He probably just feels tired. On the other hand, this is obviously my fantasy, so if I feel he doesn't want to stop touching me, he does not, right?

He looks directly into my eyes. "Thank you," he says for the second time. "That helped so much." Such a soft voice, and his smile lights up his face. It lights *me* up, and I smile in return. We stay like that for a few more seconds, and then he asks, "Do you only do women?"

What?! I thought we were having an amazing moment, and then he so brusquely asks me if I'm gay?! But he touches his face, and the movement makes me realize he means the makeup. I'm the makeup girl—woman—after all.

"I will ask for you." His smile widens.

Oh, my.

"For my makeup." He bends quite far to be on par with my face and delivers a chaste kiss. Although we barely touch, in that fraction of a second I feel his lips, so firm and smooth. He says, *"Buenas noches,"* holds the gaze of my eyes once more, gives me his charming, disarming smile once more, then turns and walks away.

I stand in place for the few more seconds it takes for him to disappear behind the curtain.

Well, that had to be just about the best damn dream of my life.

Chapter 4

GLAD I CAME

SUZANNE SHOULD BE WORKING, BUT she has a hard time concentrating. She leaves her cubicle—the intensely non-private four foot space with sides hardly higher than her head—for the third time, taking her cell phone with her, and looks for the privacy of an unoccupied huddle room.

She finds one and quickly and quietly enters, closing the door before she dials. The last two times she tried, Lori's phone rang and then went to voicemail. This time, Lori answers. "Everything ok? I see you called a bunch."

"Everything's fine."

"Good. I got nervous. You don't usually call during the day. Aren't you at work?"

"Yeah, but I just had to tell you about this dream I had last night."

"Seriously? A dream? It's juicy?"

"Yes, I would say it's juicy."

"Yum. Oh, hold on one minute. I think that's Hal." Lori clicks off.

Well, that's the end of that, Suzanne realizes, and a moment later, Lori returns, confirming. "I've got to speak to him. I'll call you back, okay?"

Suzanne says, "Okay," but she knows, as well-intentioned as Lori may be, she won't call back. Not today, anyway. Ah, well, it will just have to wait.

* * *

"I went to the dry cleaner and got your shirts." Because Suzanne got home a little late, finishing up the work she had neglected during regular hours, she and Joe dine on cold sandwiches for dinner.

"I was going to do that."

"Okay. I did you a favor."

"I have to go over to CVS anyway, so you wasted your time."

Sometimes, many times, it doesn't pay to be nice. "Apparently so," she mutters and takes a bite of her mayo-less turkey on wheat, moistened only by veggies in her constant battle against her widening hips and drooping stomach.

Joe's sandwich does not miss the flavorful and more fattening condiments, since he has no bulge in his midriff. "So, did you talk to your boss about adding that position?"

Suzanne doesn't like her boss much and tries to speak to him as little as possible, especially today when she preferred to remain in her dream-world bubble. And, honestly, it proved hard enough just to squeeze in work between daydreaming and trying to talk to Lori, who still hasn't called her back.

"Nope. Didn't get a chance today."

"You should have spoken to him," chides Joe. "Your busy season's coming up. If you don't get that position filled soon, all that extra work will fall totally on you—again."

It's not even worth responding to him. It's Suzanne's business, and she does, indeed, know what she's doing.

Except, in Joe's mind, Suzanne's business is *his* business—and that's not limited to work. If she goes to the bathroom, it's, "Where are you going?" If she gets a text, it's, "Who's texting you?" And he pushes until she answers. But reverse the situation...?

As if on cue, Joe's cell phone rings. He puts down his sandwich and takes the phone out of his pocket. After a quick look at it, he hits reject and puts it away once again.

"Who was that?" she asks.

He responds just as she expects—a shake of the head, a click of the tongue and silence.

Silence through the rest of the simple meal, including the washing up, and extending to television time as well. She sits on the couch and watches. He occupies the love seat in the same room but seems miles away, paying attention only to his laptop.

After a while, Suzanne leans over and gets really comfortable. Of course, lying on the couch and watching television after a day at work means she quickly falls asleep. Fortunately, Joe has learned not to wake her up. It took many years to convince him, but now, instead of startling her awake with, "Wake up, you fell asleep. Why don't you go upstairs to bed?" he quietly turns off the television and the family room light and leaves her to come to bed herself.

When she wakes in the darkened family room, it's close to midnight. She stumbles up the stairs, goes through the master bedroom where Joe already sleeps, and passes into the master bathroom. Half, or more, asleep, she manages to clean her teeth, wash her face and brush her hair, cursing herself the whole time for not thinking to take care of all this before she even sat down to watch her shows, so that now she could have swiftly fallen into bed.

She climbs in next to Joe—not too close, of course, because of the big, separating bump in the middle. As she moves her pillow around so it cradles her neck in just the right spot, she touches something. She'd forgotten to remove the necklace from her bed. Literally too tired to move another muscle, her hand stays right there, touching the thin charm. She quickly falls asleep, with only enough consciousness to hope she'll repeat the dream from the night before. One never seems able to dream the good ones again, but no harm wishing...

*   *   *

I can't believe it actually worked! I'm here, backstage again, near the makeup mirrors. I quickly take a peek in the closest mirror. Yup, that's me. Well, not the real me, but the me from the dream last night. Curiously, though, I'm in different clothing. My dress—a deep purple with an empire waste—seems a little shorter. The shoes differ as well, with thin straps crisscrossing up my calf. What else can I say—it's all incredibly sexy. *I'm* incredibly sexy. Well, no time to waste, and I take the same turn I did last night when I ran into Rafael. I realize I'm holding my breath. I desperately want to find him here, but I'm trembling with fear at the same time—or maybe it's in anticipation—as I look around for him. I'm immediately disappointed. I don't see him, at least not where I found him last night. So much for dreaming the same dream. My mind has played a cruel trick on me. Probably I'll be bumping pelvises with that crazy guy on the show, the one I can't believe wasn't kicked out yet, the one I can't believe made it onto the show in the first place because I've never even heard of him before. He looks like a gigantic lollipop, with bright orange leggings and a multicolored shirt fitting snuggly over his overly round torso. Eye candy with a whole new meaning. I hear footsteps. Great, I bet that's Mr.

Lollipop now.

But it's not him. It's *him*, Rafael. My heart starts pounding immediately. So I *am* having the same dream, after all. I realize he won't recognize me and brace myself. Once again he looks straight at me as he approaches. His eyes don't leave mine, and I wouldn't shift mine from him for anything. But, wait. A smile? He's smiling at me? He didn't smile at me the first time, did he?

He's almost next to me when he stops and looks me up and down. "You look even lovelier than last night."

What?

"I asked for you, you know. Did they tell you?" He's right next to me now. He takes my hand, lifting it to his lips. He kisses me—my hand—and looks into my eyes. "*Did* they tell you?"

I give my head a little shake. If I tried to speak now, it would come out gibberish. Can I really be this lucky? Continuing my dream, not repeating it? Of course, that explains the different clothing!

Then he leans in close to my ear. "I really loved dancing with you last night."

"Me, too," I manage to say, my voice not shaking *too* much.

He continues, "I like to show you how I appreciate— is that how you say that word? Appreciate?"

I nod. It may be a thick accent, but he can say whatever he wants, however he wants to, and I wouldn't mind.

"So, I appreciate you helping me, and I want to show you by having dinner." He still holds my hand, and I feel his thumb gently stroking my palm. "At my home?"

Hyperventilation. He wants me to go home with him? Rafael wants me to go home with him.

"You know, the show, people see me and stop me all

the time now. We eat out in a restaurant and... I don't want you should have to be, um..." He struggles to finish the sentence. He shrugs. "You understand? It's too much. Too many peoples want to see me."

Too many women.

"So, maybe a quiet dinner, just for us? You understand?"

I understand. I think I understand. I *hope* I understand. I nod my head.

"Yes? You'll come home with me? Now?" He seems genuinely pleased—a little surprised I think, but definitely happy.

"I would love to," because, of course, I really would. For a split second I think of Joe, but, really? This is my dream. Guilt-free time. It's a *dream*.

*　*　*

A short while later I'm in the back leather seat of a luxurious Town car. Rafael, ever attentive, sits close to me, his hand on my knee and his eyes not leaving my face, even for a moment. With the privacy window up, we can't see or hear the driver.

"Is there something you don't like?" he asks.

Why? Am I giving off some strange vibe that I don't like something? I'm liking, I'm *loving* everything about this moment. I'm young, being driven to the home of a famous, not to mention absolutely gorgeous, hunk of man, about to have dinner, and I think, I hope...

"I eat almost anything, but some people, what is the word, 'pick?'"

Oh. He's asking if I don't like some foods. Right, we're about to have dinner. "Picky?"

"Yes, 'picky.'"

"I'll like anything." I certainly will. He's doing that thing with my palm again. How can something make me so absolutely relaxed and so incredibly turned on at the same time? *Mon dieu!* Wait—he speaks Spanish, not French. I don't know Spanish. I took French for six years. Why am I starting to panic? So many feelings, I think my head may explode—or something else. How much longer to his apartment?

He speaks again. "For how long you danced?"

Another question I can't answer, since I don't know how to dance, which won't make sense, since obviously I *do* know how to dance. So I redirect with, "Do you think maybe we can..." I feel so embarrassed asking and can't finish the sentence.

He senses my awkwardness. He's not really trying to make me feel worse, but he does seem to revel in my self-consciousness. It's like the experienced man-of-the-world knowingly seducing the innocent virgin. "Whatever you want, baby, I will give to you," he whispers in my ear.

Shit. This whispering thing, so exceedingly effective.

I gather up my nerves—it's a dream, it's *my* dream I remind myself—and shyly, looking away from his eyes, say, "Can we maybe... dance together again?"

"You want to dance with me again?" he asks.

I nod.

His dazzling smile broadens. "It was in my plans." With that, the car stops. Rafael looks out the window. "Home."

Before I know it, Rafael has jumped out of the car and come around to my side, opening it before the driver can do so. I see the driver step back as Rafael takes my hand and leads me out of the car. I look up. It's a tall apartment building, and, judging from the outside, quite fancy. He escorts me to the front door.

"Good evening, Mr. Derosa," says a well-clad doorman who pushes on the revolving door, starting its slow motion. It has two oversized sections rather than the usual three, and Rafael enters first, pulling me into the same section with him. It would usually fit two comfortably. With his large frame, though, I'm sure we're a tighter fit than most, but I don't complain about the proximity of our bodies in such a small space. He doesn't seem to mind either.

When we exit into the building's lobby—posh, like I thought, with more chandeliers in one place than I would normally see in a year—another similarly clad doorman greats us.

"Mr. Derosa," says the doorman to Rafael.

He gives me the once-over, at least I think he does. Aren't they supposed to be neutral and non-judgmental? So, why do I get the feeling he judges me, judges the fact that I'm going up to this terribly attractive, terribly young man's apartment to be alone with him?

"Miss," he adds.

Okay, maybe it's not a once-over. Maybe he's just greeting me. Is that guilt creeping in again? I push it away and smile back at the doorman as Rafael squeezes my hand and leads me to the elevator. "Have a good night," we hear as the elevator chimes, opens, and we walk in.

On the short ride up, I think about the doorman's choice of words. He said, "Have a good night." He could have said "good evening," which would mean he would see me again most likely before the evening ended. But he said "good night," implying he wouldn't see me until morning. Does he know that from experience? Does he say that to all of Mr. Derosa's *dates*? Crap, am I acting jealous now? Or maybe it's more like slutty guilt, going to an apartment of a man I hardly know. Because, of course, I *am* married.

I look up and see myself in the mirrored wall of the elevator. A young woman with long wavy blond hair, a slim physique, uplifted boobs. No gray, no dark circles under my eyes, no ring on my finger. And next to me stands a magnificent man, young but older than the me in the mirror, his hand gingerly touching the small of my back. As I watch, the hand moves up to my shoulders, where it plays with a few strands of my hair. The slight tug has that magical effect again, the one that's calming and stimulating at the same time. My mind suddenly frees itself of the nonsense thoughts of a moment ago, and my body responds to his touch.

The elevator chimes again, and the door slides open. We exit, and Rafael leads me to the end of the hall. He unlocks the door to 23F, pushes it open and stands aside to let me in. The apartment is dark except for one small light, which allows me to see my way in. As soon as I pass through the threshold, he joins me and turns on the high hats. They shine brightly, but he quickly turns the dimmer down to low.

Even in the faint light, I can see stark white walls and white, modern, minimalist furniture. It all looks cold and uninviting.

Rafael watches for my reaction, which I try to keep hidden. "The show, they give to me while I live here in New York. My home, it does not look like this," he apologizes. I guess my negative thoughts about the décor show.

He gestures to the extremely low, white couch. "Please, sit." I feel terribly awkward standing here, so I quickly do as he offers. At least it gives me something to do.

He leaves me and walks to the kitchen, which opens on the living room, but from my seat I really can't see him. I can hear some clinking of glasses and other movements, though.

I look around the room once more. Large, but not

ostentatiously so. Hard wood floors, a few enormous paintings on the wall which look like the generic decorator type, not a personalized collection. I look again at the couch I'm sitting on and hope I'll be able to stand from it later without looking like a clumsy old lady.

Rafael comes back into view with two wine glasses. Ignoring the rest of the long couch, he sits right next to me and holds out one of the glasses.

I can feel the heat off his body, or maybe it's just my own nervous sweat?

We both take sips. Well, mine seems more like a gulp. I can't believe I'm sitting next to Rafael. And so close. Another inch and I would be on his lap. And what a lap. Okay, now I'm not just sweating; I'm blushing.

I take another sip aka gulp. Silence. I take another. I'm such a lightweight, I think I'm starting to feel the effect of the alcohol, not that it stops me from taking another swallow, anyway.

What we need here is some small talk. "So, when you're not living in New York for the show, where *do* you live?"

"Los Angeles, most of the time. But I don't love it. And for now, as long as I stay on the show, I am here."

"That's good."

"Yes? You're happy I am here?" He has once again gotten hold of the ends of my hair and twirls it gently.

I have always loved having my hair played with, but his charged touch shoots electricity through my hair and into the rest of my body. I can hardly voice a simple, "Yes."

I take a sip. He takes a sip.

"The wine, it is okay? I should have ask what you like, but this is all I have."

"No, it's great. I like red."

"You're very sweet. It's okay, you know. You can say I am not the best hostess."

I chuckle. It feels good to laugh, not as awkward, but when I look at him again, he seems a little wounded.

"I say something wrong?"

Now I feel terrible. I put my hand on his leg for reassurance. Despite how obviously in shape he looks, the firmness shocks me, and, feeling awkward, I pull my hand away. He puts his on top of mine to stop me. I'm thrown for a loop and forget what I meant to say.

He prods me. "I think my English, it's not so good."

"Well, your English is better than my Spanish, which is non-existent. I took French."

He strokes my hand ever so softly. "Ah, *la lange d'amour. C'est bien.*" A Latin god speaking French. Just shoot me and my New Jersey accent now.

"So, what I say wrong? I need to learn."

"It's nothing."

"Please."

"Okay. A man is a 'host.' Not a 'hostess.' A woman is a hostess."

He laughs, which makes me feel better. "See, you help with more than my dancing. Oh." He suddenly puts his wineglass on the chrome table in front of the couch then jumps up, with ease and grace. "I promise to you a dance." He crosses the room to the entertainment unit. As he fiddles around with the electronics, I take a look out the floor to ceiling window. The lights of Manhattan seem to twinkle from far below. He sees me looking. "It's beautiful, right? Go. Take a closer look."

"No thanks. A little afraid of heights. I'm good from here."

"Oh, no, that's not good. You can't be afraid of things. Then you miss out. And life is short, you don't want to miss." He stands in front of me and grabs my hands, pulling me to my feet. That solves that problem. It's easy to get off the couch with his strong arms helping. He brings me over, closer to the window. When I resist, he does stop, but we're already a little too close for my comfort. He seems to sense this, and puts his arms around me from behind. He bows his head and rests it on my shoulder, our faces side by side. Well, that's much better to think about than the sheer drop that lies behind the glass window, except, really, it's probably more disturbing, with his hot breath teasing my neck.

Rafael lifts his head, and his arms turn me towards him. "I have been waiting all day to dance with you again." It's a whisper, a beseeching plea. I would love to say the same to him, but I find myself completely unable to speak, my breath so shallow. He keeps hold of my hand and leads me towards the entertainment center, where he selects a song.

The singing starts immediately as Rafael lets go of me and heads for the glass and chrome table. A soft male voice begins the song, crooning. Rafael pushes the table away from him, moving it easily, as though it were made of cardboard instead of thick glass. He gives it a final shove, and it rests against the couch. I realize he has just maximized the living room "dance floor." He turns and looks at me as the song continues to play. I know this one. It's *Glad You Came*. He smiles, and I get the sense he didn't pick this randomly. He starts walking towards me, beckoning for me to join him in the middle of the room. Although my legs feel like the clichéd jelly, I do as I'm told. The singer has temporarily stopped, leaving only the instruments. The tempo doubles. When we meet, he places his hands on the top of my thighs. The vocalist starts singing again, and we're off, dancing the cha cha. At least I think it's the cha cha. It's fast but still sensual, Rafael's hips so in time to the music, I would think he's a professional dancer.

With the space just large enough for our movements, Rafael leads me around effortlessly, covering every inch of open floor but never taking his mesmerizing eyes off me. He turns me around so my back touches his front, his hips moving against mine, guiding them in a wide circle. His feet, my feet, move so fast it's a blur even to me, and the beat of the song pulses as he continues to move me around the room. I have no power over my own body. He has total control. The turns, the steps, the way he thrusts his hips, as though he's inviting me, showing me what he is, what we are, capable of. It's a good thing I have no time to think. He moves my arms and my body follows, back and forth, away and back to him. Even when we stand still, he moves, rolling the bottom portion of his body against mine. I let myself just react. Hips, arms, circling, pulsing—don't think, I tell myself. Just move.

My back once more to his front, the pounding beat eases. He turns me to him, and we sway with the new tempo, slowing, until, by the last words, we hardly move.

When the music has come to a complete stop, we both breath heavily, as we did last night. I wonder if he feels this, too, this strange pull between us. As if in answer, he bends down, gently placing his index finger under my chin, his expression one almost of pain. He pushes up with his finger so that my neck stretches towards him. With great restraint he slowly leans closer, closer, until I finally feel his lips on mine. I can tell immediately this kiss—long and sensual, with full lips—does not resemble the first peck. He pushes into me so hard it backs me up until I am against the white wall, and still he pushes. I respond eagerly, reaching on tiptoes so I can throw my arms around his neck. I have never been kissed like this in my life.

Suddenly he stops, and I want to protest, but he quickly takes my hand and pulls me towards a doorway at the other end of the living room. As we walk he looks at me, as though asking for permission. I nod in silent acquiescence as we cross the room and enter the short hallway. A few steps in I see a door, and with his free hand, he opens it and swiftly leads me into a bedroom. I take little note of the room, except for an oversized bed. He wastes no time, taking off his shirt in one smooth movement. If I thought him glorious before, I had no concept. The smooth muscles on his perfectly hairless chest glimmer with the sweat of the dance. His arms bulge, and I can see how he can move furniture with ease, how he can move *me* with ease. Absolute perfection. The sight of him proves the greatest aphrodisiac I have ever experienced. My blood pools, and I yearn so much it hurts. Before I even see him moving, he rips off my dress. I catch a glance in the huge mirror across the room. Thank goodness I'm wearing a lacy bra and matching panties. Hardly anything to them, but that's probably what makes them appealing. And Rafael does seem to approve, as he gingerly touches the sides of the bra, feeling my breasts. He takes in a deep breath and sighs.

"I am afraid this won't be slow. I am sorry," he says, and then pushes me down onto the bed.

I expect him to follow, but he reaches instead to the side of the bed, opening a drawer. He pulls out a condom, and, in a flash, stands next to the bed, taking down his jeans and his underwear at once. When he stands again, I think a short squeal escapes from my lips. His patented smile follows. "You like?"

"Yes, very much," I say sincerely. And who wouldn't?!

His ass is so rounded and firm, with dimpled cheeks. Like a chiseled statue. And also hard like a statue is... oh, my.

He watches me look then quickly rolls the condom on. Before I can say I don't think the condom is necessary—it *is* a dream, after all—he joins me once again on the bed, on top of me but supporting his weight with his arms. I reach up to feel those arms, his triceps so perfect they must have been modeled by a master sculptor. If I was hot before, I think now I will incinerate.

Desperate to feel him on me, I try to pull him down, but he doesn't seem to notice. He pushes my skimpy bra aside with his mouth, and his tongue hungrily sucks my nipple. With every pull I feel a deep, agonizing tug of desire. Maybe in his world he calls this fast, but to me it's painfully slow.

As if reading my mind, in the next moment he has my panties off and thrown halfway across the room. He slips his hands under my ass and kneads it, moaning slightly. He looks me straight in the eyes and, without further hesitation, slams into me with the same controlled force he used so expertly on the dance floor. He moves himself and me at the same time. I feel these exquisite sensations over and over as he pulls out slightly and slams into me again and again.

This raw, physical sex, with everything steered by the unspoken, feels so unlike sex with Joe—where every movement ends up guided by words—I'm astounded. No, don't think of Joe. This is my dream—this incredible, porn novel sex—and I deserve to just sit back and enjoy. Well, not just sit back. I push into him, and this time he does feel it. He follows my lead and turns onto his back, swinging me on top of him. Now I can feel his hard chest underneath my hands, and it makes me want him even more. I can already feel myself quickening, and I move myself, the delicious friction finally starting to satisfy the ache. It takes only a few seconds to build, then I cry out as I feel myself exploding, a bright light bursting behind my closed eyes. Rafael stays still for about a half minute, except for a gentle stroking down my back. When he can feel I've completely finished, he turns us over, and I'm once again on my back. He starts moving, faster than before. I can feel myself building, and, in a moment, I come a second time. No scream from me now, but he lets out a long, low moan. His body relaxes, and I finally feel his full weight lying on top of me. If I weren't so spent, I could come again, just feeling him. After a moment, he pulls out, deftly holding the condom. He gets up and crosses to the bathroom, leaving me completely exhausted. He's back before I can catch my breath, laying on the bed to the side of my body but resting his head on my shoulder, above my breast. He moves his head and plants a soft kiss on my cheek.

"I'm sorry," he says. "I was too hungry for you. I should have given you food first."

"I like that type of hunger," I respond.

"Yes? It was okay?"

"No, it was not okay." Oh, no, he looks wounded again. "It was so much more than okay," I smile. He smiles back. I guess he's reassured.

He takes my head in his hand. "Thank you, Shoshanna."

Very obviously, I should be the one thanking, but I don't get a chance as he gives me one more long and very satisfying kiss.

*   *   *

From my high stool at the breakfast bar overlooking his ultra-modern, stainless kitchen, I watch Rafael prepare our simple dinner. He keeps apologizing for it, but, with food not really top of my mind at the moment, I'm absolutely fine with sandwiches. I enjoy watching him cook, though. Okay, so I would enjoy watching him do anything, especially in the shorts and tight tee shirt he threw on after our... time in the bedroom. I'm wearing one of his tee shirts as well, long enough on me to act as a dress. I think he spends as much time looking at me as I do watching him, which makes for a slow dinner preparation.

He's making traditional Cuban sandwiches, layering pork, ham, Swiss cheese, pickles and mustard on Cuban bread, making a point to say it's Cuban, not Italian bread.

"It's not fancy, but at least I show you something of my culture. So next we spread a little olive oil on the bread," which he does using his fingers. He looks intently at the bread and then suddenly turns his hand so he sees his dripping fingers, then he looks at me with that pained expression he had right before he kissed me in the living room. This time, though, he shakes his head, mumbles, "Later," and turns back to the sandwiches.

Well, I can certainly say the sight of olive oil and the word "later" have never had quite the same effect on me before. I squirm in my seat.

He puts both sandwiches into a large, flat pan then reaches into the cabinet overhead and pulls down two big cans of tomatoes. Before I get a chance to say I didn't know Cuban sandwiches have canned tomatoes in them, he places the cans on top of the sandwiches. I get it—a homemade press.

"You like to cook?" I ask him.

"I love to eat," he answers as he washes the oil off his fingers. "And feed pretty womens." He dries his hands on a towel and walks around to my side of the breakfast bar. "Because, you know, if you don't feed the womens," he reaches my chair and gently parts my legs so he can slide in between them, "they might leave." His firm thighs now press against mine, spreading them a little more. "And there is so much more I need to do to this woman."

He smiles, regrettably pulls back and returns to the sandwiches.

Really, this seems more like torture than dinner.

"My momma, she taught me how to cook. I used to sit with her in the kitchen, then she said I was lazy, so I had to help." He expertly turns the sandwiches over as he talks. "It's good to know, right? Oh, you want some more wine?"

"I'll get the glasses." I'd rather do something other than just sit here watching him. I won't make it through dinner if I keep getting so distracted. But do I want to make it through dinner? Okay, you see? Exactly why I need something else to do.

I go to the living room area and retrieve our glasses from the chrome table. Mine's not quite empty, and I down the rest in one big swallow. By the time I get back to the kitchen, I already feel a little lightheaded. Ah, well, I don't think I'm driving tonight, especially since I'm already sleeping. Okay, push that thought right out of your head, Suzanne. Shoshanna.

I uncork the wine sitting on the counter and pour us both some more. I'm actually starting to like this stuff. I mean, *really* like it. I look at the label. It's a Chappellet Cabernet Sauvignon. I wonder if it actually exists, outside my dream. I'll have to look it up.

Rafael takes the sandwiches out of the pan, cuts them diagonally and places them on two plates. He walks with them to the alcove dining room table and places one at the head and the other at the seat to the left before returning to the kitchen. He opens a glass cabinet door, takes out two tumblers and asks me what else I would like to drink. I raise my wine glass, but he insists I drink something non-alcoholic as well. He doesn't want me to get a hangover. I'm thinking that's pretty unlikely, considering the circumstance, but I indulge him. "Just water," I say. He fills one tumbler with ice and water from the refrigerator's dispenser then opens the stainless door and pulls out a tall bottle filled with a dark purple liquid.

We both head to the table. I place his wineglass at the head at the same time he goes to put my water at the catty-corner seat. Our arms touch. He looks down at me, a small shiver seeming to ripple through his body. I wonder if he can see the shiver pulsing through mine.

"We should eat. The cheese is not so good when it is cold."

We sit, and he immediately shakes the bottle he still holds, which looks like some kind of juice. He pours a bit into his glass. When he sees me looking intently, he asks, "You would like?"

"What is it?"

"Pomegranate juice. You never had?"

I shake my head. I've heard about it, of course, but we generally stick to boring old orange juice at home.

He lifts his glass to my lips. "You know, the pomegranate is also called a Chinese Apple." The liquid looks thick and has a strong, unfamiliar, although not unpleasant, smell. "Some people think this was the type of apple Eve off—what is the word? Gave to Adam." He tilts the glass a little more, pouring maybe a teaspoonful into my mouth. I'm surprised that it's not thick, but it does have a sweet and sour taste I'm not used to in a juice. I'm not sure I like it at first, but that doesn't stop Rafael from lifting the glass and forcing a second try.

Actually, when it sits on my tongue another moment, I realize I'm starting to enjoy this exotic flavor.

"It's good," I have to admit.

"Good. You share mine, and I share yours." He picks up my tumbler and takes a long swallow of the water. "We eat," he says as he puts down the glass and picks up a half of his sandwich, which he holds out towards me. "*¡Buen apetito!*"

That much Spanish I can understand. I pick up a half of mine and we "clink" the sandwiches together.

I take a first—completely satisfying—bite. The warm sandwich tastes slightly tangy from the mustard and oozes melted cheese. I feel a little olive oil on my fingers from the outside toasted bread. I look at Rafael, who eats hungrily. I realize I'm famished as well, and we both silently devour the first halves quickly.

Rafael downs the rest of his juice in one long gulp then reaches to the bottle for a refill. I notice the bottle itself has a bit of an unusual shape. He sees me looking and comments, "It's a sexy bottle, no?"

Funny, but I can see what he means. It's curvy, shaped like a well-endowed woman in a long, flowing A-line dress.

We pick up the second half of our sandwiches simultaneously. I've slowed down, with *that* part of my hunger somewhat satisfied. He takes much bigger bites than I do, and he's almost done when he looks at me again. I lick the oil and crust off my fingers. He throws the last bit of his sandwich back onto his plate, stands while pushing back his own chair and grabs the back of my seat, pulling it out from the table. He bends and picks me up. "I'm tall. The counter is good," and into the kitchen we go. He quickly but gently places me on the edge of the countertop. Like before, he pushes my legs apart, and I feel his strong, muscular thighs on mine, but this time he presses in much closer, and I can feel so much more...

Chapter 5

HAVANA ON MY MIND

SUZANNE SITS ACROSS FROM LORI. It's the first time either of them have visited this restaurant. They haven't tasted the food yet, but the décor seems authentic enough. Not that either of them have travelled to Cuba, of course, but the tropical artwork in blues and greens, the dark mahogany ceiling fans with the matching wood shutters separating the sections of the seating areas, all support their image of what it looks like, anyway.

"Why are you so hot for a Cuban lunch all of a sudden?" Lori asks.

Suzanne brushes her off with a half-assed reason. "It's a new place. I want to try it, but you know Joe. Not interested." That works but isn't the true answer. Except the real explanation—that she "ate" Cuban food the night before and wants to see what it actually tastes like—wouldn't really make sense.

The waitress brings the appetizer order of *empanadas* the friends will share. They each take one, filled with spicy chicken. The waitress had called them mild, but Suzanne sweats after just a couple of bites.

Despite the heat, she likes the *empanadas,* yet as she takes another mouthful, she feels the greasiness of the fried food and can't help thinking of the phrase that has the doughy goodness spending the rest of her life on her hips. She wiggles in her seat, and, even though she hardly moves, feels her weight shifting with her. When she bends her head while cutting another piece, she becomes acutely aware of her double chin. She weighed the same yesterday, so why is she suddenly so uncomfortable in her skin? It's obvious, of course. Last night she spent time in a healthier, younger, thinner, no-extra-flaps body. From the moment she woke up and rolled over, her body has felt heavy to her today.

Suzanne puts down her knife and fork.

"Don't like it?" asks Lori.

"Just saving room."

Lori has only taken a couple of bites of her own piece. She rips a packet of artificial sweetener and pours it in her iced tea. "So, talk. What's the deal? The *real* reason you wanted to do lunch today?"

"How can you drink iced tea when it's cold outside?"

"Don't avoid. How come you're here with me instead of spending your Saturday with your husband?"

Suzanne looks down at her hands. She sees Lori's well-manicured hands mixing the sugar substitute into her drink. Suzanne's hands pale—literally, since they lack nail polish—in comparison to Lori's.

"I had to talk to you."

Lori puts down her glass. "What's he done now?"

"Joe? No, it's not him."

"It's always him."

"It is not. He's not a bad man."

"Of course he's not a *bad* man. We've talked about this how many times? He's just annoying as hell and doesn't bother doing anything to make you happy."

"Oh, is that what he's supposed to be doing?"

"Don't make a joke. Your marriage shouldn't be a joke."

Lori sips her tea. Suzanne sips water with lemon then tents her hands by her mouth and nose and leans against them. She breathes in the citrus, a calming scent she has always loved.

"Okay, so you want to hear the real reason why I asked you here?"

Lori nods and sits back against the booth wall, waiting.

"Well, I asked you here," Suzanne gestures around her, "because I kind of had Cuban food last night, but I still have never really tasted it, and I wanted to try it."

"You know that doesn't make any sense, right?"

Exactly what Suzanne figured. "It does, really. I ate Cuban food but in a dream."

Lori takes another sip of her tea. "Okay..."

"The dream involved a hot man. A *very* hot man."

Lori puts down her knife and fork. She's listening now, full attention. "How hot?"

"Like... Rafael hot. Rafael dancing hot."

"You had a dream about someone who looks like Rafael? Ooh." Lori fans herself with a napkin. "You are one lucky lady!"

"He didn't look *like*, Rafael. I had a dream *about* him. Rafael and me." Suzanne stops talking for a moment. "You know, now that I've said that out loud, I can't believe how ridiculous it sounds. I think we're going to forget this."

"No, I think we are *not* going to forget this."

The waitress saves Suzanne by bringing their main course. Suzanne ordered a Cuban sandwich. She never had one before—well, before the dream—and she couldn't resist getting it, to see if it tastes anything like her mind had conjured. It looks pretty similar, with its crispy, slightly darkened bread, flattened, cut on the diagonal. This one, though, has a side of plantain chips. She takes a chip and bites into its crunchy saltiness. She looks up at Lori who tastes her *Pollo Ensalada*—mixed greens, cheese, tomatoes, red onions, and topped with grilled chicken, as the name implies.

"How's your salad?"

Lori has to chew her large mouthful before she can answer. "Good, but don't change the subject. I want to hear everything."

Until this moment, Suzanne had been desperate to pore over her Rafael exploits with Lori, but now? Now, she quickly takes a big bite of her sandwich, because with a full mouth, she can't talk. Her teeth meet the bread with a satisfying crunch, but when the food hits her tongue, she almost stops chewing. It tastes exactly like the one from her dream. The rich flavor of the pork, the salty ham, the zest of the mustard, the tart pickles, the oozing Swiss all mix in her mouth—provocative, spicy and smooth like... the tango. But has she actually eaten this before? She must have, the mixture of flavors so familiar.

"He's Cuban, isn't he? Rafael? That's why you insisted we come here."

Oh, well. Lori's gotten going, and there won't be any stopping her now. Suzanne nods. "And he made dinner for me." She lifts up her half sandwich.

"He *made* you a Cuban sandwich? What, were you at his house?"

"His apartment. In New York City. The producers give him a place to live while he's doing the show." Anyone hearing this conversation would think it had actually happened. Suzanne shakes her head and rolls her eyes. "This is absurd. Look what I'm talking about. I don't know *any* of this. I've made it all up. Well, my subconscious has." Suzanne absentmindedly takes another bite of the Cuban sandwich and sighs. "But it did feel so real. It *tasted* so real." Suzanne thinks about much more than the sandwich and can't help a huge smile.

"Look at you, all happy. I never see you this happy. Come on. I want to hear the beans. Spill them all. Now. Shit, if you're this happy after eating his food, imagine if you'd actually dreamed of having sex with him."

Suzanne raises her eyebrows.

Lori raises hers. "You did not."

Suzanne says nothing.

"But you're not me! You shouldn't be having sex in a dream with some stranger!"

"Just because I don't talk about it incessantly, doesn't mean I don't think about it. Dream about it. Whatever."

Lori's mouth drops open. "You got fed and fucked by Rafael."

"No, I had a *dream* I got fucked by Rafael, then fed and then fucked again." Suzanne takes great joy in shocking Lori, since it's not easy to do.

As they continue eating, Suzanne recounts the night for her dear friend, and since Lori favors details—constantly interrupting to ask for specifics—the story takes a while to tell. When Suzanne has indeed spilled all, Lori's mouth drops wider, and after staying uncharacteristically quiet for some time, blurts out, "You came seven times?!"

"Yes. Not including the two before dinner."

"Were they real ones?"

"Real orgasms? Well, maybe some were little aftershocks..."

"Aha! Little ones."

"Not so little."

"Hmm." Lori puts down her fork, cooling herself with a big swig of her tea—her third tea, since the waitress had been by several times refilling as they talked. "Did you blow him?"

As long as Suzanne has known Lori, it's still hard sometimes to get used to her blunt sex talk, but she might as well not be shy, especially considering all she has just described. "I kind of wanted to, but he was, I guess he was too busy concentrating on *me*."

"Hence the 'dance of the seven orgasms.'"

Suzanne chuckles. "Let me tell you, he was a great dancer." Suzanne wipes the sweat off her water glass with her napkin.

"Speaking of which, which one was better—the tango or the cha cha?"

The waitress approaches them. "Can I get you something else? Dessert, coffee? We have *tres leches*. It's a traditional cake made with three milks."

"No dessert for me. Do you have any herbal tea?" asks Suzanne.

The waitress nods. "We have regular decaf, and then some chamomile..."

This is the first time Suzanne realizes the waitress' accent resembles Rafael's. "No chamomile," says Suzanne. "Too early for sleeping."

"I think also I have some pomegranate tea."

Suzanne and Lori look at each other. Judging by her almost-drooling facial expression, Lori had particularly liked the part of Suzanne's evening when Rafael had her drink from his glass of pomegranate juice.

"That's weird," says Suzanne.

Lori nods in agreement.

"You know what?" decides Suzanne. "Just the check, please."

*   *   *

Before they leave the restaurant, they both pay a visit to the Ladies Room. It's not a far trip home, but with all the iced tea and water, they don't feel like waiting.

As they wash their hands, Suzanne looks up into the mirror and immediately sees the weight that makes her feel so heavy today. She also sees the abundance of gray topping her head. "Okay," she says.

"Okay to what?" asks Lori.

They haven't talked at all since they entered the bathroom. This "okay" is a continuation of conversations long past. "Okay, I'll go to your hairdresser," concedes Suzanne. "Finally fix the gray."

Lori's eyes light up.

Suzanne continues, "And I'll try going to the gym with you."

Lori smiles a broad grin. "I think I'm loving your dreaming thing."

A moment later, Suzanne and Lori climb into Suzanne's car for the short ride home. With both her girls now in college, you would think she would have downsized and upgraded from the mommy-mobile, but she hasn't had the time or the energy to shop for something to replace the minivan. Lori brings it up every time she rides in it.

"You're a hot fifty year old having sex with a man who's close to half your age. You're getting rid of the gray, going to get into shape, now it's time to get rid of the car."

"There's so much wrong with that sentence, I don't know where to start. Not to mention, I have another *eight* months to go before I turn fucking fifty."

"Exactly, and eight months is not far off. You have to plan." Lori gets distracted so easily, sometimes Suzanne thinks her friend was a cat in another life. "What are we doing? A BIG party? You know Joe's not going to throw one. We'll have to take care of everything."

Suzanne realizes she can pretty much bet on that. "Anyway, I just get done telling you about this wild dream that made me so happy, where I was a young woman having incredible sex. I'm telling you I'm going to work on all the things you've been hounding me to work on, and you have to slam the looming fifty right in my face?"

"It's just a number, sweetie. So, it *was* incredible, wasn't it?"

Suzanne hesitates. "I think it was the best of my life." Suzanne pulls up to the driveway of Lori's house and puts the car in park. "Don't say it. I know. Pathetic."

"Which is exactly why you need a party. Think about it, Dancing Girl," and out of the car she prances.

Chapter 6

ALARMING

STILL FULL FROM LUNCH, SUZANNE decides a supper on the lighter side will be best, so she defrosts some turkey burgers and throws them in the broiler with some garlic powder, onion powder and Worcestershire sauce. She could spend more time and try for more finesse, but Joe will likely load it with ketchup and mustard, so what's the culinary point?

The turkey burgers done, she puts a salad on the table and calls Joe in for their Saturday night supper. Of course, it really makes no difference if it's Saturday, Monday, Thursday. The only real difference is what will be on television later. Tonight, yes, it's *Dance*.

During dinner, Suzanne notices Joe seems even more uncommunicative than usual, but tonight it seems something more than silence. He almost seems uncomfortable. She thinks he's about to talk a couple of times, but then he looks away. He manages to say, "Turkey burgers are good." Suzanne thinks hers is a little dry, but she keeps the thought to herself.

After dinner, after the washing and straightening up—amazing how even two people eating a simple meal can generate so many dirty dishes and cooking utensils—Suzanne goes to the family room couch and takes a seat, stretching her right leg lengthwise down the couch and tucking her left leg, bent, next to her. To her surprise, Joe enters the room and sits on the love seat, catty-corner to Suzanne. He never watches this show with her, and he doesn't even have his laptop to keep him busy. She looks at him, puzzled, but then the music introducing *Dance* starts, and her attention diverts to the television.

After they show a few glimpses of tonight's episode—the taped portions, since most of it will be live—they go into the regular taped introduction. Suzanne has momentarily forgotten the presence of her husband when he asks, "You like this show?"

"Mm-hmm." Really, she thinks, why is he here, tonight of all nights? She really would like to be alone when *he* comes on. Okay, so she's sounding stupid to herself already, but still...

After the introduction, and after the plethora of commercials that follow, the first few couples perform. Suzanne feels the first does a flavorless, dull tango, and the judges seem to agree with her armchair assessment. She's also spot on for the second pair when they perform a rather lackluster quickstep.

When they go into the next commercial, Joe stands and announces, "I think I've wasted enough time. How does a smart woman like you sit here watching this show? Isn't it the most boring thing ever?"

"Some of the dancing's pretty good," Suzanne answers. Inwardly, she assures herself tonight certainly won't be boring. In fact, with what's coming next, she's more than happy when Joe leaves the room.

Indeed, right after the next commercial, the anticipated moment arrives. Rafael stands next to his partner—what's her name? He has on tight black pants and a loose and almost translucent lime green shirt that seems to be missing all of its buttons. He looks so familiar to Suzanne, just as he looked in her dreams. Such a strange feeling, thinking you know someone so intimately, but he's only a remote figure on the television.

The host has finished talking, Rafael and his partner (what *is* her name?) are in place, and the announcer's voiceover booms, "And now, dancing the Argentine tango—"

Really? The *Argentine tango*? How did she know? Okay, it must have been on some commercial or coming attraction.

The announcer continues, "Rafael Derosa and his partner Heidi Von Hellerman." Oh, that's right. That's her name. Heidi Von Hellerman. How could she possible forget a name like that?

The music starts, but the two stay absolutely still for a moment, looking intently at each other. Then, with only the slightest motion, his leg travels from her foot and on up her leg, his movements as tantalizing as Suzanne "remembers." The sultry music... wait, that music. Is it? Yes, absolutely, it's the same. The *Assassin's Tango*. Again Suzanne pushes the coincidence out of her head. She *must* have seen a coming attraction.

She continues to watch Rafael, the beautiful dancer, as he leads Heidi smoothly through the moves. It's as though he has been dancing all his life, not just for a few weeks. He seems better practiced than last week. And then Suzanne's breath hitches in her throat as she sees a series of movements. Rafael "flicks" Heidi and Heidi returns the move, after which Rafael picks Heidi up and twirls her around, her legs wrapped around him. Didn't

Suzanne do these moves, these very same moves? Okay, now her mind must really be playing tricks on her. It's one of those moments—a déjà vu with a twist—when you think you recognize something, but it's all in your mind.

Suzanne takes a series of deep breaths as she watches Rafael and Heidi perform probably their best dance of the season—*her* dance. At last, in their final hold, the audience thunders applause, with many, most, up on their feet.

The judges exhibit their happiness as well, both with their enthusiastic comments and with their near perfect scores. Rafael smiles widely as he's asked how he feels. "I had a good week," he says, straight into the camera. "A very good week," he repeats.

Joe walks back into the room just as Rafael walks offscreen. "Oh, did I miss your boyfriend?"

Irrationally, Suzanne's stomach drops.

Joe continues, "What's his face, that Cuban guy? Don't you like him?"

"He's the best of the dancers," responds Suzanne meekly.

"Hmm," replies Joe as he sits down again on that damn love seat.

They remain that way for the rest of the show, with Suzanne repeatedly stealing glances at Joe. Ill-at-ease, he doesn't really watch the show, but he's not talking, either. At the end of the program, Joe mumbles something about needing to do some work and wanders off again.

Suzanne's nerves have settled, but she feels unusually tired and decides to go to bed early. She walks to the extra downstairs room they use as the office and a sometimes guest room. Joe sits at the desk, looking blankly at the computer screen, his hand on the mouse.

"Night," says Suzanne.

"Oh, you're going to bed? Okay, then. Night," he replies, only barely turning towards his wife.

Back down the hall, Suzanne turns off the family room light and walks up the center hall stairs. As she walks into the bedroom she sees a bare bed with blankets in a heap, pillows on the floor missing their pillow cases and the mattress devoid of its sheets. Once again, Joe has stripped the bed but neglected to put on new sheets. Now, bleary-eyed, Suzanne must pull out fresh linens from the closet and make the bed.

As soon as she finishes this unexpected task, she quickly changes into her sleep shorts and tee shirt, turns off the light and climbs into bed. Forgetting herself for a moment, she reaches for the charm under her pillow, where she had left it the night before, thinking she should move it off the bed. When she doesn't find it, she remembers the bed had been bare. As she drifts off, she wonders what happened to the necklace, but she's asleep too quickly to ponder it any more.

That night, she has no dreams.

* * *

The next morning—a Sunday morning—no place to be, no reason to get herself out of bed, Suzanne wakes to an obnoxiously loud alarm. Joe's alarm, the one screaming from *his* clock on *his* night table next to *his* side of the bed. It keeps on ringing, and Suzanne finds herself fully—and none too happily—awake.

She looks over to Joe and sees him sleeping, alarm blazing in his ear. When their girls were younger and living at home, Suzanne used to bolt out of bed on the weekend mornings to silence Joe's early alarm. These days she hurries only when the girls are home from college, but not quite as fast as before, since the soundness of their sleep seems to have increased with their age.

This morning, with only Suzanne and Joe at home, she finds no real reason to rush to shut off the alarm, except to stop the annoying trill from getting on her last nerve. She gets up, walks around the bed, slams her hand down on the alarm button and then returns to her side of the bed. She knows she'll never fall back to sleep but lies down anyway. She turns onto her side, facing Joe, and gives him a little shove.

"Hmm," he groans.

"Your alarm."

Nothing.

"You wanted to get up?"

He moves onto his back, showing a small sign of life.

"Why'd you set your alarm?"

"Have to start the day," he grumbles.

Since Joe never gets up with his alarm, it really means *Suzanne* has to start her day.

Suzanne gives Joe another push, by this time so annoyed to be woken up—today and all the days before—she figures Joe damn well should get his ass out of bed, too. But he doesn't. She lies back on her pillow and tries to relax. If she can at least rest for a while, it will be better than nothing.

As she shifts herself, trying to get as comfortable as she can, her right hand slips under her pillow. It reminds her of the missing necklace from the night before. Good. It gives her something to say to Joe, so, in a loud voice, she asks, "Did you see a necklace when you stripped the bed?"

"Huh?"

"Yesterday, when you stripped the bed—remember, when you left me to put the sheets on late at night—I had a necklace under my pillow. Did you see it?"

"Why did you have a necklace under your pillow?" he says groggily.

"Does it matter? I just want to know if you saw it."

"Why? Is it missing?"

Oh, brother. "That would be why I'm asking."

"Where did you last have it?"

Yes, that's the logical question, since if she knew where she last had it she would actually have it. "Never mind. Go back to sleep."

As expected, Joe does—or, rather, he probably was never really conscious. Suzanne, of course, does not fall back to sleep. Instead, she thinks about the necklace and how she had intended to return it to Cybil today, but one can't give back what one has lost. She gets off the bed and, on her hands and knees and not as nimbly as in her younger years, she searches in the area around and under the bed, turning up a big fat nothing.

She eventually heads downstairs, checks her emails on the office computer—delete, delete, delete—and heads into the kitchen for her favorite breakfast of cottage cheese and strawberries. Okay, not really her favorite, because she'd much rather be eating Belgium waffles with real, warm maple syrup and sliced sugared strawberries, but strawberries and cottage cheese tastes yummy, too, right?

Quite a while later, Joe finds his way downstairs and joins Suzanne in the kitchen. "Morning," he says and goes directly to the drawer that holds all the non-kitchen stuff. He looks through the mound of papers, pushing many aside. "What happened to that unpaid lab bill?"

"I paid it."

"You paid it?" He sounds slightly annoyed.

"It was past due, been sitting here for months, so I

paid it last week."

"I wanted to look into that bill." He sounds more than slightly annoyed. "I'm not sure we even really owe it."

"I'm sure we do owe it, and it was only $20.34."

Joe slams the drawer shut and exits the room.

Chapter 7

IT'S TOO LATE

IT'S SUNDAY MORNING, AND A little chilly in the house, especially the frosty downstairs where Suzanne now drinks a cup of hot tea to warm and wake her up.

In a short while, Lori will pick her up to go to the gym. At least Suzanne's finally making good on her promise to work out. She had lost some of her enthusiasm since she hadn't "seen" Rafael again. Hadn't had any of those dreams—the really dreamy dreams—for a long time.

It's also been a while—almost three months—since Joe left. Still hard to believe. Well, it should finish quickly, anyway, her uncontested divorce.

The girls came home for their winter break and went back to school already. For the first time ever, Suzanne is living on her own. Twenty-two years married—would have been twenty-three coming up soon. She has these almost-regretting moments once in a while, but she allows herself the indulgence of melancholy, allows the "what if" game, because most of the time she's fine with it.

It was the end of October, another Saturday morning

filled with Joe's usual crap. They had no big blowout, he did nothing different, nothing horrible, just all the things she'd had enough of and knew would never change. Everything—the early-morning alarm clock, the lack of conversation, the penny-pinching with money she had earned just as much as he had—everything seemed to converge in one fed up and unhappy moment.

In that one moment, she felt overwhelmingly tired from so many things.

Tired of his wanting to control every dime, of him trying to control *her*. Tired of him putting himself first all the time. Tired of being a casual observer during sex. Tired of having no connection to the man who should have been her best friend.

Tired of just not being happy.

They were eating lunch. She finished her tuna on wheat but found herself not quite satisfied. She went to the refrigerator and saw a small, nonfat chocolate pudding snack and grabbed it. As she turned holding the tiny cup, Joe said, "You just ate lunch. Why do you need that?"

"I want a divorce." It blurted out of her mouth without thinking, except, in reality, she'd been thinking it for years.

And then silence. Fifteen seconds, five minutes, Suzanne didn't know how long.

Finally, Joe nodded, said a soft "Okay" then got up from the kitchen table. As he turned to walk out of the room, he said an even quieter, "If that's what you want."

In fact, he said precious little for the next few hours, and she figured his ready acceptance meant he had been thinking the same thing, thinking about divorce, for years.

A short while later the doorbell rang, not a usual circumstance in the suburbs when you're not expecting someone. Suzanne went to the door and saw a miniature ghost and an even smaller hippie. "Trick or Treat!" She'd forgotten it was Halloween. Well, at least something kept her busy that day as life as she knew it packed up his own life and headed out the door.

* * *

"When did you last visit a gym?" Lori asks over her shoulder, holding the door for Suzanne to follow her through.

Suzanne is immediately hit by the unfamiliar smell, the bright lights and colors, the impossibly high ceilings—and by the sheer volume of equipment and equally large number of people. "High School, I guess."

"Oh. I didn't realize it was that bad. Okay, we'll go slowly."

Suzanne looks around to see men running on treadmills, women climbing on climbing machines, young people moving the various parts of weight machines up and down and others lying on the floor doing sit ups. So much going on at once, how can anyone go slowly here? Suzanne has a sudden urge to flee this foreign land, feeling as out of place as Gulliver in Lilliput, but Lori has already signed her in as a guest and beckons her forward. Too late to run.

Lori takes her into the colorful locker room. Suzanne sees a couple of other women, both walking around unselfconsciously, one in bra and panties, another wrapped in a large towel. Lori leads Suzanne to a vacant spot next to a row of lockers. She takes off her jacket to expose her short cropped but tight exercise pants and a halter type workout top. Suzanne takes off her coat to expose her extra-large and baggy pair of cotton shorts and an oversized tee shirt.

Suzanne can feel Lori's disapproving eyes observing her wardrobe choice, but, to her credit, Lori's only comment is to ask if she brought a lock.

"You didn't tell me to."

"No problem. We'll shove all our stuff in one," and Lori proceeds to do just that after choosing one of the longer lockers. "Next time, bring a lock."

"Assuming there will be a next time."

"There will be. Let's go, an elliptical's calling your name."

Suzanne knows what an ellipse is, but an elliptical? The land of Lilliput stretches vast and wide.

Lori talks as they exit the locker room. "We'll only do some cardio today. Got to get you into a little bit of shape before we start with the weights. If we ever do them, because, you know, I'm really not a fan."

Suzanne inwardly breathes a sigh of relief. As scared as she is to try anything in this place, the thought of trying to work those clanking machines or lifting those dumbbells—who thought of that apt name?—would put her over the edge.

She follows Lori to her doom...

Chapter 8

THE IDES HAVE IT

IN YEARS PAST, MARCH FIFTEENTH proved to be a gorgeous day—basking sunshine, warm but not hot, with a sweet spring breeze. Like the day twenty-three years ago, the day Suzanne got married.

Today, a wintry mix pelts from the gray sky. Suzanne can see small pieces of ice bouncing off the walkway as she peeks out the curtain for the tenth time, waiting for the delivery truck already an hour past the three hour window they had quoted her. It's not how she wanted to spend her anniversary, her first non-anniversary. She wanted to spend this day anywhere *but* at home, but she also badly wants the new mattress, a mattress without two big dips and a ridge, the every-night reminder of her failed marriage. She'll reuse the bed frame. Not one for a fancy headboard, she feels no need to get rid of the simple metal frame that won't be seen after the new box spring and mattress go on top.

The large truck finally pulls up, and she leads the one delivery person—shouldn't there be two?—upstairs, since the price includes removal of the current bed. He's a husky man, probably older than she by a few, but by his physique and his brusque demeanor, she figures he's been doing this for years, especially when she sees how he deftly handles the old king size mattress. By the time she grabs the vacuum and a rag, he's already stripped the bed down to its skeletal frame. While the delivery man finishes removing the old pieces, Suzanne hastily vacuums those hard to reach places. She puts the vacuum aside just as the delivery man returns with the new box spring and asks him to hold for a moment as she runs the rag quickly over the frame. Might as well clean while the cleaning is good. Just as she nears the last bend, the rag pushes something onto the floor. She picks it up, surprised to see the charm necklace she'd almost forgotten about these past five months.

"Ready?" asks the delivery man. She suspected he is a man of few words, and since this is the first word Suzanne hears him utter, her suspicions prove true.

She puts the charm in her pocket. "Yes, sorry. Go ahead."

A short while later, the delivery truck has driven away, and Suzanne finishes putting a new sheet—bought especially for the occasion—on her new mattress. She slips off her shoes and lies down. The mattress feels even better than in the showroom. After another moment, she realizes she's on "her side" of the bed and quickly scoots to the middle, easily accomplished on this level and smooth surface. "Happy un-anniversary" she says to herself.

The doorbell rings again. She figures the delivery man forgot something, maybe some paperwork? She regretfully leaves her new comfy bed and goes downstairs. Through the small glass part of the door, she does not see the delivery man. She opens and Lori enters.

"Gym." Lori, *not* usually a woman of few words,

seems all business today. When Suzanne doesn't respond, just stares at her, Lori continues, "You're going. Get dressed."

"I don't like to go. You know I don't like it."

"You're lazy, that's why."

"Bullshit. But I'll go. I need to get out of the house. Come upstairs while I change. You can see my new mattress."

"Ooh, you got it? When are you going to christen it?"

"When I sleep on it tonight."

The two women walk to the second floor and into Suzanne's room.

"You know that's not what I meant."

"But that's what's gonna happen." Suzanne points to the bed with a big flourish. "So, you like?"

"Nice. Looks like a bed. How does it feel?" Lori asks as she stretches out on it.

"Like a bed." About to change into her sweatpants, Suzanne reaches into her pants to empty the pockets. She pulls out the charm necklace.

"What's that?"

Suzanne doesn't feel like getting into the who what why and when, so she simply says, "A necklace I found when the old bed was taken out. Thought I'd lost it."

Lori puts out her hand for it, and Suzanne drops it in her palm before escaping to the bathroom to change. When she comes out a few minutes later, Lori sits on the edge of the bed, still turning the necklace over in her hand. "Interesting piece. Come here. Let me see it on you." Lori stands and puts the necklace on Suzanne. "I like it."

Eager to get the next hour or so over with, Suzanne says, "Let's go."

* * *

Suzanne and Lori work out at the gym on side-by-side recumbent bikes. Suzanne likes this piece of equipment because it is nowhere near a mirror, not an easy task in this hall of looking glasses. Even after a couple of months since joining the gym—okay maybe she has hardly visited—in any case, she's remained terribly uncomfortable here. A stranger in a strange land, a fish out of water—all the clichés rolled into one. Everything here seems a cliché, from the perky young things working the front desk—both genders equally perky—to the narcissistic gym rats with the insatiable appetites for their own reflections, which is why the endless mirrors come in handy. And how self-conscious she feels as she looks around, surrounded by one perfect body after another. All the women must consume only juice, and the men must juice on steroids. Why else would such perfection abound? What makes this place so unusual, at least to Suzanne's eyes, is that the shapely young women and the hunky, bulked up young men seem virtually oblivious to one another. They only have eyes for their own selves. Again, hence the mirrors.

An older woman walks up to Lori and Suzanne. Suzanne has seen her every single time she's visited the gym. In their talks, Suzanne has discovered this woman, Sandy, ten years her senior, comes to the gym six days a week, and has been doing so for "more years than most of these kids here have been alive." And she has the arms, legs and abs to prove it. Sandy chats for a few minutes, which makes the time go a bit faster, but then takes off to do some reverse pyramids. Suzanne has no idea what that means but smiles as if she understands gym talk.

With Sandy gone and Lori reading a magazine as she sits back and bikes, Suzanne tries to watch some television, but she switches stations quickly, nothing holding her attention. No one to talk to, having forgotten something to read, nothing good to watch on the small screen positioned where handle bars should be, Suzanne has just her own self to keep her company, her own head to be in. She's sometimes quite bored being in this head. How does everyone stand it? Close to fifty years, imprisoned, so to speak, with the same person. She wishes that, just for a brief while, she could get out, have a little relief from her own thoughts. Divorce herself, or at least a temporary separation.

As she thinks, her pedaling automatically starts to slow. She looks down at her feet and pushes her legs to move faster in their useless circles.

*　*　*

"Look at those tits. What a lucky son-of-a-bitch I am. Smooth, full, soft. I've got to taste them. She's putting up zero resistance. She's into me. I am a lucky, lucky mother fucker. Looks, body, willing. I must be good 'cause she's moaning. Oh, she likes it when I suck and run my tongue over her nipple at the same time. Are those real moans? Yeah, they sound real. Her ass looks good, too. Wow, it feels as good as it looks. Okay, man, don't come yet. You don't want this over too quickly. Don't want an unsatisfied customer.

Enough playing. Time for some serious stuff. Will she like the abc thing? They all like that. Perfect position, she's half-sitting already. Just spread those beautiful gams a little. There you go. Got to love that spread eagle look. Would have preferred a little less hair there, but she smells pretty good. Mm, tastes good, too. Okay, now one letter at a time: a b c d e f g—yeah, baby, that g gets them every time—h i j—j is just as good as the g—k l m—man, she's going to come, just look at her—n o p— nice and slow—q r—that's it, that's it, baby, and when I get to z, I'm going to fuck the living shit out of— "

*   *   *

"What's the matter?" Lori has her magazine down and looks at Suzanne with concern.

"Huh?" says Suzanne, a little dazed.

"You were sitting here on the bike, and I was talking to you. Wow, it was weird. Like you were in this mini-coma for a few seconds. Totally blank."

"But I was sitting here?"

"You don't remember?"

"Well, I remember something... Must have been a daydream. I guess." Suzanne feels freaked out, and all she can think is, "Ick, ick, ick." If that was a daydream, that was the freakiest one she's ever had. She looks around at the sea of men—some on treadmills, some lifting weights, some doing stretches on the floor—and she tries to push the thought out of her mind, but she can't help herself. What exactly are they thinking right now? And what the hell—why the hell—was she just thinking what she thought?

"We still on for tonight?" asks Lori. She's gotten off her bicycle. "Girls night out, dinner and a movie?"

"Let's make it a comedy. Nothing about sex."

Lori looks at Suzanne like she's got two heads, but says, "Anything you want. It's your night."

"A sexless comedy it is. You drive. I may need a drink or two."

Chapter 9

USE IT WELL

THE BIZARRE DAYDREAM BY NOW a dim blur—with the help of some Kahlua and cream—Suzanne arrives home close to midnight after a delicious seafood dinner and a pretty funny movie. Perhaps it wasn't truly funny, but, again, the Kahlua and cream helped with that as well.

Still feeling slightly buzzed, Suzanne locks up downstairs and climbs the center hall steps. As she reaches her room, dead tired, she remembers her new bed awaits. She quickly rushes through her nighttime rituals and jumps in. How long will it take to get used to this feeling—this firm, comfortable, great new bed feeling? She sits up again, takes a long swig of water—no hangovers, please, she has work in the morning—and lays back down. Taking a look at the clock, she sees it reads 11:34 pm.

What a strange day, especially that thing at the gym, which she doesn't want to think about. In fact, she prefers to think about anything else, even her pathetic performance at the gym. She hasn't been able to get herself to try anything except the treadmill, the elliptical and the recumbent bike. She wishes she had the guts to try the weights. She really wishes she had the guts—and the money—to take some lessons with a personal trainer, but, she has to admit to herself, she's a complete wuss and will forever avoid that whole world, that strange, unfamiliar, uncomfortable world. But the bed sure feels comfortable to her. So comfy she could just drift off to sleep...

*   *   *

Wow, this is one of those vivid dreams again. Wait, I hope to hell it's not like this afternoon. Where am I? I don't think I've been here before, but it's hard to tell from a bathroom stall. Oh, but if it's a bathroom, then there are probably mirrors. Let's hope to hell I'm a woman.

And, yes, I'm a woman. Not only a woman, but *the* woman. The young woman who had sex with Rafael Derosa. Hey there, where you been these past five months? Things seem much more exciting when you're around.

Okay, why am I talking to myself, and as though I'm a bimbo? Let's size up the situation. I'm looking blond and beautiful today, and I have on—what are those? Black yoga pants? I think so, and a little cropped strikingly bold blue top that really holds in the sisters. Gives me an even nicer cleavage than the last time.

I walk outside the bathroom area and discover I'm actually in a locker room. I continue through the little hallway until I get to a cavernous room. Sure enough, I'm in a gym, but it's not the gym I belong to. I can see out the front window a little, and it looks to me like it's on a pretty busy street. Like New York City busy. Okay. Why not a gym in NYC? Might as well go big or go broke. You know what? I wonder if I'm still a little drunk. I sure am acting pretty stupid. But why shouldn't I act like an idiot? Dreams are not a place for inhibitions.

But I *am* inhibited. I'm all dressed up for a real workout, except I don't know how to do anything besides some simple aerobics. I catch another glimpse of myself in a mirror. (What is it with gyms and their embarrassment of mirrors, anyway?) I *look* like I should know what I'm doing.

Okay, I march over to the closest unoccupied treadmill and step on. I only know how to work the one in my gym, but I guess I'll figure this one out. If I choose the manual override, then I should be able to push a couple of buttons and get moving... Got it. Oh, look, I can even get it to incline. Level one it is. Actually, this feels almost easy. Okay, let's go for level two.

As I'm playing with the controls, out of the corner of my eye I see someone—a tall, lanky someone—get on the treadmill next to me. I look up. It's a man. He's got a kind of a shaggy, scraggly way about him. Mop of black hair, needs a shave. He punches some settings onto his treadmill's console then raises his head and catches me peeking.

"Hi," he says. I can see his face better now. Young-ish. Well, younger than the real me, but quite a bit older than the me he's looking at right now.

"Hello," I say back, not wanting to be rude.

But, come to think of it, wouldn't it maybe be fun to be rude? "I'd prefer not to talk while I'm exercising," I could say. Or, if I really want to be a bitch, I would say, "You think a hot young thing like me wants to talk to *you*?" Okay, that is *too* horrible. And because I was even thinking of saying it, I feel compelled to be nice to this stranger who I thought to insult but didn't. "How are you?"

Well, that is some smile. I guess he's really happy I'm talking to him. "I'm just great. The night's starting off well." Okay, so, obviously, a pleasantry from this hot young thing (that would be me) is all the encouragement this guy needs. "Hey, you here alone?"

"I'm sorry?" I can't help keep the undertone of surprise out of my voice.

He quickly corrects himself. "I mean, if you're alone, maybe you want to work out together? Lift some weights?" He increases the level on his treadmill, even though he's starting to breathe with difficulty already. "Helps keep me motivated when I pair up."

Okay, so he's not asking me out after thirty seconds and a few words. Phew. "I'm not really... I don't actually... I don't really know much about weight lifting." Honestly, I'm not sure if he knows anything about it, either, with all his huffing and puffing.

"Oh, that's okay. I haven't been doing it that long myself." He stands up a little, trying to reach his maximum tallness. I may be reading into it, but I get the feeling he's showing himself off, sort of saying, "See, a pretty good body for someone who's only been doing it a short while."

Now I'm in a bad position. I really don't want to work out with him, but, well, he seems nice enough, and kind of desperate, and that makes me feel for him. I might as well work out, since I've come all this way into my dream to get here. "Um, yeah, sure, okay."

There's that smile again. I really have made this guy's night. "Great. So, just let me know when you're all warmed up and want to start." He slows his treadmill down. I guess he's done with *his* one minute warm up. "What do you think? Bench press? Is that okay?"

I figure you sit on the bench rather than lift it, so I guess it's okay. "That's... fine." At least Rafael is not here to see me in my idiocy. I slow my machine down, wait until it's at a complete stop and carefully step off.

No point falling off and looking like a moron before I even get started.

I follow... wait I don't even know his name. "Hi," I say. "I'm Shoshanna." Oh, that came out of my mouth before I could think. Well, we'll go with it.

"Bartholomew. Bart."

"Nice to meet you, Bart."

"'Shoshanna.' Hmm, you don't hear that every day." Like *Bart* is a common name? "What do people call you? 'Shosh?'"

How would I know what people call me? But I would hope to hell it's not *Shosh*.

"Okay, well, follow me, Shosh. I think there's a bench with our names on it."

Maybe I *should* have insulted him.

Bart leads me to an area with lots of benches. They're only about a foot or so off the ground and at one end, suspended about two feet above each bench, hovers a pole. The poles rest on thick stands bolted to the floor. Bart approaches one of these contraptions and puts his water bottle next to one of the stands. "So, have you done a bench press before?"

I shake my head. I've seen people do it at my gym, but I've never gotten up the nerve to try it myself.

"Why don't I demonstrate first, and then you can try?" He makes a big show of taking a circular weight off the bottom of the stand and putting it on one end of the pole, then strides to the other side and adds one to that end as well. He starts to lie down, but jumps up. "Forgot the cuffs."

Huh? Is he going to handcuff himself to the pole? What does that do? Make sure he doesn't stop?

Duh. Not a handcuff. It's a strange, small metal thing. He squeezes it, slides it up next to the circular weight and then lets it go. Ah, I see. It holds the weight on the pole. He puts one on the other side, too, then lies down on his back, this time staying put. His face stares up, positioned right under the long pole.

Oh, disgusting. Now that he's lying down, I can see he wears a pair of black, very tight fitting, long shorts (oxymoron, but true), leaving *nothing* to the imagination. Really, dude? I know it's a gym, but how about a little decorum? And what's that smell? I can't quite place it, but it's wafting off of him. Some weird cologne?

"Okay, so you put your hands about shoulder length apart, like this." His palms face upwards, with his thumbs and forefingers making *O*s around the pole. "Then you lift up and pull the bar a little forward." Ah, it's called a "bar," not a "pole." Good to know. "Then slowly lower... and... push... back... up." The bar is extended once again, away from his chest. "See? And you do about maybe eight to ten reps." A rep? Is that short for repeat? Well, he seems to know the lingo at least. He lowers the bar again, but it's not smooth. He's only on rep number two and already he seems to struggle. He puts the bar back on the stand then sits up. "Ready to try?" He gets up and takes off the cuff (yes, I'm picking up the lingo). "Maybe you should just try the bar."

"How much does it weigh?"

"Oh, not sure. But with this weight it's a bit heavy for me, so we should go down as much as possible."

With the way he was moving that weight, it seemed to me that a small stick of wood would have been too heavy for him, but, hey, I'm not one to talk. I'd probably have a hard time with a toothpick.

The bar free of all its extra weight, I lie down on the bench and position my head just as I had seen him do. He stands right behind me, next to my head. Oh, don't look up, because you'll see—oh, why did I look up? And there's that smell again. What *is* that?

I position my hands as he had. It's a little frightening, looking at the bar—not to mention his unmentionable threatening to obstruct my view of the bar—thinking I have to hold that heavy metal thing up or it will crush me. I remind myself you can't really get crushed in your dream, then I count to three and push up. Well, that's not so bad. A little wobbly, but, hey, it feels okay. Here goes. I lower it slowly, closer to my chest, and then push it back up. Feels kind of cool. Not too heavy. Didn't kill myself. I try it again. It still feels good, and I repeat the movement a few more times.

"Okay, I think that's enough," Bart says, and, before I can protest, he pulls the bar out of my hands and places it back on its stand. "Don't want you getting hurt on my watch." Except I was still feeling pretty strong, and I'll bet I was looking a whole lot stronger than he had looked, too. "What would you like to do next? We should try some bicep work."

"Wait a second. I want to try this again. It wasn't too hard." Actually, it seemed kind of easy, and kind of fun, I have to admit. I get up, select the same size weight he had used and put it on one end. He makes a bit of a face, but I try not to look at him. He does put the cuff on that end as I put a matching weight on the other end. He finishes it off with a cuff there, too.

"You sure about this?"

"Yeah, I just want to try one or two."

"Okay, well, don't worry, I'll stand right here and help you if you need it."

For some reason, I'm not worried. I lie back down, and reach my hands up. The metal feels cold. Most of the bar is smooth, but where I place my hands, the metal is crisscrossed and feels a little rough against my skin. It's a strange sensation, but I like it. I get myself settled and take a breath, then push up. It feels okay, not too heavy. I take my time and let the bar down, but not too far—don't want to chance it. Then, letting out my breath, I push back up. This feels great. It feels— odd to say—natural. I do another and another.

"You okay?" Bart asks, disbelief creeping into his tone.

I do one more then decide to call it quits. Better to end on a high note. I settle the bar back onto the stand.

I sit back up on the bench. Before I know it, Bart has taken off the cuffs and the weights, clanging them as he puts them back where they belong. His voice has lost some of its cordiality as well. "Follow me," he says. As he passes in front of me, I get another dose of the smell. It hits me suddenly. Oh, you have got to be kidding me! He smells like sex. A really strong smell of sex! He must have fucked someone then immediately come to the gym, no shower, nothing. I bet he left his partner high and dry and said, "See ya later, baby." And now he's working out with me, and, let's be honest, hitting on me. Wait a minute. Maybe there *was* no partner. Maybe he just jacked off in the locker room. Gross with a big old capital G! I have definitely had enough of him.

"Um, you know, I think I'm done for now. I think I'll just finish back up on the treadmill. It was nice meeting you, Bart."

Bart turns, and the geniality has most definitely disappeared. There's anger on his face and in his increasingly louder voice. "Oh, I see. I know what you are. You're one of those ball-busting women who like to make every man she meets feel like shit, aren't you!? I suppose you've been working out for years, and you get off making fun of a poor shmo like me, right? Well, Shosh, you can take your stupid name and go shove it up your ass!"

Well, he's a pleasant chap, isn't he? I'd sure like to get away from him right this second.

*　*　*

Suzanne opens her eyes, happy to be awake in her wonderful new bed, far away from NYC and its fictional athletic facilities. Where is a good Rafael dream when you need one? She turns over and looks at the clock. How can that be? It's only 11:35 pm? Since when does a dream that long take so little time? Her brain must be on overtime. But, still, how could she have fallen asleep so quickly and dreamed that much? Maybe it's the alcohol. She takes another few gulps of water and lays back down, hoping the rest of the night will prove dreamless.

And sans dream it is.

The next morning she wakes, just slightly hung over. Thank goodness it's no worse. As she performs her morning *getting ready for work* rituals, she can't help but think about the wildly weird dreams—one dream and one daydream, actually—of the day before. Unfortunately, all the time she eats, dresses and brushes her teeth, she can't stop thinking about them, and as she enters the bathroom to perform the final routine of makeup application, she wonders to herself why she's had two of these bizarre, horrible dreams in such a short time, especially since she hasn't had any dreams at all in months. Nothing's changed in her life, really, to have brought these on. She decides maybe she'll search the internet tonight, to try to figure out the cause. She picks up her light green tube of liquid base, squirts out a tiny bit onto her finger and looks up into her mirror, dabbing and spreading out the cream starting on her forehead and moving down. When she gets to her chin, she notices she's still wearing the Cybil necklace. She'd forgotten somehow that Lori had put it on her yesterday right before they went to the gym. She puts down the base and picks up her blush. As she brushes the pinkish rose blush onto her cheeks, she sees the necklace jiggle with her movements. Lori put the necklace on her right before they went to the gym. Right before she went to the gym where she had that...

Could it be? No, the necklace can't have anything to do with this. Could it? She racks her brain to remember. Has she only had these incredibly vivid dreams since she's had the necklace? It couldn't be. But wasn't the first of the dreams, the first one with Rafael, wasn't it that Bunco night, when Cybil first presented the necklace to her? And then, after, when she lost it temporarily, she didn't have any dreams for a long time, until... yesterday.

Of course, Suzanne realizes this is utterly ridiculous. A necklace giving you dreams. A weird necklace from a woman who said... what? That she wanted her to use the necklace well. That's normal, isn't it? Use it well— isn't that a common thing to say when you give a present? Except Suzanne also realizes that's not all she said. She also claimed that Suzanne had lost her way, or something like that. So was she saying this necklace would get her back on the right path?

Suzanne impulsively removes the necklace. She walks it over to her bed and deposits it in her night table drawer.

"Enough," she says to herself. "I've got to get to work."

Chapter 10

THE TWELFTH OF JUNE

JUNE TWELFTH. A BIG DAY for Suzanne Stern, especially because she's not Suzanne Stern anymore. Or is she? She can't decide. With the divorce papers finalized, today of all days, she should go back to her maiden name, but after twenty-three years as Stern— almost half her life and certainly the majority of her adult years—does it make sense to go back to Tilman? She thinks about asking her daughters, now home for the summer, but she's tried to avoid talking about the divorce as much as possible with them. They seem happy not discussing it, and she certainly has no desire to add mood-altering conversations. The girls may need to work this all out, but they're close enough—especially now that they attend the same college—to lean on each other and old enough to do it without her.

For now she decides to stay with Stern. It's her name at work, it identifies her as her children's mother, and, at this point, it's who she's been for years. And it's not like she had one of these messy, acrimonious divorces and can't stand the sight or sound of him. Hers had been short. Short and sweet. Well, not so sweet. Maybe bittersweet, which would certainly describe receiving the divorce papers today, June twelfth, Suzanne Tilman Stern's birthday. Her *fiftieth* birthday.

How the hell did this happen? She feels like she's still in her thirties, and yet here she is, turning fucking fifty. Turned. She was born in the morning. Fucking fifty and single. Who would have thought? How the hell *did* this happen?

Suzanne thinks about this as she gets ready for her birthday dinner party. She's gone back and forth for months about how she should "celebrate" this day. Big party? Little party? No party? Totally ignore it? In the end she settled on a catered at-home dinner for twenty-odd people, including her daughters, a few close relatives and a handful of close friends. Not invited? Joe—which still feels strange.

The party all ready to go—the caterer expected soon and the girls having decorated and set out the art deco black and white paper and plastic products—and Suzanne's name decided, Suzanne moves on to the next, and arguably most difficult, task. She needs to decide what to wear. For weeks, Lori had encouraged her to shop for a special outfit, but Suzanne never got around to it, most probably subconsciously on purpose. For one, she prefers to spend the money on the food for the party, and, for two, even after the last few months of going to the gym, she still feels uncomfortably heavy, with no desire to add to her larger size wardrobe. Maybe if she had learned to work out with the weights she would have gotten some better results, but the closest she'd gotten to that was the one dream months ago.

Suzanne steps into her walk-in closet and stares at the various possibilities for the evening. A dress? The only ones she owns appear too formal for this laid back party. Jeans? She's a little too large for the ones that aren't worn-out, and the worn through the upper thighs look? Maybe a little *too* laid back. She pulls out a few nice slacks and some blouses to match and lays them down on her bed. She hasn't tried some of these on for a while, and when she does, she realizes why. Nothing seems to fit right, and she prefers not to look like an overstuffed sausage—let alone feel like one—on a night when everyone will look at her, the main attraction.

After a disheartening twenty minutes, Suzanne settles on a pair of basic black pants she often wears to work, and a white and black loose fitting, to-the-thigh blouse. She looks in the mirrored door to her closet and decides the ensemble will work. The blouse hides most of the body parts she hates and goes with the black and white decorating theme to boot. She's not sure if Lori will like or hate that idea, but Lori would have preferred a private party for a hundred in a restaurant with a dee jay, so, at this point, it certainly doesn't matter.

Suzanne hears Abigail shout, "Mom, the caterer's here!" She makes a mental note to return for some jewelry and heads downstairs.

Suzanne and the girls help empty the caterer's minivan of all the food. The caterer has brought one assistant, and they work to set up the grilling station in the backyard as Suzanne, Hannah and Abigail set up the side dishes inside. As per Suzanne's direction—and certainly without Lori's blessing—the caterer will be grilling the main course—hamburgers and hot dogs— through the dinnertime hours. Suzanne's favorite birthday dinner has always been a good, juicy hamburger, some well-cooked French fries and a gooey hot fudge ice cream sundae. She keeps within that theme, but since this *is* a special birthday, and since she *is* feeding a couple dozen people besides herself, she had the caterer bring fancier side dishes: an arugula salad with beets; an Israeli couscous with orange zest, cranberries and walnuts; *haricots verts* with an herb sauce; a sweet corn salad and, Suzanne's favorite barbecue accompaniment, cole slaw. Okay, so cole slaw doesn't count as a fancy side dish, but, again, it *is* Suzanne's birthday, after all.

Since everything always takes more time than one thinks it will, once Suzanne comes downstairs, she never gets a chance to return to her room, so her fingers, wrists and neck stay unadorned. At least she'd gotten a mani-pedi earlier in the day and had time for a full face of makeup. More importantly, on Saturday she had finally colored and highlighted her hair. She may have been a light-haired child, but never, ever this blond. A little of the young woman from her dreams of months ago creeping in.

Even with the extra help from the caterer and her assistant, Suzanne finds herself "working" during most of the evening. Hannah and Abigail had promised they would help during the entire party so their mother could talk to and enjoy her guests, except the girls haven't seen so many of these people for quite a while, and they keep getting hung up in conversation. In the end, despite her well-intentioned girls, Suzanne spends more time replenishing food and drink, cleaning up spills and what-not than she does speaking with her guests. Still, she's happy to have all these people here. She needed some special recognition of the day, she needed family and friends around her, she needed, on her fiftieth, not to remember how quickly these fifty years have passed, and, for all this, the party proves a great success. Not to mention the beyond amazing hamburger Suzanne gets to eat.

A couple of hours into the party, the caterer stops grilling, cleans up and departs. Hannah and Abigail manage to tear themselves away from family and friends to set up the cake and other desserts. They had wanted to get something fancier, maybe from a boutique bakery, but Suzanne had insisted upon her favorite huge chocolate cake from the local members only warehouse. They had also gotten some gorgeous and decadent truffles along with a mixed fruit pie. As Suzanne stands in front of the smorgasbord of delights waiting for the singing of the birthday song, she thinks to herself she has to make sure none of these desserts stay in the house after tonight—not if she wants a chance in hell of fitting into any of the clothing she had passed over for tonight's shindig.

The rendition of *Happy Birthday to You* could not be more out of tune—the norm with that hard to sing song—but the people Suzanne loves belt it out with great sincerity, so perfect pitch be damned.

A short while after the serving of the cake—hungrily devoured by the same guests who said they could not possibly fit dessert into their already full stomachs—the doorbell rings, surprising Suzanne. She becomes even more surprised when she reaches the door and opens it to none other than Cybil, right there on her front doorsteps.

Cybil enters immediately, not waiting for either a "hello" or an invitation. The crowd parts as she and her long, white dress float their way into the center of the group. The living room filled with loud voices suddenly becomes silent, and all hear her low and sing-song words. "Dear child, I saw all these cars in front of your house, and I deduced it must be an important event, so I said to myself I must pay Zuzanka a brief visit." Cybil slowly looks around, the decorations giving away the exact nature of the important event. "Ah, I thought so. Your birthday. Your fiftieth."

Everyone in the room stares intently at Cybil. Some clearly recognize her, some do not, but she captivates all.

Cybil steps closer now to Suzanne. "Such a special occasion," she continues, "and you decorate your home but not yourself." As she speaks, Cybil lifts her right hand to her own throat, resting her pointer finger on the indentation at the base of her neck. "Such a shame, allowing a beautiful piece to languish in the drawer of your bed-side table, wouldn't you say? Today of all days."

To almost all, Cybil sounds completely nonsensical, but Suzanne knows. She *alone* knows what beautiful piece lies in her night table drawer. The only other person who even knows of the necklace's existence is Lori, but Lori doesn't know where it came from, hasn't a clue where Suzanne put it, and certainly has not been talking to Cybil. And yet, Cybil knows...

Suzanne's heart races as Cybil turns from the living room back towards the front of the house. Taking Suzanne's hand along the way, she pulls her outside the door, out of sight and earshot of the rest of the group. "For your birthday," Cybil croons in her mystical voice, "I wish you everything your heart," she hesitates a moment before continuing, "desires. The necklace will show you the way. Do not be afraid."

Suzanne finds herself unable to utter a sound as Cybil lets go of her hand and walks away.

A moment later, Suzanne hears her name and turns to see Lori standing in the doorway. By the time she turns her head back around, Cybil has disappeared, just as she had that night months ago.

"What the hell was that?!" demands Lori.

Even if Suzanne could find the words, it's neither the time nor the place for this discussion. With a small shrug of her shoulders, she turns to return inside.

"Well, I guess the party wouldn't be complete without a little crazy-assed drama," Lori says, shrugging her shoulders as well and following Suzanne into the house.

Suzanne has a strong, overwhelming suspicion that the crazy-assed drama has only just begun.

Chapter 11

Long Days, Short Lives

AFTER THE LAST GUEST LEAVES, Hannah and Abigail insist on cleaning up together, and high-speed Hannah has the place in shape in no time—with some help from the less energetic Abigail. When they finish, the girls retreat to their bedrooms, and Suzanne retreats to her own room. Exhausted by all the goings on, she puts on her least dowdy nightgown—no sense looking like an old maid, even if she happens to fit the bill—and climbs into bed.

As much as she tries to avoid it, after just a short while, she can't help herself and bends over to the nightstand. She slowly opens the drawer and pulls out the necklace. Considering the evening's strange incident, Suzanne half expects something magical will happen, like maybe the charm will start glowing, or maybe even heat up as she holds it, burning her skin—but then she shuts down those thoughts and opts for logic. Nothing's burning, glowing or, for that matter, even mystical. Cybil hadn't seen the piece on Suzanne's neck and took a lucky guess as to where she had put it.

Suzanne stares at it a moment longer. It looks pretty

much as she remembers, but she leans over once more to the night table and picks up the pair of one and a half times magnifying reading glasses she keeps for reading things not on the iPad. After all, you can't automatically enlarge the font size in a printed book. With the magnification, she can see more of the intricate work, but she still can't figure out what the hell this symbol, or whatever it is, represents. The one thing she does know is that she now feels guilty as sin for having neglected it. She puts the necklace on.

Suzanne yawns, completely and utterly worn out by this long, emotional and full day. She leans back onto her pillow. "Long days, short life," she thinks as she drifts quickly off to sleep.

*   *   *

I'm back in the gym. The same New York City one, I think. Oh, I hope that sleaze bag—what was his name? Bart—I hope he's not here. But if he *is* here, it's just a dream, right? It feels like a dream. What else could it be?

"I haven't seen you for a while."

I turn to see the young man who speaks to me. I quickly steal a look at one of those ever-present mirrors to make sure to whom the young man talks. Don't want to assume, but, yes, it's me, or rather Shoshanna. And compared to Shoshanna, he's not that young.

He continues to talk. "You came in once, but I haven't seen you again."

I notice many things at once about this young man. Of course, you can't miss his black shirt with the word "Trainer" across his chest in large, bright red, block letters. I'm guessing he works at this gym. I also notice that, while he's taller than me, he's probably not more than five foot ten, but he's one well-built son-of-a-bitch. Said tee shirt fits tightly—a walking advertisement for his training abilities—and if there's truth in his advertising, then he's a damn good trainer.

"Have we met?" I ask, because I don't remember seeing him before. I have a feeling I would have noticed.

"No, unfortunately." He smiles. Yes, he's certainly selling something. "I was watching you work out with that... black-haired man. Is he your boyfriend?"

Direct, aren't we? "No, I don't know him. And, thankfully, I only saw him that one time. He asked to work out with me. I didn't want to insult him." Why do I feel the need to explain myself?

"Good. I didn't like him yelling at you like that, in front of everyone. Kind of a prick. But I haven't seen him for a long time, too." He winks at me. "You're safe."

I can't help but smile. This man—boy?—what a charmer. And there's something about his voice. He has a slight accent, like he wasn't born in the U.S. but has been here a long time, although I can't quite place it yet.

We're in the middle of the large room of the gym, the one with the benches. The gym seems pretty quiet though, with not much of the equipment occupied.

"Would you like me to help you work out?" he asks.

"Don't you usually get paid for that type of thing?"

He laughs. "I do get paid—usually—but if you like what I do with you, then maybe you'll want more. That's when you'll pay."

"I see. A free sample, trying to get me hooked."

He shrugs, smiling. "And, believe me, you'll get hooked."

Smug bastard.

He continues, "You did pretty good when I watched you last time, but I can make you better. Much better, I think."

Now I laugh. "I bet you say that to all the girls."

He shakes his head. "I know what I see," he says,

looking me up and down, which, by the way, makes me more than a little uncomfortable. "And I know what I can do."

He lifts and bends his left leg and places his foot against a rare piece of non-mirrored wall. He leans back making a triangle with the floor then purposefully crosses his arms over his chest, a pose which seems to show off his arms and their protruding muscles in quite the, um, attractive manner.

"Well, I like a trainer with confidence." Did I say that out loud? I think I meant to say it to myself.

"You've trained before?"

"No."

"Then, baby, you don't know what you like. But you'll find out. Let's go."

Why not? Because, really, why the hell not? I follow him to the room with the majority of the treadmills, ellipticals and some other equipment I've never used. Of course, he marches right over to one of the unfamiliar ones. It looks like a short staircase, with the first step pretty far off the ground. He nods his head towards it.

I don't like the looks of this. "I don't know how to use that. It looks scary."

"Scary?" he asks, as though not believing I've said that. Why *did* I say that? "Ever climb stairs?" he asks in what can only be described as a no-nonsense tone. "Get on."

All kinds of alarm bells go off in my head. But it's *all* in my head, right? Forget about my fleeting thoughts otherwise—this is nothing but a dream. And if I'm scared off in my *dream*, then I'm one sad, sorry fifty-year old.

I guess I've been hesitating while I've been sorting through these thoughts, and my friend here isn't putting up with any of that.

"You look pretty fit, so I know you can step up onto this all on your own, but if I have to, I'll pick you up and put you on it myself. Let's go. You need to warm up."

Okay, here goes. I reach up and grab onto the handle bars on either side of the stairs first, then raise my right leg way, way up and put it on the first step. It moves slightly down and I immediately pull my foot off.

He crosses his arms over his chest again. "Up."

Yeah, well, I'm not loving him or his teaching methods so far.

"Both hands, pull up, start climbing. You have to start walking right away. Don't hesitate," he commands as he pulls himself up on the side of the neighboring machine, leans over to mine and starts pressing buttons. The console on my machine lights up.

He stares at me, and I do as I am told. Both hands on the rails, right foot lifted onto the bottom step and pull up so my torso becomes level with the short staircase. The stairs move of their own accord, but when I step with my left foot, I start to feel a little resistance from the machine, and this time I gain my balance. Okay, a little high off the ground for my liking, but I can manage. And the climbing's not too difficult.

He pushes a couple more buttons and the resistance gets harder. So much for feeling good about it. "How's that?" he asks.

"Um, tough."

"Good. Ten minutes. It's just a warm up." He hops off the machine he's on and stands between the machines in the spot right next to me. "I'm Rami, because maybe you want to know my name."

He looks up at me and I understand the silent question. "Shoshanna." Might as well use my pseudonym.

"Hmm. 'Rose,' right?"

Does he have a hearing problem? "Shoshanna," I say a little louder.

"I know. 'Shoshanna,' it translates to 'Rose' in English," then adds, when he sees my blank look, "from Hebrew."

"Oh." I guess I look pretty stupid not knowing. Oh, well.

The climbing gets progressively harder, but not because he changes any levels—he doesn't touch my machine again—it's just freaking tiring. "What's... Rami... mean?" I struggle to ask.

He shows me a wicked grin. "'Supreme.' Also Hebrew."

That's it, the accent. He's an Israeli. I would ask him to be sure, but it's getting too hard to speak.

I climb in silence for quite some time until I feel a bucket of sweat pouring off my face. How can this be? I thought Shoshanna has an in-shape body! She should be able to take this. Are those numbers the time ticking down? Thank goodness. Ten more seconds. Damn, how slow can ten seconds be? Okay, done. Get me the hell off of here!

"Great," says Rami, rubbing his hands. "You're warmed up, and we can get started."

Started? I think I'm in trouble.

I follow Rami—as quickly as my jelly legs allow—back into the large room.

We pass a man who looks like he's in his fifties, body a bit on the heavier side. He's on one of those rowing machines.

"Hey, Rami," says the man. "Another victim?"

"Hey, Allen. If she knows what's good for her," Rami says, winking at the man. So, he's friendly with everyone. Well, come on, I knew that charm wasn't just for me, but still...

"A client?" I ask when we're a distance away.

"A very *good* client," Rami answers. "He does very well," Rami rubs his fingers together, so I understand the man does well financially, "and he likes to spend it on himself, which means he spends it on me."

"Well, I hate to say it, but he's not the best advertising for you."

"Really," chuckles Rami. "Want to guess how old he is?"

I don't hesitate. "I'd say about fifty-four, fifty-five?"

"Allen just had his sixty-ninth birthday. Plus, as of a week ago, he's lost eighty pounds."

I think my mouth drops open.

"Hey, Allen," Rami calls across the room. "How long have you been on the rowing machine tonight?"

"Forty-three minutes so far," Allen calls back. "Why?"

"Just wondering," Rami calls in return. He looks at me, smugly. "Told you I'm good. I'm the best."

"You're 'Supreme.'"

"Make fun all you want, but you'll see."

Rami stops by one of the benches, like the one I had worked on with Bart.

"I know this one."

"I know. You used this with the creep."

"You know what's creepy? That you were watching me."

"It's my job to watch. And if it had gotten out of control, I would have stepped in."

"Is that part of the job, too? You rescue girls in distress?"

"Only the ones who are helpless."

"I'm not helpless." Except I don't say it with much enthusiasm.

"You are. You know you are, but you won't be for long. And if you're very nice, I'll teach you some self-defense, too." He puts up his hand before I can talk. "No, it's not part of the job, but it's what I did in the army. The Israeli Army. I trained women, and part of *that* was self-defense."

Rami lies on his back on the bench, his head under the bar, and demonstrates how to do a proper bench press. He tells me I want to feel it both coming down and going back up. Many people, he says, think it's all about the pushing up part, but you want to work your muscles in both directions, get the most out of the exercise. He does it with just the bar—no weights on the ends—and it looks so incredibly easy for him, as though the bar is made of cardboard.

He replaces the bar on the stands and gets up then gestures for me to take his place. I lie down. "That's right. You can bring your head up a little more towards the top. Good. If you want, you can have your feet up. You want to make sure your lower back stays firm on the bench." I pick up my feet and place them on the bench. It feels weird, like I have my shoes on the good furniture. He squats down and looks at my midriff—I guess he's seeing if my back is in the right position. He nods his head then stands and circles around to the top of the bench. "Hands on the bar. Not quite there." He puts his hands on mine and moves them a little further apart. "Too close and you'll use your arm muscles more. You want to use your chest for this."

"How much does this weigh?"

"Your 'boyfriend' didn't tell you?"

"Yuck, don't call him that. And he didn't know."

"Forty-five pounds—just the bar alone. Usually I would start you with some dumbbells—a lot less weight—but you can handle yourself." He winks again. "And I'm trying to make the best impression I can, so I need you sore tomorrow. Well, the day after. Tomorrow won't be as bad as the next day." A sly smile. This guy must spend hours in front of the mirror perfecting that smile.

I'm all set to lift, but I don't. "You know, I thought that was an Israeli accent. How long have you been here, in the States?"

"Long enough to know you're stalling. Ready or not, here we go." He spreads his feet and puts his hands palms up in the space between my hands. "I'm here for support only. You're going to do this. One, two, three, push up and get the bar off the stand. Good. Now bring it forward a little."

And I do. It's weird and disconcerting, but I'm able to handle the weight.

"Okay, don't lock the elbows, and lower, slowly. That's it."

I know his hands are there, so I feel more confident than I would otherwise, and I lower the bar. It feels heavy but not too heavy.

"That's right. Bend those elbows and bring the bar down to your chest. Good, good. Now up. Keep going. Don't lock your elbows. Great. That was one. Seven more reps."

Eight in all? One was pretty easy, two and three, still a breeze, but four through eight get progressively harder. With Bart it had seemed easier, but I guess I wasn't doing it exactly right. In any case, I manage to do them all. He helps guide the bar back onto the stand, and I sit up. About to stand, he says, "Where are you going? We have two more sets."

Now, I don't know the lingo, but I'm guessing it means I have more of this exercise to do. Two more rounds of the same, I'm thinking, and it turns out I'm right.

The second "set," my arms feel tired already, but he

shows no mercy. Eight more, slowly up and down. By the time we get to six, I'm starting to really struggle, but he says, "Let's go, don't slow down. Now, back up. Come on, push it. Good, that's six." And somehow I manage to squeeze out two more.

"Okay, thirty seconds rest, then one more set."

I start to protest, but he wants none of that. "Twenty more seconds." Then, in less than the twenty seconds, he has me lie back down. "Last set. Give it all you've got."

This time, I even struggle with the first rep, and two through eight? Damn near impossible. I'm thanking the fact that his hands stay on the bar, and, to be honest, I think his hands do a little more than safety patrol on the last couple. With my arms so exhausted by the time I get the bar back in its holder, I don't even get up. I just cross my arms over my chest and let them hang there.

Rami laughs. "Baby, we're just getting started. Legs next. Ever do any presses? Come on. We're going to have some fun!"

Exactly whose idea of fun *is* this?

* * *

I'm back. It's the next night, so to speak. At least I woke up, went to work, came home, fell asleep again, so I guess it's the next night in my dreams as well. I'm surprised I fell asleep so quickly, because I wasn't feeling at all well today. My body was kind of aching— just a little, like I'm coming down with something. I hope I'm not. I hate being sick, especially home alone and sick. I haven't had that in a very long time. Come to think of it, I don't think I've ever had that. My mom took care of me when I was sick. Then Joe did, at least a little bit. He opened up a mean can of chicken soup. Okay, I don't mean to make fun of him. He did try.

Looking around, I see a few more people here in the

gym tonight than last night. Not too many of the same people, anyway. Oh, I see that old man who looks not so old. Allen. He's on the rower again. I think I'll say hi.

"Hello," he says back. "Nice to see you here again. What's your name, sweetheart?" He doesn't miss a stroke of his rowing as he talks to me.

"Su—Shoshanna."

"Pretty name for a pretty girl."

"Why, thank you, kind sir."

"So what did you think of our friend Rami? Pretty tough guy, right?" He's still not breathing hard, even with all this talk. "Let me tell you, he's an ambitious one, that boy. While he has me pumping the iron, he's pumping for information about my business. He's saving, he'll invest, and I'm telling you, he'll go far. Certainly farther than me on this damn rower, that I can tell you. You ride and ride, and you don't even move an inch."

"Well, since that's a rowboat to nowhere, I think you've gotten there already—many times over. How often do you do this, anyway?"

"The rowing machine? Oh, I do it every day. Gets the ticker moving but not so hard on my ailing ankles."

"Every day?"

"Every week day, anyway. But I mix it up so I don't get bored. For one thing, I do it at different times of the day. For another, on Mondays, Wednesdays and Fridays, I do an hour."

I can't believe it. This sixty-nine year old does an hour on that thing?!

"And on Tuesdays and Thursdays, I do sixty minutes."

I chuckle. "You should open up your own comedy club. Call it the 'Rowboat.' Get it? Instead of 'The Showboat?'"

"Keep your day job, sweetie."

"Hey, where's Rami anyway?"

"Night off. So, you going to do the personal training with him?"

"Haven't decided. Should I?"

"He's good. And a nice kid. And the ladies sure do like him." The bell rings from the console of the rower. Allen slows down and stops. He picks up a nearby cloth and towels himself off. "Really damn good at what he does."

Chapter 12

A PAIN IN THE...

SUZANNE WAKES UP THE NEXT day, still not feeling well. Worse even. She knows it as soon as she opens her eyes and senses an overall malaise. She lies in bed without moving for a while, waiting for as long as she can before she needs to get going to work. It takes quite an effort, but she reluctantly swings her feet over the side of the bed. Is it some sort of flu? But she doesn't feel feverish at all. Her legs ache, though. As in *really* ache. She tries to reach her feet down to the floor, but they feel as stiff as Frankenstein's monster's legs. She manages to set them down, but the excruciating pain in her calves radiates up as soon as her legs touch the floor.

Suzanne's heart starts pounding. She's truly scared. Nothing has ever happened to her like this before, and she's not sure what to do. Should she wait it out, see what happens? Or should she call the doctor immediately? One thing she knows for sure—she can't make it into work. She can't walk, for goodness sake.

Instead of calling—because she truly hates to speak to her boss and especially does not need to talk to him while in panic mode—she picks up her iPad from the nightstand and sends him an email, calling in sick. Still not knowing what to do next, she swings her legs back up on the bed and massages her calves. Her legs have never felt this stiff before. What the hell?! Does your body fall apart the *moment* you turn fifty?

The pain does not start to ease, not in the least, so, after a short while, Suzanne decides to call the doctor's office. None of the medical staff has arrived yet, so, with no one to talk to, Suzanne makes an appointment for a little later. When she hangs up, though, she realizes she needs to get there, somehow. How will she get to the car, let alone drive it?

She calls Lori. "Good, you're there."

"Where else would I be at eight in the morning?" Lori, in tune as always to the slightest changes in her friend's voice, quickly adds, "What's wrong?"

"My legs. They hurt."

"Both of them? Why? How bad is it?"

"Yes. Don't know. And I can't even walk."

"You can't walk? What do you mean you don't know? It started out of the blue? Maybe you slept wrong."

Slept wrong? Is she joking? How are you going to hurt your legs while you're sleeping? A stiff neck, a sore arm maybe. And the only thing Suzanne did while she slept was to dream about an hour long workout. Yes, during that workout she annihilated every muscle in her body. Yes, the hardest hit part of her body was her legs, but this dream happened the night before last. And, oh yeah, it was a *dream*!

"I didn't sleep wrong. Listen, this is serious. I need your help."

Before Suzanne can even explain that she needs Lori to drive her to the doctor, Lori says, "I'm coming over," and hangs up.

Suzanne immediately calls her back, and just about gets the words in, "Use your key," when Lori hangs up again.

Five minutes later, Suzanne hears the key in her front door and then Lori calling, "Where the hell are you?" Suzanne tells her to come upstairs.

When Lori gets there, shock registers on her face to see her friend laid up in bed. She quickly insists on taking Suzanne to the emergency room. Suzanne counters that she already has a doctor's appointment, asks if Lori can take her there, and, while Lori persists with the hospital idea, Suzanne insists she will stay with the doctor's visit. Suzanne can't imagine it will result in anything of consequence, and she's already embarrassed just going to the doctor.

Even more embarrassing? Actually getting to the car, since Suzanne can't even walk down the stairs. After quite a bit of discussion—always the case with Lori involved—Suzanne ends up going back to her roots. Her roots as a baby. With great effort and a lot of leaning on Lori, she makes it to the landing, but then she "baby bumps" down the stairs on her derriere.

* * *

A humiliating and excruciating hour later, Suzanne at last makes it to her doctor's examining room. Lori helps her in and reluctantly retreats to the waiting room. A short tap on the door and in walks Suzanne's doctor, a woman just a few years younger than herself. They've known each other a long time, and usually Suzanne has no problem asking questions and voicing her concerns, but this time she already feels uncomfortable, and the exam has not even started.

Suzanne reluctantly explains her problem as the doctor washes her hands. The doctor prods, asks questions, prods some more. Suzanne cringes when the doctor straightens Suzanne's legs and pulls her toes up towards her face.

"So, Suzanne, what type of exercise have you been doing?"

"Oh, um, mostly the elliptical, but I'm not doing it too often lately. I've been bad."

"I mean, what did you do a couple of days ago?"

"Nothing."

"You didn't do anything out of the ordinary involving your legs?" Suzanne shakes her head, and the doctor shakes hers in return. "You don't get this way—this charley horsed—doing nothing. That doesn't make sense."

Suzanne decides to put it out there, but in a way that won't make her look ridiculous. She fake laughs and says, "Well, unless you count my dream." The doctor looks at her, obvious confusion in her face. Suzanne explains, "I had this weird dream where I was in a gym, working out with a trainer. I worked my legs pretty hard. Really hard."

The doctor seems to take her remark seriously, but lets her know that even moving around a lot in your dream, or tightening your leg muscles, won't produce such an extreme muscular reaction. And even if she had been on the elliptical, that wouldn't account for it either. The doctor says this only happens to people who over-use their muscles in a way they never have before.

Even though the doctor feels positive it's not the issue, she decides to take some blood work to make sure Suzanne's potassium and electrolyte levels are okay, and, after getting some basic instructions to help her at least feel a little better, a short while later Lori helps Suzanne back into her car.

On the drive home, Lori pumps Suzanne for the results of the exam. Suzanne, lost in her own thoughts, gives terse responses, but the quieter Suzanne stays, the more verbal Lori becomes. "She doesn't know? How can she not know? She's the doctor. You need to get another doctor, maybe. I can still take you to the hospital."

Suddenly, Suzanne blurts out, "I had a dream."

Lori hesitates then says, "What are you, Martin Luther King, Jr.?"

"The doctor said it comes from extreme and unfamiliar exercise. I had a dream where I had the most wicked workout of my life."

"Okay, so you have the answer, then, don't you? You tensed up your muscles while you thought you were exercising in your dream."

Suzanne shakes her head. "The doctor says no. It wouldn't be this bad."

"Maybe she doesn't really know. Maybe your body is different."

Suzanne takes a deep breath in. "Maybe it's..." Suzanne fights with herself. Should she say it? Once she says it, she can never take it back.

Lori stops the car at a red light.

Suzanne plunges. "Maybe it wasn't a dream."

"Huh?"

Suzanne's terse moment over, her thoughts rush out. "I thought they were dreams, I kept telling myself they were dreams, but they weren't like any I've ever had before. So real, like I was living them. I mean, dreams aren't usually so logical, right? Aren't they usually a mishmash of things? But these, these happen in sequence, they're long, they make sense. Well, I don't know how much sense it was that I could snag a hot hunk twenty years my junior—except, of course, Rafael is only younger than *I* am, but he's older than Shoshanna, who is also me. And... and dreams are fast, but if you dream of something for a couple of hours, it can't be just a few minutes fast, can it?"

The light turns green, but Lori stares at her friend, not moving the car until someone behind her honks. Lori then starts driving but stays uncharacteristically quiet.

"I'm crazy, aren't I," asks Suzanne after a couple more silent moments.

"Yes. Yes, you are. Let's forget the hospital. Maybe I need to take you to a different type of institution, my friend."

Suzanne allows her head to drop backwards to the headrest. "Electrolytes, then. Or the potassium."

"Bananas."

"I'm admitting it's not a dream; you don't have to call me crazy."

"I'm not. I'm giving you dietary advice. Go home and eat some bananas—you know—rich in potassium? Eat some bananas, do some stretches, you'll be as good as new. After about a week."

"Gee, thanks, Dr. Lori."

That's all for the talking for the rest of the short drive. Suzanne thinks about how Lori thinks she's crazy. She also feels extraordinarily tired, the pain and the stress of the day already catching up to her. She can't wait to get home, grateful not to be working, and looks forward to a rare, long, uninterrupted nap.

* * *

I don't feel much better here, in the dream—because, as we've established, it most definitely *is* a dream. I lay down on my couch, fell asleep and now I'm here.

But where is *here*? I don't recognize this as any of the places I've recently imagined. Or do I? Wait, something seems a bit familiar. I don't think I ever sat on this high-back sofa before, but the room beyond this alcove, this really large room with tremendously high ceilings and top-to-bottom windows on the one wall I can see... definitely familiar. I try to get up, to check my surroundings, but my legs hurt here as much as they did in the real life I just left. I sit back down, feeling as dejected as I had when I got back to my house.

A few seconds go by, and I hear footsteps. A few more seconds, and I see the feet producing those steps. Polished men's shoes and handsome tailored trousers come to a stop right in front of me.

"Baby, they told me you were here. Are you okay?"

I can't mistake that voice. Rafael. I look up, confused but thankful to see him. I guess he can see the pain in my eyes when he says, "Oh, you don't look okay." And seeing his concerned face, before I know it, I start to cry.

He sits down next to me and immediately lifts his hand and brushes my hair out of my eyes, and some of the tears along with it. "What? What happened?"

I can't stop myself from crying.

"Come, come upstairs." We must be in the lobby of his apartment building, which answers why it looks familiar. He stands and tries to pull me to my feet, but, when I grimace, he stops immediately. "You're hurt?"

I nod my head. "My legs."

Before I know it, he picks me up, carefully cradling my back and legs with his strong arms. I bury my head against his chest. I don't want anyone to witness this, and, like a child, I feel if I can't see them, they can't see me. Fortunately, we're in the elevator in a flash, and I look up from my hiding spot and into Rafael's eyes. I start to calm down. He pulls me closer and kisses my forehead tenderly, the gentle giant with the full, soft lips.

We get out of the elevator, but Rafael hesitates in front of the door to his apartment. "The keys," he says, and looks down. It almost looks as though he's staring at my chest, but I figure out he wants me to grab the keys from his jacket. I slip my hand inside and feel for the breast pocket—of course knocking into his hard chest at the same time. I have to twist my body slightly, but I get to the keys. He leans down with me, and I insert the keys into the lock and turn. I feel his hand move behind my back, and he has the door to his apartment opened.

It's as stark and white as I remember it. He carries me through the threshold—don't even think about that one too much, Suzanne—closes the door with his foot and swiftly continues across the apartment, depositing me on that all-too-low couch.

Thankfully, I've stopped crying, but he's still concerned and attentive. "Okay, now you tell me what happen."

Well, at least he won't call me crazy, because telling him, it won't be a dream. "You're going to think I'm silly. It's really not a big deal."

"You cannot walk, so I think maybe it is a 'big deal.'" Oh, I'd forgotten how cute, how sexy that accent sounds. Hearing it on television, seeing him on television—well, it's just not the same. And I'm here, alone with him in his apartment, the scene of the first—and multiple— "crimes."

"I exercised." Does he think I didn't see that? The raising of the eyebrows. "A lot. I mean a whole lot. Exercises I've never done before."

"Ah," the light bulb goes on. "That happened to me, also. When I started with the dancing. What did they say? Charley hose?"

"Horse. Charley horse."

"Why do they call it that?"

"Beats me."

"Wait—somebody beats you? I thought you said it was your exercising?"

"No, sorry. Just an expression. 'Beats me' means 'I don't know.'" I need to lose the idioms around him. Changing the subject, "Were you able to walk when you had it?"

"Oh, yes. Mine was not so bad. But I am sorry you cannot walk."

A smile? Why is he smiling? "You don't look sorry I can't walk."

"No, sorry. I smile because I can help you. You know, before, when I was younger, before I started to act, I make money a different way." He moves the fingers on both hands, kneading the air. "I did the massage."

I think I like the direction of this conversation.

"Would you like me to give you one?"

I definitely like this direction.

"I have very good hands."

Well, that I already know.

And before I can answer, he picks me up once again and starts walking towards the hallway, the one that leads to the bedroom. He responds to my surprised expression—which he can easily see because he's looking straight at my face instead of where he's walking—by letting me know the couch is too low and narrow for a big man like him to give a massage. Anyway, I really wasn't asking. Who cares about the sofa right now? I'm cradled in his arms, and he's so tender, the way he holds me. I'm so not the damsel in distress, never have been, but I have to admit, it feels incredible, him taking care of me.

He gently puts me down on the bed, taking great care not to touch my legs. Then he surprises me again by asking me to take my clothes off, but I quickly understand his real intention. He wants to give me a full body massage. He holds up a sheet and averts his eyes, which I find quite touching, since, you know, he has seen all of me before. A beautiful gesture to make me feel comfortable.

I lie down on my stomach, and he covers me with the sheet. The linens have an incredible calming scent, and I feel like I'm in a spa, especially when he turns on some ultra-relaxing, Zen-like music.

I'm completely covered up to my neck as he lays his hands on my back. Honestly, his soft touch alone could melt my muscles. He rocks me back and forth ever so slightly, his hands getting used to my back, allowing my body to get used to his touch. After a few moments, he peels back the sheet from my right arm only. I can't see him, but I hear what sounds like the squeezing of a bottle. Must be massage oil. Now, so slowly I can hardly tell when the touch starts, he begins to massage my arm. Ahh. His professional background sure shows, even down to the perfect ocean scent of the oil. Somewhere in the room a fan blows, and a gentle breeze plays across my body, a counterpoint to his firm touch. His remarkable hands magically release the tension from the muscles in my arm, muscles I had no clue even existed until he started working them. His attention to detail surreal, he pays as much mind to the smallest parts of my hand as he does to the large muscles above my elbow.

I already feel so relaxed I doubt I can lift my arm, which he now covers up. He moves to the other side.

He speaks not a single word as he finishes the left arm and moves on to my neck, back and shoulders, lingering a long time wherever he senses the most tension, with no sense of time or rush. I have no idea how long he spends on each area, or how many minutes pass. I feel the warm air, I smell the island smells, I luxuriate in the sensation of the oils on my skin. Mostly, I succumb to his strong, insightful hands exploring every part of my bare body.

After ample time, he covers my back, and I know the serious part will now begin. He moves the sheet from my right leg to the empty vee between both my legs. I hear the squeeze of the bottle once again—a long squeeze. I know he'll take extra care, but even in my relaxed upper-body state, I'm scared.

He lays his hands on my upper right thigh as gently as his first touch. I grimace involuntarily.

"So sorry," he apologizes, his first words since we began. "It will hurt, but it will be okay. I promise." He continues. I can tell he's holding back his strength, but even his slightest touch proves excruciating. He alternates a soft kneading with running his fingers lightly across my skin, feather-like. He repeats the motions over and over, muttering, "It's okay, it's okay" until, finally, I can feel my leg start to relax. He feels it, too, and begins to massage a little deeper, then deeper still. When he seems to sense—correctly—I've had enough, he covers the right leg up and attends to the left, with the same agonizing but gentle regimen. Finally, the muscles in my left leg also respond and release.

I think he must be done, but no. He covers both legs leaving only my feet exposed, his hands as skilled with them as with the rest of the massage, and I feel the effects throughout my body.

I'm so relaxed. I can feel myself drift off to sleep...

*   *   *

I don't know how long I've slept, but I wake up groggily. Maybe no sex that time, but I'd rate that dream as one of my best. Hmm, I must be bringing a little of the dream-state into my reality, because I can still smell the scent of the ocean on the sheets. I roll over, eyes closed, but I feel something hard in bed with me. I open my eyes in alarm.

Oh, I'm still sleeping. Well, Rafael lies next to me, anyway. He's not sleeping, though. He looks at me, and I get the feeling he's been watching me as I sleep. We face each other, both propped on our sides. We share the same sheet he covered me with during the massage.

"Have I been snoring?" I ask. I kind of want to know, but, really, I'm trying to cover what could be an awkward moment.

He shakes his head, then lifts his hand and starts stroking my arm, the sensation now completely different, unlike his professional masseur touch. Maybe it's because he's looking at me so intently. "The massage, it was good?"

I sigh and allow myself to fall onto my back, looking up, remembering. "The massage, it was heavenly."

"Good," he says, sounding genuinely pleased. He scoots closer to me. I realize I'm not the only naked one. "You feel better now."

I flex my feet. Yes, better. Not great, but I can move them, and the pain has lessened. I nod my head.

He moves even closer. "Very good. So, now, I'm the one with the problem. He lifts the sheet and looks down, drawing my attention to his "problem." "Maybe I need a massage."

I can't help myself—I laugh. "I'm sorry, that just sounded so..."

He also laughs. "That was not so good. But, the problem..."

Well, I wouldn't call that a problem. And this kind of massage I'm more than happy to provide. I take hold of him, his "problem," and his intake of breath, his eyes closing, the feel of him so hard in my hand—it's all I can do not to jump him immediately. Inside or outside of reality, it's been a very long time since I last had sex, and the pain I'm feeling hits me suddenly, an aching, a yearning that seems to match his own. And, oh, how I've missed the sight of his Michelangelo-inspired perfect body!

"Let me know if you hurt, and I'll stop," he says.

"Don't you dare!" I warn. Maybe he wants to laugh again, but instead he presses into me. I think he's still being careful not to hurt my legs, and I feel his glorious weight on my upper body. He starts to kiss me hungrily, and I respond, just as hungry. I want him desperately, but he stops and reaches under his pillow, pulls out a condom and hands it to me. So, obviously this all was planned. Well, that's fine with me. I happily open it and roll it onto him.

"Now!" I demand.

"Baby, whatever you want." And he proves once again that he understands the body, a woman's body, like no one else I've ever known. Not only does he move against me in just the right way inside, he uses his hand for pressure from the outside. I explode so quickly I'm almost disappointed, but I should know not to be with Rafael. He waits a few seconds for my orgasm to subside, then turns me over onto my stomach, putting a hand on the area still throbbing. He lies down on my back, leaning himself against me, still kneading me with his hand. "Come, baby. Come for me again." The way he's holding me, the feel of him on my back... before too long, I oblige. Again he waits until this orgasm has died down, and he turns me once again to face him. "More?" he asks.

I nod my head.

"This one for both of us," he croons and enters me once more. I see his expression change, no longer intent upon me but adrift in his own sensations. This is the first time I'm watching him lost in extreme pleasure, and it's so hot I drive up into him with as much force as I can muster. He responds by speeding up his movements. I respond as well...

* * *

I seem to have fallen asleep again, but waking up next to Rafael is a treat, no matter how many times I do it.

I open my eyes to see his are closed now. I study his beautiful face, masculine but gentle, and his body, unmatched, strong with a massive chest one could gaze at—and lean upon—endlessly. I could not have done a better job making up the perfect man—so caring, so sweet, and, of course, exceptional at massage *and* in bed. Well done! Especially the dancing part. Well, that's where my imagination *has* failed me, since my legs certainly won't allow that activity this time.

Rafael's eyes open. He smiles. "You're watching me?"

I smile. "You're an actor, aren't you? Don't you like to be watched?" Oh, that reminds me—why didn't I think of this before? "Why are you still here, in this apartment? I thought this was for while you were on the show. But that's over, right, and you're still living here?"

"Why? You don't like this apartment? This bed?" he asks. "Right now, I like it very much." He once again runs his hand up and down my arm.

Oh, I like it all right. Very, *very* much...

Rafael continues, "I got used for it, and I make arrangements to stay a little longer, but—"

A cell phone on the night table next to Rafael rings. He looks at the number, smiles and says, "Excuse me, please." He pushes a button and talks into the phone. "Hello?" A hesitation as he listens to the person on the other end. "Only a minute." He listens again then swings his feet to the floor, pulling back the sheet and standing in all his glory for the world—okay, right now it's just for me—to see.

"I did not see it, but I look." He goes over to the dresser and moves a few things aside. "Ah, it's here." He picks up what looks to be a woman's bracelet. "Of course, baby, but not tonight. Tomorrow."

What is that? "Baby?" And he's using the same seductively soothing voice he uses with me.

"No, it must to be tomorrow. I leave the day after." Listens. "Here. Perfect. I'll make you some dinner. *Hasta mañana.*"

He's asked a woman to dinner tomorrow. While I'm lying here naked. And we just finished fucking.

I watch as he puts the bracelet down, turns towards me and then practically runs into bed. He catches me on the way in and pulls me towards him, but I stiffen against him.

"Something wrong, baby?"

He's quick to sense my rejection, I'll give him that. "What was that just now?" I blurt out before I can stop myself. Of course, I have no right to this man at all.

"Oh, I understand. Sorry, I was wanting to tell you. I'm leaving, but I didn't want for you to hear it on the phone. That's what I saying but then the phone, it rang." Yes. Another woman calling. "I stayed in the apartment, the producers, they agree, because I need a place until my next job. But I leave to be on the set in England in two days. I want to say this earlier but we were, you know, a little busy."

Even though I really don't know this man, even though I've only slept with him a couple of times, even though he's obviously been with another, bracelet-forgetting woman—recently—even though he's a figment of my imagination, even though all of this, it hits me, and my heart drops into my feet. He's leaving.

I try to focus on what's important here. "You're sleeping with another woman."

"Yes?" It's a question, as though asking, 'So?' "I sleep with many womens."

Okay, well, as proud of myself as I was a short while ago for imagining such a perfect man, such a perfect scenario, that's all down the toilet now.

Chapter 13

THEY MEET AGAIN

THE DOORBELL RINGS. SUZANNE HEARS it through the fog of sleep. It rings again. She decides not to get up. She'll let the intruder leave. They shouldn't be interrupting her nap, anyway.

But it rings once again. Persistence pays off, and Suzanne rouses herself.

"Coming," she calls, because she realizes her strained legs may slow her down. She tentatively pulls them off the couch and places them on the floor, standing slowly. So far, so good. First step with the right leg. It still hurts. The left leg still hurts, too, but she continues and happily finds the pain easing with each step. By the time she reaches the door, she realizes it feels as it had in her dream, after the massage from that two-timing (Two-timing? Maybe more-timing) no good, but incredibly good at it and strong-handed and unbelievably sexy man. As Suzanne opens the door, all that she can think about is how the best sex she ever had in her life has likely gone for good, since her imagination has sent him packing.

The man at the door has his back turned, looking

across the street at the neighbor's house, but Suzanne immediately knows who stands before her. "Hello, Joe," she says.

Joe turns as though startled. "Hi." He has a miniature shopping bag in his hand. "Hey, Suze." His tone gives away the awkward way he feels.

Suzanne finds herself at a bit of a loss. What should she do? Good manners win over, and she invites him in.

The two go to the living room. As Joe sits in one of the barrel chairs, Suzanne offers him a drink, although it feels more than weird, treating him as a guest in what had been his home for decades. He declines, and Suzanne feels grateful she will not have to serve him.

"I see you're walking a little funny," Joe comments.

And Suzanne had thought she's doing so much better...

"What happened?" says Joe, punctuated by a nervous laugh. "Rough sex?"

Really? Did he just say that? Why would he be so stupid, and how could it get any more awkward? Suzanne smiles weakly. "Sore muscles. They're getting better." She really should have said yes to his rough sex joke, though. Would serve him right. "So, what brings you here?" she continues, hoping the conversation-changer will lead them to more comfortable ground.

Joe lifts up the small bag and holds it out to Suzanne. "I hear you had a great soiree."

Suzanne hesitantly takes the bag. This ground is just as awkward, considering Joe had not been on the invite list. "Very nice. The girls helped throw a wonderful party."

"Good to hear."

Suzanne gestures to the bag. "You didn't have to."

"Well, the fiftieth... You know, if we were still married, I would have really had to go all out, so I kind of got off easy."

Okay, so either this is now way past awkward, or it's kind of funny.

"Um, why don't you open it?" asks Joe looking as though he finally realizes he should be quiet.

Suzanne looks into the fancy faux leopard paper bag and pushes aside the crinkly paper. Hidden inside she sees a small white box. She's momentarily taken aback, because it's certainly not his usual iTunes gift card.

"I never got you anything like this before, so I figured it was time," he says as she takes off the lid of the box.

Suzanne cannot believe her eyes. On a small, white cotton bed rests a stunning pair of delicate, dangling earrings, with a thin sliver of a silver rod and a round crimson ruby orb at the bottom surrounded by a leaf shaped out of tiny diamond chips.

"I never see you wearing any earrings, so I figured it's about time you had a beautiful pair." Joe scoots to the edge of his chair to get a better look. "At least *I* think they're pretty."

Suzanne nods her head. "Yes. Exquisite, actually."

Joe smiles, obviously pleased with himself and his great purchasing accomplishment. "Great. Use them well." He sits back in his seat.

Suzanne's not quite sure what to say. Lovely, they most certainly are, but, although, she had her ears pierced as a teenager, she had several severe infections since then and she let the holes close years ago—hence why Joe's never seen her wearing earrings. And these earrings are most definitely for pierced ears, Suzanne is at a loss. "That's very... thoughtful, Joe."

He beams again.

Suzanne gets up to take the bag with the earrings over to the table at the far end of the living room.

Joe watches her strained walk. "So, sore muscles,

huh? You okay?"

"Yeah, getting there. Will be soon."

"I can help you."

That's funny. Isn't that the same thing Rafael said? Suzanne is taken aback at how strange it feels to think of Rafael while in the same room with her husband. Her *ex*-husband, she reminds herself. *And* Rafael doesn't exist—at least in her real life. And how would Joe help? The same way? But he's never given her a massage before. Does he even know how?

Joe interrupts her reverie. "Here, I'll show you." He stands and walks next to the couch, putting his hands on the wall. He stretches his right leg back, making a triangle with his body, the wall and the floor. "It's a great stretch. You hold it for a half minute or so—don't push too far—and it'll really loosen things up for you."

See? Stretching instructions. Just as good as a warm-touch, ultra-intimate massage, isn't it?

"You try it," Joe insists.

Suzanne has absolutely no desire to stretch—at this moment or in front of Joe—but she also knows he won't give up until she does, so she heads over to the wall and starts the exercise.

"A little more," he encourages

"A little sore, here. It hurts."

"I got that, but you need to stretch."

"Yup, I am."

"Okay. Now hold that for a little while. And I'll just visit the bathroom while you do." He starts towards the main floor half bathroom but stops. "Um, if that's okay with you?"

Will this ever not feel weird?

"Of course," she says.

While Joe visits the bathroom, Suzanne finishes the stretch on her right leg and then does the other leg. It actually does feel pretty good.

By the time she's done with that second leg, Joe has returned from the bathroom. "You know," he says, "you really shouldn't use that brand of toilet paper. If you don't flush right, it's going to clog."

Seriously? There's really nothing Suzanne can say to that. "Mind your own business" pops into her head, of course, but that doesn't feel quite right after he generously gave her a beautiful pair of earrings. Of course, she'll never be able to wear them...

Joe interrupts Suzanne's thoughts. "I've been wanting to talk to you about something."

Suzanne wonders to herself what he wants to talk about now. More toilet paper choices? Maybe the proper way to floss her teeth? Or maybe how much money she should spend at the grocery store next week? That was sure a big topic of discussion in their married years.

"I know you're not going to like hearing this—"

Suzanne's mental answer involves suggesting that then maybe he shouldn't say it.

"But I think maybe Abigail should stay home with you this year. Go to school locally, live at home, keep you company. It's no good, you being here alone."

Suzanne, stunned, doesn't respond for a moment, thinking whether she *should* respond. Finally she does. "What the hell are you talking about?! Is this about money? Tuition money?"

Joe seems taken aback by Suzanne's yelling. "What? What's your problem?! I'm trying to help you."

"By kicking our daughter out of school?"

"Kicking her out? I'm suggesting she go to school closer to home. What's wrong with that for one year? And, yes, it would save a little money. What exactly is wrong with *that*?"

"What is wrong with that is that I would even have to

explain to you what's wrong with that, which is pretty much why we're no longer married, and I no longer have to explain what exactly is wrong with that."

To which Joe does not reply. He goes to the front door, opens it and walks outside then turns and says, "Enjoy the earrings," closing the door with some force as an untold exclamation point.

Enjoy the earrings, indeed!

Suzanne spends the evening first on the phone with Lori discussing the idiocy of her afternoon visit and then watching television to stop her mind from obsessing about it. A long while later, her blood pressure drops enough to finally fall asleep.

* * *

Well, this is scary as shit. I'm back in the gym. At least I can walk again. Maybe I should do some stretches while I'm here. It can't hurt. And Joe, the asshole, was kind of right. That calf exercise did actually help.

And speaking of assholes, if it isn't the King of Pain, Mr. Rami Sadist himself. He's not torturing anyone tonight, it seems. Too busy looking at himself in one of the many floor-to-ceiling mirrors. Who does that, holds up his shirt in a public place and looks at his abdomen? More importantly, who pulls down the elastic of his gym shorts at the same time to expose those, okay, I've never seen that in person before—how did he get that perfect ridge right below his six pack?

And what a six pack it is! You know, on second thought, I can totally see why he's pulling up that shirt to show the world. Holy hell. He may not be as tall as Rafael, but, man, in a competition for the well-sculpted body of the year, I'd be hard-pressed to pick between the two.

I think I must be about the most frustrated woman in

the world to keep conjuring up these perfectly shaped men. And this one will turn out to be an asshole, too. Trust me.

He's seen me. At least he has the decency to pull up his pants and pull down his tee shirt as he smiles at me.

"You're not my favorite person," I say as he approaches. His smile does not falter in face of the harsh words. "I could hardly walk," I add, feeling the need to explain myself.

"Let me see," he answers, beckoning me. I walk towards him. "You look okay to me."

"I had help."

"So, you came back to start private sessions?" It sounds more like a comment than a question.

"And what are you smoking?" Rami looks at me blankly. Apparently, here's another one who doesn't get American slang. "Are you out of your mind?" I rephrase, an easier expression to understand.

"But your legs feel good now, right?" He looks at my legs. "They look good."

I'm pretty sure he's playing me.

"You liked lifting the weights. I saw that. It won't hurt you anymore. The first time, it's the hardest. In weightlifting." He smiles at me again.

"You're selling sex, you know," I blurt out.

This remark doesn't seem to bother him either. He just clicks his tongue on his teeth and shakes his head, then lifts his shirt a little and gestures to his abs. "For the men, I'm selling how they want to look."

"The fantasy, you mean. They're not going to look like that."

"Hey, they only have to work hard. Very hard." A sly smile now. "For the women, I sell, well... a chance to be close to me."

Wow. Wasn't expecting that kind of honesty. "So,

you're selling sex," I insist once more.

"No." He comes up right next to me, so close I can feel the heat of his body. "I do not sleep with my clients." He looks into my eyes. "Like I said, you have great possibilities, and you'll learn a lot from me. I think you should take lessons."

You know what? I think I should, too.

*   *   *

So, tell me now, why I'm such an idiot? Was it just last night I signed on that contract line? Twenty-five one hour sessions. Now who's out of her mind?

And Rami's sensual yet oh-so-scary response when he learned I had signed up for him? "You're mine now," he had said, sadistic yet sexy.

In the here and now, though, we have only the sadistic. "Let's go, next set. Slowly this time," Rami barks.

It's called a "lat pulldown" and he wants me to do *everything* slowly *every* time. Pull down to my chest, then release but, yeah, I know, *slowly*. Except the bar connects to weights. Heavy weights. I complain, and Rami asks if I thought it would be easy. Easy, impossibly hard—isn't there a lot in between? Okay, I think I better concentrate. Pull down—slowly—keep going, to the chest, let it up one two three four. Rami stands directly behind me, the extremely attentive trainer. His hands touch my back, the muscles he wants me to work. A hands-on trainer. He tells me to concentrate on those particular muscles as I raise and lower the silver bar.

Okay, so I have to admit, despite my bitching, I actually really enjoy this. And it's not just the touch by this all too attractive young—emphasize the *young*—man. I like the sensation of the weights. I like the rough feel of the place on the bar where I put the palms of my hands. I like the power I feel in my muscles. And his touch, I have to admit, helps me concentrate so I can really feel the muscles working. But I can't really show Rami how I feel, because then, I have a strong suspicion, the exercises will go way beyond what I enjoy and, most importantly, what I can handle.

We're done with the third set, and Rami claps his hands and pronounces, "Biceps. Come."

Even *I* know this means we're going to work my arms. I get up from the lat pulldown and realize how tired I already feel, but I dutifully follow him to the next round of torture. He points to a bench shaped almost like a straight-back chair. I happily sit as he heads to the rack of weights directly in front of it, on the wall of mirrors I face. He thankfully selects two of the smaller dumbbells and brings them over to me. In his arms, they look pretty light, so it's a bit shocking when he places them in my hands. I look on the ends and see they weigh ten pounds each. Doesn't sound like much, but lightweight? Not so lucky.

Rami returns to the rack and picks up two more dumbbells, larger than the ones I hold. He sits down on a similar bench a few feet from mine. "Watch," he says as he starts the demonstration. He sits with his back straight, weights held in his hands, hanging down at his sides. He starts with his left hand, controlling it as he lifts it in an arc so it's almost, but not quite, touching his shoulder. He slowly lowers it, just as controlled, and when it's hanging down all the way, he repeats the movement with his right hand. He then puts down the weights. "Okay, let's see three sets of ten reps each arm." When I don't move, he continues in a bark. "Now."

And so it goes...

Chapter 14

NOW, THAT'S WHAT I CALL A BICEP

THE PHONE RINGS. LUCKILY, THE phone sits next to the bed, so Suzanne can answer it without moving anything more than her arm. She grunts a greeting. Lori, of course. No one else would be calling at this ungodly hour. "And good morning to you, too, Sunshine. Time for wakey. We're going to the gym before they decide you've abandoned your membership and take you off their books."

In her early morning *I had no intention of getting out of bed don't you know it's the weekend* haze, Suzanne almost says, "But I've been going to the gym four times a week for a month and a half," except she catches herself after the "But," since the gym she's been frequenting does not exist in the real world.

"'But' what?" answers Lori.

Suzanne has to think fast. She does not want to have another conversation about her dream life, especially with her non-functioning morning brain. "But is the gym open this early?"

"This *early*? Many worms have been devoured by this time of day, let me assure you. Get dressed—in your workout clothes—and I'll pick you up in fifteen."

What Suzanne really wants to say is, "Screw you, I've worked out enough and I want to go back to sleep," but, in reality, she *has* neglected her *real* gym membership. "Ugh," she says, which, unlike the earlier greeting groan, means, "Okay, I give up."

"Look cute," Lori says before she hangs up. "You're a single lady these days. The gym is a great place to pick up men."

It takes all the energy Suzanne can muster to get herself out of bed and into some probably not so cute shorts and tee shirt, let alone brush her teeth and hair, before Lori arrives. Lori, on the other hand, lands on her doorstep, a ball of energy adorned in a pair of deep purple capri yoga pants and a lime green spandex top.

"You're still in pajamas," Lori complains as soon as Suzanne opens the door.

"Huh? You told me to be ready in my workout clothes." Suzanne gives a Vanna White motion to show her outfit.

Lori sighs and taps her foot at the same time. "Okay, grab your purse. We're stopping at the mall first."

If there could possibly be one thing Suzanne wants to do even less than go to the gym early on a Saturday morning, it's go shopping, especially in shorts and a tee shirt. But what she wants, she doesn't get. Off to the mall they go.

*   *   *

A short while later, Lori and Suzanne enter the locker room of the gym. Despite Lori's teasing warnings, they allowed Suzanne through the front doors without even mentioning the fact that she has not been there in months.

At the mall, Lori had insisted on everything new—except she did let Suzanne keep the sneakers, since those had been purchased just a few months before. But *everything* else Suzanne puts on her body still has the tags from the shopping spree just completed. The biggest fuss Suzanne put up was on the underwear, if you can call this new item something to wear. In Suzanne's mind, it's the clichéd dental floss underwear. When Suzanne had initially said a firm no, because who wants to see a fifty year old woman in a thong, Lori countered that anyone these days who would possibly be seeing Suzanne in her underwear would rather see a thong than the matronly butt covering cotton whites which undoubtedly were taking up a full drawer in the dresser she had, until recently, shared with a husband who had not paid any real attention to her in many years. Hard to argue with a woman of so many words in the middle of a crowded, Saturday morning store, so Suzanne now owns a half dozen lacy unmentionables that sewn together could maybe add up to just one of her old completely mentionables.

Lori helps Suzanne pull off the tags, and soon enough Suzanne stands in front of the locker room mirror gazing with a critical eye at the stranger in tight black long workout pants and a skimpy, tight-fitting lycra watermelon top.

"Wow. I know I'm a good shopper, but I didn't realize I'm *that* talented. You look great!"

Suzanne has to agree. This wonderful bra is truly a wonder, and these pants a perfect fit. Who knew clothing could do so much for a body?

The two women head out to the workout floor and over towards the ellipticals. They snag two side-by-side and start their machines.

Both women have their headsets with them. Suzanne plugs in and turns on the television, but she quickly realizes Lori has not connected her ear buds and instead stares at Suzanne. Finally, starting to feel uncomfortable, Suzanne takes off her headset and blurts out, "What? What are you looking at?"

Lori hesitates then says, "Something's not right."

"Well, it's your fault if you don't like the outfit. You picked it, remember?"

"The outfit's fantastic. I told you, you look great."

"So, what's wrong?"

"Nothing's wrong. It's just not right. Didn't you see, in the mirror?"

"See what? I thought I looked surprisingly good. Now I'm starting to think not." Suzanne turns back to the control panel of her elliptical. She's finding the beginning level a bit too easy and increases the speed.

"Yes, clothes can make your ass look curvy, your legs thin and shapely, your boobs a bit perkier than usual, but you're wearing a sleeveless shirt. How come your arms look so much tighter than last time I saw them? That's not the clothes, honey-pie."

Suzanne looks across the way at the mirrors. It's a little hard to see herself, but she tries her best to get a view of her arms. Are they looking better than before? She shrugs. "Haven't the slightest."

They both plug back in and for a while concentrate on the small screens in front of them as they move their legs in endless circles. After about twenty minutes, Suzanne turns to Lori and asks, "Have you been using any of the weights?"

"Are you kidding?"

"I think maybe it would be fun. To try."

"I've made a fool of myself every time I've tried. Anyway, I'm happy over here in my aerobic world."

Suzanne keeps moving her feet around and around, but at the same time, her mind keeps going back to the weights. About ten more minutes go by, and, on a whim,

Suzanne unplugs, shuts down her machine and steps off.

"You done?" asks Lori.

"I'll be back."

Suzanne has spent enough time looking around while on the aerobic machines to know where to find things. She walks over to a place where she's seen the gym rats working with dumbbells. It's not exactly the same setup as she concocted in her dreams, but it looks familiar enough. She puts her water bottle down by an upright bench and goes over to the racked weights. In her dreams, she's up to fifteen pound dumbbells. She knows she won't be able to handle that for real, so she looks for the lightest ones she can find. She sees ten pound weights and thinks maybe that's pushing it, but there's nothing less than ten in this section, so she selects two and returns with them to her bench. She sits down with a straight back and holds the weights close to her body, one in each hand. Concerned she'll have a hard time, she puts all her concentration into her right arm and slowly lifts the dumbbell up, just as Rami had "shown" her. It feels surprisingly natural. Very surprising. And light. She tries her left arm. Also very easy. She doesn't bother doing any more and returns to the rack to exchange them for something a little heavier. She means to take the next weight up—twelve pounds—but they seem to be missing from their designated spot on the rack. "What the hell," she thinks to herself, and grabs the fifteen pounders.

Sitting back down with them, her heart beats loudly, not from exertion but from fear. She has no right trying to handle these weights. Dreams aside, she has no training, no experience, but she's already all set, and she doesn't want to back down now. Concentrating even harder than before, she lifts the right dumbbell up. It feels... exactly as it had in the "other" gym. Not easy, but not too hard, and the heavy resistance in her hand, and the effort it takes to lift it smoothly up almost to her shoulder, it's exhilarating. She lowers her right hand and begins again with her left hand. That's two, she counts to herself. She continues, unaware of any of the noises around her, putting all her thoughts and efforts into her two arms, feeling the muscles contract and elongate with each repetition. Before she knows it, she's gotten to sixteen. She feels great and could easily do more, but she puts them down, figuring she'll do a couple more sets.

After placing the weights on the floor, she looks up and sees Lori standing next to her.

"What the hell, Suze?! So, that's why your arms look so good. What have you been doing, sneaking around to come to the gym? Why would you lie about this?" Lori turns and starts to walk away from Suzanne, not waiting for an answer.

Suzanne stands and defends herself as she follows her friend. "No, really, no. Lori, I haven't been here for ages." Except as soon as the words come out of her mouth, she feels guilty, as though speaking a lie. What a confusing feeling, telling the truth but, at the same time, feeling as though she's not.

Suzanne follows Lori, who currently appears not to be talking to her, all the way into the locker room. Lori heads into a bathroom stall, leaving Suzanne in the bathroom area, facing the mirror. "I'm telling you the truth, Lori," Suzanne asserts again. She leans her hands on the sink area. "I swear, the only times I've been to the gym are in my dreams."

Suzanne hears a small "Humph" coming from the stall.

Suzanne looks up at the same moment, seeing her

reflection. It does feel almost like her dream right now, because the body she sees looking back at her is not the body she knows. It's still her—not the young girl Shoshanna by any stretch of the imagination—but certainly a somewhat smaller Suzanne, and those arms—trim, firm. She looks almost like one of those photos, where you put your head into an oval hole and take a picture of your face on someone else's body. That's an exaggeration, of course, but those arms especially, so not her arms. No wonder Lori got so upset. Especially to see Suzanne lifting the weights as though she's been doing it forever. Suzanne's heart starts to pound once more. What is going on here?

Suzanne turns away from the mirror, no longer wanting to see herself, and quietly waits for Lori to come out. When she does, finally, she looks at Suzanne then looks away.

As Lori washes her hands, Suzanne tries once more to speak to her. "Look, Lori, I don't know any more of what's going on here than you do."

Lori shoots her a piercing look.

"Really. I have not been in this gym, I swear. The only gym I've been in—"

"Hah!" Lori interjects.

"The only one I've been in is the one I've been dreaming about."

Lori rolls her eyes in an expected reaction. "Oh, the one that landed you in the doctor's office? That mythical place?"

"I know. That was crazy. This is crazy. But *I'm* not crazy. Look at me! Look at my arms."

Lori does look as Suzanne fists both hands and does the clichéd body building pose, with both arms curled to show off the biceps, much bigger bumps than her arms have ever shown. Then she drops her right arm and turns it slightly. There's a small tricep starting to protrude from her upper arm.

"We talk all the time," says Suzanne after dropping both her arms from their poses. "You know where I am all the time. Have you ever called me and heard gym noises?"

Lori reluctantly shakes her head.

"See? I'm telling you, I don't know what's—" Suzanne cuts herself off as she becomes overwhelmed suddenly by a sickening feeling. She leans back against the sink area.

Lori comes over to her friend's side. "Suze, are you okay?"

Tears well in Suzanne's eyes. It's her turn to shake her head.

"Come on," insists Lori. "Let's get dressed and grab a drink."

* * *

The "drink" in this case is bottled water, which they grabbed from the refrigerator section at the gym, put on Lori's tab and took to Lori's car, which has now become a temporary mobile think tank.

Quite apparently, something a little stronger than water may have been a better choice for this particular conversation.

"If I saw this in a movie," Lori says, "I would be rolling my eyes, it's so ridiculous. And I still don't think I believe it."

Suzanne has stopped crying, but just barely. "You did roll your eyes."

"Can you blame me? It's so not logical to me."

"To me either," admits Suzanne.

They sit in silence for a moment. Each woman takes a sip from her water bottle.

"But how can you explain it?" asks Suzanne after a

long swallow. She touches her upper arm. "How did I get muscles?"

"It sure isn't from housework," Lori gibes.

"Kick a girl when she's down, why don't you?"

"Sorry. Just some nervous joking. It's not every day your friend tells you she thinks she's actually been physically going places in her dreams."

Another silence and then a sudden confession from Suzanne. "It's not just when I'm asleep. It happened once at least—once for sure—when I was awake. Here. At the gym."

"What? You were here at this gym and then, poof, you were at that other gym?"

"Um," Suzanne can't even look her friend in the eye. "Uh, no, I didn't go to the other gym. I, uh, went somewhere else. Except it wasn't me."

"Huh?"

"You remember that time? You asked me if I was okay? You thought I had zoned out?"

"Oh, yeah. That was weird."

Suzanne explains that it was even weirder than Lori thought. She explains that she was inside the head of some man, *while he was having sex.*

Lori screws up her face. "Okay, I'll play along for now. What was he thinking?"

Suzanne screws up her own face and tries to shake off the memory, but one gnawing thought won't go away. "Is that really a thing, doing the alphabet with your tongue? On a woman. You know."

"Ooh, I've read about that! I don't think it's ever been tried on me, though. Well, if it has, I haven't recognized it as the alphabet... Anyway, if this really is some time travel—"

"Not time travel," corrects Suzanne. "More like, I don't know, some alternate reality or something."

"Okay, so what is it? You just randomly show up in different places?"

Suzanne argues that it can't be that random considering that most of the time she visits the same places with the same people. And it's places she wants to be.

Lori asks her how, then, she can explain this flight into some loser guy's head while he's doing some young thing. Suzanne admits that, right before she ended up there, she was thinking how tired she was of being in her own head, day after day, month after month, year after year, and how she desperately wanted some relief from that, a break from her own head. And, next thing she knew, and bizarre as it may seem, her wish had come true.

The two women stop talking for a moment and lean back in their seats.

Lori breaks the silence. "This is crazy. You really think you've been travelling to some new reality? Even saying it—it's just, it's crazy! I sound like an idiot. And why all of a sudden now? Or has this been going on for a long time, and you've been keeping it to yourself? It's crazy. I don't even know what I'm saying."

"I know. I know. But, I've got to tell you, it doesn't feel crazy when I'm in it. It feels real."

"Right. Really crazy."

"Bunco."

"Completely bonkers! That's what I'm saying."

"Bunco is when it started. Bunco night."

"Yeah, well, I'm not the one having supercharged sex-on-steroids dreams—fantasies, realities, whatever—and I'm not the one growing muscles while I sleep—so, to be honest, I have no idea what Bunco has to do with it."

"When we played, that was the night I saw Cybil. The night she gave me this." Suzanne pulls the necklace out from under her shirt. "I've gone over this, again and again, but it makes sense now, in a strange way. When I lost it, I didn't have any of these 'dreams.' As soon as I found it again, months later, they immediately started up again. It can't be coincidence. It's not logical."

"Right, so it's logical that you're wearing a magic necklace that mystically transports you to other realms where you're a young, hot macho-man-magnet having sex with superstars—"

"Only one superstar."

"Oh, sorry, one superstar—so that's all logical."

Lori looks intently at Suzanne, but Suzanne doesn't back down. "I've told you before, I'm not crazy. And I'm not imagining things." Suzanne takes Lori's hand and places it on her own upper arm.

Lori pulls her hand away. "Sorry, it's just, it's weird."

"Believe me, I know. Do you believe in aliens?"

"What, now you're switching to aliens? Is that a way to make me a necklace believer?"

"But it wouldn't make sense, in the vastness of the universe, that we're the only ones, the only living things, right?"

"Your point?" Lori puts her cool bottle of water up to her forehead.

"The point is, there's a lot about this world, this universe, just being alive that we don't understand, and there's got to be a lot more out there, a lot more to it, than we could ever imagine. Why is it so hard to believe other realms—or alternate realities, whatever—exist? There almost *has* to be something else, don't you see?"

Apparently Lori doesn't see, because she seems to remain unconvinced.

Suzanne takes another swig of her water then suddenly realizes what they need to do. She almost spits all over Lori in her rush to get her idea out. "*You* put the necklace on. *You* try it out."

"Are you kidding me? You're just full of great thoughts today!"

"No, it makes perfect sense. Then we'll know for sure. If you have an 'experience,' that is."

"And if I don't?"

"Then it's Plan B."

"Which is?"

"Non-existent. The bridge yet to cross." Suzanne reaches behind her neck and unclasps the necklace, then hands it to Lori. "Here. Put it on."

Lori takes the necklace, staring at it in her hand. "What's it supposed to be, anyway?"

"Haven't figured that out yet. It's pretty, though."

"That it is."

"So, put it on."

"I don't know. It feels—scary."

"That from the woman who doesn't believe. It's a necklace. It's not going to come alive and suddenly tighten around your neck, choking you to death."

"And you think that makes me want to put it on? You know, your imagination is entirely too active. It's gone wild. Bonkers, if you will."

"Put it on."

Lori reluctantly does just that. And then they drive home.

* * *

That evening is a rare event when both Suzanne's daughters are at home. It gives them time to catch up as well as discuss the upcoming school year. And to eat some delicious food Abigail cooked—roasted chicken with *herbes de province*. Suzanne will miss this when the girls go back to school. She likes to cook, but it's better when someone else does it for her.

"Dad's an ass, you know," says Abigail as she takes a

bite of the chicken.

The food may be fabulous, but the conversation does not make a very good accompaniment.

Hannah verbalizes her reaction even before Suzanne gets a chance. "Abby!"

"Well, he is. Did you hear what he said to me?"

Hannah shakes her head. Suzanne braces herself—he didn't, did he?

"He wants me to stay home from Vassar this year and babysit mom."

Oh, shit, he did. That's what Suzanne thinks to herself as a sound inadvertently escapes her lips.

"What?" asks Abigail. "Did you know about this, Mom?"

"Only in that he mentioned it to me the other day, when he came to give me a birthday present."

"Why didn't you tell me?" Abigail slips into her pouting teenager tone.

"Well, number one, I hardly get to see you."

"Um, there's such a thing as texts, Mother."

"Okay, then, number one and a half, it's not the type of thing you put into a text. 'Ur father says no college. Mom pathetic. Needs nursemaid.'"

"Okay, I'll give you that."

"And number two, you're not going to do it—I don't want you to—so why get you upset over nothing. You're going to college this year. Your college. Vassar."

"I love school."

"I know you do."

"And my friends are there. And it's so short. I don't want to miss a whole year. I don't want to miss *any* of it."

"Preaching to the choir, sweetie. You're going, like I said."

"Dad's an ass."

"The only thing I can say—besides that I don't want to talk about it anymore—is that at least your father was trying to do something good." Because she would rather not bad-talk her ex in front of their kids, no matter how much she would like to agree. The King of Asses. "Okay, now, let's change the subject. How are you two getting to school, since my car is definitely not big enough to fit all your stuff? Have we worked something out? Since it's only about an hour and a half from here, I'm willing to go up two different days to help out my two most special girls."

"Well, okay," says Hannah, and you can tell she's about to break some bad news, "this kind of brings the topic back to Dad. He promised he'll help one of us move up. Well, he did before he decided one of us should stay home. But I think he still will, won't he? Take one of us and you can take the other?"

Abigail obviously has not moved on yet. "Well, he'll have to take you, Han, because I'm not getting in the car with him!"

"Abigail!" chides her mother.

"What? He might highjack me to the community college for all I know. You have to take me, Mom."

"That's fine, that's fine. I'll go with Dad," says save-the-day, make-everybody-happy Hannah.

"Did you make dessert?" asks change-the-subject-Suzanne.

"Of course," says queen-of-sweets-Abigail. "Homemade bread pudding with rum raisins. But store-bought ice cream for on top. Sorry."

Well, it will just have to do.

Chapter 15

THE PERFECT FRUIT

SUZANNE WAKES THE NEXT MORNING to the ringing of her phone. Her eyes may be full of sleep, but when she sees Lori's number on the caller ID, Suzanne sits straight up in bed and picks up the receiver.

Not even waiting for a "hello," Lori states, "I had a dream last night."

Suzanne's heart starts to skip.

"You were in it," continues Lori. "An ultra-modern room, minimalist, stark white, padded walls."

Suzanne, skipping heart over, understands immediately there was no dream. Happily, though, Lori does not truly feel Suzanne is in need of a white, padded room, and, after a bit of further convincing from Suzanne, she agrees to one more radical step to figure out just what the hell is going on.

With her *no time like the present* philosophy—or maybe *wants to get it over with* attitude—Lori convinces Suzanne to call in sick so they can get started immediately. Suzanne does just that, and a couple of hours later, the two women sit in Lori's car on the way to Manhattan. Lori drives so that Suzanne can freely look for the gym that may or may not exist, the one she has no clue where to find or even what it looks like from the outside.

"I'm a good friend," Lori reminds Suzanne for at least the third time this morning.

Suzanne absentmindedly fingers the charm of the necklace. Lori had returned it as soon as Suzanne had climbed into her car, eager, it had seemed, to get rid of it, although it had not produced any type of Lori-fantasy world. Or maybe *because* it had not.

They plan their strategy as they approach the city. First, they whittle down the possibilities so they won't have to drive through every single part of the city. Lori asks if Suzanne saw a lot of trees when she looked out the window of the gym. When Suzanne answers no, Lori says they can cross Park Avenue and anywhere right near Central Park off the list.

"What about the Village?" asks Lori. "Do you think it could have been the Village?"

Suzanne thinks for a moment and decides no. However, those areas seem to be just about the only ones they can exclude, leaving a whole lot of territory to cover.

The thermometer reading the temperature of the world outside the car already shows eighty-five degrees, and, as the day progresses, the temperature climbs steadily. Nothing seems to resemble the gym Suzanne has come to know so well in her mind, and, with each passing block, the tempers inside the car seem to rise at the same rate as the temperature outside. By mid-afternoon the two women decide to call it quits. In the thirties and wanting to get to the FDR Drive going north, Lori turns from Madison Avenue onto Thirty Fourth Street. Whereas earlier in the day Suzanne eagerly looked out the window in hopes of finding the gym, she now stares out her side more to avoid talking to Lori, wallowing in her disappointment in relative peace. She watches first as they slowly approach and then pass Park Avenue. Once they've crossed over Park, something begins to gnaw at Suzanne, and after another few car lengths, she calls out to Lori.

"Stop the car," she demands.

"We are stopped," Lori answers. "There's traffic. Remember that—the stuff we've been sitting in for hours?"

"This is it!"

The building Suzanne gestures to has a recessed front, all windows, with tons of exercise equipment clearly visible. The large sign over the entrance reads, "The Athletes Complex."

"Pull over, pull over! We have to park." Excited Suzanne overlooks the fact that no such spot exists. After a few minutes, though, Lori finally turns the corner onto Third Avenue and, miracle of miracles, finds parking. Lori stops to read the muni-meter as Suzanne rushes up ahead, turning back onto Thirty Fourth Street. As Suzanne stops directly in front of the gym, she stares up at the huge window from the outside in for the first time.

Lori catches up a couple of minutes later. "You think this is it?" she asks.

Suzanne nods her head.

"Okay, so then what's the plan?"

Suzanne shrugs her shoulders but answers anyway. "I guess we go in."

A small but shapely young brunette—not anyone Suzanne recognizes—mans the reception desk. Suzanne immediately starts to look around. The feeling is beyond freaky, knowing a place so well but knowing she has never set foot—a real foot—in it.

Lori decides to speak for them. "Um, we're thinking of joining here, and we're wondering if we can just take a quick look around."

"Of course. We'd love to show you around. If you can just wait a minute, I'll ask one of our membership associates to give you a tour."

Lori tries to get her to agree to them looking around on their own, but that's a no go due to liabilities, against policy, blah, blah.

As they wait for their unwanted tour guide, Lori whispers to Suzanne, "So?"

Suzanne whispers back, "It's so weird. Looks just like I've seen it."

They sit for a couple more minutes, Suzanne anxiously peering around. After another moment, Suzanne's nervous bladder starts to signal her. She goes up to the front desk and asks to use the restroom. The brunette looks around, presumably unsure if she should allow Suzanne bathroom access on her own, but thankfully finally points down the hall. "There's a bathroom in the lady's locker room," she says, and Suzanne quickly takes off in that direction.

When she returns up front, another young twentyish girl, this one a striking, tall redhead, speaks with Lori. She greets Suzanne with an almost-sincere toothy smile. "I'm Deidre," she says as she extends her hand.

"I'm Suzanne. I guess you've already met Lori."

"I sure did. Well, Suzanne, Lori, welcome to the Athletes Complex. Let me tell you a little about us, and then we can take a tour, okay?"

Not having much of a choice, the two women follow Deidre to a small alcove and take a seat. Deidre rattles off her speech—obviously one given many times— consisting of a short history of how the gym started as a squash club and then became the gym of today, with lots of aerobic classes, lots of equipment, trainers always on the floor to help, personal trainers for hire—at which Suzanne's heart takes a dive into her feet—full shower amenities in the bathroom...

At Deidre's first real breath, Lori says, "Great, can we take the tour? We're kind of running on a schedule."

Deidre breaks out her really big smile and stands. "Sure. Right this way, Ladies."

They first pass by a door Suzanne has seen but has never entered—and doesn't know what it leads to, either. Deidre enlightens them. "As I said, the club started solely as a club for squash, and, because of these beginnings, we keep a squash court. We still have some of those members, and this is a popular exercise."

"I guess it's not just a vegetable, then," smart mouths Lori.

Deidre responds with a weak laugh. "Our busiest time of day," she informs, "is the evening. Right now you won't see too many people here, but the place hops after five until about nine at night. We're open until eleven, of course."

They next enter the room with most of the aerobic equipment. As Deidre predicted, no crowds, but when Suzanne looks over to the rowing machine, a wave of nausea overtakes her.

"Oh, good," says Deidre. "My favorite member is here. Everyone's favorite."

Deidre leads the way until they stand in front of the older gentleman on the machine.

Suzanne yanks at Lori's sleeve and whispers in her ear. "It's Allen. His name is Allen."

As soon as Suzanne finishes her covert sentence, she hears Deidre say, "Al, I have some visitors who would like to say hello." The man looks up. "Allen, this is Suzanne and Lori."

Lori's eyes go wide. Suzanne starts to panic, illogically wondering if she will be recognized.

Allen smiles. "Afternoon, Ladies." He bows his head to the side in greeting. "*Dear*dre, I love when you bring in these young ones."

Deidre laughs. "You're such a charmer." She turns to Suzanne and Lori. "We're not going to take credit for his energy—"

"*You* shouldn't, but my trainer should."

"That's true. But, anyway, Allen is one of our regulars. Al, how often do you ride the rower?"

Suzanne again grabs Lori's arm and puts her mouth to Lori's ear. "Three days a week for one hour and two days for sixty minutes," she manages to whisper quickly before Allen answers.

"Well, Monday, Wednesday, Friday I do it for one hour," he pauses for effect, "and then Tuesday and Thursday I like to mix it up, so I do sixty minutes."

Suzanne sees Lori's face go ashen.

Deidre notices, too. "Are you okay?"

Allen uncharacteristically stops his rowing.

"She's okay," assures Suzanne. "Maybe just a cup of water?"

"Of course," Deidre says. "Why don't you come and sit down?" She shows Suzanne and Lori back to the seats in the little alcove and rushes off to fetch the water.

Lori has found her voice again. "You've been here, right? I mean for real. You're playing a trick on me, aren't you?"

It's suddenly obvious to Suzanne that Lori had just been playing along with her, trying to placate her. She never had believed. Maybe *Suzanne* hadn't really believed before this moment, either.

Suzanne's voice shakes, but she answers. "I didn't even know where this place was, remember?"

Deidre returns with the water and gives it to Lori. "Are you sure you're okay?" she asks, genuinely concerned.

"I'm fine," says Lori, still looking anything but. "Can you give us a few minutes?"

Deidre nods and leaves, heading for the reception desk.

Suzanne and Lori sit quietly, Suzanne's thoughts so jumbled she can hardly think. Now that she's faced with the reality of her dream-life, she feels completely lost. How *can* it be true? How *can* it be real? Suddenly, she wants nothing more than to leave.

"Let's go," Suzanne says, and stands up and walks out of the alcove. As she does, she hears a voice that stops her completely. Panic in her eyes, she turns to Lori, who has followed her. "It's him," she mouths.

She turns back towards the corridor and sees him. Rami. He's walking, in fact, with Allen. In his hand he holds a cell phone, and he's flipping through some pictures, showing them to Allen.

Rami. In the flesh. In the real world. He looks just like the Rami she's been spending so many evenings with. He sounds like the Rami who's been driving her night after night to do more reps, slowly, with better form. He's dressed in the same shorts and trainer tee shirt. The slight accent, the cadence of his voice both sound the same, the smile...

Suzanne has never felt as frightened in her life as when this young man turns towards her. Her first thought is that he recognizes her, too. He must, because he's so familiar to *her*. But he does not. How could he? They've never met.

Allen talks first. "Your friend okay?" he asks.

Suzanne doesn't trust herself to speak. She nods.

Rami extends his hand. "Hello, I'm Rami."

Still not trusting that her voice won't give her fear away, Suzanne realizes she must respond. "I know," she starts to say, without thought, but quickly adds, "um, nice to meet you. I'm Suzanne. Are you Allen's trainer?" Her voice is, indeed, shaky, but since this Rami hasn't heard it before, perhaps he doesn't notice.

If Rami heard her first remark, he ignores it. "Yes. Impressed?"

Through all the other emotions, Suzanne has to laugh. It's so typical Rami, trying to get more business. At least the laughing sounds almost appropriate in this situation. "Yes," she concedes. "Very impressed."

"Oh," Allen chimes in. "You have to see these pictures." He turns to Rami. "Show the one of that pomegranate."

As Rami looks at his phone, flipping back through a bunch of pictures, he explains that these pictures are of Israel, where he comes from. His grandmother still lives there, and she sent him some recent photos. The pomegranate tree is his grandmother's prized possession, and she sent this photo of a perfect pomegranate. She also sent him an email with a whole long lecture, apparently. About how the pomegranate symbolizes love and marriage. "A little hint," he says as he smiles and winks at Suzanne. Just like how he smiles and winks at Shoshanna, she realizes.

"Ah, here it is." Rami turns his phone around for Suzanne to see. It's a gorgeous reddish almost burgundy color. His grandmother is right—it does look like a perfect fruit.

As Suzanne hands the phone back to Rami, Lori, apparently having recovered somewhat, steps up to the trio.

"Lori, this is Rami," says Suzanne, her voice still quivering slightly. "Rami is Allen's trainer," continues

Suzanne.

"I can be yours, too," Rami says with his patented smile.

Allen pipes in. "He's the best."

"So I've heard," says Lori quietly.

"Pardon?" asks Rami.

"You know what," Suzanne quickly interjects. "That muni-meter, our parking time is going to expire, isn't it, Lori?"

Rami looks surprised. "Oh, I thought you were looking to join the gym. You don't live around here?"

Suzanne offers up a smooth lie. "No, we work nearby. Just checking out the place for some lunchtime workouts."

Rami nods his head in understanding. "Okay, well, I hope to see you soon."

"Oh, you will," mumbles Lori.

Suzanne abruptly takes hold of Lori's hand and leads her out. "Nice to meet you all," she says as she turns and leads her mouthy friend away. As they pass the reception desk, she sees Deidre and says a quick thank you both to her and to the brunette.

As soon as they step outside and the door has closed, Suzanne turns to her friend and angrily questions, "Hey, what the hell was that?!"

"It's not like they understood what I was saying. What's the difference? And, you know, I'm having a hard time dealing with this, if you haven't noticed. Being a smartass is just my own personal way of helping myself through this situation. I'm a little freaked out, honey bunch!"

Freaked out would be putting it mildly in Suzanne's mind.

They walk down the block, back towards the car. Suzanne can hardly feel her feet on the pavement, her body has become so numb. Suddenly Suzanne stops. Lori looks at her with an expression of "okay, what happened *now*?"

Suzanne leans against the wall of whatever store she stopped in front of. "Oh, shit," she exclaims. "If Rami really exists, then I... I... "

"Spit it out," yells an increasingly impatient Lori.

"I fucked Rafael Derosa."

*　*　*

Although Suzanne and Lori speak very little on the way home, they do decide on their next step. They will pay a visit to Cybil. She gave Suzanne the necklace. She should be able to tell them what is going on. Maybe. If it *is* the necklace.

But, reminiscent of their younger selves, both women worry about going to see her.

"Are you kidding? I don't want to go by myself," says Suzanne.

Lori points out, "You're being a baby."

"You come with me."

"I don't want to go into that house. It's creepy."

"Who's the baby?"

"I know," says Lori. "Let's let Mikey do it. He'll do anything."

Now that they've dated themselves—with thankfully no one else in the car—the tension breaks a little, and they laugh.

"We still need to go see her," Suzanne points out but also suggests she talk to her own mother first. Apparently the two of them knew each other somehow— her mother had never told her, but Cybil had mentioned it—so maybe she'll have some input for their visit. Lori agrees it's a good idea.

They hit a little traffic on the way home, and Suzanne, suddenly feeling the emotional exhaustion from one of the most, or rather *the* most bizarre day of her life, lays her head back, closes her eyes and relaxes. She wonders how this all works. Is this gym they just saw, is it the same gym she goes to, or some parallel universe one? Was it the very same Rami? If she, Shoshanna, were talking to her Rami right now, would he remember meeting her, the Suzanne her? How she wishes she had more answers.

* * *

"You're early."

I turn. It's Rami talking to me. Well, that was fast.

"That's good," he continues. "You can warm up longer on the treadmill." He's dressed the same way as the Rami I just left, but since it's a uniform, that doesn't tell me anything. "Your sneaker is untied," he warns me.

I lean down to tie it, and the necklace slips out from its usual hiding spot under my top.

"That's an interesting necklace," Rami notes. "Haven't seen you wear it before."

"That's because I wear it under my tee shirt."

"Hmm. Pomegranate?"

I look at him blankly as I'm thinking this bizarre day just got even stranger. Just a few minutes ago he was showing me, or rather Suzanne, his grandmother's prized pomegranate, and now in one glance he identifies the symbol I've been wondering about for months.

He mistakes my bewildered stare for ignorance. "A pomegranate," he repeats as he takes out his phone, and, yes, shows me the very same photo he just showed the Suzanne me. "It's a fruit. This one is in Israel, but it's popular here now, I think. Mostly the juice."

I'm letting him go on talking, because I'm beginning to feel a bit overwhelmed. And that would be the understatement of the day.

Out of the corner of my eye, I see an older gentleman,

dressed in smart street clothes, coming through the workout room where I stand with Rami.

"See you later, Allen," says Rami.

"Have a good one, Rami," answers Allen. "Oh, hello, Shoshanna, dear. Nice to see you."

I smile at Allen. So he is here, too, just like the gym I left a short while ago. But still, he's always here, as is Rami.

"I'll be looking out for those two hot chicks." Rami says. "I hope for your sake they join."

Allen laughs. "Oh, I think maybe they're a little too young for me. But yes, very attractive. What were their names?" he asks. "Just in case?"

"Um, Suzy, or something like that, was one of them. The other? Lauren, maybe?"

I feel like I may crumple, like some creeping, unseen marauder has hit the back of my knees with a long pipe. I see Allen leave, and I see Rami turn to talk to me, but it takes a moment until I truly understand these simple motions and can focus on what Rami says.

"Shosh, you don't look good. You want to sit down?" Rami takes my arm, leads me over to one of the benches and helps me to sit. "What's going on here today? One of those women we were talking about, she almost fainted, too. Okay, maybe you don't do a long warm up today. Maybe we'll take it a little easy. Hey, we can look at some more pictures."

I figure the worst shocks are over, so I nod my head. He shows me photos of his grandmother first. She looks pretty young to be a grandmother. I see some of where he grew up, a small city, not too far from Tel Aviv, apparently. He shows me one of a friend from the army, too.

I've never gotten to ask him about the army. Usually we're concentrating on me and my exercises. If I ask him now, it might take the attention away from me for longer. I need that right now.

I steel my voice to try to talk normally. "So, you were in the army, but you've never told me much else. How long have you lived here? When did you move here? You were born in Israel, right?"

He holds up his hand with the thumb, forefinger and middle finger together, the back of the hand to me. "*Regah*," he says.

It looks almost like an Italian gesture, but that's pretty unlikely.

He translates. "It means 'wait.' You're asking but not giving me time to answer."

"Sorry."

"It's okay. At least it looks like you feel better, no?"

"Kind of."

"So, maybe instead of my story, some extra time on the treadmill?"

"Not feeling that great."

He laughs. "Okay. So, yes, I was born in Israel. My parents both are Israeli. But when I was five, they decide to come live in New York. My uncle, he's here. Then, I'm fifteen, and they decide this was not such a great idea, and we move back to Israel."

"So you had to move back after ten years? How was your Hebrew?"

"We spoke only Hebrew at home, and my mother, she made me keep up the writing—she's a teacher—so it was okay. Then, of course, because you must to, I went into the army when I was eighteen, and I stayed in the army for the full three years. So, two years ago, I finish, and I decide to come back here and stay with my uncle."

"Wow. You left your home and came here by yourself, kind of."

"Well, there's more for me to do here, for work. And I

always liked it. I love Israel, too, but I want to come here for now."

"So, you're twenty-three. So young. Still a baby."

That's a slip. I realize it when Rami gives me a strange look. I'm feeling like Suzanne, not Shoshanna. Maybe it's because I was just Suzanne here. I'm getting so confused. I feel so much older next to him today.

"I'm a baby?" He takes my hand, pulls me to standing then walks me to a mirror. "I think we look about the same age, don't you?"

Okay, now how do I fix this? "Well, I *am* a couple of years older than you." A couple? Yeah, right. Better change the subject. "So, the army for three years, huh? What did you do there?"

"I told you, remember? I trained women. It was a good job. For me. I learned how to train. I'm around a lot of women." There's that patented smile. "A very good job. Okay, enough of talking. You look okay. Go warm up. I'll wait for you." The charming smile turns devilish. Oh, brother, I don't know that I'm ready for this today.

*   *   *

"Where the hell did you just go?"

Suzanne is back in Lori's car. "I... I wasn't sitting here?"

"What do you mean? Of course you were here, but I was talking to you, and you didn't answer. Only for a minute, but, oh, my god, you scared the shit out of me. Are you okay?" Lori is driving but she keeps looking at Suzanne, quick glances as she tries to keep her eyes on the road. "Oh, shit! You went somewhere else, didn't you?! You did that fucking thing!"

"Calm down, Lori."

"I can't calm down. I can't fucking calm down! This is crazy!"

Suzanne tries to keep the driver of the car from

driving off the road, so she makes her voice as even as she can. "We'll talk about it when we get home okay? In one piece. So just concentrate on the road, all right? It's okay. I'm here."

For the moment, anyway.

Chapter 16

A Visit

True to Suzanne and Lori's plan, Suzanne goes to visit her mother, Jana, to pump her for information on Cybil. Even though her mom lives in the same town—across the small town actually—Suzanne does not usually see her all that much during the week. Life usually gets in the way, especially with the girls home. There's no pretending, therefore, this is just a normal social visit.

Jana makes some tea, probably more for something to do than as any real sign of hospitality. Suzanne grew up in this house, and no matter the years since then, it still feels—to both herself and to her mom—like Suzanne's home, too. But Jana, a sprightly seventy-something year old, likes to keep busy, especially when she knows something's afoot.

"How are my grandchildren? Ready to go back to school?" If you didn't know the situation, you may think she's talking about little kids getting their book bags ready for grade school.

"Eager, I would say."

"You need help to drive them up?"

"You want to help schlepp their stuff?"

"I can chauffeur, and you and the girls can do the schlepping."

Suzanne thanks her mom, but she lets her know that Joe volunteered—as he, the father, should—so they'll be okay.

To Jana's credit, she has never said a bad word about Joe, throughout the divorce and before. She actually never said *anything* about the divorce, pro or con. Suzanne wonders if her mother disapproves that she's taken this action but figures better left unasked than disappointed in the answer.

Both women add a splash of milk, no sweetener, to their English Breakfast decaf tea and start sipping. True to her reserved form, Jana still does not ask the reason for the visit.

Suzanne eases into it. "You had a good time at my party?"

"We talked about it, didn't we? I thought that was super, you made yourself the party. I never would have had the guts to do that. I should have, though, since your father isn't the party-maker type."

"I thought you didn't like parties."

"I like parties. Just not for myself."

Sometimes talking to her mom was like being on a mad teacup ride.

Suzanne tiptoes one step closer to the intended conversation. "Um, strange that Cybil showed up, don't you think?"

Jana chuckles. "Well, Cybil's behavior is not known for being normal, now is it?"

Suzanne plays cohort and chuckles, too.

"You know," Jana continues, "Cybil was in and out of your house so fast, I didn't even get to say 'hi.' I haven't spoken to her in ages."

Her mother already headed in the right direction, Suzanne encourages continued conversation with a well-placed but meaningless, "Really?"

"We were quite good friends, you know. You remember, don't you?"

"Remember what?"

"How could you not remember? I used to watch her kids."

Suzanne barely stops herself from spitting out her mouthful of tea.

Jana puts down her own teacup. "No, you wouldn't remember, would you? You were just a baby. How's your tea? Did you want a little bite with it?"

Suzanne shakes her head. "You used to watch Cybil's children?" she asks, outwardly shocked.

"Why are you looking at me like that? It's not so strange. I was home with you, anyway. Her two girls, they were older, and they helped me, actually. I'd say it was a two-way street. I got help keeping an eye on you—those girls *loved, loved, loved* you—and Cybil, she was a single mother—not so usual in those days—she definitely needed the help. Needed to be out making money, of course."

Suzanne takes a few sips of her tea, letting all this sink in. "What did she do, to make money?" she asks finally.

Now it's Jana's turn to look perplexed. "You know, I don't remember. Hmm, that's odd."

No more information to be had, so, after finishing her tea, Suzanne takes her leave and heads towards Lori's house, alone with her bewildered self for the few minutes' drive.

* * *

Suzanne hardly waits for Lori to open her front door before she starts talking. "My mom used to watch her kids."

"Whose kids?" asks Lori, standing back so Suzanne can enter her foyer.

"*Cybil's* kids. Cybil's kids used to watch *me*! Do you think there's a connection? I mean, with what's going on now?"

"Like we have any idea what's going on now?"

"Which would be why we're going to Cybil's. You ready?"

"No."

Suzanne will have none of that. She's too hungry for answers to her long list of questions, too eager to understand. "Well, too bad. We're going. Get your shoes on, Missy."

None too happy, Lori obliges, and a couple of minutes later, she and Suzanne walk together on the sidewalk nearing Cybil's house, which is hard to see even when they reach the edge of the driveway. The junipers planted along the front walk have grown tall, each plant invading its neighbor's space, forming an impervious fence of green. Suzanne and Lori walk up the driveway, continuing until they reach the line of trees, where they hesitate for a moment as they finally get a good view of the house.

Suzanne speaks first. "Okay, at least it's not creepy," she whispers.

"It's... hideous."

"But not scary."

"Are you kidding? I'd call that scary. Scary ugly."

"Shh. She may hear you."

"Honey, anyone who would paint their house bright robin's egg blue deserves to hear the truth. It's a fucking eyesore."

"But you can't see it from the road, so that's... neighborly?"

Lori glares at Suzanne then heads for the brightly painted unsightly front door. "Let's get this over with." She pushes the button for the doorbell. "Did you hear anything? I didn't hear anything." She pushes the button again, but still no sound. She knocks loudly on the door.

As they wait, the two women take a closer look at the front of the house, with its wall of blue broken only by a few, narrow windows.

"Hideous," remarks Lori once again.

"Shh."

"I don't think she's even here."

The door opens. "I'm here," says the woman in white. "Well, can't say I'm surprised to see you. Or maybe a bit surprised it's taken this long. Come," she says as she sweeps her hand back, drawing the women in.

Another surprise for Suzanne and Lori, because, as colorful as the outside of the house appears, the opposite holds true of the inside décor—at least of the first space they see. A sea of beige greets them in the living room, including light tan walls, a matching taupe couch and taupe chairs and a few accent pillows in yet another shade of beige. The light wood of the coffee table fits in perfectly.

The effect appears quite, well, Suzanne would have to admit, beautiful. In fact, she's so surprised, she involuntarily lets out a little gasp.

Lori goes one step further. "Gorgeous," she says, not bothering to filter out the shock.

Perceptive Cybil smiles. "Not a fan of the blue?" she asks. "Well, as they say, it's what's on the inside that matters. Please, have a seat," she adds as she waves her arm towards the couch, the long white sleeve billowing in the breeze created by her grand movement.

Suzanne eagerly does as directed, with Lori taking a

more reluctant seat beside her. From this position on the sofa, Suzanne notices an oversized ceramic bowl placed exactly at the center of the coffee table before them. It holds the only splash of real color in the entire room, about a dozen pieces of reddish purple fruit, each so perfect they could well be made of wax.

Cybil sees Suzanne staring. "Pomegranates."

Suzanne unconsciously reaches for the charm on the necklace.

"Ah, so you figured it out," says Cybil, smiling.

"Well, not me. Someone I... met."

Lori does not understand the conversation. "Figured what out?"

"The necklace I bestowed upon your friend,"— Suzanne knows if she looks at Lori at this moment her friend's eyes would be rolling at the word "bestowed"— "it's a picture, a symbol, if you will, of a pomegranate." Her arm waves towards the center of the table as she says that final word.

"Are they real?" asks Lori, just the question on Suzanne's lips.

"Yes, indeed."

"But why would you give Suzanne a necklace of a pomegranate? I mean, come on, whether you wish it on her or not, this lady is well past her fertile days."

Lori laughs, but Cybil does not. "Ah, you see, that's a common misconception. A pomegranate is not just a symbol of fertility. There is so very much more to this magnificent creation."

This time Suzanne does not have to imagine Lori's eye-rolling. She catches a glimpse of it herself.

"Shall I tell you a little about the history of the pomegranate?"

"Well—" starts Lori.

"Sure," says Suzanne, cutting her friend off.

"Lovely," responds Cybil. She explains first that many people believe the apple in the Garden of Eden was a different type of apple, or actually not really an apple at all, but rather, yes, a pomegranate. She pauses after that revelation—which, of course, Suzanne already knew since Rafael had told her months ago—then continues, sounding more like a lecturing professor than an elderly woman standing in a living room. She describes how pomegranates are not just about their health benefits or a symbol of fertility, as most people think. Suzanne and Lori learn that the fruit, one of the first to be cultivated, has a long, strong history, depicted in artwork and architecture through the ages.

If the two women think that's the end of the lecture, they couldn't be more wrong. Cybil launches into even more pomegranate specifics, outlining their prominence in many religions and cultures. She describes how depictions of the fruit were used to decorate King Solomon's temple. To the Egyptians, it represented the afterlife. Roman women wore headdresses of pomegranate twigs to show their married status. In Greek myth it also represented marriage. Hades tempted Persephone with the pomegranate, and she was joined to him forever. It is prevalent in Buddhism, Hinduism. In Christian art it symbolizes life after death. Some cultures even use a pomegranate within the wedding ceremony.

She relates her favorite pomegranate quote—her favorite, she lets them know, because of its declaration of love—from the Bible, from Song of Songs, chapter seven.

Cybil concludes by saying, "Pomegranates symbolize health, abundance, prosperity, posterity and a joyous future full of blessings." And as a grand gesture symbolizing the completion of her speech, with a flourish of her arms and the resulting flowing of her white dress, Cybil takes a seat in a chair directly across from her guests.

Suzanne says not a peep, trying to remember all of the information just imparted by their hostess.

Lori reacts slightly differently. "Wow," she says. "You must have spent a long time doing research."

"Not really," answers Cybil. "It's all on the web. The internet makes life delightfully easier, wouldn't you say?"

Suzanne tries to picture Cybil sitting in front of a computer, surfing the net—a hard image to conjure.

"Well," Cybil continues. "I have a feeling you didn't come see me for a lecture on the history and symbolism of the pomegranate. So let's start on your questions, shall we? I shall endeavor to provide the best answers I possibly can."

Suzanne thinks how unusual this is—well, in truth, everything about everything lately seems unusual—but in the here and now, how unusual for an older person to want to get down to business. Most want the company and will prolong the niceties. In this case, though, no niceties are expected or requested, apparently, and Suzanne gratefully dives into the questioning.

The most obvious first. "What does it do?"

Cybil, perched at the edge of her chair, looks right into Suzanne's eyes. "Dear, if you didn't know what it does, you wouldn't be here asking me questions, now would you?"

Suzanne doesn't expect that answer and gets flustered, but she doesn't let it stop her. Perhaps this next question is a bit more straightforward. "Why did you give it to me?"

"Because you need it, of course."

"Lots of people need it, but you gave it to *me*."

"By the way, how is your mother? Please say hello when you speak to her next."

"Okay, but—"

"And to your lovely daughter, Abigail, too."

How does Cybil know Abigail? Anyway, Suzanne starts to get a little annoyed. Cybil promised to answer her questions, and here she is, doing anything but.

Suzanne tries another one, hoping to get Cybil back on track. "Why won't it work for Lori?" Suzanne describes how Lori had taken possession of it, but nothing like what happens to Suzanne happened to Lori.

"Because it was intended for *you*, not your friend." Cybil's tone in delivering this answer could definitely be described as annoyed. Suzanne looks over to Lori to see a few ruffled feathers.

Suzanne continues before Lori can open her mouth. "How long will it last? I mean, for how long will it work?"

"Why, as long as you need it to, of course."

Suzanne, definitely getting tired of this "of course" business, wonders how Cybil could be so good at making her answers appear to be answers when they answer nothing at all. Still, she tries one more. "*How* does it work?"

"My dear, how does anything work? The stars, the planets, time, life itself?"

Suzanne can't contain her frustration and blurts out, "You're not answering my questions."

Cybil looks quite sincere as she answers this one. "But I am. I'm answering them completely. Perhaps, though, dear child, if you're not getting the answers you want, perhaps then you're not asking the *correct* questions."

"Okay," says a startled Suzanne, hesitating. She

looks at Lori, who shrugs. "What questions *should* I be asking?"

Cybil rearranges her body in her chair, pushing herself back into her seat. "Well, if I were you, I think I would ask what you should be gaining from these experiences. Of course, I have no idea where the necklace actually takes you—that's a very personal journey, isn't it? But I do know that usually it will include some... ah, shall we say *physical* elements, as well as those of a more *intellectual* nature," she says.

Well, the physical part sounds about right. Different types, and lots of it. Intellectual, though? Can't say there's been much of that. But Suzanne plays along. "Okay, then," says Suzanne, "what *should* I be looking to gain, and which should I be concentrating on? The physical or the intellectual?"

Although Cybil had actually posed this question herself, she leans her head into her hand and purses her lips as though in deep contemplation. After a few moments, she answers, "The mind and the body—are they not completely connected? Or maybe, perhaps, they are not in the least. After all, on your journeys, your body remains in this realm, does it not?"

And one more non-answer.

"So," says Cybil as she claps her hands together and stands up, a clear signal their time is coming to an end, "any more questions?"

"I have one," Lori says, which makes Suzanne quite a bit nervous. "You gave us the history of the pomegranate, but what's the history of the pomegranate *necklace*? Did you give it its special powers, or did you find it that way?"

"Excellent question," says Cybil, "but a woman has to have *some* secrets, does she not?" And with a smile, she turns and walks towards the front of the house. She does not stop there, though, opening the door and leading the way outside. Suzanne and Lori follow her out the door, down the front steps, along the path and onto the driveway. Before turning back towards her house, she looks at Suzanne and says, "Please send my love to your mother and to your Abigail." And, laughing, she adds, "If she ever wants to come back and do more weeding, there's plenty to keep her occupied."

"Abigail used to *weed* for you?" Suzanne had no idea. Her Abigail? Her lazy Abigail used to come to this woman's garden and do yard work? That's certainly not an activity she ever volunteered to do in her own home!

"Just like your dear mother. They saw my need and never hesitated, never asked. They just did." With that, she briefly places a hand on Suzanne's shoulder then slowly walks back toward her house.

As soon as the door closes, Lori turns to her friend. "And I thought our time at the gym was weird. Come on. I still have some of that Melon Liqueur and vodka left over from Bunco. It'll go down pretty damn easy right now."

Yes, thinks Suzanne. Yes, it will.

Chapter 17

You Don't Know Squats

BACK IN THE LOCKER ROOM of the gym, the place I used to think I had dreamed up. Now I know, of course, it's no dream, no figment of my imagination. There is no rational way I could have known about the gym, about Allen, about Rami. No logical explanation for how my body in real life has made leaps and bounds improvements without very real workouts involving a very real trainer.

So, I've accepted it. Kind of. Sort of. To the best of my ability.

Apparently, though, Lori's way to deal with the situation is to ignore it as much as possible. She hasn't spoken to me once, not since cocktails after the Cybil incident. If Avoidance were an Olympic sport, Lori would win enough gold medals to rival Michael Phelps.

Okay, time for my training. And there he is, waiting right outside the locker room.

"Look at that," says Rami, who seems to be checking me out. "Come here." He takes my hand and brings me over to a mirror. He likes to do that, I've noticed. "Here, make a muscle, like this." He does the typical flexing of the biceps. I almost want to laugh.

"That's cheesy," I can't stop myself from saying. But when I see how good he looks while he's flexing, the musculature of his chest showing through the tight, black tee shirt, I can't stop myself from gawking, and, also, I must admit, getting more than a little hot and bothered, as they say.

Snap out of it. He's a boy. Okay, so not a boy, but closer to puberty than to my real age.

The boy is talking. "You see the difference from when we started? Look at you!"

I do look different. Not that I knew my body—this body—well before, but it didn't have that definition for sure.

"Let's see the legs," Rami demands. "Like this." He hikes up the bottom of his shorts and moves his right leg forward, pivoting on his big toe while flexing the muscles. That's a nice view, his dark, smooth skin taut, and the long muscles underneath bulging in David-esque fashion. "I'm waiting," says the impatient Israeli, putting an end to my innocent ogling.

I try to imitate his motion. My legs don't look bad, but I'm not seeing any of the outlined musculature I saw on my arms. Rami puts his hand on my thigh, shakes his head and clicks his tongue.

"I haven't spent enough time on these legs. Hmm." I can see his mind churning. Suddenly, he claps both his hands together. "Okay, legs today. It's about time we do some squats. You know squats?"

"I know they're dangerous, aren't they?"

A kind of evil smile. "That's why you have me, right? Come on." He starts walking, and, with his powerful legs, a few steps take him into the next room. I scramble to keep up. "Don't worry. I'm going to work very close with you. This is when the fun will start."

Don't worry. Don't worry? Don't worry! Okay, so now I'm worried.

He leads me to an area we've never visited in any of our sessions. I've worked with free weights before, but this corner has always seemed taboo. I've only seen the really big, rough looking guys over in this part of the gym.

Rami looks at me strangely.

"What?" I ask.

"I'm talking to you."

"Sorry. I was too busy being scared." Wow, I hadn't even noticed he was speaking.

"No being scared," Rami instructs. "Okay, so what I was trying to say to you is that squats are really, really great for you—like for all of you, your whole body—but, you know, the workout it gives to your legs, that's the really great thing."

"But people get hurt, don't they?" I'm not letting this line of questioning go.

"If you don't do them right? Yes, you can get hurt, so if you're not going to do them right, don't do them. But you, you're going to do them right, because I'm here. And until you are used to them, and I mean, really, really used to them, you're not going to do them without me."

If I wasn't scared before, now I'm scared shitless.

"So, are you going to squat when I'm not with you?"

"No, sir, I will not squat."

He laughs, but then he says, "No laughing. We have to be serious with this. Okay, so first you're going to squat without weights."

"I thought it was done with the bar on your shoulders."

"It is, but you're going to learn with nothing first. When your form, it looks good, then we add the bar. And then we add more weight and then more weight and then this already great body of yours is going to *really* kick ass."

I don't know if I should be insulted that I don't already have a kick-ass body or happy that at least he thinks it's great. Of course, it's not really *my* body, at least I still don't think of it that way. "Aren't squats really hard?"

"Yes. They're going to be the hardest thing you've done so far. Probably the hardest you'll *ever* do."

"Okay, well, then, I have a question. So, if I've got such a great body already, why would I put myself through this?"

What's he doing? Why's he walking up so close to me, his face drawing closer to mine?

"You like sex?" he whispers.

Huh? What did he just ask me?

"Because," he continues, his whispering tickling my ear, "you may be hot to men now, but when I'm done with you, you'll be fucking irresistible." He pulls his head back, a little away from my ear. "And believe me, sweetheart, you're pretty damn hot already. I think more than once it's too bad I have a rule not to have sex with my clients."

What?!

I think I may throw up.

He wants to have sex with me?

But next he says, "We'll have to see if I can resist you, when I'm done with you," and I can hear it now, that teasing, playful tone. It was there all along, I think, but, sometimes, I guess we hear whatever we want to hear.

And, in the next breath, the playfulness over, he claps those demanding hands and says, "Okay, let's get started." He places me facing the bar, and I have to push all these other thoughts out of my mind. The mirrors seem to be all around me. I see my front reflection, but when I look to my left, I have a great side view as well. And whether Rami is all-teasing or not, I have to say I do look pretty damn good. Of course, what's even hotter is him standing right next to me. Holy shit, he is such a turn on. Too bad he was only joking. Wait, I've got to stop thinking about this! Stop it right now! Concentrate. I'm about to do squats.

"You're going to follow everything I'm saying," instructs Rami. "There's a lot to do during the squat, a lot to remember, and you will remember all. So, watch what I do." He pretends to have a bar on his shoulders. As he's demonstrating, he barks out everything I need to remember while doing a proper squat. Feet pointed outward slightly, a little more than shoulder width apart. Butt should protrude out but knees shouldn't be farther than the toes. Heels should be firmly on the ground. Head should be straight or looking slightly up, never down. Chest out and shoulders back, slightly arch the lower back. Breathe slowly in on the way down and let it out sharply on the way up. Keep squatting down until your thighs become parallel to the floor. "Got it?"

Well, I heard it, but I didn't absorb it, that's for sure. I got that you're supposed to stand with your feet a little more than hip distance apart. "Some, I guess."

"Look again." He demonstrates once more, repeating all the orders, this time a little more slowly. "Okay, now you're going to try it, no weights." He stands to the side of me. "Go."

I position my feet correctly, point them out a little and bend.

"Butt out," he shouts.

"I'm trying."

"No, you're not. Head up, shoulders back, chest out."

I try again.

"No, no, no."

What the hell am I doing wrong? I stand up again, and Rami moves up behind me. He puts his hands on my hips. Okay, like now I'm supposed to be able to do a proper squat, with him touching me like that? He takes his hands off my hips to put my head into position and pushes my shoulders back, towards him, and then he holds my hips again, my butt just about touching his groin. "Now down," he says, and as his hands guide me down into the squat, he's right behind me, bending also. Crap, this is hard, not only on my legs, but on my libido. He feels so strong, moving me down and then up, down and up again. He's rubbing slightly against me.

"Better." He steps back, away from me. Damn. "Okay, you try it by yourself."

I try hard to concentrate. I keep my head up, my shoulders back, my chest out, and slowly I descend.

"Keep your heels down and your *butt out*."

"It's out."

"Don't talk back." He steps over to me again and pulls my hips back, truly making my ass protrude. "That's what I mean. Now keep it that way, really sit back on your heels. Good. Now up, slowly. Right. Again."

Oh, so that's what a proper squat feels like.

After about ten more of these, he beckons me over to the squat rack, which looks like the rack for the bench press, except the two poles holding the bar stands much taller. The bar lies across the two poles on the u-shaped holders at the top. Rami steps right up to the squat rack to demonstrate, ducking his head under the bar and stepping up to it so that the bar lies across his broad shoulders. He stands to his full height, lifting the bar at the same time, and steps back, fully clearing the rack.

"Watch again," he says and does the squat with

perfect form. He repeats it two more times then returns the bar to the rack, making sure it sits securely before ducking his head back out and walking towards me. "Okay, your turn. Make sure you don't hit your head on the way in."

I follow that advice closely, because I'd hate to make a fool of myself right before I make a fool of myself. I take care to bend low enough under the pole and then ever so carefully raise myself up until I feel the cold metal on my neck. "Like this?" I ask.

Rami moves me a little forward. "You want it on your shoulders, not your neck. The neck would be bad."

How many pounds sitting directly on my neck? I can easily see why that would be bad.

"Okay, now stand up and make sure you've got the bar lifted up high enough to clear the rack. That's right. Now walk back a couple of feet."

I do as I'm told, and the weight across my shoulders already feels heavy. All of a sudden, it hits me, and I begin to freak. I can't believe I'm doing this. A squat, with free weights. This is the most scared I've been in the gym, any gym, in real life or this life. Maybe I'll tell him no. He'd have to let me put the bar back, right? He'd have to.

I think he senses my fear, because he's right behind me again. "I'll stay with you the whole time." Damn him and his sixth sense. "Okay, ready?"

"No."

"Yes, you are. And down."

Once more, he holds my hips and guides me through the squat, but this time, with the weight of the bar on my shoulders, it's a completely different feeling. Besides making sure my legs don't give out, I have to balance the bar. It's heavy and awkward and did I say heavy? And he's yelling at me again.

"Butt out, chin up, chest out, shoulders back."

"They are."

"Didn't I say no talking back? Heels down. Keep the bar straight."

I don't say another word.

"And up. Slowly, slowly. And down again."

This time he just moves with me, but doesn't say anything.

"Nice. One more. Good."

When he backs away, I start to take a step forward toward the rack, figuring I'm done.

"Where are you going? Give me three on your own."

He's glaring at me, and as much as I want to get rid of this weight across my shoulders, as much as I'm panicking, I set up my stance, rocking the bar a little to get it back in balance. I lower myself into squatting position, careful, careful, not as far as before when he helped me.

"A little lower," he says, catching me at my cheat.

I squat down ever so slightly lower, keeping my head straight, my shoulders back. Boy, do my shoulders hurt, and my neck, too. This bar gets heavier by the minute. Is my ass out? I guess so, because he's not screaming at me. Okay, I don't care what he says, I'm standing up now.

Oh, fully upright, that feels so much better. But I know not to get used to it, because he's expecting two more. Okay, let's get this over with. I dip down again, running through everything I'm supposed to be paying attention to and trying to squat down as low as I can.

"A little more," says the drill sergeant.

A little more is all I do, and then up I go as fast as I can before he can stop me.

"Okay, last one for today. Not so quick this time."

For today? Like I'm ever going to do these again? The

bar is so heavy, I feel as though I'm wobbling, but rather than succumb to the wrath of Rami, I do the squat.

Before I'm as low as I'm willing to go, he calls to me again. "Hold it for a second, when you get to the bottom."

Maybe I hold it for half a second and back up I come. And I'm not waiting for his permission to be done. I walk straight up to the rack and carefully lift up a little to sit the bar back in its proper place. I've never in my life been so happy to get rid of something. I duck my head under the bar and walk away as quickly as I can.

He's got his hand up to high five me. Really? He's happy with how I did? Because he sure didn't sound happy while yelling at me.

"Good job. You're really something," he says, smiling.

"It didn't feel like I did a good job."

"Your form was good. You went nice and low, steady."

"I only did a few."

"You did enough. Remember the time when you couldn't walk after doing too much legs?"

Not going to forget that for a while.

"We don't want that again, right? You did enough. We'll let you rest a few days before we do them again. Next time, maybe we'll even put a few pounds on each end."

My face must have an extreme horrified expression, because he quickly adds, "You can handle it. You're my star client."

Hmm. "Don't let Allen hear you say that."

"Allen won't have a problem with me calling a beautiful woman my star. Come here."

Surprising me yet again, he wraps his arms around me and pulls me in close, kissing the top of my head. This time, I think he actually shows me some real affection, and, wow, it feels good here in his arms. The arms of a beautiful man. Boy. Man. Okay, so maybe it was worth doing those squats.

"I don't think I should be your client anymore." That pops out without thinking.

Rami pulls back. I see his expression, and I know I've wounded him, shocked him, even. "Was it that bad?" he asks. "You were ready for it. I was watching you, taking care from you, all the time. I would never let you get hurt. You did great."

Oh, no, I shouldn't have said that. Crap! "No, no, not that. It's just that... "

"What did I do?"

"Nothing. It's because, well... "

"Please."

"Because... because you don't sleep with your clients."

And guess what? I shouldn't have said that either.

Chapter 18

READY, SET, GO

IT'S A GOOD THING IT'S already mid-August and time to get the girls prepped for school. Suzanne needs something to occupy her mind. Life seems a little twisted right now, what with having a secret, alternate life controlled by a pomegranate necklace where she fucked a superstar and made advances on a boy/man who's making her alter-body into some type of sex machine.

The embarrassment she feels from her slip up with Rami continues to torture her. Her only consolation is that she had been somewhat successful in glossing over it, lamely pretending she was joking. Apparently she was convincing enough at least to allow them a pretense of normalcy, not to mention the ability to continue her training. And since Rami wins as the best trainer she has seen—in either of her lives, in either of her gyms—she desperately wants to keep him.

Of course, obsessing over her stupidity with Rami is also just another way to stop her brain from reflecting on the bigger issue, the really big issue, the fucking elephant that's so big it's not just in the room, it's taken over the entire neighborhood. What the hell is really happening?

Suzanne thinks through all of this *again* as she mindlessly walks the aisles of Target with Abigail, a small shopping spree for some college essentials, and, of course, non-essentials.

"I need a husband," says Abby.

That startles Suzanne into the here-and-now. "What?"

Abby points to the top shelf. "I like to work on my bed, but it isn't comfortable. A lot of people bring husbands. That one. The purple one. That would be cool."

Suzanne looks up and sees that Abby points to an oversized pillow with arms. Right, it's called a husband. A pillow that holds you. "How much?"

"It's on sale. Besides, you don't want me breaking my back, do you? And it will fit in the minivan. Somehow."

Into the cart it goes.

Abby continues to chat as they go up and down the aisles, looking for things on the list and any other must-haves. "Did you see the list of suggested items on the website?" asks Abby. "Really needs some updating. A stereo? Who would bring a *stereo*? Who *owns* a stereo? Have they not heard of iPods? Or, this one's good—a telephone and answering machine. Wow. Reality check. But the best? The best? I should bring a typewriter. Can you imagine? Where can you even *buy* one?"

Suzanne had never thought of it that way. Just in terms of what you bring to college now, it's so different from when she went away to school. The means of communication then? You had a pad stuck to the outside of the door, and people wrote notes. "Meet at dining hall at 6:30," or "In library near copy machine." No cell phones, no texts. If you weren't in person or near the pad, you had no way to get in touch. And if you wanted to add a sentence to page one of your ten page paper, you had to type it all over again. Everything's changed in what feels like such a short time. Probably not so short. A lifetime. Her daughters' lifetimes.

"Speaking of typewriters," says Suzanne, "they have ink cartridges on sale. We should pick up a few for your printer."

They continue down the rows, filling the cart with Abigail's semester needs. Tomorrow night will be Hannah's turn. Suzanne learned a long time ago not to shop with the two of them together. The eyes of the daughters become much bigger then, and the hit to her wallet much more severe. Besides, they'll be leaving soon, and it's nice to spend the time with them individually...

*   *   *

True to expectations, the weeks have flown by. It's the Sunday of Labor Day weekend. Although classes don't start until the day after Labor Day, today is the day the upperclassmen are expected to return to school. Both girls are eager to get there, so, although they will drive up in separate cars and will be living in two separate areas on campus—Abby to share a double with her best friend in the dorm called Josselyn, and Hannah to live with three friends in the college-owned Terrace Apartments, about as far from her sister as she could physically manage—they both want to leave at the same time. Early.

Joe shows up with his car but has already been warned by organized Hannah that he will not be driving his Camry up to college. Since Hannah is moving into the apartment, she needs to bring some things for the communal kitchen as well as small pieces of furniture for the shared living room. And since Abby remains too angry to speak with Joe, Joe has been told he will drive Hannah up in mom's minivan, where the back two rows can be taken out and a big empty space left for all the college crap. The Camry should do just fine for Abby's stuff, although Suzanne has some concerns with the addition of the oversized husband.

Even with all the extra stuff, Hannah gets the minivan packed up before they've loaded all of Abby's things into the smaller car. "Okay, Dad, let's go," she says.

"Let's help your sister," he counters.

"I don't need help," retorts Abby.

Joe seems about to resist, but Hannah pulls his hand. "They'll be okay," she says to her dad, although she's looking at her sister. "We'll see you up there."

Joe reluctantly allows himself to be pulled by Hannah, looking back towards Abby. "I'll get Han's stuff in the apartment, and then I'll come over to help you unload," he insists.

"See you up there," Suzanne calls, mostly to Hannah, who a split second later sits in the front passenger seat of the minivan.

With a bit of rearranging and a whole lot of pushing down and scrunching in, the Camry gets packed up. Even without a typewriter, a stereo, a telephone and an answering machine, the car fills to capacity. Abby sits in the front passenger seat resting her feet on a couple of small boxes.

The ride to school proves a totally different experience than the year before. Last year, Abby had to make the journey a week earlier, to attend the freshman orientation. Hannah, as an old-hat junior, had one more week at home. Suzanne and Joe drove Abby up together, the three of them in the minivan. Scared of the unknown, Abby sat quietly in the middle row, surrounded by all the things she thought she would need. Many of those things didn't make the list this year. Now, Abby chats freely, talking about the friends she misses, the classes she's taking, how she's going to try to watch her caloric intake in ACDC, aka the Deece. This year she doesn't have to worry about running into her sister at the All Campus Dining Center, since Hannah and her friends will be cooking for themselves in their townhouse.

When Suzanne can finally get a word in edge-wise, she brings up a topic she's wanted to discuss for a few weeks. "So, you used to help Cybil in her garden?"

Abby looks at her mother blankly. "What? Who?"

"Cybil. Crazy Cybil, who lives near Lori."

"Oh, the one who crashed your party. You didn't know I used to help her? I thought you knew. Oh, wait, maybe I didn't think you knew. That's right. I didn't tell you because I didn't want you to get any ideas that I would weed at our house."

"I see."

Suzanne's not quite sure if she should be proud or pissed off. She settles for concentrating on driving, as well as concentrating on getting through the day, a day to say goodbye to both of her daughters at once, a day where she gets to go home to a large and lonely house.

The ride takes a little under an hour and a half, since not too many people share the road at this time on a Sunday morning in the middle of a holiday weekend. The timing at campus also proves to be good, and they secure one of just a few parking spots next to the corner of the building where Abby's room is situated. Josselyn House is in the shape of a squared off U, and her room is on the second floor of the east side of the building. Making things even easier, someone has thankfully, albeit illegally, propped open the door at the southeast end of the dormitory, the one that leads to the staircase which lets out almost directly next to her room.

Abby's roommate, Charlotte, has not arrived yet, but the two had already agreed upon the room assignments, so they are able to move Abby's things right in. This particular double consists of two rooms. The first is the room into which one walks from the door in the hallway—quite large with immense windows overlooking both the southern end of the building with a view towards the library as well as the western view where you can see the inside of the U and the rest of the dorm. The second room is a much smaller one reached through the bigger one. This space may be much smaller, but it has its own door. Charlotte cares more about having a larger room, and Abby wants her privacy. A roommate match made in heaven. Neither girl minds being at the edge of the campus either, especially since the dorm is a short walk to the dining hall and to the library as well.

With a primo parking spot and two pairs of willing hands eager to finish the job without the roommate underfoot and blocking the doorway with her own massive amount of "necessities," Suzanne and Abby make quick work of unloading the car. Organizing and prettifying the room will be a different story, of course, but Suzanne knows better than to try to help with that.

Just as they bring up the final couple of boxes, Joe arrives. He's not quite out of breath, but he does look tired and a bit sweaty. "Hey, you want some help?"

Suzanne and Abby both decline, but Joe takes the box from Suzanne and walks up the staircase trailing her. The day is still summer-hot and Suzanne wears shorts. She knows her legs look pretty damn good, so she doesn't mind Joe climbing the stairs right behind her, giving him a view of what he's missing. She may have been the one who asked for the divorce, but she's not above wanting him to feel badly about it. Out of the corner of her eye she can see him looking. Good.

"What's this?" Joe asks as he follows Abby and Suzanne through the big room and into her little slice of solitude. "This doesn't seem fair. Why does Chartreuse—"

"Charlotte," say Abby and Suzanne together.

"Whatever. Why does she get this huge room and you get the puny one?"

"It's not puny," argues Abby. "And it's because I wanted the inside room. Privacy. You know, in the old days, when the girls used to have servants accompanying them to college, this used to be the maid's quarters."

"Oh, that makes me feel better. We're spending all this money for you to go to school here so you can live in the servant's quarters? And what do you need privacy for, anyway?"

Abby beseeches Suzanne. "Mom."

"What 'Mom'? I'm talking to you," says Joe.

Suzanne tries the age-old ploy. "You know what? I'm hungry. Anybody for lunch?"

Abby shakes her head. "Charls texted me. She'll be here soon. I'm going to help her unload, and then we'll do the Deece together."

"Figured," says Suzanne. She turns to Joe, deciding to be nice. "You want to grab some lunch in the College Center before we head off? Oh, what's up with Hannah? You think she wants to join us?"

"I think she's as ready to set up her place and get reacquainted with her friends as this one is."

Suzanne can hear the touch of sadness and regret in his voice. She'll sound the same if she's not careful. "Fair enough. Well, the two of us can grab a bite then go say bye to Hannah."

Joe agrees. Before they take their leave, they each take turns giving a big hug to their youngest daughter. Abby gives a big squeeze in return to her mother and, to Suzanne's surprise, a big one to her father as well. Maybe she's getting over her anger. Or maybe she's just a bit emotional, as is evidenced by the moisture in her eyes. Joe looks like he wants to linger, but Suzanne grabs his arm. "Let's go. I'm famished."

Suzanne tries not to remember that she's leaving her child as she and Joe walk the diagonal sidewalk through the common area surrounded by the four dorms that make up the quad. She can never remember their names and wonders how the occupants can keep straight which one they live in, or at least what the neighboring dorms are called. Besides this, she and Joe know their way around. This is their fourth year coming here, so they should by now. They pass Rockefeller Hall on their way out of the quad, and Suzanne turns her head to the right for a great view of the library. Hannah always said it reminded her of a castle, and it's what she fell in love with even from her first visit to the school more than five years ago. Suzanne fell in love, too.

They head towards Main Building, at the back of which sits the College Center. Main is the oldest on campus, a huge regal old-world magnificent building onto which the modern College Center was added.

Suzanne sighs.

"What's the matter?" asks Joe.

"Nothing. It's just such a beautiful school. I love being here. And I'm happy for our daughters that they get to come."

"Is that a dig, because I wanted Abby stay with you this year? Because, you know—"

"No dig, Joe." And now a sigh for a totally different reason. "Let's just go eat some lunch, okay?"

A short time later, having picked up some sandwiches and drinks from the snack bar, the two sit at a small, silver round table in the atrium of the College Center. It's a bustling place, with the co-eds talking in groups from two to many, some grabbing lunch or a coffee or an ice cream, others taking money out of the ATM, and others just passing through. Every once in a while Suzanne and Joe hear enthusiastic and happy screams as old friends meet up for the first time in many months.

After some chit chat—mostly Suzanne filling Joe in on news about the girls, about the classes they will be taking and about their roommates—Joe puts down his sandwich and says, "Boy, I wish I were back in college."

Suzanne looks up from her own food and catches Joe looking at a pack of attractive young women, obviously of round-about her daughters' ages. "What for?" she asks. She nods at the girls. "Because of them or because you miss the academics?" she asks sardonically.

Despite Suzanne's openly obnoxious tone, Joe looks at his ex-wife wistfully and answers, "Not because of the girls—I wouldn't have a chance in hell with them, anyway. No, I'd go back in a second—for the simple life, the innocent life. Remember then, when we thought the late night, all night studying was hard? That finals were hell on earth? Remember that? When the expectations and anticipations of our lives to come held the wonders of the world? No sorrows, no sadness." Now it's Joe's turn to sigh. "No failures. The simple life before we could even imagine the mistakes we would undoubtedly make, once, twice and again and again."

Wow. That was unexpected. Suzanne had taken the last bite of her sandwich at the beginning of Joe's soliloquy, but by the end she finds it hard to finish chewing. She chokes it down, though, washing the remnants away with her remaining bottled water.

And then Joe surprises her one more time. Looking down at his almost empty plate, he says, "I miss the girls." Then he picks up his head and looks directly into Suzanne's eyes. "I miss... the girls," he repeats, his voice so low against the happy roars of greeting friends that Suzanne has to strain to hear.

"Come on," Suzanne says kindly. "Let's go say bye to Hannah."

Chapter 19

THE START OF SOMETHING NEW

AN HOUR LATER, SUZANNE DRIVES her minivan south. The hollow car—missing the necessities of college along with the second and third row seats—seems void of everything. Everything except her already lonely and empty self.

The fact that she will be completely by herself when she arrives home suddenly hits her hard, somewhere along the New York State Thruway. Yes, the girls were away when Joe moved out of the house, but it was all so new, so much to get used to, so many loose ends to tie up, the paperwork, the moving of his things. And then the girls returned for the summer. But now? Now there's none of that.

Was this what Joe was thinking with all his melancholy?

It strikes her, and in a rush, overwhelms her. The tears—for her ended marriage, for the end of her daughters' childhoods, for the years of her life that have flown with cruel speed—the tears she has willfully refused to shed for all these losses suddenly shatter the quiet of the cavernous minivan. Overcome, she pulls onto an exit ramp off the Thruway and stops the car along the side of an unknown road. She brings her hand up to her heaving chest, thinking, "If only..."

*   *   *

Okay, where the hell am I? Wasn't I just crying in my car? But my eyes, yes, they're dry. Wait a second. In the car, I put my hand on my chest. Crap, I wasn't thinking. The necklace. I made a wish, kind of. No, I can't be here. A tiny sparse room with a bed, a dresser and a desk? What is it with these places and their white walls? It can't be. Okay, one way to find out. Just look out the window. Just a quick peek.

Oh, shit! I *am* here. Here, where I just left. And I know this type of room, I think. I'll know for sure if I open the door.

I do open it a crack and look out carefully. Holy hell, it's true. I'm in a Vassar dorm. Noyes. I know it well, since both Abby and Hannah lived here their freshman years and Hannah her sophomore year as well. She had one of these small rooms that year, a single, all to herself, but freshman year both girls lived in the rooms across the hall, on the other side of the building. Divided doubles, I think they call them, with a wall of dressers separating the two roommates.

I quickly close the door and look for the mirror—I remember there being one built in. Here it is, set back on top of the dresser. Oh, it *is* me. Shoshanna me, kind of. Wait a second, I'm younger than the gym Shoshanna me, maybe five, six years younger? Maybe Abby's age? College age. Holy shit, this room is mine! I'm in college. I'm at Vassar.

Thank goodness I don't have a roommate.

Thank goodness I'm not in the same dorm as Abigail.

Now what?

Okay, I better sit down before I faint. Have I ever

fainted? No matter, because if ever there was a time to start, it's now. Back in college? This is crazy, crazier than a night with Rafael, crazier than the many nights—very different nights—with Rami. Oh, how come I never thought about that? They both start with the letter "R." Does that mean something? Okay, now I'm really going crazy. Well, either that or I'm getting hysterical. Well, of course I'm getting hysterical. I'm back at fucking college! Not back, though, because I didn't go to Vassar. And my kids, they're here. I can't meet up with them. I better not run into them. I won't know how to act. I'll be a blithering idiot. Not much different than I'm sounding right now, but, of course, I'm by myself right now.

Okay, well, maybe I should just stay put. If I don't leave the room, no one will see me. But what happens when I need to pee? And eat. But if I don't eat or drink, maybe I won't need to use the bathroom, so I'll be okay.

This is ridiculous. I know. I'll just wish to go home. That should work, right? I mean, usually I just end up at home, but it should work both ways. In the car, driving home, I kind of wished I could go back to college, and here I am, so if I wish for home now, I should end up there, too, right? Okay, so I'll just hold the necklace, and, well, better say it out loud.

"I wish I were back home."

Nothing.

"I want to be back at my home, as myself. As Suzanne."

Still nothing.

It's not working. Why is it not working?

But, if I'm being truthful, I know why not. And might as well be truthful, since I'm the only one in the room. It's because I might be saying the words, but really, truly, I don't want to be back home. I guess the necklace knows. I guess this is where I want to be. For now.

I guess I'm back at college.

Okay, so... like I said, now what?

Now what?

What now?

Let's take a peek around the room. It kind of feels like spying, but, really, I'm spying on myself, right? And what have we here? It looks like, why yes, it's a class schedule. Looks like I'm already signed up for my courses. Excellent. What am I taking?

"Introduction to the History of Art." Art History? Oh, I remember both the girls talking about that one. Each of the department members teaches his/her specialty. They both loved that course. Wow, it meets four times per week. Oh, I see why. Three of them are lectures and the other is a smaller section with one of the professors. Should be good, at least that's what the girls said.

Okay, what else do we have? "Introduction to Cognitive Science." What the hell is that even about? And this one and the art class are both 100 level courses? Am I a freshman? No, I can't be. I've got a dorm room to myself, but freshmen always have roommates. And, right, look here. I'm also taking "Nineteenth-Century British Novels" and "Metaphysics," which are both 200 level classes. And, well, here's a course that really seems to go with the rest of them: "Intermediate Squash." Firstly, that's a strange coincidence, considering the history of the Athletes Complex, and, secondly, who really plays squash anymore? Who *ever* played squash? Well, I guess the answer would be me, since I'm at an intermediate level.

This seems to be a pretty harsh course load. Wait a minute. It looks like there's one more. Classical Guitar? I don't play the guitar, classical or otherwise. Do I? And what does this course number mean, Music 068? That doesn't look right. I've never seen a course starting with a zero before. Maybe it's a Vassar thing, like that they give their diplomas in Latin, so my girls will receive an AB (can't remember exactly how you say it in Latin, though) instead of a BA.

Hold on—there's a laptop here. I bet I can look the course catalog up on line. Okay, it's starting up. Let's just hope it's not password protected...

Well, at least something's going my way. I'm in. Getting onto the Vassar website and, yup, there's the catalog. Okay, easy enough to navigate to Music, scroll down...

Ah, okay, I see. It's no-credit music lessons. Wow, like I wasn't taking enough courses, I had to sign myself up for guitar? *Classical* guitar? At least it's not for credit. But, come on, am I really worried about this? I'm not *really* in college. This is only some strange cosmic side trip to college. In real life, I work full time. At a job I hate. But the money's good. At least I'm supporting myself.

Oh, while I'm in the catalog—or catalo*gue*, as it's written on the website—I might as well look up those other two classes. Let's see... click on Cognitive Science and... okay so it's multidisciplinary... and it explores... how physical things get a mind. Well, then. Yeah, okay. Maybe I should look at the next one. That's in... oh, you've got to be kidding! Philosophy? I've never taken a philosophy class in my life. Finance majors don't do philosophy. Okay, here it is, the description. I'm going to be studying about reality, existence. Ha. Very funny. I can't resist and pull out the necklace. "Is this some kind of joke?" I ask it, but it doesn't answer me back. I guess that's a good thing.

Okay, enough of this. I might as well go out and

explore a little. I *look* like a college kid, anyway, so no one will suspect anything, unless I say something really stupid. Probably best if I try not to speak at all. That should be relatively easy, because I don't know anyone. Except my daughters, but they won't know me, right? Okay, I'm getting out of here.

It's a simple building to navigate, this thin semi-circular structure. I'm downstairs and walking through the lounge in a snap and heading outside. One door would be the way my room is facing, towards the cemetery that marks the northern border of the campus. I scoot out the door opposite, the one that leads into a large, empty grass area. I'm pretty sure it's called "Noyes Circle." "The shortest distance between two points kills grass." Isn't that what the girls used to say as they led the way directly across the circle? I head that same way, since it leads to the main part of campus. On an impulse, I turn back around and take in the view of the dorm I just left. It's modern, elegant, simple and completely different from the architecture of the other residence halls. I wish I knew something about architecture. Oh, wait, I will. I'm going to be taking Art History. For the first time since I "arrived," I think maybe a little of the overwhelming fear might be morphing into excitement. Back at college. Who would have thunk it?

I turn once again in the direction I was headed, and in a moment I'm through the ring of trees that surround the Circle and headed towards the back of Main Building. Walking around the front, I have a wonderful view of the magnificent library. And there's Main Gate, with the art gallery. It really is an amazing museum, an incredible collection, especially when you consider the small size of the school. Wow, I sound kind of funny, don't I? "Magnificent," "amazing," "incredible." I think I sound more like Chef Gordon Ramsey than a Vassar Girl.

So, do I stop in at the library? The art gallery? Hmm, no, I'll save that for later. Skinner Hall is where I'm headed. That's where my guitar lessons will be, and I've never seen it before. Why would I have? Abby and Hannah don't have a musical bone between them.

Hold on. I'm pretty sure I'm going somewhat towards the right place, but I really don't know where I'm going. Good thing I'm not a male. I can stop and ask directions.

*   *   *

Yes, I definitely have not been in this remote corner of the main campus before. Feels kind of secluded, a little dark, even, compared to the rest of the grounds. Wow, but that's a beautiful building. Not quite as castle-like as the library. Not fairy tale like. More like imposing. Looks like what I'll probably read about in my Nineteenth-Century British Novel class. The tragic heroine's estate, passed down from generation to generation. Or not. I've never read any Nineteenth-Century British novels before—at least, I don't think I have. This place seems pretty damn remote, and this huge building—why is nobody here? "Body of unknown girl found under walking bridge leading to liberal arts college music building. Foul play suspected." Oh, look. A couple of people are coming out the front door. That's better. I'm not the only one here. And now I also know the front door is open. See, now that's the front door of a tragic heroine's estate, for sure. Wood and iron, heavy, tall.

Okay, now that I'm inside, with these dim lights and wide corridors, I really feel like I've stepped back in time. So many doors. These can't all be classrooms—way too tiny. Wait, what's that? A piano? Oh, duh, of course it is. These are practice rooms. Ooh, I wonder if one of them is open so I can see inside, preview what I'll be practicing in, or taking lessons in, or maybe both? Not quite sure how all of this works. Here's one. Okay, don't want to just barge in. What if someone's in there already? I'd better listen first, make sure no one is in there. A quick check around—don't want anyone seeing me with my ear up to the door... coast clear. Let's have a listen.

Silence.

More silence.

Now slowly, in case I walk in on someone, slowly... wait, why the hell am I being so dramatic? What's the big deal if I walk in on someone? I catch them in the middle of what? A scale? Mortifying. Although, these rooms are pretty remote. Come on, over the years, you can't tell me there was never a little something more than music lessons going on in these rooms. At some point, Dinah must have been blowing something other than a horn, right? I mean, it's just the law of averages. Wow, do I sound like a teenager or what?

Enough of that. I'm just going to ease this door open and, yes, there you have it, an empty practice room. Well, empty except for the fact that almost the entire space is taken up by this shiny black Steinway piano. I can't resist—I have to tickle those keys. Wish I could play this thing. So, if someone *were* having sex in here, how would they do it? Standing up? Because the other choices would be either on this way too narrow bench or right on top of this beautiful baby grand. Okay, now that really does sound teenager-ish and downright blasphemous. I think I better leave now.

This really is a quiet building. Wonder if it's always like this, or just because the semester hasn't started yet. I can hear the tap of my shoes echoing in the hallways. Well, I'll be out of here soon enough.

Wait a moment. What's through there? I don't remember that door being open when I passed before. Hmm, that looks pretty. An auditorium. Wow, well that's really something. Plush, turquoise seats on a sharp slope and an intimate stage. That is one magnificent pipe organ. Makes sense, an incredible music building like this having its own recital hall. "Nice," I say out loud, before I realize I've done so.

Something—someone—stirs in the center of one of the front rows. Crap. I hadn't noticed anyone when I walked in. He's getting up, hastily making his way out of the row.

"I'm so sorry," I apologize. "I didn't mean to disturb you."

"Oh... no... that's okay," he says in stilted fashion.

"Really, please stay. I'm just taking a quick look."

He's out of the row and starting to leave the hall before I even finish the sentence. This is one shy, awkward young man. He can hardly look at me, darting glances as he moves by me. "It's fine. I was... I was leaving... anyway."

Before he's out the door, though, I can see that he's really not a boy. Late twenties, could even be early thirties. A professor, maybe? I'd say maybe a timid first year professor? Okay, I hope I don't have him for any of my classes. Looks like he would pass out even if you just said his name. But cute. I mean, did you see that dark, full hair? I think his face was not bad, too, if he had let me take a better look. Tall and... ugh, there are those teenage hormones again. Think it's time to get back to civilization now.

*   *   *

I may be a little hungry, and it may be time for dinner, but I can't resist a short stop in the library before I head over to the dining center.

I smell it as soon as I step through the doors of the Thompson Library. I know I haven't spent so much time here, but from the first time we toured with Hannah, I remember this smell. Musty, maybe, but an inviting musty.

I walk up the short set of stone stairs—say that one ten times fast—and find myself in a square area with a lofty ceiling that reaches up, I don't know, maybe fifty feet? It could be one hundred, for all I know; I'm not good with these things. All I do know is that this is the "turret" of the castle, the center tower. A group of maybe fifteen people—a mix of younger than college age and older women and men, probably around my real age—stand together, eyes up towards the tower. Off to the side stands a perky, college-age woman. She points her hand upward as she addresses the small crowd, obviously a tour group, most likely an admissions tour judging by the ages of the attendees. I've taken a couple of these tours myself, each in turn with my kids, but, at that time, I was thinking more about the kids and their reactions, their futures, how fast they're growing up. I was thinking about lots of things on these tours and probably did precious little listening. I listen now.

"As you can see," says Miss Perky—I can tell right away she's perfect for this job—"above us hang five tapestries. And while Vassar was founded in 1861 by Matthew Vassar, a brewer—more on that a little later—and this library, the Thompson Library, was completed in 1905, these Flemish tapestries hail from an earlier time—the seventeenth century. They depict the romance of Cupid and Psyche, a story that first appeared in the middle of the second century in Lucius Apuleius' *Metamorphoses*. It's quite a story, but the gist of it is that beautiful Psyche had to suffer through and successfully complete multiple dangerous tasks in order to earn the right to be with her love—that would be Cupid—and an eternal life of joy."

I crane my head up as do the others in the group, but Miss Perky moves on.

"So, if you'll follow me now to this next room..."

Her group follows, and I follow the group. We don't walk too far, though, stopping in the middle of a large area facing a massive stained-glass window.

"Now we've gotten to one of my favorite parts of the tour. The Great Window, also known as the Cornaro Stained-Glass Window, was commissioned for the library and installed in 1906. The scene it depicts is an actual event of 1678, one of great significance to Vassar and its beginnings as an all-women's college. It is the conferring of the first Doctorate—ever—to a woman. The recipient of the degree, and the focal point of the scene, is Lady Elena Lucretia Cornaro-Piscopia of Venice, Italy. Lady Elena was a brilliant linguist—she spoke eight languages fluently—and an expert in philosophy, literature and more."

Miss Perky the Informative takes a short break from talking as she watches her group gazing at the exquisite glass.

"Okay, well, while I give you a couple more minutes to get your fill of this remarkable window, let's talk for a moment, as I promised, about the founder of Vassar, Mr. Matthew Vassar. Vassar, inspired by his niece, founded the college for women in 1861 with four hundred and eight thousand dollars, half of the fortune he had made as, yes, a brewer, making beer." She pauses for effect; the crowd dutifully chuckles. "Many people know of Vassar College's auspicious beginnings, but very few know what happened just seven years later. On June 23, 1868, Matthew Vassar was giving his annual speech to the board of trustees, reading from the pages he had written. About to remark on how fortunate the school had been so far not to have experienced any serious illnesses or deaths among either the students or the trustees, Vassar stopped mid-sentence, dropped the papers he held, fell back in his chair and died."

Hmm. Well, that's irony for you. And sad. He died so soon after the school started, he never got a chance to really see its success. *His* success.

Miss Kill-the-Moment and her flunkies move on without me. Instead, I take a seat facing the Great Window. It may be evening, but the light still shines through the window, with its western exposure. The deep purples and crimsons glimmer, warming the entire room. Lady Elena Whatever-Whatever beams from her throne. What had she thought at that moment? Pride in herself, thanks to her parents, to her teachers? Had she understood the significance, the courage, the major historical role she was playing in her city, her country, the world? And, once she had her degree, what did she do with it? Did she accomplish whatever else she set out to do? At the end, was she proud of herself then?

Well, she had a lot more to be proud of than I do, that's for damn sure.

I take a deep breath as I gaze at the benevolent face of Lady Elena once more. My lungs fill with the heady library smell I shouldn't find so appealing but do. I can hear the tour guide's voice in the distance as she subtly tries to sell the benefits of the strong liberal arts education to be gained at Vassar. Not at all like the education I received that led me straight into a "good" job, a job of daily grinds, daily crap for a company I care little about, a company that cares nothing for me. I practically learned a trade in my schooling, but my kids? No, they're not learning anything they can translate directly into cash upon their convocation.

They, my children and all their schoolmates, are learning how to learn, learning how to live.

Good for them.

Is that why the necklace brought me here? To learn about life, to do better things with my life? Or did I bring myself here, in a moment of extreme loneliness? Or does it all boil down to a whim, a fleeting thought? "Wouldn't it be great to be back in college?"

The light dims behind the Great Window. Lady Elena and her throngs of observers must say goodbye for the night, invisible in the darkness.

I head out to the darkness as well, headed for the light and life that awaits in other parts of the campus.

* * *

As soon as I hit the fresh air of the cool September evening, as soon as I see the campus laid out before me, I feel a moment of clarity. I *want* to be here at Vassar. I *want* to go back to school in this very unusual way. But what if the necklace won't bring me back? What if this is a one-time thing? I know the necklace takes me to the gym constantly, but with Rafael it was different. I only got to be with him a few times. Of course, that probably had more to do with me, since I wasn't too happy with his, shall we say, amorous extra-curricular activities, and, on top of that, he did say he was moving away. Wonder where he is now, while I'm meandering the Vassar campus in my even younger body. Would he want this body?

Hold on. How did I get from lofty thoughts of women and degrees and learning about life all the way to sex, in thirty seconds flat? I've got to stop this. I need to focus, focus on my education, just like I would say to my girls. That's what I'm here for. I'm not Psyche, looking to win my Cupid, the love of my life. I'm no Lady Elena, either, of course, but the necklace can't be just about having sex, or constructing the perfect body. It has to be about more than that. I mean, as much as I loved having sex with Rafael, the way he moved, the way he touched me... stop that! Control your teenage hormones, Shoshanna!

You know what I need? Food! Good thing I have a dining card on my keychain. And, yes, right on cue, here I am, smack dab in front of ACDC. Perfect. A nice, quiet dinner; that's what I need. I open the door and enter. There's a line to get in. Okay, I know I won't see Hannah here—she's eating in her townhouse, terrace apartment, whatever you call it—so I just have to make sure I don't run into Abby. Except what would it really matter if I do? She won't know who I am. I keep forgetting that. But it does matter, because it would be too awkward for *me*.

At least the line moves pretty quickly.

What is that man behind the counter yelling? Sounds like "Two linus, two linus." Oh, I think he's telling everyone they should make two lines. Greek accent, maybe.

Hey, I thought college food was supposed to suck. This looks pretty good. Smells pretty good, too. No wonder there's the gaining of the freshman ten, or twenty. I better be careful. Rami would kill me if I derail this body. But if I got out of shape in this Shoshanna body, would that mean my older Shoshanna body, the one that works out with Rami, would be out of shape as well? Better not chance it. Lean meats and veggies.

I put sensible-sized portions on my plate and set off to find a quiet place to eat. I turn first to the closest seating area I see. No, definitely not this side of the dining center. That's just one big room. Too loud, too overwhelming and too much chance to see a real-life daughter. How about the other side? I weave in and out of the maze of people picking up food and drinks and cross over to the other side of the hall. Yes, much more like it. One central larger room, but look at all these closed off rooms surrounding it. Let's look in—yup, this seems perfect. Just a few tables in this small room, with one of them completely unoccupied. And no Abigail.

I set my tray down on the table and am about to sit when I realize there are a few things missing, namely, utensils. I leave the food—doubtful anyone will bother it—and run back into the cafeteria area to grab a knife and a fork. I have to hunt for them for a moment and finally discover they logically sit next to the trays, in the place where you first enter. I grab the institutional cutlery I need, but as I turn from the row of silver cylinders that hold them, I nearly crash into a young woman.

"Sorry," I say automatically, and look up into none other than Abby's face. You have got to be kidding!

"No problem," she says with a smile. "Good thing you weren't holding the knife sharp edge out, right? But, come to think of it, with these knives, you probably wouldn't even have broken skin." She smiles at her own joke. "No worries," she says.

What a nice kid. But she's *my* kid, and I absolutely do not want to talk to her. Run away, run away—which I do with another quick "sorry" just so she knows I'm not a total boor.

With my heart pounding, I high-tail it back to my secluded little dining room to find it's no longer so secluded. Someone has joined my table at the end opposite to where I had left my food. A male someone. A male someone who possibly looks vaguely familiar?

I hardly look as I sit down to concentrate on my dinner, putting my hard-won knife and fork to work.

Abby's right. It's not the greatest knife, a little thin and not so sharp, but the strips of tender London Broil cut easily enough and taste of a well-balanced marinade. The broccoli tastes pretty good, too, and not the limp consistency of a normal cafeteria vegetable. This is why I've never heard finicky Abby complain about the food here. I wonder what she's eating tonight—the London Broil, too? I could look, if I wanted to, which is a pretty funny thought. But I won't.

I raise my head for a second and see the male someone looking at me. He quickly looks down at his food but not before I realize why he seems familiar. I just saw him a short while ago. The man from the recital hall, the possible professor. He's alone, no other students dining with him, so that kind of supports the professor theory. Of course, I'm eating alone as well, but he's definitely a number of years older than I am—than Vassar-Shoshanna.

With him looking at his plate, concentrating on his food, I'm able to examine him with some extended and more edifying scrutiny. He eats quickly and with little relish, with one foot under the table but the other on the side of his chair as though ready to make his great escape from the dining hall as soon as he finishes his last bite. He has the London Broil and vegetables, too, but he also took the rosemary roasted potatoes. They look and smell great. I wish I could afford to eat those, but I can't risk all those white-potato calories. And is that pineapple upside down cake on his tray? Oh, I *really* wish I could afford to eat *that*. I used to make it sometimes. Joe liked it. *I* liked it. Doesn't look like Music Hall Man has to worry about those calories, though. I would call him "trim." Not skinny, but well-proportioned. And, yes, my first glimpse of him at Skinner Hall proves correct. He's quite the attractive looking man. He's got a shadow of a beard that makes him look rugged, brooding and a little dangerous all at the same time—the kind of beard you wouldn't really want rubbing against your face but that looks hot as hell. Hot as hell, yes, that's the way to describe him. Movie star features that don't say perfection individually but work together to seduce the millions. Is he really that good looking? I steal another glance. Yes, yes he is. And he's sitting all alone, which means he'll probably be sleeping all alone tonight as well. Oh, Suzanne, shut up! This guy's at least twenty years younger than you—or a dozen years older than you if you look at it another way—and you haven't really even talked to him yet but you have yourself fucking him already? On the other hand, why the hell not? I can introduce myself, just start talking... no, no I cannot. Well, I *can* but I *will not*. Did I not just experience some extreme soul searching, not a half an hour ago in the library? Did I not say I'm choosing Lady Elena's lofty educational intentions over Psyche's quest to win happiness through securing a man? The necklace clearly is not sending me from place to place just for me to satisfy some unquenched sexual thirst. On the other hand, the necklace *did* give me these looks, right, and this unbelievable body? There's got to be a reason for that, too. And, look at him! Just watching him chew his food—look at his mouth, look at his hands...

Is this what all the young women feel all the time? Heat and desire taking over their bodies? I don't remember this from when I was young. Well, I don't remember much about my youth at this point. Do my daughters feel this? Are they acting on it? Maybe the necklace sent me here to keep an eye on them, guide them?

Right, like that would really work. Imagine me

walking up to Abby as Shoshanna, a complete stranger. "Uh, Abigail, you know you shouldn't be having sex with this boy you hardly know." To which she'll say, "Oh, you're right. I'm going to kick this gorgeous junior out of my bed and sleep alone from now on. Thank you so much, Miss *Strange Sophomore I've Never Seen in My Life*. You just saved me from an embarrassing orgasm."

Besides, she's in college. As much as I don't like to think about it, I shouldn't be stopping her from any type of orgasm. Yuck, I'm talking about my daughter. Get over it. I shouldn't be stopping *her*, but I should and will stop myself. The bottom line is, I want this college time again. I want to visit here at Vassar, often, and I don't need any Rafael-type baggage that might stop me. I want to find out the real reason I'm here. No men. Do you hear me, curvaceous and sexy Shoshanna? No men! I wasted my college years the first time around, I didn't appreciate it then, but, you know what? I'm not going to waste it this time.

"Youth is wasted on the young."

Oops. Did I just say that out loud? I must have, because Music Building Man just looked up.

"G. B. Shaw."

Oh, that's a nice voice. Husky but low. "I'm sorry?"

"'Youth is wasted on the young.' That's a quote. From George Bernard Shaw."

He sounds as awkward as he did in our brief encounter earlier this evening. But, yes, that is one sultry voice. I didn't notice it earlier.

"Right. Sorry, I was thinking of something, and it just slipped out."

He kind of grunts in return and turns back to his food. Not much of a conversationalist, this one. But a fast eater, apparently. In less time than it takes me to chew one more piece of beef, he devours his slice of upside down cake in about four rapid-fire bites.

As soon as the last forkful hits his lips, he awkwardly pushes back his chair and gets up. He gives me half a nod, picks up his tray but almost drops it, then heads out the door, narrowly missing a pair of laughing students on their way in. He almost looks like he's had a few too many, but not quite. He looks more embarrassed than drunk, like he's just not comfortable in his own skin. And being that his skin—all of him—is pretty fucking hot, that's a damn shame.

Suzanne Shoshanna—whatever the hell your name is—YOU STOP IT RIGHT NOW!

Chapter 20

FROM BAD TO WORSE

SUZANNE SLAMS THE DOOR TO her gas guzzling, four-door, good for nothing pain in the ass car. Well, it's good for two things, actually—giving her aggravation and gobbling up money. This morning it did both. Not only did her day start late—since she forgot to set her alarm last night and only woke because her full bladder demanded her to—but then, when she hurried into her car with a breakfast bar in one hand and her computer bag in the other, she couldn't start the damn thing. Completely dead. AAA came quickly enough, and thankfully it doesn't take long to replace a battery, but now she's an hour and a half late to work. She tried calling her boss multiple times, but he didn't pick up. She hopes he at least got her voice message, but, still, that won't stop the glaring stares to which he'll surely subject her.

She takes several deep breaths as she nears her work entrance and reminds herself she should be grateful the car died in her own driveway. At least she didn't get stuck somewhere. "Positive attitude," she tells herself and then repeats the phrase three times, a mini-mantra to start her unusual morning.

As soon as she walks in the door, she realizes this is no ordinary day for everyone else as well. People congregate outside their cubicles, their muted conversations forming a low but audible buzz. No one even notices her as she walks towards her own cube. She quickly puts her purse away in her drawer and joins the closest huddle.

"What's going on?" she asks.

The answer is not good. The company just announced it sold off their Ace division. It may be in another state, but the home office, that would be *this* office, no longer needs all the staff to support it, especially in Finance and Customer Service. The executives and Human Resources are calling people in one by one to give them the pink slip. The packages they're giving—a week salary for each year of service—aren't as good as they used to be, but at least they're something. Then they rattle off who has gotten the axe so far. No one she's too close with, so that's a good thing, but some really nice people.

Suzanne looks around and sees, over the tops of the low cubicle walls, a couple of people standing in their own cubicles, heads bobbing as they clean out their desks. Her stomach falls into her toes worrying she may be next. But as she looks around at the gloomy scene, she realizes this place has been sad for a long time. It used to be fun here, nice to come to somewhere you wanted to spend so many of your waking hours. But it's been a daily grind for a long time, and with the arrival of her boss a year ago, the daily grind became an hourly drudgery.

Maybe it wouldn't be so bad if she were laid off. She's been with this company for fourteen years. That's over three months of severance...

Except she's divorced and helping to put two kids through college. And three months pass very quickly, especially in a job market like today's job market.

Suzanne leaves her desk and heads over to where the three people reporting to her sit. Of course, they're not sitting now. They stand together in a group and ask her what's going on.

She's a manager. Of course she should know, but "I honestly have no idea," she answers. To herself she wonders if someone from her group will be let go. But it couldn't be, right? Wouldn't they at least have given her the courtesy of telling her if someone reporting to her was losing their job?

"Suzanne." The voice startles her, and before she even turns to face its owner, her heart starts racing the Indy 500. The voice belongs to her boss. "I need to see you. In my office."

How long does it take for Suzanne's feet to start moving? It seems like minutes, although likely it's seconds, and when they do start moving, she can't really feel them. Is her entire world about to change in seconds? It would only take a few words. *I'm sorry to tell you...*

Suzanne realizes she's in his office. The room smells like cigarette smoke. He's a smoker, her boss. He doesn't smoke inside his office, not even in the building, but he must have recently gone out for a smoke, and the stink emanates from his clothing, permeating the room. He gestures to a seat, which she gladly takes. As she sits, she realizes she and her boss are the only ones in here. No one from Human Resources. She thinks to herself that it's a good sign. They need HR in here if they are letting her go, right?

He clears his throat. "I'm afraid I have some bad news."

Then again, maybe they don't.

Suzanne's heart no longer races; it now feels as though it's not even beating. She wonders for how long it can stop beating. She wonders how long it will take her boss to say his next sentence.

"We have to let Mary go."

Suzanne wrinkles her face, stumped. "Who's Mary?"

"Mary, who works for you," he answers in that tone he likes to take, that tone that says he hates talking to idiots.

"I don't have a Mary reporting to me."

"Well, you know who I mean."

Suzanne hopes she doesn't. "Mandy?"

"Yes, Mandy. They're telling her right now." Amazing how he doesn't change his tone.

Suzanne is almost speechless. Almost. "How come I didn't know about this before?"

"Well, if you had been here on time this morning, I would have told you when you first got in."

How he can so massively miss the point is beyond Suzanne. She has to keep the words in her response to a minimum in order to ensure she doesn't lose it all together. "Car trouble. I meant before today. Why didn't I know ahead of time? I'm her boss."

"The division was sold. I couldn't tell you that. Was on a need to know basis. Anyway, why would you need to know? *You* still have a job. The rest of it doesn't concern you."

All of a sudden, Suzanne's heart remembers how to beat. More than beat. It pounds. Her hand unwittingly reaches for her chest...

*   *   *

I'm sitting in the office, across from my boss, except with several key differences from a moment ago. One, I'm in his seat, and he's in mine. Two, my heart beat is perfectly paced. Three, one more person occupies the room—Phyllis from Human Resources.

"I'm sure you've heard the division has been sold," I say to my boss, now obviously not my boss. "Many people are getting laid off today. But you're not one of them." I see him let out a sigh of relief. "You're getting fired instead." I look at him to watch his reaction. He's speechless and turning pomegranate red.

"But... but..." he sputters.

I don't give him the courtesy to allow him to struggle through to the end of his sentence. "You're incompetent, nasty and lazy. Here's your stack of warnings," I say, placing my hand on a thick file of papers. "Phyllis here will show you out."

Phyllis stands and gestures to the door, through which my ex-boss leaves, his tail between his legs.

*   *   *

Why do the good ones have to end so quickly, thinks Suzanne as she finds herself back on the other side of the desk, her boss still talking to her. She realizes she probably should be listening.

Except as she listens, she thinks she probably does not want to listen, because all he talks about is how, with "Mary" gone, Suzanne will need to spread those now unattended responsibilities among those left in her group. And, since "Mary" is not the only one getting laid off in Finance, Suzanne and her group will be taking on some new assignments as well.

To which all Suzanne can think to respond is, "It's 'Mandy,' not 'Mary.'"

Her boss responds with an eloquent, "Whatever."

What started off as an unexpectedly short day becomes a painfully long and deeply unproductive one. The march out of the building holding a box of meager personal belongings and accompanied by a representative from Human Resources gets repeated over and over by people from various departments. Since Suzanne's cubicle sits along the path to the outside door, she sees them all—some she knows well, others have just vaguely familiar faces. And all Suzanne can think as she watches these scared and somber faces pass by is how much she must really hate this place to think she may be better off as one of them.

Chapter 21

FROM WORSE TO HELL

SUZANNE THANKS LORI. A TRUE friend—once she started, a while back, to talk to Suzanne again—Lori dropped her plans for the evening and has accompanied her to the gym, the two trying to work together to stave off the inevitable toxic reaction to this horrendous day. They decide to take a high-intensity, high-frustration-release cross-training class together—a class so demanding, Suzanne figures she'll have little time for thinking, which she finds necessary after a day like this.

The class starts with a slow warm up, though, providing a dangerous time for evil thoughts to intrude. Suzanne pushes them out of her mind by constantly reminding herself to have a positive attitude. "You have a job," she tells herself as she stretches her left arm over her head and towards the right side of her body. "Your work is interesting. Sometimes." Following the instructor's directions, she stretches to the other side. "You still have a job," she repeats in her mind as she exhales and holds the painful stretch.

Thankfully, the class quickly picks up mind-numbing steam, and both Suzanne and Lori can do little more than breathe heavily as they try to keep up, stealing an occasional furtive glance at each other as they commiserate. It's during one such glance...

* * *

"What the hell was that?" booms Lori as soon as she finds Suzanne, who sits on a couch just outside the classroom.

"I got tired. I had to leave."

"You asked me to come here tonight, you asked me to change my plans, and then you walk yourself out the door halfway through? What the hell!?"

"Not here," answers Suzanne, looking around for possible eavesdroppers.

Lori seems to ignore Suzanne's request for privacy. "Wasn't the point of doing this class to make you tired so you could go home and pass out and not think about things? I think I'm missing something here."

Suzanne realizes she has to nip this tirade in the bud. She pulls her friend's arm so that Lori sits next to her. "I went to the gym," she says in as hushed a voice as the din from the surrounding noise allows.

"Okay, do I need to take your temperature or something?" asks Lori, obviously not understanding the signal to speak in something below a shout. "Hello? We *are* at the gym."

Suzanne tries again for an inconspicuous volume. "The *other* gym."

Lori finally lowers her voice. "Oh."

"I'm almost at the end of the private sessions I bought. Rami's acting like a madman. He's complaining I'm not giving my all, and he's working me harder than ever. Incredibly exhausting. I just couldn't finish this class after doing all of that with him. Sorry."

"You're sorry," repeats Lori, sounding unconvinced.

"Yes, I am. Listen, it's out of my control. Well, maybe

not, but if I can control it, I haven't figured out how yet."

Lori doesn't answer but gives Suzanne a puzzled look.

"What?" asks Suzanne.

"Nothing," says Lori seemingly shaking off whatever thoughts she had. "Hey, I have an idea. Why don't we go to the movies? Girls night out, a good comedy. Just what the doctor ordered. How does that sound?"

"Like a spoonful of sugar."

*   *   *

Six concession stand lines and each one has a long wait, as usual.

"Do they give them a test and hire only the slowest people possible?" asks Suzanne in her irritation.

"Wow, you sound like me," answers Lori. "You're usually the generous soul, and *I'm* the bitch."

"You're right. I'm sorry. Positive attitude."

"That's right. We're out for a good time. Forget about all your troubles. Tonight's about a good chick flick comedy and buttery movie popcorn, the bastardization of an otherwise healthy snack food. Screw the woes!"

"Screw the woes!" Suzanne agrees emphatically.

Somebody waves to her from the line two over from where they stand.

"Oh, fuck me," curses Suzanne.

"That was fast," says a surprised Lori.

"It's Joe. Over there. He's here." Suzanne waves feebly back. "Can't I go anywhere and not see him?"

Lori looks confused. "You've been seeing him a lot?"

Suzanne explains she just saw him at Vassar, when they dropped the kids at school.

"You know, he's the father of your children. You should talk to him once in a while," Lori advises.

"Yeah, because you know so much about this topic."

"I'm just saying."

They finally make it to the front of the line and order their indulgence. The cashier obliges in an exceedingly pleasant and pathetically slow manner.

As they come off the line and head towards theater number five, they bump into none other than Joe, of course.

"Evening," he says almost timidly.

"Joe, what's up?" asks Lori in her patented loud voice. "Hey, I'm going to grab us some seats," she says to Suzanne without waiting for Joe's answer.

"We have time. It's okay," says Suzanne, trying to stop Lori from running off and leaving her with the ex. Up at Vassar, dealing with the kids—that seemed fine to be alone with him. Here? Not so much. "You know they're going to play fifteen minutes of commercials and coming attractions."

The argument does not dissuade Lori. "Yeah, but I hate if I have to sit in one of those front row, crane-your-neck seats," and off she runs with a wave, leaving Suzanne and Joe standing across from each other.

Joe looks more awkward, more uncomfortable in his skin than even the young professor at Vassar. Suzanne can kind of understand. It's beyond weird seeing him in a place they used to come to together. They never went on frequent dates in their married life, but when they did have one, it was almost always at the movie theater. *This* movie theater.

Joe shifts back and forth, looking more at his giant popcorn and colossal soda than at Suzanne. Suzanne looks at the drink, confused. Joe drinks only water, not soda. Well, he used to drink only water.

He interrupts her thoughts. "So, um, you doing okay?"

She thinks for a second to tell him about her latest work woes, but in the next second decides not. "Yeah.

You?"

He nods, followed by an awkward silence. After a moment he asks, "The girls doing okay, starting off the school year? I don't hear from them much when they're at college."

Suzanne's stomach drops at the mention of "college." Another thing she's not telling Joe about. "I don't either," Suzanne says, shrugging.

"Hmm. That's funny. I thought you did." Joe shifts his weight once more, staring again at his snacks. "I know I haven't lived in the same house with them for a while now," he continues after a moment, clearing his throat, "but, you know, at least I felt, you know, kind of close to them, since I was in the same town." His voice starting to crack, he continues, quietly, "It's hard for me, not being near them."

Suzanne tries not to show the shock on her face. He's continuing that openness he shared at their lunch.

And, even more shocking, he quietly adds, "Well, you know how that feels, too."

Suzanne can't respond. She stands in awe of his candor, his demonstration of the affection he has for his children. A new side to Joe. He's being so open—he's never been open—and she's acting so deceptive, not telling him about her own time at Vassar. It doesn't feel right. It feels like lying.

Suzanne realizes she should say something, but what? Should she be opening up to him, too? Should she say "screw the movies" and ask if he wants to chat over coffee?

The longer Suzanne does not speak, the more uncomfortable Joe seems to grow. He breaks the silence, his tone trying for normal. "So, work okay?"

Great, Suzanne thinks to herself sarcastically. He asked a direct question. Now she's really torn. Should she answer it honestly? She panics. "Well, you know, trying to keep a positive attitude."

He chuckles. "Good for you," he says, and Suzanne sees a hint of something she hasn't seen in, well, decades. Joe's smile is what won her over all those years ago. "Good for you," he repeats.

Joe shifts his weight again, and Suzanne's attention is drawn from the sweet smile on his face down to the clothes he wears. She hadn't realized before, but his clothes have definitely taken a step up in style. Not his boring non-descript navy blue slacks with a simple button down shirt. Tonight he's wearing nicely fitted jeans and a black tee shirt, both quite flattering. He looks nice.

"Hey," he says, bringing Suzanne's attention to his face once more where his momentarily relaxed smile has turned back to a tense one. "I wanted to call you. I wanted..." he struggles to speak, "I meant to let you know," he can't spit it out. He takes a deep breath and tries again. "I'm sorry."

Suzanne looks at him quizzically.

"For that whole Abby staying home thing. It came from... it was a stupid... I... I'm sorry. I should never have brought it up."

Well, that was unexpected. Like the rest of this encounter.

Apparently Joe's confessional time has finished. "I guess we should... I guess your movie should be starting soon, right? And this popcorn's not getting any fresher..." Now his smile would be classified more in the uncomfortable range than relaxed.

Suzanne nods. They start walking towards the theater entrances. Suzanne expects him to keep walking as she starts to turn off towards theater five, but, to her surprise, he follows her. "You're seeing this one?" This is not Joe's type of movie at all.

"Oh. Yes."

Suzanne notices Joe's soda sloshing in his cup and a few pieces of popcorn fall off the large mound.

"Need some help with that?" she asks, surprised at how unsteady he appears.

"Nope. Just fine. Yup. Just fine."

As they walk into the theater, it's Suzanne's turn to feel awkward. "Um, did you want to sit with me and Lori?"

"Oh, um," and there's that deep breath again. "Actually, I'm not alone."

Suzanne looks up in the direction Joe looks. Her eyes might still be adjusting to the darkness, but she can sure see the attractive long haired buxom thing smiling and waving enthusiastically at her ex-husband.

And the thing that pops immediately into Suzanne's head?

Fuck the positive attitude.

Chapter 22

THE SIMPLER DAYS?

BACK AT COLLEGE. I FEEL like I can breathe again. Breathe hard, at the moment, since I find myself on the squash court. I'm surrounded by three white walls in front and a clear plexiglass back wall. My opponent wears all white—white tee shirt, shorts and sneakers. I'm in an out-of-place but adorable looking red pair of shorts and pale lemon top.

How can I think about my cute wardrobe and smash the hell out of the ball at the same time? My opponent might look more the part, but I appear to be beating the shit out of her. The small, hard ball comes careening off the side wall and SMASH. Take that! Wow, I'm really good at this. Really, really good! This is my second obliteration today.

I have to say, I love this college life. Everything seems in control, and all I have to think about is getting my next assignment in on time. Beats the hell out of struggling with work, cars breaking down, ex-husbands who date. When I was in college for real—the first time—I worried about all the little stuff: the assignments, the tests, my grades. Now? Hell, now I know that was one big waste of worry. I should have saved all that energy for much later in life, when I really need it.

One more SMASH and I complete the creaming. I shake the girl's hand and wait for my next victim. I guess this little girl doesn't have all the frustrations I do to work out on the court. Too bad for her. Well, good for her. I'd be better off, too. Ah, well.

I hear the door open and close and look over to see my new opponent. Crap! It's not another little girl. It's not a girl. It's the squash teacher, a man. The kind of teacher who turns the heads of the entire female population—profs and students alike. Full and curly dark blond hair, the handsome boyish looks of the athletic elite, a smile that puts Joe's heyday smile to shame and a trim V body that even draws attention from the magnificent face. *Crap* on so many levels!

He saunters up towards me, turning his racquet in his hands like you see professional tennis players do as they wait for a serve, though I'm drawn more to his strikingly clear blue eyes than to his hands. I notice this despite his protective glasses, clear on the bottom but red and yellow along the top, looking very much like a more fashionable version of what you may find in chemistry class. Hey, the red and yellow—I should have those. They match my outfit.

Ugh. Focus, Suzanne. Shoshanna.

When he's about a foot away, he leans up towards my ear and quietly comments, "Doing pretty well today, aren't you?" As he pulls back, he winks, smirks and then walks to the other side of the court.

Did he really just say that? Did he really wink at me? Well, baby, it's on. Remember, I haven't missed a single shot today.

"Shoshanna, right? Well, Shosh, I'm letting you

serve."

An accent? He's an Aussie? Okay, not the time for this. I'm serving.

I set up my stance and serve, intending on giving him one of my meanest ever. It barely clears the service line, but it's still good. He doesn't wait for it to land in his quarter court before he slams it back, hitting one sidewall, the front and the other sidewall in rapid succession, before I am able to get my racket ready. His point. I hear giggles from the stands on the other side of the plexiglass. I turn around and the giggling stops. Really? You're Vassar Girls!

I turn back around. He's readying himself to serve. Wow, he's certainly one gorgeous squash coach. Focus! Here it comes. A fast serve, but I can get it. Move into position, ready your racket... how did that get past me?

Okay, shake it off. Just get ready for the next one. That's right, I'm set. Okay, so he's taking it easy on me, lobbing this serve gently. I can get this one for sure, no problem.

Shit, how did I miss that?

He's looking at me, smirking. He knows. He saw me playing those other girls, not letting a shot get past me. He knows I can play. But as soon as he walks on the court—gorgeous, god-like, young, Australian accent, smiling, smirking—as soon as he steps onto the court, I can't hit the easiest of plays. Pathetic. I turn as red as my shorts. Pathetic and humiliating!

*   *   *

I run quickly back to my dorm to change out of my so-called squash outfit. With my book bag and guitar, I head towards Sanders for my English class. Right after English I'll have my music lesson, and Skinner is near there, so it wouldn't make sense to return to the dorm for my guitar before my lesson. The gray sky threatens rain, but for now my guitar and I stay dry.

As I enter Sanders, my body slows down enough to allow my brain to take over. I realize I'm jittery. Why's that? Maybe because I just made a fool of myself and hope to hell I don't do it again? This professor's a woman, right? Better be. I've had enough of these men. Life is not about sex and men and attraction and... haven't I been through all this before? Isn't the necklace supposed to be guiding me through the path of enlightenment, not disarming me with schoolboy charm so I can't even hit a fucking ball?! Dammit. No more sexual sidetracking for me. I'm here to learn. Learn about life. Learn what I've been doing wrong all my life.

I find the classroom easily enough. With all my rushing across campus fueled by mortification, I seem to be a little early, with only about a quarter of the dozen or so chairs set in a circle already filled. The professor— relief, she's a woman—occupies the desk in the front of the room.

I sit and take advantage of the extra time to settle myself down with a few slow, quiet breaths. After taking out a spiral notebook and a pen, I take a moment to look around, take a gander at my fellow classmates. I notice a couple of them have dressed themselves all in black. Thought that look might have gone out when I left college, but I guess it never does. They all look like an intelligent bunch, though. Hmm. I haven't really thought about this, but this is one hard school to get into. That means no slouches here. How will I stack up? I'm out of my element in the courses I'm taking, for sure. Who picked them for me, anyway? I feel the panic start to set in again. Deep breaths.

A few more students enter and take seats. No one talks, but lots of fingers text busily. I'm out of place already, behind the times with my still digits. Look at them all, so intense, even in their innocent communications.

The teacher stands and clears her throat. Texts get completed in a hurry and cell phones deposited in pockets and bags. The class begins...

* * *

Really, why the hell did the necklace bring me here? To enjoy back-to-back humiliations? First getting squashed by the squash teacher, and now demeaned by Nineteenth-Century British Novels?

I leave Sanders accompanied only by my guitar as the others in the class leave in twos and threes, still seemingly discussing... what? I just sat in class for an hour and a half and have no idea what any of them said! Okay, so I understood the teacher, but these kids? And that's weird, right? That I understood the teacher but not the students who kept happily answering the teacher's questions, but I had no clue what their answers meant? So freaking pathetic! What the hell am I doing here? Is my purpose maybe to show off my stupidity to make the other students, the real students, feel good about themselves? Or maybe there's some value I'm missing in being ridiculed and feeling like an idiot?

For the umpteenth time today, I try to calm myself with deep breaths. Whoever said this works is the real idiot.

Okay, Suzanne, get a grip. I'm probably reacting like this because I'm nervous. And I have a right to be. If I thought the British Novel was out of my league, then my next class—not a class, really, but the guitar lesson—will be twenty thousand leagues away. Jules Verne—no, he's French, not British, right? Scatterbrain! Stop it.

The threatening clouds that had earlier dotted the

sky have now obliterated the remaining light as I approach Skinner Hall of Music. The building looms, a dark edifice against the early evening gray. I hurry inside, but it's more to beat the rain than to get to the dreaded lesson.

I can tell by the room number that the practice room the lesson will be held in is on the second floor, so I find a staircase and slowly climb the wide stone steps. I follow the flow of room numbers, my steps echoing down the cavernous hall. I can hear various bits of music as I walk, including a couple of pianos, one classical, the other jazz; a singer's operatic scale; a stringed instrument of some kind. Almost at the end of the hall I see a door slightly cracked. This is it, the practice room written on my class schedule.

I can't concentrate on the squash court, I can't understand what my fellow students are saying in English class—how am I supposed to learn an instrument from scratch at fifty years old? The body may be young, but inside, this old dog seems a little resistant to learning any new tricks.

I step closer to the partially opened door. Are those gorgeous sounds coming from this room? It's a guitar I'm pretty sure, but not all chords, strumming and rock and roll. It's classical, I think, and intense, with some passages so fast and layered I think there may be more than one guitar player. The tempo changes constantly, the theme romantic. Now I understand when people describe a "singing" instrument. I creep up to the room, enthralled, and gently push the door open wider. Just one guitar player, but the sounds—sweet, sad—fill the room. His back faces me, and he's hunched over his instrument, so intent, as though nothing but the two of them—the guitar and its master—exist in this world.

Thankfully, he does not hear me enter. The theme of

the piece repeats one more time, slowly, then he plucks a chord and, with a flourish, plays the last notes. I don't breathe, and neither does he as the sound hangs in the air for several seconds. Suddenly, footsteps from out in the hall cause him to look up at the door towards me.

Oh, Sweet Petunias, you've got to be kidding me! The awkward professor from the dining hall? *He's* my teacher? No, maybe I've got it wrong. Maybe he's just playing in here. Maybe the instructor hasn't arrived yet.

This man, who just a moment ago played with incredible confidence and emotion, gets up and has a hard time even uttering a word. "Um, you're, um, you're Miss Kaplan?"

I sneak a look at my schedule. That's right, I don't even know my last name. Well, crap, I guess he really *is* my teacher. "Um, yes."

"Oh. Okay. Well, imagine that. It's you. Yes. Okay. Well, come in. I see you brought your, um, your guitar. That's um, that's good."

And this man will be teaching me? He can play, that's for damn sure, but he can't even talk. And besides that, he's hot. Well, when he's not talking. That wouldn't make him a bad teacher, of course, but I don't want that. I don't need that, hotness in a teacher. I'm here to learn, dammit! What the hell is this idiot necklace doing?

"Okay, well, I guess you can take out your guitar— oh, let's close this door—and, okay, well, let's see..."

He looks lost, absolutely lost. I understand why *I* would be—I've never even picked up a guitar before— other than today, to get it here, to this building—but I've never played it. Why's he acting like he doesn't know what the hell *he's* doing? Amazing—how could this be the same man who just moments ago played his instrument magnificently, with full, enchanting control?

"I'm sorry," he says.

What's he apologizing for? His apparent bumbling inability to teach?

He answers my unasked question. "I'm new at this, this teaching thing. Not playing the guitar," he quickly adds. "That I've been doing for a while, kind of..."

What? He's not making any sense. "So, you're new here?"

He nods.

"And you haven't taught the guitar before?"

"You're, um," his weak voice gets even lower, "you're my first."

His first? Come on! But... hold on, maybe this is not such a bad thing. If he's never taught anyone before, maybe I won't look like such a fool. "Oh. Okay. Well, I'm new at this, too."

He seems to brighten a little. "You've never played? The guitar?"

"No. Never. My h—" Careful, Suzanne, you're a bit too young to have had a husband. "My boyfriend used to play, a long time ago, but that's as close as I got." Good save. Except now he thinks I have a boyfriend. Well, really, what's so bad about that? You're going to be working intimately with this guy, with men off limits here. Let the necklace do its work. Quest of enlightenment! No men allowed!

Mr. Music Man has been talking during my internal discussion. I let my brain catch up to my ears, and then I follow his directions and place my guitar on a small table and open up the case.

"Do you mind if I ask your name?" I ask. And before I look stupid, I add, "It wasn't listed on my schedule."

"My name?" he repeats.

Really, I didn't think that was such a hard question.

"Um, David."

"I should call you 'David?'"

"Yes, that's fine. Yes. Okay, well, we'll start with the basics, you know, like how to hold the guitar."

I have to say, the next fifty minutes go by exceedingly quickly. Turns out David—feels funny to call a professor that—is a surprisingly good teacher. When he's teaching, he's confident, concise and helpful, and I don't feel like an idiot when we're done. I actually feel like I've learned something. Quite a lot, in truth, about the strings, how to hold the guitar, how to pluck. I've even played some notes that make sense. All this has helped cheer my foul mood substantially. I'm not a total failure as a student.

David seems more at ease, also, at least while he teaches, but as soon as I start to pack up, the pre-class demeanor returns. "So, um, I guess, um, I suppose you're off to dinner with your, um, your boyfriend."

It's almost a question, not quite, but he's definitely fishing. Before I have the good sense to filter myself, I start to answer, "No, I..."

"Oh, he doesn't go here, to college?" David nervously interrupts, looking anywhere but at me, it seems.

And I miss my second opportunity to edit myself. "He's my ex, actually. And, anyway, he's nowhere near here right now." Open mouth, insert bomb. Why the hell do I not keep this information to myself?

"Oh. Sorry to, um, sorry to hear that." And he does look sorry. Or maybe just awkward again? "Would you, then, would you, it's dinner time now, um, so, would you like to eat together? At the dining hall?"

Crap. I stupidly left myself open to this. Now I have to fix it. "I, you know, I," now it's my turn to struggle getting a sentence out. I mean, really, he's my *professor*. Why the hell is he asking me, anyway?

He turns red—my squash court red. "Oh, my god, I

can't believe I asked that. I'm completely... I'm sorry. I didn't... I shouldn't... please, just forget I've said anything."

Okay, so now I feel badly for him, but I can't waiver. But look at him, all embarrassed. Yeah, he's even hotter than Squash Coach. He must be able to get anybody, anyone he wants. What's his deal?

He turns towards the window, away from me, and says, "I just, I didn't want to eat alone again," so softly, I'm not sure I'm supposed to hear it. Unless he's playing me. No. No one can play that color red.

"Okay," I say, the acquiescence slipping out. He's just so sweet, so sad. It's only dinner.

"You're sure?" he asks, his mood brightening immediately and then darkens again, just as quickly. "No, I... it's probably not right."

"It's fine, it's good. It's only dinner. I'd be eating alone, anyway, too."

Visible relief washes over his face.

Well, well, well, I *am* as stupid as I think.

*   *   *

We're back in that same room, in the dining center, the room we ate in last time, except a big difference this time, since we're sitting across from each other, with each other. Kind of.

He's slightly more relaxed. Only *slightly*. I am not relaxed. Why am I here? Well, that's the general question I have every day—why am I here at Vassar, at the gym, in Rafael's bed... oh, I haven't thought of him for a while. Anyway, that's not what I meant. Why did I say "yes" to dinner?

But it's okay, actually, besides the sideways glances I've received. Not many, though, since this room has little traffic. And maybe I'm imagining them. Does anyone really care if a student has dinner with a professor? Okay, I'm sure they do, but, really, I'm no student, and, judging by the way he acts and his complete teaching inexperience, he doesn't seem much of a professor. Well, he *is* a professor, but still.

He eats a little more slowly than the first time. I guess he's not in such a rush, since he has some company. He seems satisfied with just that, not talking too much, not demanding too much conversation from me. It's kind of nice for me to have company, too, I have to admit. I've been spending a lot of time by myself recently it seems.

I've finished my plate of grilled chicken breast and mixed vegetables and have started on a salad—how European of me, eating salad after my main course. I'm enjoying the fresh greens, a little bit of sunflower seeds for some crunch. David's on his seconds of meatloaf and corn. I wonder if my Shoshanna metabolism would tolerate that meal.

David's slowing down and seems to have some questions of his own. "So, what is your major?"

That's a good question, since I don't know, but I'm only a sophomore, and not all sophomores know yet, so I'm in the clear. I shrug. "We'll see," I say, and then add, "Don't think it will be guitar."

He smiles. It's a nice smile, an honest smile. "You know, you're going to have to practice a lot."

I can't tell if he's insulting me. "Was I that bad? I guess I was that bad. It's not because I'm just a beginner?" Actually, I thought I'd done pretty well for my first time.

He blushes slightly, getting all awkward again. "No, that's not... no. You did okay. You did fine." He takes a breath. "What I meant was that it's the rules. You have to show a lot of progress in order to keep getting the lessons. Because you're getting the lessons through a scholarship and all."

Oh, I am? Okay, that makes sense.

"You did well so far. Very well. I guess you play some other instrument?"

Does he mean it, or is he trying to compliment me? No, he's too flustered to be complimenting. "No other instruments, no." But I add, "I sing a little." A very little. At home, in the shower. Corny but true.

"That explains it, then. Some musicality in your background. I'd like to hear you sing sometime." Then he turns colors again—does he ever *not* blush? "You're not thinking this is, you know, rock and roll guitar, with singing and all, right? Because, you know, it's classical guitar lessons."

Man, does this guy need a chill pill. And I thought *I* was high strung...

He's getting so concerned over nothing, I can't help myself and start to laugh. To my surprise, he joins me. I have to say, the nice smile has a laugh to match.

"I'm sorry," he says, still chuckling. "I tend to do that. Get a little too worked up over nothing."

"You think?"

"It's just," he leans over the table so he can lower his voice. "This place kind of gets me a bit nervous."

I lean over from my side of the table as well. "Me, too," I whisper.

He chuckles again, grateful, and leans back, instantly more relaxed. He takes a bite of his dessert, some type of cream cake. "The food's good, though."

I nod, pretty happy with it myself.

"I'm not the best of cooks," he explains, taking another spoonful. "My... ex used to do the cooking. Wish I'd paid more attention."

His "ex," huh? Totally inappropriate for me to dig further, so I leave it alone, but I'm curious. An ex-wife or an ex-girlfriend? Maybe ex-boyfriend?

We finish dinner in pleasant conversation. It's nice to have someone to talk to here. It feels normal, comforting.

Too bad it's not another place and time—literally. I think we could be friends.

Chapter 23

VEILED

HER LATEST TIME AT VASSAR hadn't started too well, but it had ended agreeably enough, and Suzanne would be in a decent mood now because of it, were it not for a couple of things. For one, she had another backbreaking session with Rami last night. She's starting to think he's *trying* to make her hate him. Either that or he's a sadist in trainer's clothing. In any event, she's now in resentful pain.

And then, to top it off, just a little while ago, when Suzanne called Lori, Lori brushed her off completely. Suzanne had just started to talk about her odd professor-student dinner when Lori got off the phone, giving some flimsy excuse about needing to check on something in the kitchen. It was such a fabricated exit from the phone call that it made Suzanne wonder if she had done something to make Lori angry, but absolutely nothing came to mind. In the end, she figured something else must be up in Lori's life. She would have to follow up with her later.

For now, well for now Suzanne has no one else she can talk to about David, so in her desperation to talk it through, she decides to talk to herself—well, herself as herself and herself as Lori, at the same time. Maybe it's a little crazy, but, after all, no one else will know, and besides, she's already a time-traveling or quantum leaping or alternate reality poser anyway, so what's one more bit of craziness?

"That's gross. You're a student, he's a professor," says Suzanne playing Lori.

"But I'm not really a student," Suzanne argues back. "Yes, he's a professor, but he doesn't really seem like one."

"Those are the ones you have to watch out for. He's playing you," warns the pseudo-Lori.

"He's not playing me. No one's that good an actor. You can't fake a blush."

"What do you mean? Put a little makeup on..." Hmm. Is she going too far? Would Lori really say something like this?

Regardless, Suzanne answers herself. "It's not a movie. He doesn't stop the scene, call 'makeup' and then start the action again." It feels good to be obnoxious.

"Just watch out with him, that's all I'm saying." Yes, *that* is certainly something Lori would say.

"He's a friend. I need a friend." This Suzanne says out loud to the empty air, the irony not lost on her.

* * *

Her one-sided conversation over, Suzanne sets herself on a mission. Despite her Rami-induced sore muscles, she decides to clean the house. She knows it's not born out of anything positive, rather it's a result of her feeling out of control, but she might as well run with it. Who cares if she's divorced, living alone, her job a mess? Who cares if she's bouncing back and forth between worlds? Maybe she can't keep her eye on a ball when there's a squash coach on the court, and maybe she can't answer questions posed by kids younger than her daughters in English class, and, okay, maybe this is not how she had envisioned her life when she turned fifty, but, dammit, she might as well have a clean and organized home. Her home. Where she lives. Most of the time. A bit of the time lately.

Some people use shopping as therapy. For a while, Suzanne thought she might use sex as therapy, but for now she'll settle on cleaning.

She starts with the linen closet. Joe had always put away the towels haphazardly, and his method of folding sheets seemed more like rolling them in a ball than actual folding. More times than she can count, Suzanne had asked him not to fold and put away the sheets, but he liked to say he was helping her. In the end, she let him take care of putting away the sheets and towels, because she couldn't bear to look inside the closet any more. On one occasion when she did just that, when she recklessly opened the door to Joe's linen closet, white puffs erupted outward, like an expanding Stay Puft Marshmallow Man. She stayed away from then on.

But now it's no longer Joe's closet, and Suzanne gets down to business. For close to three painstaking hours, she meticulously folds sheets, towels and washcloths until the linen closet is the neatest it has ever been, with its organized, symmetrical stacks. You can even see a bit of the shelves. She steps back and admires her job, then quickly moves on, a woman on a mission.

She goes to her bedroom and opens the door to the walk-in closet she used to share with Joe. It may now be all hers, but it's still as much a mess as when Joe's crap ate up more than half of it. To Suzanne's surprise, she finds some of Joe's possessions—a pair of old sneakers ripped along the side, a small box of ties wide enough to belong to a clown and an even smaller box with cuff links. Judging by the looks of them, he left them on purpose, using her closet as a garbage dump. Anyway, she never saw Joe wear cuff links in his life, except maybe on their wedding day.

The next find proves much more of a stunner. It's a guitar—Joe's old guitar. How bizarre. He stopped playing not long after they met, and he never did play in front of her. He seemed too embarrassed. He must not have been all that good.

She pulls it out of the closet and lays the case on the bed, then opens it up. She realizes it looks similar to her guitar, the guitar at Vassar, but what does *she* know? They all look the same, pretty much.

She leaves it open on the bed and goes back to the closet. No more of Joe's stuff, so she can concentrate on her own. Thankfully, this goes much faster than straightening the linen closet, but she finds herself taking repeated little breaks to step out of the closet and go over to the bed to steal glimpses at the guitar. Finally, she takes it out of its case and sits down with it, trying out the few things she's learned. She certainly can't do much yet, and even *she* can tell the poor neglected thing is horribly out of tune, but she likes the way it feels. She's interrupted after a few minutes, though, by the guilt starting to creep in. Joe might have left the guitar in her closet, but for sure he did so unintentionally, and she should give it back.

She puts the guitar back in the case and returns to the closet to finish her self-inflicted chore. When she emerges once again, leaving behind an organized space she can proudly call her own, she gazes one more time at the instrument sprawled out like a full-figured woman on her bed. Before she allows herself to think about it, she finds her phone and dials Joe.

"Hey," she says. "It's me." Like he doesn't know.

"Hi," he answers. She can tell he's trying for nonchalance, but she knows he's surprised to hear from her.

She dives right in, not bothering with those pesky pleasantries. "So, I was cleaning out the closet in our— the bedroom—and I found your old guitar."

She hesitates, expecting some type of a response, maybe a chuckle or a mild curse, but nothing, not a word. After a moment, Suzanne asks, "So, do you want it?"

"Um..."

He's taking too long answering, and Suzanne loses patience. She gets on with it, asking what she really called to ask. "Because I'm thinking of taking up the guitar. So if you don't want it, I'll buy it off of you." It sounds weird as soon as she says it, but it's out there now.

"Wow," he answers, but she's not really sure what he's saying "wow" in response to. After another long moment, he elaborates. "That's very odd, because I just decided to get back to it. The guitar, I mean."

Okay, so not at all the response Suzanne expected. Not a happy one, either, since she figures now he'll want to keep his guitar, and Suzanne will be SOL. "Oh, that's nice," she says weakly. Can he tell she doesn't mean it?

Joe keeps the surprises coming. "Yeah, it's been a long time. But, anyway, I just bought a new one, a new guitar, so, you know, keep that one, if you'd like. That sounds great, you taking it up. I'm... happy for you."

He bought a new guitar? While Suzanne knows she should be happy, since he offered his old one to her, the only thing she can think about is that he damn well better not claim he doesn't have money for the girls' tuition if he's going and buying himself a guitar.

She tries not to let her irritation show. "Yeah, should

be fun. And that sounds great for you, too." Was that natural enough? Surely he could hear right through her. Then again, Joe never had developed an ability to understand her subtext. Just to be sure, she gets off the phone quickly.

Once off, she marches over to the closet, but as soon as she looks in, she remembers she had already completed the job. She marches back to the guitar, opens the top of the case and runs her fingers over the strings. The discordant sound makes her realize she needs to ask Music Professor David to teach her how to tune a guitar. She closes the case again.

*   *   *

I'm getting the hang of this. At least, it feels more natural to be in the practice room, holding the guitar. I don't feel *too* much like a faker. Well, not too much like a faker at playing the guitar. I still feel very much the fraud pretending I'm a college student.

I like it here in this space, secluded. I like listening to the others holed up in their own small rooms, hearing bits of violins and pianos and trumpets as I walk through the halls. I like not worrying about seeing Hannah or Abigail.

Since the dinner, it's better to be here by myself than with David. Surprisingly, considering how well the meal went, the lessons since then have been so formal and stiff. But he's still a good teacher, so I guess I shouldn't complain.

Okay, I'll complain. I don't like the beyond uncomfortable feelings of being near him now. I guess professors and students shouldn't share a meal—just too damned weird. And, as long as I'm complaining, I don't like that I still look like an idiot in front of my English class. Let's not stop there. I hate feeling isolated—not making friends at college because I'm worried I'll give myself away if I get too close to anyone. And it's not at all fun trying to stay away from the two people on campus I'd most like to talk to, because how could I ever hide who I am from my daughters?

I put the guitar back in the case and get ready to leave.

What's wrong with me? I'm back in college! Okay, maybe I still look like an idiot in English class, maybe it's freaking weird to have dinner with a professor and then have him treat me like I'm a complete stranger the next time I have a lesson with him, but so what! I should be making friends, enjoying learning just for learning, taking advantage of this amazing school. What I should definitely not do is cloister myself in this beautiful but dungeon-esque building and mope about my existence. Where will that get me?

Okay, now off into the world of Vassar, to experience, to learn, to meet people and to have fun! Let's do this!

*   *   *

I love the fall, the woodsy smells, the air getting cooler, the quiet of the evening. I love the simple act of walking on this magnificent campus, enjoying the smells, the evening and the beautiful and beautifully tranquil setting. But, I have to say, walking in the dark, I don't love. I hate that it's getting dark so early now. It's a little creepy, my walk tonight from Skinner back over to Noyes. Wish my dorm didn't sit way at the other end of campus.

I'll just keep chatting to myself, and then maybe I won't realize I'm so alone. In the dark. Stupidly taking the road less traveled shortcut.

Wasn't I just reading something about the campus in the *The Miscellany News*? Not a bad newspaper—they do a nice job with it. What did that article say? Oh, I still have it in my bag. Where was it? Ah, here.

The campus, with its array of regal, striking buildings and its abundant and majestic trees, shines spectacularly during the day. In the early evening hours it all but glows in the warmth of the waning sun. But after nightfall, the very same glorious buildings and towering trees assume an alternate reality, what could almost be seen as a...

Right. Well, probably shouldn't read this just now. But, at least I'm almost out from behind the Chapel, and then I'll be in sight of both the Library and Main Building. Maybe I'll walk a little faster. Okay, I think my breathing can calm down now. I see people, I see lights on in the buildings, and it's really not all that late.

Someone's going into the Art Gallery. That's a good side trip for me on my trek back to the dorm. A two-birds, one-stone side trip, so I can get rid of the willies from this lonely walk, and, at the same time, I can start taking advantage of some of the best things about being on campus. I haven't been at the Gallery since my first tour with Hannah, way back, but I remember it as an extraordinary place. And I'm right here.

I walk in, and the light in the glass entranceway surrounds me. The student sitting behind the counter looks up from his book and welcomes me with a smile.

"I'm surprised the Gallery's open this late," I say, more to chat than anything else.

Despite the smile, the young man looks as though he'd rather lean his head right back down towards his book, but he answers cordially, "We're open late one night a week." He notices the guitar. "You can put that in the room by the lockers, right before you get into the exhibit area."

With a "thanks," I head down the glass corridor and into the main part of the building. It's relatively quiet inside, but a few people my age—I mean my real, Suzanne, age—and a few more, well, my Shoshanna age, ramble around. The first entrance gallery holds a couple of Calder's mobiles. I don't think of myself as someone who loves modern art, but I have to say, I like the mobiles. There's a balance, a simplicity. I walk to the right, moving from modern to antiquities in a few steps. Japanese drawings, Egyptian sculptures, artifacts from ancient times. It boggles the mind how people, thousands of years ago, shaped these pieces. How many lifetimes have passed between then and now, between them and me? If thousands of years can go so quickly, and if pieces like this can still hold up after all this time, what does that say about our own brief time here? And yet, how do I have the right to complain about time moving quickly? Me who received a second chance at youth? Almost like getting two lifetimes at once.

I move on to stand in front of a section of a sarcophagus, a child's coffin, extraordinary in its relief work, still so intact, and exceedingly sad in its purpose for being. I wonder if the students react to this object in the same way as the more mature visitors. Can you truly understand the sadness of losing a child if you have not begun a family yourself?

I think I'll leave this area. I'm all for art invoking emotions, but right now, my quest is to recall and regain some of my youthful happiness, isn't it?

The next room contains treasures of a totally different kind, with its walls of paintings by such artists as Picasso and O'Keefe. So many remarkable pieces by so many influential artists.

I continue on and walk through a couple more rooms. Oh, I remember this one. It's a bust of a woman. I remember how fascinating this sculpture was both to me and to Hannah. Hmm. It's not so old, well nothing like the pieces in the first room. From sometime in the latter part of the 1800's, it says. The artist—that's some name—Albert-Ernst Carrier-Belleuse—aptly called it *Veiled Woman*. She's just that, a woman whose face, whose entire head, is shrouded in a veil that flows over her face and then ties on her shoulder. Except it's completely made of terracotta—the face, the clothes and the veil. You can see her eyes "beneath" the "cloth" as they look demurely down and to the left, but you can only see half of her mouth. The veil covers the other half entirely.

I stare at this lovely young woman intensely for a moment. As I do, she becomes more and more realistic, so much so that it becomes unnerving, seeing her encased, imprisoned in this glass box. I turn to move away from her and almost charge directly into a man I hadn't realized had stepped behind me. I look up to say "sorry."

But "I'm sorry" are not the words that come out of my mouth. "What, are you following me?" I ask David, my mouth coming to that extraordinarily unlikely conclusion before my mind can control it.

"No, I'm... no, I just..." sputters David.

Well, he looks contrite enough. I guess I should believe him, that this is an innocent encounter rather than a deliberate stalking.

"It's okay. I'm sorry." Well, at least I got to the sorry. But, I have to say, a small part of me remains unconvinced.

Damn. I was having such a nice, carefree time here this evening. Why did he have to show up? Anyway, probably he'll scoot away as soon as he can. From how he's acted at the lessons, it's obvious he feels too awkward to be around me, so if I just wait it out for a moment, he should disappear.

But he doesn't disappear.

He looks like he's going to speak. "Ahem." What is that? Clearing his throat? Who does that? "So, um, are you well?"

Am I well? He looks around thirty and acts twice that age sometimes. I nod because, really, what am I going to say?

Even more awkwardly, he gestures towards the bust. "You like this?" he asks, a funny lilt to his voice. It almost sounds as though he's sneering, as if to say, "Out of everything here, *this* is what you like?"

"I do. Very much," I answer. I've nothing to be ashamed of, certainly not of this incredible sculpture.

David turns to the glass case and examines the *Veiled Woman's* face with great scrutiny. "I think it's my favorite piece in this museum," he says quietly.

Okay, so, yes, obviously I got that idea about him sneering totally wrong.

"Funny, right?" he continues. "All this art by super-famous painters and artists, and this little bust is what catches my eye, every time. This bust and also this." He points to a painting hanging on the wall a few feet from the bust. It's of a young woman in an apron, hanging a cream colored sheet outside to dry, with the shadow of a nearby tree forming a decoration on the otherwise plain linen.

Even though now *I* should be the one acting contrite, I can't help my snarky thoughts. Maybe it's because he likes young women, maybe that's why he likes these two pieces so much. At least my filter is now in place, and I keep my snarkiness to myself.

"They both look sad, don't they?" he asks, mostly to himself, and sounding a little sad himself.

All right, then. Happy I've kept my mouth shut.

"What else do you like here?" he asks.

I don't get this. Is this the same man who asked me to dinner, who enjoyed speaking to me at that dinner— at least it seemed so at the time—but then who acted so aloof, as though it had never happened, when we saw each other again? What's going on, and why hasn't he run away? Why haven't *I* run away?

I think all this and try to come up with an answer to his question at the same time. It's challenging for my confused brain, but I say, "O'Keefe. Her work's so colorful." And what's not to love about that? Besides, I don't want to talk about depressing artwork with my music professor whom I hardly know.

He smiles. "Hmm. Good choice. And you're right." He starts to walk back towards the room where the O'Keefe hangs. He does not seem to be walking away from me, though, and I get the sense he expects me to follow, which I do. "Except for that piece."

What is he talking about?

He looks at my puzzled face and gestures towards a narrow and small all-gray painting next to the vibrant, oversized, very apparently Georgia O'Keefe painting right next to it.

"I think it's called *East River*. It's so unlike anything else I've ever seen from her."

He's so obviously wrong, I don't click the filter on. "What are you talking about? That's not a Georgia O'Keefe. It looks nothing like an O'Keefe!"

"Exactly," he answers, and walks closer to the painting.

I follow and take a look at this painting I hadn't noticed before. Foot in mouth again, because, sure as hell, it's called *East River* and it's by none other than Georgia O'Keefe.

"My grandparents lived on the Lower East Side of Manhattan," I say, because I'm not man enough to admit out loud how wrong I had been.

"Mine, too," he says.

And all of a sudden, I start to relax. Maybe it's because we have this commonality, or maybe it's because we've had a bit of an argument, an itty bitty argument, but recovered quickly, or maybe it's because he's speaking to me again the way we spoke at dinner.

A short while later, we're out in the hall. When I stop to pick up my guitar, David smiles. I remember that nice smile.

"That's right," I say. "Just came from practicing."

He smiles wider. "Glad to see you're taking it seriously."

"Yes, well, I tend to take all of life too seriously, I think."

"At your age?"

"Especially at my age," I say and leave it at that.

As soon as we walk outside, into the space between the gallery's entrance and Main Gate, the atmosphere between us becomes awkward again, as though neither of us knows what the hell to do next. *I* certainly don't.

He talks first. "I was wondering—"

Oh, shit. Please, no. Please don't ask me to dinner. I don't think I can do this whole thing again, the nice dinner, the uncomfortable moments.

"—tonight... "

Crap.

"In the Chapel, tonight—"

Oh, not dinner. That's good, right?

"Have you seen, I mean heard—well, seen and heard, I guess—have you seen the Night Owls?"

That's unexpected. I shake my head. "I don't think I ever have, come to think of it."

"It's not just them, the concert. It's a bunch of a cappella groups, even from other schools. One of my, um, one of my students is in it. I thought I would, you know, go and support her." He's getting a bit red again and looking like he might pass out. Yup, here it comes. "So did you—would you—would you like to see it? The concert? I didn't really want to go alone. I mean, I could go alone, but it would be nice, and I thought it might be something you would like..."

Double shit! Why can't he ask some other professor—or student, for that matter?

He's still talking, but with a voice that quiet, it's more like talking to himself. "I'm really bad at being by myself."

How the hell does he do that? How does he know just what to say to make me feel sorry for him? Sorry and willing to do the things I know I shouldn't be doing. "Sure, I'll go. What time?"

Nice going, Idiot.

Chapter 24

GOING TO THE CHAPEL

MAYBE IT'S A GOOD THING I'm here with David. I can keep an eye on him. I mean, why did he want to come to *this* event? The Night Owls is an all-female group, isn't it? All *young* girls. On the other hand, he *is* a music teacher. And he did say he wants to support his student. It all *seems* logical, doesn't it?

Look at him. He seems so nervous. Certainly not the look of a pedophiliac serial rapist, right?

And look at those girls, staring at us. Really, isn't it rude, even if I am a student with a teacher? They don't know anything about our relationship—our lack of relationship.

Wait a second. For all they know, I'm just sitting next to him. We're not even talking to each other, so they have no idea we're here together. They aren't looking at me and him. It's him. They're staring at *him*, aren't they? Talking behind their hands, glancing over, laughing. These girls have crushes. Oh, what a moron I am! In the dining hall, here, I keep thinking girls are looking at us disapprovingly, but they don't see *me* at all. He's one of those professors all the girls fawn over.

I take a sideways glimpse at him. He gives me a nervous but oh-so-sweet smile. A very sweet smile. A sexy, adorable, like his eyes and his tousled hair and his...

Shit, think of something else.

I look around—anywhere, everywhere but at him. Must be a big event, with the Chapel almost filling up. I wonder how many people this place holds? A lot. All filling up.

The straight back pews feel narrow but comfortable, with their thick cushioned seats.

Why is this moron looking to sit here? No, buddy, not enough room here. Damn, well, I guess there is, if David moves over closer to me like he's doing. I did not ask for that, now unavoidably touching knees. He's noticing, too, judging by his increasingly red complexion. Look away, look away.

Look at the beautiful, massive pipe organ. Not every day you get to see an organ like that. Wonder if they plan to play it tonight. When do they usually play it? I've never heard it, not that I remember.

David glances around, too. He's new here. I wonder if he ever set foot in the Chapel before.

Should I say something to him? We kind of came together, even though we're acting like strangers. Except for the fact that our knees keep touching. My inner thigh will be sore by the end of the evening, with all this effort to pull my leg away from his.

Oh, thank goodness. A group is coming onstage. From Yale, so says the program. The Spizzwinks(?). It's a large group, all male, tuxes with tails. Good, this music will keep my mind occupied and off other things.

They look so young, these Spizzwinks(?). What's with the parentheses and question mark? Is that really part of their name? Do they look younger even than the

Vassar kids? No, but I guess when you think "Yale Men" it seems like they should look older.

I sit and listen, enjoying the concert. We have good seats. David insisted on sitting pretty close up. Said he doesn't have his glasses with him, except I've never seen him with glasses.

They just finished *Billie Jean*. Quite a young comic, the soloist on that one. Doing Michael Jackson high-pitched grunts, but the MJ moves performed by this boy in his tux, that's what you would call comical incongruity.

Now they've started *Somebody to Love*. Know how to pick them, these kids.

Why did that seat hog have to squeeze into the seat next to David? My leg's so tired.

I enjoy the rest of their set. It does take my mind off of... things... temporarily. And, happily, there's literally no break between the Yale group and Vassar's own Night Owls.

The announcer just said the Vassar Night Owls is the oldest continuous all-female a cappella group in the US. Didn't know that. Not as large a bunch as the Yale group. They look adorable, though, each one in a different little black dress. I like the one with the partial pink hair. A few of them wear hats. Look at that one, so huge and floppy I can hardly see her face. Another peek over at David and I can see she's really caught his eye as well. Wow. I mean *really*. Don't think he's spending a single second looking at anyone else. Oh, he's caught me looking. All right, now he's looking at them all. Maybe it was the hat, a fairly ridiculous thing. Twice the size of her little face. Can't see her all that well still, but she kind of looks a little like Abby. Oh, crap! Hadn't thought of that. I could easily run into Abby here. She likes these types of groups. A real shower singer, that girl.

Well, if I haven't seen her yet, doubtful she's sitting anywhere near, anyway, so I should be okay. Not to mention, of course, the little fact that SHE WOULD NOT RECOGNIZE ME. I have to keep reminding myself of that.

Okay, getting right to it, they start with *Rolling in the Deep*. I know I'm old and supposed to be out of the popular music scene, but, I have to say, I really like Adele. And this girl here, she's doing a beautiful job with this song. David's smiling. I guess he likes this, too. Of course, he's much younger than I am, more in tune with this music.

That's right. Keep reminding yourself of that. He thinks he's older, anyone seated around here would, too, but older I am. A lifetime older. I-could-be-his-mother older. Okay, well, that thought's pretty damn disgusting.

How about just listening to the music?

Another good one—*Dream a Little Dream of Me*.

You know? Why am I freaked out, being here with David? Right here, right now, I *am* younger than he is, but well over eighteen. And he's my pseudo-kind-of date, a popular and wildly attractive man about campus. Much better than eyeing some young freshman boy. Relax, will you? Sit back and enjoy.

I literally do just that. I sit back in my seat and let my tensed up leg relax. I can feel his jeans, the side of his thigh brushing against me. I leave it where it falls. Enjoy the evening! Enjoy the moment!

The girl with the ridiculously large hat takes center stage. This is a good one, too—*Tell Him*. She has a lovely voice, and it really resonates through the building. Kind of sounds like Abby's voice. Not that she likes to sing in public, but sometimes I hear her through her door. Don't know why she never wants to join any singing groups. Well, I do know why she wouldn't join *this* one. Abby would never be caught dead wearing a little black dress. Maybe they do all get to wear whatever little black dress they want, but, nonetheless, a dress they wear.

Oh, good, she's taking off that distracting hat. David smiles more than before.

The hat's off, and she turns.

No.

I...

Can't...

Abby? It's Abby? *My* Abby? In The Night Owls? Since when? How beautifully she sang! Listen to that applause. Especially that girl in the front row. Wait, that's Hannah, whooping it up for her sister. But it's not just her. The whole audience loved her singing. I loved her. David loved her, clapping so loudly, and he's a music professor. Holy cow! I can't believe it! She was great. How did I not know? How could she not tell me? I feel my eyes start to well but push back the tears as quickly as I can.

David leans over to me. "She was good, huh?"

I want to scream a big old "Yes" at him. I want to say, "That was my daughter!" But I can't. He definitely can see my odd expression, though, and he looks at me with an odd expression of his own, probably trying to figure out why I'm so damn emotional over an unknown fellow student.

They continue with the concert, but I hear nothing after Abby's *Tell Him*.

*   *   *

We're at the snack bar in the College Center, aptly named The Retreat, since that's exactly what I'd like to do right now. I've already retreated from Hannah, but that proved easy, since she seemed to hang around after the concert to congratulate her sister. Her sister, my daughter, who sang in a concert, who sang with a group she's obviously been rehearsing with, without ever telling her mother.

And all this I can't even discuss with my escort.

I almost said no to coming to The Retreat with David, but at the last second I figured I might as well. Better than going back to my dorm room to sulk by myself.

We prowl the snack bar, both trying to figure out what treat to buy. I know what I *should* get: a salad or a healthy vegetable soup. I know what I *want* to get, but I feel strange in front of David. Ben & Jerry's keeps calling to me, though, and David, catching me looking in their direction, reaches his hand into the freezer and pulls out two cups of Cherry Garcia.

"Good for you?" he asks.

"I can't; I shouldn't," I say, an image of Rami dancing in my head.

"We can, and we should."

We pay—well, uncomfortable as it is, he pays for me—grab some napkins and spoons and go looking for a table, but they've filled up quickly after the concert, so we make our way upstairs and find a little seating nook to park ourselves and our ice creams.

It seems quiet here, the crowd downstairs a gentle background hum.

David opens his ice cream and digs right in. I follow suit. Yum, one of my favorites. I let the ice cream melt and slide down my throat, and then my tongue plays with the remaining piece of cherry and some chocolate bits. With the pieces sucked clean of the creaminess, I crunch the chocolate and the fruit together and savor the flavor mix in my mouth.

David seems to relish his ice cream as well. After a few bites, he says, "See? Eating ice cream. That's what's nice about being young, right? No middle age middle tube to worry about. Not yet, anyway."

What a weird thing to say. I guess I can't help showing my thoughts on my face, because the next thing he says is, "Hey, no comments. I *am* young, just not as young as you."

Ha.

Both of us sit back and attend to our dessert. I've got to say, he looks so damn cute as he eats, the way he almost smiles with every mouthful, relishing each bite.

After a moment, I can't take it. I just have to ask, "How old *are* you?" I keep wondering, and he certainly left the door open.

"I don't know."

Huh?

The spoon stops, almost at his mouth. "I meant I don't know that we should be talking about my age."

I nod. He's right. We shouldn't even be sitting here together, eating our innocent ice cream.

And yet here we are.

I dig out one of the bigger pieces of cherry and bring it up to my lips, holding it there on the spoon as I lick off its ice cream coating.

He's kind of staring at me, I think. I pop the cherry into my mouth. He lets out a small sound—what was that, a sigh?—but then quickly returns his attention to his own spoon, his tongue licking it clean.

Am I staring back at him? I've got to stop.

"So, the *Veiled Woman.*"

Is he talking about me? What did I do? Wait, that's the name of the statue at the gallery. "I love that piece." I continue with fervor, because, one, I really do love it and, two, it's a safe topic of discussion. "It's amazing, right? It's all terracotta, all one piece, but it looks exactly like she's draped with the thin material. And so transparent you can see all of her."

"Well," he responds with a wistful chuckle, "women are never *that* transparent, are they?"

Wow. Okay, well, I *thought* it was a safe topic. I mean, what am I supposed to do with a comment like that? I'm a fifty year old woman, and I can't think what to respond. And what should my twenty year old alter ego Shoshanna say? Nothing probably works best.

Back to the ice cream.

So completely different, this man. So completely different from other men I know, from other professors. But he's not a professor right now, quietly sitting next to me, unconsciously licking some melted cream from his full bottom lip. Do I like the difference? Well, I think I do. I sure could use getting away from the usual right now.

Unwanted, an image of Joe enters my thoughts. I try, but I can't keep the logical thought sequence from forming. Does he know about Abigail? Did he know before I did that Abby sings with The Night Owls?

I look back at David and try to push Joe out of my mind.

"No one is transparent," I say and take my final bite of Ben & Jerry.

Chapter 25

HOT AND COLD

I GET THE FEELING LATELY I'm spending more time in my alternate universe—my alternate *universes*—than in real life.

Is that a bad thing?

Rami saunters over to me, slowly slipping on his black weightlifting gloves, all the while looking at me with a crooked smile. The gloves match his black tee shirt, which clings to his thick chest but tapers at the waist, a thin material almost showing off the six-pack that lies beneath.

Yeah, wouldn't say it's a bad thing. Not a bad thing at all.

He does look young, though, even in comparison to David.

I've got to stop this, all these thoughts. I touch the pomegranate necklace and wonder for the umpteenth time—this array of men, this can't be what the necklace is trying to show me, is it?

Or is it?

Hell, all I know for sure is that I'd rather be here than at work fielding a hundred useless emails a day and answering inane questions for the executives of a company who could care less about me, as long as I finish the month end reports on time. Well, maybe I *have* learned something after all.

"Less thinking, more doing," says Rami, his gloves now on, flashing his pearly whites.

I put my gloves on as well. "Hey, I'm still angry with you," I let him know.

"'Still,' Shoshanna? Since when are you angry?"

I don't answer the *when*, but I do let him know the *why*. "You've been so hard on me lately. What's your problem?"

He's laughing at me. "My problem? Come." He takes my hand and leads me over to a nearby wall with floor to ceiling mirrors yet again. "There's my 'problem.'"

He has his hands on my shoulders, forcing me to look at myself. I have never liked mirrors, not for a long time, but to see my Shoshanna self, especially now—that's one reflection I could learn to deal with. A few months ago, the stranger in the mirror seemed sleek, slim and pretty. Now, the not-so-much-a stranger peers back, complete with her athletic build, her sinewy arms and her shapely and powerful legs.

In the mirror, I see Rami moving his head closer to mine. "Tantalizing," he whispers, then pulls his head back. "I learned that word from a movie yesterday and thought of you. Look? See what I've done with you? If I didn't push you so hard..."

He has done wonders. But, on the other hand... "You didn't do this alone, you know." He can't take all the credit. I did the work; I did the sweating.

He looks at me a little too closely, a little too long. And then a non sequitur. "Today's your last session."

How did that happen?

"You know what that means." He's whispering again,

his breath in my ear. His hair smells of fresh citrus.

What *does* it mean? That I'll never see him again? That now I have to work out only in the real world? Well, not that, since he doesn't know this isn't really the real world. For me.

He pulls his head back and admires my reflection once more, still speaking quietly. "No more rules after tonight."

My stomach takes a nose dive. No more rules. *His* rule. The no-sex-with-clients rule.

But wasn't he teasing me the last time we spoke about this particular rule? Playing around that maybe someday he may find me too hot to resist? Is he joking now? Was he joking then? That does not look like the face of a man—boy—man joking about sex. Oh, hell!

Rami claps his hands together in his bossy way. "You warmed up? We're doing squats today, baby."

What's that wink mean? Playful? Suggestive? I'm so confused.

As I follow him, I see a man out of the corner of my eye, mid-twenties, maybe five ten, five eleven, dark blond, gawking at me. I think he's gawking. Even if he's not, that look is a little too intense in my book.

I quickly turn my attention from this stranger back to Rami and jog a few steps to catch up with him. "Where are you going?" He's not headed over to our usual area. "I thought we're doing squats."

"We are. Here." We're at a machine that looks like you can do squats on it, but the weights lie on a built-in lever—not the free standing squats we've been doing all this time.

"This?" I ask. "Not the free weights?"

He steps a little closer and talks in that same quiet voice he used in front of the mirror. "Because I don't want you to get hurt if you lose your concentration."

"What are you talking about? I haven't had a problem with losing my concentration in squats. Look at these legs." I say as proof of my focus.

"I *have* looked at those legs," he says and smiles slowly. "I know you haven't had a problem with concentration, but you will now."

What the hell? Frankly, I'm a little scared.

To make matters worse—or maybe not, because it thankfully draws my attention away from Rami's strange behavior—that dark blond stranger has followed us. Okay, I don't know for sure he *followed* us, but he's here and still looking at me intently. Who am I kidding? He's staring.

I turn my back to the man so he can't see my face. "You see that guy behind me?" I ask Rami. "Wearing the long gray shorts and the burgundy polo?"

"I see him."

"He's staring at me."

"So?"

"He's *ogling*."

"So? He likes what he sees. He better. Okay, let's go."

Okay, then.

Rami has me scoot up right close to the machine. Looks easy enough, I guess, especially since I'm used to the free weights. Kindergarten stuff in comparison, so why's he making me do this? And not only that, but he's standing right up behind me, like the first time, like he has to spot me and show me what to do.

"Now, let it down real slow," he says, squatting with me, his hands on my hips. His hands on my hips and his body tucked close to mine. Holy shit! Can't say this man has ever seemed shy touching me, spotting me, pointing out which muscles I should contract. But now?

"You're doing great, baby," he says as we pull back up. "Again." And down we go. "Feeling it yet?"

I turn my attention back to the weights. To be honest, they feel light. "Not really."

He stands and walks away for a moment, adding some weights. When he returns, he stands closer than before. "Again," he demands. "Squat nice and slow, nice... and... slow."

Now I feel it, only it's not the weights. I feel *him*. So close. So... yes, well, this explains the foretold concentration problems. *Oh, crap.*

He inches closer still and guides me through the next squat, hands on my hips. At the bottom of the squat, I feel almost as if I'm resting on his lap, but only for a moment, until his hands guide my hips slowly back to standing. He leans his head forward, but with our nearness, he doesn't need to lean far. "Do you like this?" he whispers.

Beet red, I nod my head almost imperceptibly. His hands still linger on my hips.

"I like this," he continues, and I can feel his smile against my neck.

Holy shit, how can this be so fucking sexy? I'm sweaty, in my gym clothes, at least a dozen strangers share the room with us, and yet I can only think about his strong hands cradling my hips and how much I'd like them to be touching so much more.

He pulls me down again into another agonizing squat, painful only because of his teasing proximity. On the way back up, he leans in once more. "Nothing will happen."

"What?"

"Between us," he answers. "Nothing will happen between us." As soon as we stand fully, I can feel his hands ride down to the top of my thighs, my back flat against his front. I could swear he kisses my hair gently. "Not tonight," he adds, then releases his hands, backs up and walks away.

If that's not a fucking kick in the pants.

As I gather my wits and start to follow him—I have another forty-five minutes left to my last session—out of the corner of my eye I notice the dark blond, still gawking.

Chapter 26

EVERYTHING'S GONNA BE ALL RIGHT (YEAH, RIGHT)

"SAME OLD," SAYS ABIGAIL IN response to her mother's usual "How are things?" question during the obligatory Sunday night phone call. Suzanne had insisted from Hannah's first week at college that she would speak to each of her children at least every Sunday. She prefers three or four times a week, but she keeps that overprotective thought to herself.

Usually Suzanne takes her daughter's succinct answers at face value, but not tonight. Suzanne knows damn well it's not the "same old." Singing with The Night Owls is a "different new," but, since she shouldn't know about it, instead of accusing "Liar, liar, pants on fire," she tells Abby "I love you" and quickly gets off the phone. Sunday night calls ordinarily lift Suzanne's spirits, but lying Sunday night calls seem to have quite the opposite effect.

* * *

The clock on Suzanne's computer shows the time in

the lower right corner of her screen. Only ten in the morning and yet her eyes already feel bleary from the incessant and insipid flow of emails. So many emails, she can't even get to her real work. It wouldn't seem so bad if only a single missive contained one insightful remark, one judicious question, but no. Each email proves once again that stupidity abounds.

The phone rings, an uncommon but welcome interruption. "Suzanne speaking. May I help you?" The company mandates a specific, not to mention long, phone greeting, but Suzanne never remembers it and doesn't see the reason to use it if she did. No clients call her—only fellow employees or the occasional friend or family member.

One of the few people Suzanne admires in the company speaks brightly on the other end, a saleswoman with a lot on the ball and a nice personality to boot. She and Suzanne gossip a bit then get to the point of the call. The saleswoman needs some margin information on one of the clients. Wrapping up the call, the saleswoman innocently asks, "When are you flying down to Orlando?"

"Orlando? For what?"

"Aren't you going to the annual summit?"

Not often that a short phone conversation and a simple question can so completely change your perception about a major part of your life, but this particular question slices Suzanne in two.

It takes several moments before she finds herself able to get up from her cubicle and knock on her boss's office door.

"I'm not invited to the annual summit," she says, not mincing words.

"They're doing things differently this year."

"I've been here 15 years. I've always gone."

He doesn't answer, except for a blank stare and perhaps the tiniest of shrugs.

How should she respond? Numerous possibilities simultaneously flood Suzanne's head. She could scream, punch, storm out. Quit. All excellent and completely out of the question choices, but satisfying to imagine, nonetheless.

She and her wounded pride walk out, sans storming, and return to her puny desk in her pitiful cubicle. The cubicle that once upon a time had been an office, in the time before the new president took over, in the land where she had clout, had a say, had an invitation to the annual company summit.

A loud woman two cubes away gets a phone call, and the sound of her nasal, high-pitched voice quoting chapter and verse of the company's policies effectively makes it impossible for a single helpful thought to form in Suzanne's head. She gives up thinking and once again returns to her emails, which have multiplied in the short time since she last left them.

* * *

Lori sits at her vanity, tweezers in hand, prepping for a late evening dinner out. Suzanne sits nearby, thankful that her hot and cold friend is at least warm at this moment.

"The only thing worse than having to pluck hair from your chin," Lori tells Suzanne, "is having to pluck wiry white hairs from your chin." Out comes one of the nasty white culprits on the word "chin."

Suzanne chuckles and nods. "What restaurant?"

Lori shrugs. "It's *his* work. I let him pay attention to the details." Lori has never liked these obligatory dinners, at least these many years Suzanne has known her, but she likes getting dressed up. "So, you wanted to talk? We've got half an hour until I leave. What's up?"

Suzanne has a smorgasbord of starters, but she begins with her child. She explains that Abby joined the a cappella group and asks the mother's question, "Why would she keep something like that from me?"

"Kids keep things from their parents all the time. You know that. Why's it bothering you all of a sudden?"

Lori has a point. Suzanne's always known the girls keep things from her. All children do, to some extent, so why should this bother her so much now?

Lori quickly answers her own question. "You know why it does? You need to get laid. It's been too long." Lori smiles and nods at her own suggestion.

Suzanne laughs—in Lori's book, it always comes down to getting laid—but then, because it *has* been a long time, she sighs. "It does feel like Rafael happened a long time ago."

Lori's smile disappears. "Oh. I was thinking about Joe. Right."

"I guess I am craving sex," Suzanne admits, noticing and confused by Lori's sudden change in mood but choosing to ignore it.

Lori plucks a final white hair from the crease beneath her chin. She picks up a small tube of base, the start of her lengthy makeup application process, but suddenly bunches up her brow and nose. "If she didn't tell you—Abby—about the a cappella group, then how do you know?"

"Because I went to her first concert," Suzanne explains, thinking it should be obvious.

"Why would you go up to Vassar for a concert if you didn't know she was singing in it?"

This question totally baffles Suzanne. "Because I was there? You know, as Shoshanna?" Maybe she and Lori haven't spoken for a little while, but it hasn't been *that* long, and Suzanne remembers having at least a few conversations about her "travels" to Vassar.

"Oh, right. Got it. Sorry."

Lori puts a small dab of the base on her finger and then touches it to her forehead, immediately spreading it all around. She repeats this for her nose and cheeks, until her entire face appears smooth with its healthy hue.

Despite the strange vibe from Lori, Suzanne has so much to confide in her friend, she decides to go on.

"So, I didn't get to tell you about Rami. The other day, he... not sure how I should say this... he positioned himself really close to me, during squats. I mean *really* close, so that I could feel him. All of him. Anyway, I think he wants me, now that my sessions are over. *Wants* me," Suzanne repeats, making sure Lori understands exactly which type of "want" she's talking about.

Suzanne looks to Lori for a reaction. Sex in any way, shape or form always elicits a response from Lori, but this time, her only reaction consists of putting down the base and picking up the eye shadow.

Suzanne tries to hide her shock. Her mind quickly shifts into fast forward. If Lori has no reaction to Rami's wanton moves, how can Suzanne broach the subject of David—and isn't that what Suzanne really wants to talk about? It's certainly the most confusing of all her many confusions. And if she does talk about it, what will she say about him? Suzanne herself doesn't know what she thinks. Does she like him? Does she *like* him?

Abruptly, Suzanne stops her chaotic thoughts. Even to herself she sounds like a teenager with a teacher crush. How can she possibly raise this with Lori?

Except Suzanne doesn't have to worry about that, because as Suzanne nears the end of her internal debate, Lori puts down her makeup and turns towards her friend. "This has to stop, Suze."

Suzanne, not quite sure what exactly needs to stop, tries to sort through her muddled thoughts to recall what she last said to her friend. Rami. "You think I shouldn't be around Rami anymore?"

Silence for a moment, and then Lori turns back to her mirror, concentrating her eyes on her reflection as she continues to apply her makeup. "I'm getting worried about you."

To Suzanne, Lori sounds more irritated than concerned. Skeptically, she asks, "About?"

"Rami didn't make a move on you, Suze, because he doesn't exist!" volcanically erupts Lori, and then, immediately contrite, she puts her hand over her mouth. A moment later, her demeanor changes. She looks at Suzanne with true compassion, the concern clearly showing in her voice. "I mean, we saw him, he exists, but he's a stranger. He's not your trainer. You don't have a trainer."

"But—" Suzanne tries to cut in. Lori does not allow it.

"The only place you work out is at *our* gym, Suze. I don't know what's going on in your mind, I don't know what kind of dreams you're having, and I believe they feel real to you, but, honey, you have no 'alter existence,' as much as you would like one." Lori gestures around the room. "This is it. This is life."

Lori may have stopped talking, but her speech so throws her friend that Suzanne can't respond, although after a pregnant pause that feels long enough to birth two children, Suzanne finally finds the words. "But you were there, with Rami, when I knew about all those things I shouldn't have, couldn't have. Allen's name, his Monday, Wednesday, Friday thing."

Lori gives a slight nod. "Remember when you went to the bathroom, when we were at the gym? You must have heard something without realizing it, heard Allen talking."

Suzanne does not concede. "But Rami. I recognized him, Lori. I knew him. And what about Cybil?"

Lori does not concede, either. "I think maybe that was some kind of déjà vu or something. You know? Like you've been dreaming about someone and then you see someone else, and this someone else becomes that dream person. Maybe they looked something alike, and then, after we met him, you have this déjà vu that you've seen him before, and that's the image that you now have in your brain."

"Then explain Cybil, okay? Explain her!"

"Are you fucking kidding me? Explain a psycho? She was out of her mind years ago. You think she's got a full deck *now?*"

Suzanne struggles to calm herself. How can she argue with Lori when her friend has gone to such lengths to make up excuses? She takes a deep breath, steadying herself. "You really seem to have thought this all out."

"I have. And you should, too, Suzanne. It's not healthy, all of this. Abby's not in a singing group, you don't have a personal trainer, and, I'm sorry, honey, I wish it were true, but you don't have hot guys throwing themselves at you every night. I'm worried." She does sound worried, looks quite worried, but at this point Suzanne's not quite sure she gives a flying fuck about her friend's concerns.

Suzanne gets up, and, without another word, leaves Lori's room, walks down the center stairs and out the front door.

* * *

Suzanne does not get far—only to the edge of Lori's property—when she has an overwhelming desire to stop, drop and cry. Her one and only confidante no longer supports her, does not believe in her, wants only to explain everything away.

The smell of burning wood from a nearby fireplace obscures the fresh air of the clear-sky night. When Suzanne tries to take a deep breath, the acrid smell and the cold air seem to stick in her throat.

Should Suzanne explain it away? Has her "other life" been all dreams, figments of the imagination, wishful thinking? Logic says yes. All these preposterous situations, how could they possibly be any type of reality?

The fall evening chill races through Suzanne's body, and she stands frozen at the end of Lori's driveway. Rafael a fantasy? Rami a twisted déjà vu? College life and the professor of her dreams a sad cry to relive her youth?

Suzanne's feet do not want to move, but she reluctantly pushes herself and starts the walk towards her car, parked a couple of houses away because of all the leaves swept into the street, taking up the spots closer to Lori's house. As she reaches her car, still feeling numb, she looks up and sees the house of the woman who started this all. The cold feelings start to melt in the heated wake of her rising anger, and instead of moving towards her car, Suzanne finds herself marching towards Cybil's house. By the time she has made it up the length of the driveway, she has transformed into a Terminator-like, cold metal machine searching for its prey. Psychotic or not, this woman needs to give her some answers. Her fists pound sharply on the door. "I want to speak to you, Cybil," she calls forcefully, the rancor surprising even herself.

The pounding brings immediate attention, and Cybil opens the door, her calm demeanor a striking contrast to Suzanne's fury. "So pleasant to see you, dear."

The woman's tranquility somewhat diffuses Suzanne's anger, but Suzanne fights back, feeling she deserves her moment of resentment. "Pleasant? What part of this is pleasant?" she asks.

"Please, I don't want you to get a chill. Come in," she offers as she steps back and gestures with her always-flowing robe for Suzanne to enter.

As if on cue, a cold wind gust seems to push Suzanne forward. She resists. "No. No, thanks. I just want some answers."

Cybil silently continues to gesture Suzanne into her home.

Another wind gust and Suzanne succumbs, walking past Cybil and into the warm, inviting hallway. The hostess closes the door and flows down the hall, leading Suzanne to the familiar living room. Suzanne sits on the couch without further invitation, and Cybil takes the seat next to her, immediately placing a calming hand upon the younger woman's knee.

"What is troubling you, my dear?" Cybil asks in her low, sing-song voice.

Suzanne's not sure if it's any one thing or the combination of the touch, the voice, the warm home and the muted tones of the soothing room, but her anger melts, leaving only confusion in its wake. Her eyes well, although she fights against the stream that wants release. "It's all crap," she says quietly, more to herself than to Cybil.

Cybil looks concerned. "Is the necklace not working?"

"Working? You mean taking me places?"

"It stops, sometimes. Rarely, but it can happen."

Suzanne does not answer Cybil's question, but rather asks the most pressing one she has. "Have I been dreaming, or are they real—the places, the people?"

Cybil pats Suzanne's knee. "Well, that's all part of the journey, isn't it?"

By now Suzanne should expect a frustrating answer like this, but the disappointment mixes with exasperation, causing a gushing release of the suppressed waterworks. Cybil moves her arm from Suzanne's knee and wraps it around her shoulders. Suzanne wants to be angry, thinks she should blame Cybil for her confusion, for her loneliness, for all the current turmoil in her life, but instead she leans her head on the older woman's shoulder and allows her tears to flow.

In a moment, when the tears subside and Suzanne somewhat recovers her composure, Cybil releases her and asks if she would like a nice cup of herbal tea. When Suzanne nods, Cybil gets up and steps into the kitchen. Suzanne can hear the running water and the soft clang of the kettle on the stove then the clattering of ceramic cups. She also hears Cybil softly humming to herself.

A short while later, Cybil emerges with a tray holding two steaming white cups, a small round white dish holding several shortbread cookies and an empty glass dish just large enough to hold the teabags still steeping in the cups. The tea-making interlude proved long enough for Suzanne to feel almost normal, no longer the crazed, angry, confused time/place traveler who had entered this home a short while ago.

Cybil hands one of the mugs to Suzanne, the tea-scented steam wafting with an unfamiliar, almost-citrusy, enticing aroma. "Mm. What type of tea?" asks Suzanne, happy to discuss something mundane.

Cybil takes a sniff of her own tea. "Pomegranate, of course," she says with a wink, and holds up the plate of cookies.

Suzanne declines the treats. She blows into her cup

and takes a tentative sip. As usually happens with such fragrant teas, the taste does not live up to the smell, but Suzanne continues to sip, finding the scent and the heat a soothing mix.

"So," Cybil says, now seated in the small armchair next to the couch, "I'm guessing the necklace still leads you places, yes?"

Suzanne nods, takes a deep breath from the steam of her tea, and lets it out slowly.

Cybil continues. "And I'm going to guess there's a man involved. Someone you're starting to have feelings for?"

David flashes into Suzanne's mind, but she pushes him away. She doesn't even know him and definitely does not have feelings. He very possibly doesn't really exist. All these thoughts swirl in her head, and she feels the same pounding confusion building up. Before it overtakes her once again, she puts down her cup and faces Cybil. "I thought... I thought the necklace was supposed to make everything all right." It's a question and a comment in one.

Cybil giggles first then flat out laughs. The movement sloshes her drink, and she puts down her cup, continuing to chuckle as she does. "The necklace— supposed to make everything okay? Well, I'm sorry to be laughing—I really am—but, you know, it's only in childhood we believe someone or something will make everything all right. As adults," she says, selecting a cookie from off the tray, "we should know better, now shouldn't we?"

Chapter 27

Misunderstood

Several days have passed since the emotional rollercoaster at the houses of Lori and Cybil. I'm sitting here, alone in a practice room at Vassar once again, waiting for Professor Music Man to show up for my lesson. I haven't seen him for a while, and it's a good thing. The distance gave me clarity. Nothing's going on between us. He needed some company and invited me to a concert. I needed company, so I accepted. We both wanted some ice cream, and found it at the College Center.

"It means nothing," I say out loud, because saying things out loud gives the words a lot more integrity. I'm taken aback at the sound of my voice, so loud and clear. These rooms really do have good acoustics. So much better than a shower. I can't resist singing a few phrases of a song I have stuck in my head. Not bad sounding, not bad at all.

And, as if on embarrassing cue, I hear a knock. I quickly stop my singing as the door creaks, and David walks in.

Thankfully, it doesn't seem as though he heard me.

Actually, he looks a bit harried, and his, "Sorry, I'm late," bears that out. He sounds winded even. Did he run here? Why was he late? Is everything okay with him?

See? That's exactly what I shouldn't do. He's fine. He looks fine. He looks more than fine, with his a-little-too-long brown hair falling at will on his sculpted cheeks and his dark jeans paired with a pink shirt and black tie. How sexy is a man in pink, right? And the way he fills those jeans...

Not good. Stop it right now.

"So, you practiced enough this week?" he asks. See? Right down to the business of the lesson. Our non-date, my personal well-being—neither item has made his agenda.

I nod and remove my guitar from its case. I pick it up, and when he checks to make sure I'm holding it correctly, he signals for me to start playing the simple piece I've prepared.

I begin the song, not really thinking about what my hands do. I actually play better than usual and, as a bonus, forget how much these damn strings cut into my fingers. Maybe that's the key—don't think about what I do too much. Except now I have time to let my mind wander, which is not the best thing, letting it wander, with David sitting so close to me, watching my arms, my hands, my fingers, making sure I hold the instrument just so...

He's so damn young, for a professor.

And gentle.

I don't know him well, hardly at all, but he emanates such a kind, true character.

Does he know I'm watching him? He sees me looking at my guitar, but does he see the sideways glances? Does he have to sit right next to me? Is that normal for a lesson?

He smells nice. Not of cologne, though. Maybe a different kind of soap? I take a deep breath. He cocks his head towards me—my face, not my hands. Oh, shit—did he see that? Maybe he thinks it's emotion for the song? In any case, he's smiling. Why's he smiling? Get that smile, that gorgeous *I don't know that I'm sexy as hell* smile away from me. What is it about him? It's not the classic magnificence of Rafael. It's not the pure hot animal magnetism of Rami. I don't even like stubble— not to feel it anyway. But on him, next to those deep, dark eyes and long lashes, the lips that...

Thank goodness I'm done with this incessant song.

As soon as I take my hands off the strings, "Nicely done," he says, still smiling, his fucking kindness just oozing through. "Here, let's go over a few of the passages together." He picks up his guitar and points to some of the bars on the sheet music. Okay, I actually have to pay attention. Let's see how that goes...

*　*　*

"You know, you hum while you play."

I nearly drop the guitar while I put it back in its case. "I do not," I say, hoping my protest proves true.

David laughs, which intensifies my embarrassment, though it seems he's being more charitable than mean. "Sorry, you do. You have a nice voice, though."

I hope—I think—he's only talking about the humming, not the pseudo-shower singing from before he entered the room. "Thanks," I say shyly. My mother always taught me I should take a compliment gracefully, but that doesn't mean I like to take them.

I think he hears my discomfit, though, because he adds, "Once, when I was sitting in the first row of an audience at a classical concert, I heard the guest pianist 'moo' while he played." David laughs.

Undoubtedly, the idea of a classical pianist mooing as he plays is pretty funny, but the happily contagious sound of David's mirth is what makes me want to laugh along with him.

"Seriously, just like a cow. The concert was live on some local channel, and I had videotaped it, but when I played it back later that night, I couldn't hear the bovine part. I guess they only put a mike on the piano. Fortunately for him. Moooo," he says, long and low.

I can't help but smile. "Videotaped, huh? You're showing your age."

He laughs again. What a wonderful sound. "I'm not much older than you, though. Except I can remember the time before VHS."

Well, buddy, so can I. How old are you anyway? I'm guessing about thirty?

"No On Demand, either," he continues. "You missed a television show, you really missed it. Anyway, quit distracting me."

I'm distracting him?

"You're a little self-conscious, aren't you? I can see it in how you play. You're tentative, like you're afraid to show what you can do. But you're doing so well already. You're very musical. And your voice, you really do sound nice," he says, but it comes off like a sigh.

I think I'm blushing. I know I lean my head down, because, a moment later, I feel his hand on my chin, lifting it up. When our eyes meet, he quickly pulls his hand—and his eyes—away.

"You should own what you do well. That's my teacherly advice." He picks up his guitar. "Have confidence in your talents. Otherwise, you'll take a different path, away from what you love." He starts plucking his guitar. Even the few notes sound so forlorn.

"That's true," I say, though my voice starts to choke a

little.

He stops playing and clears his throat. "So, what I wanted to ask you..."

He wanted to ask me something? Shit. Not again.

"What I wanted to ask was—and it's totally fine if you're uncomfortable with it, totally okay to say no –"

Oh, no. He's not going to—

"But I've been asked to participate in a professor/student kind of informal concert in the Students' Building. They want duets, small ensembles, but each one needs to be a mixture of professors and students. Popular music. Not really my thing, but, you know, I thought, maybe, if you would sing with me. That song you were singing when I came in, that was nice. I've never heard it before. What's it called?"

So, he's not asking me out. That's a good thing. Right? Isn't it a good thing? Except he heard me singing. "It's called, um, *Little Miss Understood*, by a woman called Raeya. I heard her once, singing at *Ellen's Stardust Diner* in New York City. Ever been there?" Definitely am trying to distract him now.

He shakes his head, but the distraction doesn't work. "How come you haven't tried out for The Night Owls? You have that tone—it would mix so well with the group. Kind of like that girl, you know? The one in the big hat?"

Abby. He's talking about *Abby*.

"Sorry, don't mean to be pushy. Except about this concert. What do you think? Would you like to? Sing with me? Well, you sing, I play? They're really hounding me to do it..."

*   *   *

Why did I say yes? What the hell was I thinking? I know what I was thinking. I looked at those eyes in that face on that body...

Right, I wasn't thinking. I was feeling. Feeling sorry for him. Feeling hot and flushed all over. Feeling needy.

And now I'm standing up here, finishing my last few phrases of the song, and I'm pretty sure I just embarrassed the hell out of myself in front of, I don't know, maybe seventy five students and a dozen or so professors. We got about a whole five minutes to practice, although, I have to say, David did a damn good job playing the piece, learning it by ear after downloading the song. He's really quite incredible. Um, an incredible musician, I meant to say.

Well, at least neither Hannah nor Abby showed up, although, as I keep reminding myself *ad nauseum*, they wouldn't know it's their mother standing here in front of everyone.

And who the hell is David searching for? He keeps looking up and scanning the audience.

Okay, well, there you go, the last note. And... silence. Wait a second.... I can't believe it. Claps and smiles and, yes, I hear some hoots. Although I doubt that's for me. David the Adorable has his following. They probably make up half the audience, those David Devotees. The cute young professor too hot for his own good. Well, let them clap all they like, and let him find whomever he's looking for, and let's call it a night. I have homework to finish.

The clapping winds down, and David looks at me and smiles. That's right, girls, he's smiling at *me*. Of course, it doesn't really mean anything, but, still, I bet most of those young pretties in the audience would love to switch places with me...

At least it seems I didn't embarrass myself.

And, fortunately, we went last, so the concert is over.

"Hey, just let me pack up my guitar, and I'll walk you out, okay?" David says to me as we make our way off the stage area.

I wait. I see several people, several girls, come over to congratulate him. I guess none of them is the one he's been looking for this evening, because he pays little or no attention to all of them. In a moment, he's by my side, guitar strapped to his back. Boy, he really looks young now.

Once out in front of the building, David turns to me and says, "Nice job. Thanks so much for doing this."

"You're the real musician here," I say, but remembering my mother and my manners, I add, "but thanks. And you're welcome. You did an exceptional job." I speak the truth.

The atmosphere goes quickly from mutual admiration to strange, as I'm not sure what to say next.

David thinks of something. "They—um, the audience—seemed to like the song."

"Yeah. It's catchy, right?"

A couple of girls pass by, looking at us. "Bravo, Professor D.," says one of them.

"You were the best," says the second one.

"You two were the best," corrects the first one. Better manners, this one.

Once they're far enough down the path, I tease David with a "Professor D.?"

He shrugs in return. Probably smart of him not to touch that one. "I hate that it's so dark so early these days," he says, changing the subject. "Let me walk you home, um, to your dorm."

"I'm just right over here, in Noyes." You can't get much closer to the Students' Building than Noyes. Hardly need a chaperone for that.

"Oh. That's convenient, then, isn't it? I mean, when you want to go to meals, having the dining center right next to you."

He's back to his nervous way of talking. What's up with him? One minute he's calm, the next he can't get through a sentence without looking like he's about to throw up.

"So, um, I guess... so I guess that's 'good night,' you know, right? Unless, you know, unless maybe you want to—I mean it's totally up to you and all—but maybe you want to take a walk? Um, I mean, with me, of course. Take a walk with me?"

Do I want to? Well, yes, of course I *want* to. The real question is, *should* I? Should I want to go? Should I go?

For goodness sake, it's just a damn walk. What the hell is the harm in that? But what if it's not just a walk? Oh don't be ridiculous! Of course it's just a walk. We just played a song together, and now he's asking me for a walk. All very natural, isn't it?

I sound like a pyscho, even to myself.

No more pyscho-babble. Just take the damn walk!

We start down the road and quickly pass my ultra-modern dorm to our right. The darkness of the cemetery to our left balances out the lights blazing from the windows of Noyes.

"Thanks, again," he says, "for doing the concert. I... enjoyed it."

"You mean, the audience enjoyed it."

"Who cares about the audience?" he asks with a coy smile.

I'll play along. "Doesn't a musician always care about the audience?"

He thinks about that. "Hmm," he says, then adds after a moment, "You're one of those wise college kids, aren't you?"

That's me, a wise old kid.

We pass by Noyes and walk behind the next dorm, the much older dorm called Cushing. Although probably teeming with life inside, from the outside it seems dark and almost deserted.

To drive away the awkward silence, I talk. "Such a nice night, isn't it? We won't have these for too much longer. The smell of autumn, just the right amount of warmth in the air... "

"I love autumn, too," he agrees.

We pass Kenyon on our left, home of the squash courts. Thoughts of the coach, and of me turning into a bumbling jellyfish before his eyes, spring unsolicited and unwelcome to mind. I push those thoughts away by looking to my right. Doesn't that building house the nursery school? It must, because, even in the dark, I can make out the playground equipment in the back.

Hmm. This is no good, either. Now I think about my own kids as I walk here with this man. This beautiful, sensitive, kind of quirky but incredibly sexy man who is not their father...

What's that? Guilt? Shit, why would I feel guilty? Joe might still be their father, but he isn't my husband, and I can walk with whom I like, dammit!

A car passes and we move over, out of its way. Other than that, the road remains pretty desolate, since we've moved off the main campus area. And since I have my kids on my mind now, how would I feel if one of them walked along an almost deserted road in the dark with some older man they don't really know?

But that's not how I feel at all with this man. I don't feel he's a stranger. I'm comfortable with him, even as we go further along the road, further away from the lights of the buildings.

I'm enjoying the quiet, the trees barely rustling with their thinning fall leaves. I look up at David. Okay, he's staring at me. Maybe I do feel a little uneasy. "What?" I ask.

"Oh, sorry. Nothing. It's just... nothing. Um, it's getting pretty dark. Did you want to hold my hand, so you don't fall?"

I think, from any other person, at any other time, that would sound like the most insincere, scheming, cheesiest thing I ever heard, but, you know what? I can tell that's not how he means it at all. He's offering me his guileless hand, and I damn well am going to take it.

I reach out my hand, and he takes it into his own, strong and warm and comforting. I feel protected by his touch and somehow stronger myself. Okay, so maybe I'm the cheesy one.

I notice one other thing. "You've got callouses," I can't help myself from saying. "From your guitar?"

He nods. "Sorry. Is my hand scratching you?"

He moves as if to pull it away, but I hold on to it. "No, no, it's fine. I... it's dark here."

"We could turn back," he says, but I can tell he wants that about as much as I do. I shake my head, and we continue on.

Probably to fill some of the silence, David asks, "So, have you figured out your major yet?"

I shake my head again.

"Still undecided, huh? Your parents okay with that?"

"They're fine," I answer, because, really, what else should I say? "And anyway, it's their job to give me the opportunities and the independence. Then it's my job to figure out how to use it, right?" I might as well inject a little of my own philosophy. I suppose it comes from my parents, anyway.

"You sound like my... ex," says David. "She's smart, too."

There's that "ex" again. At least now I know it's a she, although I kind of figured that out already.

"Don't know how smart I am, but I guess I've been

around the block a little."

He smiles. "You're not quite old enough for many times around the block at this point."

Crap. I feel too comfortable, and I'm forgetting myself with him. "Maybe I'm an old soul," I suggest, hoping it's a good cover up.

"Well, you certainly seem wiser than your years," he says. "You have a certain maturity."

"As long as you're not telling me I look old," I say. That's my own private little joke, isn't it?

"You look lovely," he says, but looks away from me as he does.

Lovely, huh? That's so... sweet.

We're at a fork. David leads me towards the right, the way to the Terrace Apartments. Right now, though, you can't get much more isolated on this campus than this little stretch of road, I think. A car has not passed for some time, but I'm relaxed, surprisingly, and content. For a moment, as we walk, David hums a tune, but he soon stops the humming and asks, "So, how come you haven't tried out for The Night Owls?"

I thought I'd successfully dodged this question. "Because I'm not Night Owl material," I protest.

"But you are. Didn't you hear the crowd's reaction tonight?"

"David, come on. That was *you* they were reacting to. The..."—I want to say "hot" but think better of it—"the attractive young professor."

He laughs. "Well, attractive is in the eye of the beholder, but young?"

We've come to another fork. Once again, we veer right and start up a hill.

"What are you, like thirty? That's kind of the beginning of life, isn't it? Hell, if I feel old when I'm *thirty*, what's the point of making it past puberty?"

He smiles and stops walking. "You're something else, you know?"

We're facing each other, standing on the slope. I'm a little more uphill than is he, so, despite his height advantage, we're almost eye to eye. I feel the unusually warm fall breeze gently surrounding us. I can hear some people calling to each other in the distance, the muted cries of the truly young. I can see David leaning towards me...

A kiss—swift, soft and sweet. And another, this one deeper, longer. I feel his arm around my back, pulling me closer. I want to be closer. I kiss him back. There's a poignancy in his touch, in his lips—an overwhelming desire. I feel it, too, and wrap my arms over his shoulders, my hands in his hair, tugging, pulling, kissing. He moans softly, sending an ache throughout my body.

Girls voices, this time not in the distance.

David stops kissing and pulls his mouth away but keeps his arms pressed against my back. We both breathe heavily.

I don't think the girls have seen us. They're talking, arguing, as if no one else is around, standing just outside a group of Terrace Apartments.

"*Just call security for an escort. What's the big fucking deal?*"

"*You're my sister, not our fucking parents!*"

"*Watch the language!*"

"*Are you kidding me?!*"

David pulls his arm away from me. He takes one big breath and steps back.

"*Yeah, well, I'm me and you're you.*"

"*You know, whatever. I'm fine. Thanks for dinner. It was nice, up until now.*"

I look at him, but he looks away. Is it shame? Or

something else? Maybe he didn't like the kiss?

"Come on, Twit-Face, it's a long walk back to campus. It's dark."

And there goes a bucket of cold water thrown on my head. Hannah and Abby arguing, not twenty feet from where I just kissed my professor. I can see them now. No, not cold water. It's a bucket of freaking ice!

Maybe some of that ice flung itself on David as well, because he's also looking a little frozen. I guess the kiss was not premeditated. I guess it took him by surprise, too.

Not looking directly at me, he whispers, "I think we should head back."

I nod, not capable of speaking at the moment—for so many reasons.

"Um, maybe... " his voice seems to falter, "maybe we should offer to walk her, that young lady, home."

Are you kidding me? *That's a fucking horrible idea*, I want to scream, but I just shake my head.

I don't understand why, but he doesn't let it go.

"But it's late, like the other girl said, and she won't call security. Plus she's carrying that huge book... we can't let her walk on her own."

I have to find my voice, because I really don't want to walk Abby back to her dorm. I'll screw up for sure. I'll say something I shouldn't. I'll give myself away to both her and to David. On the other hand, this is my child, and of course I don't want her to walk back to campus on her own, in the dark. "Let's wait a second. I think her sister's convincing her to call someone." Yes, the best of both worlds—let her call security.

David gives me a very odd look. "How do you know they're sisters?"

Fuck wad! See?! See how easy it is to slip up?! "Well, um," I stutter, but then I remember, "She said it, the younger one to the older one. She said they're sisters."

Phew.

David and I both turn towards the girls, and we see Abby has started off down the road, away from us, by herself.

"Okay," I say. "We'll walk her home."

At the same time, Hannah calls after Abby, "You're an asshole."

Nice language. Their mother's certainly done a good job with them.

David, a few steps ahead of me now, gestures for me to follow. When I catch up to him, he insists, "You need to talk to her. I can't approach her, an older man asking to walk her to safety."

Shit, he's right. I have no choice. I *have* to do the talking. I run up ahead, and in a moment I'm right next to her. She seems startled but calms as she gets a look at me.

"Hey," I say.

"Hi," she says.

I have a sudden clever idea. "I know you. I almost stabbed you in the Deece."

Abby stops and turns to me. "Oh, right. You haven't got any concealed forks on you, do you?" She smiles. I can tell she's still agitated from her discourse with her sister, but she's putting up a good front.

"I could have a real knife and here you are walking around in the dark by yourself," I want to say but don't. Instead, I answer, "Not this time. But my... friend and I, we're headed back to the main part of campus. Mind if we walk with you? I mean, if you don't mind? Anyway, the paths can be a little secluded this time of night."

I know Abby, and I know she'd love to tell me, the stranger, to fuck off just like she told her sister, but she's way too polite. Plus, I can see those wheels moving, and she's probably thinking by now that maybe there's some validity to what everyone's preaching.

"Sure," she says.

David scurries to join us. "Hi," he says, but stays to my right, leaving Abby to my left. "Can I carry that book for you? It looks like a monster."

A monster book, indeed. It's half the width of my darling slender girl.

"No, really. You're doing enough, going out of your way."

"This is the way we were headed, anyway. Please. I'm kind of old-fashioned. I'd really like to hold the book for you. I'll feel so much better."

Wow, he really does sound old-fashioned now. I guess he's convincing, though, because Abby, begrudgingly, gives up the book to him.

"Thanks," he says as he cradles it in his right arm.

We start walking, now headed in the opposite direction from where David and I came. As we walk along the path headed towards a small bridge, David comments, "Hey, you were in The Night Owl concert, weren't you?" Without waiting for an answer, he turns to me and says, "Isn't that a coincidence, Shoshanna? This is the girl I said reminded me of you, of your singing."

One big happy fucking coincidence.

He turns back to Abby, now not waiting for *me* to respond. "Your parents must be so proud of you, right?"

What's with him, Mr. Inquisitive? Why's he acting this way? On the other hand, he's doing me a favor, isn't he? I want to hear Abby's answer to that question.

"They don't know. My parents. Haven't told them."

"Neither of them?" David demands. Hey, that's exactly the question I wanted to ask. He's doing a good job—a great job.

She shakes her head.

Well, how do you like that?! Joe doesn't know either.

"Why wouldn't you tell your parents?" asks David, beating me to the punch—again. "Don't you think you should tell them?" he reprimands. I wonder if he has kids, because he certainly seems to be taking this news to heart.

Abby looks uncomfortable. Good. She should.

I look up and realize we're passing the College Center at the back of Main Building. Certainly Abby doesn't need an escort now, with all these lights and people around, but I'm not going to open my mouth. My daughter still has some explaining to do.

And that she does, albeit begrudgingly. "It's not like I'm not planning to. I just didn't. Yet." She has that tone now—that belittling tone she uses with me when she knows she's guilty of something but wants to turn the tables, deflect the guilt and the consequences. She is still a teenager, after all. "I'm just waiting until winter break. I wanted to try it out, see how the first concert went. I've never performed before, you know?" She lowers her voice. I have to strain to hear her. "I didn't want... I couldn't have them here and then screw it all up. I wanted to make sure I wouldn't embarrass them," she finishes, her voice barely above a whisper.

Oh.

Well. Okay, then. Not what I was expecting.

I turn away, pretending something off to the side interests me, hiding the tears that start to well.

We're walking diagonally across the quad, Abby now between me and David, all of us quiet. She has her head down. Is she ashamed of what she did, of what she did so her parents wouldn't feel embarrassed? Did saying it out loud point out her illogical reasoning? Doesn't she know we could never be embarrassed? What the hell is wrong with her?

I can't help myself. I know I shouldn't let it out, but by this time, the steam has built up and desperately needs some release. It's all I can do to keep the anger out of my voice. "I would think, you know, Abby, that the only way your parents would possibly have been embarrassed by you singing would be if you were doing a cappella in the nude."

She looks at me as though I'm from another planet. Shit, I've gone too far.

But she surprises me again. "How'd you know my name?"

Are you kidding me?! Crap, crap, crap. Think fast. "Um, at the concert, right? They said your name." Did they say her name? I have no idea. "I have an excellent memory," I lie, since the bigger the lie, the better it's believed.

Abby says nothing in response, which means she's not buying it, and, judging by the look on David's face, he's not buying it either. I guess they never said her name at the concert. Shit!

We're in front of Josselyn now, thank goodness. Time for me to make my escape. Looks like David wants a quick escape, too, because he can't wait to give her back her book and get the hell out of here. But see what happens when you're in too much of a rush? There goes the book he was holding, dropped right on the ground. For a guy who so nimbly plays the guitar, he sure has fumble fingers. I reach down to pick it up.

"What's that?" asks David. I look up and see him staring at my Cybil necklace, sprung from its usual hiding place beneath my shirt when I bent to retrieve that damn book. I don't like people seeing it, even if they don't know what it's all about.

"What type of charm is it?" he demands rudely when

I don't answer quickly enough.

To lie or not to lie? Well, the truth won't make a difference. "I think it's supposed to be a pomegranate."

He brusquely continues his drilling. "Where'd you get it?"

What the hell kind of question is that? What is with him? Why is he using this tone with me? I think about not answering him at all, just walking away, but he is my professor, after all. I shrug and say, "I've had it for years."

Abruptly, he turns from me to Abby and stiffly says, "I apologize for dropping your book."

She seems a little weirded-out by his sudden strange behavior, too, but she answers him. "Um, no problem. It's fine. At least you weren't carrying my laptop, right?" she says, probably trying to lighten the situation a little. "Okay, so I'm going inside now. Thanks a lot, both of you, for the walk home. See you around." She takes the book from my hands, and I watch her quickly walk to the front door of Josselyn House and disappear inside.

David stands, rigid, by my side.

*　　*　　*

I know I should be paying attention—not the easiest course for me, this English class, and I always feel so stupid in it—but I can't stop thinking about last night.

So bizarre, walking back to Noyes after we left Abby. It wasn't the book dropping at all, I concluded, that caused David to act so weirdly. It was the kiss, of course. That damn kiss probably changed everything between us. Hell, it probably was the reason he insisted on walking her back to her dorm to begin with. To avoid me, to avoid the awkwardness. He probably wants nothing more to do with me now.

Except *he* kissed *me*, not the other way around! So, it's all *his* fault, isn't it?

What was that? Shit, the prof just called on me.

"Um, sorry," I say, figuring that might possibly cover me for any question that was just asked of me, oblivious as I am. "I don't know the answer; leave me alone" is what it says. I guess it works, because she goes on to someone else.

Complete silence all the way back to my dorm. I mean, it's not far, but still... then him saying only, "Night," and walking away.

What was he thinking? *Was* he thinking about the kiss? Because I was...am. The strangest kiss I've ever had, I realize now. Passionate, as though he needed me, but warm, also. Strange, wonderful. Wonderful because of its strangeness. I'm not making any sense, even to myself.

But, yes I am, if I really want to be honest. I've never had a kiss like that. Not in all my years with Joe, not in my pathetically limited other experience. I've never had a kiss feel so... *right*, so... I don't know... *complete*. Sappy, but I felt something more from this kiss. So why do I feel so badly? Because he walked away from me? No, somehow I don't think so. Guilt? Can't be. I've been flirting with Rami, I fucked a superstar, why would I feel guilt now?

But I do. Because of that kiss.

Thank goodness the end of class has finally arrived. Everybody up and out, and I won't have to sit here thinking any longer.

"Shoshanna, can I speak to you?" I hear the prof ask through my self-indulgent cloud.

Oh, crap.

Everyone else files out, and I go up to the teacher.

"A little distracted today?" she asks, although obviously she knows the answer.

I can't deny it. "Sorry."

"Everything okay?"

No.

"Yes, sure. It's just... yeah, I really apologize. Won't happen again."

"Listen, no need to apologize. Everyone has an off day. I love having you in my class. To be honest," she chuckles, "you're the only one who actually makes sense."

Must be my general confusion today, but did she just say what I thought she said? I can't help myself. I laugh. The prof looks at me like I'm crazy, which, at this point, would not be far from the truth. "I'm the only one making sense?" I repeat, kind of making sure I heard her correctly.

"You know how it is. All these young people think they have something brilliant to say. Or maybe some of them just like to hear themselves talk, think they can snow others into believing the crap they're pedaling." She shrugs.

"Really? I guess they pedaled to the right person in me."

"I had a feeling," she says, picking up her briefcase. "You're the one with the insight, Shoshanna. You don't talk much in class, but when you do... I wish you would participate more. You have great perception for the literature, and you're straightforward, and that, in my opinion, is what critical analysis should be about. Getting to the heart of the matter, not performing a show with flowery language and bullshit scrutiny."

This has to be one of the most amazing conversations I've ever had.

"You know, Shoshanna, just because someone speaks with conviction and sounds like they know what they're talking about, doesn't mean they do." She laughs and picks up her short stack of books. "Anyway, I hope whatever is bothering you works out... "

And, with a smile, she's out the door.

I like this professor.

Chapter 28

KNIGHTS IN WHITE SATIN

A KNOCK ON THE FRONT door. Suzanne opens it to find Lori in triple strap leather boots and her impractical short winter jacket that could hardly keep a small dog warm let alone a full grown woman. "What the hell's so important that I had to rush over here?" she demands brusquely as she storms past Suzanne and into the house, the cold air radiating as though an ice sculpture just stepped into the room.

"Hello to you, too," Suzanne says, chastising the rude entrance.

"Hello, Suzanne, how are *you*? I see that you're actually talking to me," answers Lori, not shying away from her own thinly veiled reprimands. "Have you come to your senses?"

Suzanne tenses, ready for a fight, but that's not what she called Lori here for, and she consciously relaxes her hands which have fisted at her sides.

Lori softens her voice and continues the conversation from the other day, as though time stood still and Suzanne stands in Lori's bedroom instead of Lori standing in the entranceway of Suzanne's home. "I know you want to believe it's all true, but it's gotten out of hand, sweetie. Sometimes a dream is just a dream, even if you want it so badly you fool yourself otherwise. Hey, you're old, just like the rest of us." Forced laughter strains from Lori's throat. "Get used to it."

Suzanne would like to say, "Doesn't look like you're admitting being old, with those tight jeans, long hair and boots meant for a twenty-something." She doesn't say it, though, because she wouldn't mean it. In fact, Lori looks good, not ridiculous at all. She obviously feels good about herself, and she translates it to her clothes and to her demeanor. The difference is Suzanne doesn't judge Lori, but Lori—bossy, obnoxious, so sure she's right—wants to make sure Suzanne agrees with her.

But she's not right. What was that the professor said? *"Just because someone speaks with conviction..."*

The professor also hoped the problem would work itself out, but that's not going to happen here, because no amount of arguing will convince Lori of the impossible-to-believe truth. Suzanne has to work it out herself. She has to take action.

She grabs Lori's arm with one thought in mind. "Show her!"

* * *

I still hold Lori's arm. Well, I think it's Lori—I mean, she looks kind of like Lori but maybe what she'll look like about fifteen, twenty years from now. And we're not in my home anymore, that's for damn sure. We're not anywhere else I've been to or know either. Where are we? It's a tiny room, and behind us I see an outside door, so some type of entrance hall, and just a tad seedy looking. Black walls, low wattage lights, long strings of beads from the sixties across a doorway into some larger room, ornate gilded mirrors on the walls. Oh, I don't like that mirror, or, rather, the reflection that's in it. That must be me, a white-haired wrinkly me. Okay, I'm going to look away now and concentrate on Lori, not my aged face.

Even in the low light I can see Lori looks ghostly pale.

She's looking into another one of the mirrors, wide-eyed. "We're not in Kansas anymore," I say with a smile and then add, a little friendlier, "Sorry, couldn't resist."

Lori turns her head from the mirror to me, and, if it's possible, her eyes widen even more. "Suzanne?"

I nod.

"What the fuck is happening?" she asks under her breath. It's her usual brash way of saying things, but despite the choice of words, I've never heard her voice so small before. "Where are we?"

"Welcome to my world," I answer, a much stronger voice than hers, harsh even. "Do you think you fell asleep suddenly, talking to me? Is this a dream?"

She looks around, shaking, scared.

Three women come through the front door, dressed for a night on the town—not fancy, but put-together, with full makeup and coiffed hair for an evening out. Laughing, they breeze by us and through the beaded entrance.

Our clothes have changed as well as our bodies. Lori wears a flouncy dress, way too low cut for that body, and high heeled black boots. Looking down at myself, I see inappropriate attire as well. How am I walking in these "FM" shoes, especially at this age? And why a long sequined top over leggings? Definitely preposterous, the both of us.

"Where the hell are we?" Lori insists again.

I shrug my shoulders. "Haven't been here before."

"This can't be," she says more to herself than to me.

I let go of her arm and take her hand. "Let's see," I

say as I pull her through the beaded curtain.

It's a restaurant of sorts, but not a usual one. A huge bar on our left, lots of long tables to our right, many of them with one sided booth-like seating, with the tables towards the back of the room the longest and able to hold the most people. At the far end of the room I can see what appears to be a small stage, heavy draped curtains and all. From a dark ceiling hang dozens of mismatched sparkling crystals of various sizes.

Yes, certainly not in Kansas.

We're met by a burly woman with impossibly big boobs and a waist to match. Her tight fitting turquoise dress screams of self-confidence and an *I don't give a shit* attitude. She greets us with a huge smile and booming husky voice, saying, "I'm Charleena. Welcome to CBQ! Table for two?" with obvious pleasure at the rhyme.

Lori stiffens beside me, but I nod, and Charleena picks up two menus and sashays to one of the smaller tables in the middle of the room. She puts the oversized menus on the table and turns with another smile. "I've put you at one of my tables," she says with a wink. "You girls have fun, and I'll see you in a bit."

I guide Lori to one of the chairs and take the other across from her. She's looking around, wide-eyed and uncharacteristically silent. I may be surprised to have landed in a new location, but the "traveling" part has become old hat. I look around while I let her get acclimated. The place definitely seems slightly run down but not dirty. Although the huge, diner like menu proves this is a restaurant, the flimsy cutlery clearly states the food will not be the center of attention.

Other servers of various sizes and varying styles of inappropriate waitress attire wind their way among the closely set tables. I take a look at the front of the menu.

It mirrors Charleena's greeting with "Welcome to CBQ!" in large letters across the top. Halfway down, though, the initials are spelled out: Club Beauty Queen. The inside cover gives away more information. With a one drink plus fifteen dollar restaurant minimum, we'll enjoy tits, lips and hips galore.

Well, isn't that a kick in the pants! I've brought Lori to a drag queen show. Not quite what I had in mind, I guess. What *did* I have in mind? *Show her.* I think maybe I had Vassar in mind, or even Rafael up close. Well, anyway, I guess she won't be able to explain this one away so easily.

"Are you okay?" I ask.

She shakes her head. Guess that's to be expected, but she'll survive.

"Well, you may as well order a drink. They're going to charge you for one anyway, and I'm guessing you need one. A glass of wine?"

She shakes her head.

"Something stronger?"

She nods in agreement.

Charleena returns. "Better get your orders in. Show's about to start. You ladies know what you want for drinks and dinner?"

"What's good?" I ask, since I haven't gotten a chance to look at the menu.

"The singing and dancing," Charleena answers. "But the Chicken a la CBQ is safe. It's thirteen-fifty."

Not quite the minimum amount needed. I order the chicken with a side salad, balsamic on the side. I turn to Lori, but she's not capable of any conscious effort at this point, except maybe staring, so I order the same for her. Doubt she'll eat, anyway. I figure she'll drink the gin and tonic I order for her, though. Chances are she'll drink mine, too.

As soon as Charleena sidles away through the closely placed tables, the lights dim. All eyes turn to the small stage at the front of the room. The low strains of a vaguely familiar tune just barely cut through the hum of the crowd. The music gets louder, though, as a spotlight hits the stage. A leg juts out between the break in the center stage curtain. Completely engulfed in black pleather that seamlessly integrates with the four inch clunky heeled black shoes, the leg dangles for a moment and then firmly plants itself on the stage at the same moment the curtain opens. There stands Lady Gaga, of sorts, in all her/his glory, the rest of the body wrapped as tightly in the black pleather as the leg. The platinum blond hair and the eggshell white face stand out starkly against the dark outfit, the eyes encircled by carefully drawn thick black bands of liner. No lip synching here. This lady, um, person, not only has the shape of Miss Gaga but some pretty strong pipes as well, with the moves to match. Oh, I know this song. *Poker Face.*

Hard as it is to pull my eyes away from Lady Gaga, I glance over at Lady Lori, who rivals Gaga's washed out look. I know for sure in the "real" world, this type of show would definitely tickle Lori's fancy, but I can't say she's enjoying the here and now.

"You okay?" I ask yet again, but, before she can answer, if she even would, Charleena returns with our oversized drinks in glasses embossed with the CBQ moniker. She sings along with Lady Gaga as she sets the drinks down in front of us, winking once more. As soon as Charleena steps away, Lori finally moves, picking up her glass and taking a long, uninterrupted swig.

Half empty, she puts down her glass. "I am *not* okay. I am definitely NOT okay," she repeats emphatically as the song ends.

Women raise their hands with dollar bills, and Lady Gaga sweeps the room, graciously collecting them...

* * *

Lori stands in the kitchen of Suzanne's house, stunned once more, or possibly still. Apparently the return trip was not any easier to accept than the one going.

Not knowing what else to say in this moment, Suzanne asks, "You want a drink?"

Lori shakes her head. "Had enough," she mutters.

Suzanne has to agree, since they each had consumed three very tall, very strong gin and tonics while at Club Beauty Queen. Tall and strong—like most of the "women" singing and dancing on the stage and even waitressing off-stage.

"You want to talk?" offers Suzanne. Strike while the iron's hot, take the bull by the horns...

Lori seems to have a different cliché in mind—get while the going's good. "I think... I think I'll go home," she says, her voice no stronger than at the club a short while ago.

No way can Suzanne just let her go. "But you believe me now, right?" Get down to the heart of the matter.

"I... " Lori stumbles, "I know it sounds, I don't know, corny, but I don't know what to believe."

"Are you kidding me?" Suzanne can't help getting angry. "Are you fucking kidding me? Did we not both just see men in drag dancing around, singing their hearts out, making a bundle off of women so drunk from bad liquor and glee at getting out of their houses that they were waiving probably a good day's salary around in singles to the ones they thought made the best women? Did you not just see that with me? Did you not see *yourself*?"

Lori nods weakly.

"Then what the hell is the problem?"

"I don't know. I just can't..."

Suzanne has nowhere to go with her frustration. She wants to scream but knows it won't help her cause. So exasperated, she's ready to pull her hair out, but when she unconsciously brings her hands up to her head to give it a try, she realizes she clutches something in her left hand. She opens her palm to see a crumbled cocktail napkin, which she quickly flattens out. This small piece of paper may only measure mere inches from corner to corner, yet the story it tells could come from a full-sized book. Suzanne smiles first to herself and then looks up, grinning at her friend. She holds up the napkin and takes a few steps towards Lori to make sure she can clearly see the imprint.

Suzanne can tell the exact moment when it clicks, because Lori gasps and takes a step backwards, except she can't back away from the truth. The CBQ logo may be small and wrinkled, but it cannot be denied.

And with a soft sigh from Lori and an almost imperceptible "okay," the world changes forever for both women.

* * *

A short while later, Suzanne and Lori sit at Suzanne's kitchen table, sipping their sobering cups of coffee. Now that Lori's had some time to get used to the idea, she acts more like herself.

"There's one thing I don't understand," she says, a complaint already evident in her tone. "Well, lots of things. *Lots* of things. But one thing I care to talk about right now." Lori takes another sip of her coffee. "Why were we old?"

Suzanne shrugs her shoulders.

"You're never older, right, when you, um, go to the

places you, uh, go? In fact, seems like you're saying you're always *younger*." She looks at her friend for confirmation.

Suzanne gives a simple nod, but inside she's happy having this conversation, glad for Lori to ask all the questions she wants, because it shows her acceptance of Suzanne's strange worlds.

"That pisses me off."

Ah, that's the Lori Suzanne knows and loves.

"I mean, if I'm going to be subjected to something like that, tearing through space and time or whatever the hell we did, shouldn't I at least get rewarded with a young bod, not to mention a post-pubescent muscled-up hotty who wants to get into my skirt? What the hell?! You've got more men than you can handle, and I get the ones who only want to squeeze into their *own* skirts! And what the hell with those wrinkles?!" Lori takes one more sip of her coffee but quickly puts it down. "I think I'm ready to go back to the hard stuff. Got anything good?"

Chapter 29

THE MUSIC MEN

SUZANNE WAKES UP THE NEXT day and smiles to herself, remembering the night before. She finally has someone she can talk to, someone on her side. Her good friend. Finally.

Except that happy feeling quickly gets shot to hell when her cell phone rings.

"Mom, I need a favor."

"Hello to you, too, Hannah."

"Oh, right. Sorry. Hello, Mother dear."

"You want a favor with that mouth?" Suzanne had thought Hannah had finished her snarky teenage years.

"Please, Mommy."

Not a new trick, this reverting to childhood in order to manipulate the mother into the desired result. Of course, Suzanne walks willingly into the trap. "What do you want?" Translation? "Okay, I'm Mommy. I'll do anything you ask of me."

"I need you to go over to Dad's, find a book I left there, and then bring it to me."

"Excuse me? You want me to come all the way up to Vassar today?"

"I know it's a really big favor. Like really, really big. But you miss me and Abby, don't you? And it's not *too, too* far, right? We can have lunch together, or dinner—whatever you want. I'll cook, even. You want me to cook?"

Clever girl.

"Who says I want to spend my day driving to and from Poughkeepsie?" In fact, the thought just about puts Suzanne into a panic. A visit to Vassar—as Suzanne, not as Shoshanna? She's just not prepared. "And I don't understand—you left a book at your father's? What's going on?"

"Nothing's going on. I just didn't think I needed this book for school this semester. I had it at Dad's once and left it by accident, and now I really, really need it. Like right away. And it's one of those expensive ones, and I don't feel like shelling out the money for another copy. Shelling out *your* money."

"So, two questions. One, if it's at your father's house, why are you calling *me*? Why aren't you asking *him* to bring it? And, two, this is not some *Parent Trap* ruse to get us back together, is it?"

"Okay, mom, I'm going to answer number two first. Obviously, you don't remember what *The Parent Trap* was about if you're going to ask that question and, frankly, I'm a bit insulted you'd think that about me—and definitely surprised you think I have time for games like that. And, as for number one, you know Dad. If I ask him to do this for me, he'll only half listen, and it definitely won't go right. He'll either bring the wrong book or he'll send it by mail and I'll get it later in the week when it'll be too late. Don't deny it, because you know it's true."

Suzanne certainly wouldn't even attempt to deny it, seeing that her ex-husband's inability to listen to the smallest need was one of the reasons he's now an ex. And she would be shocked if he agreed to go that far out of his way to help. The children could always be inconvenienced, in his opinion, but never the father.

"*Please*, Mommy. I really need this book. Dad said he'll be home this morning, so you can definitely pick it up."

"So, you told him I might be coming over?

"Yes."

"And you told him why?"

"Yes, again. He said no problem."

"He didn't say he would bring it to you himself?"

"I kind of told him you already planned to come see us this weekend."

Suzanne thinks to point out Hannah had not even given her father a chance to take care of the situation, but she knows it would have just led to Hannah's disappointment—yet again—so she leaves it alone.

What's the one thing right now Suzanne dreads more than a trip up to Vassar? That would be a trip to her ex-husband's house.

Lucky her, setting off for both...

* * *

Since Hannah had already told Suzanne that Joe expects her, Suzanne doesn't bother to call ahead, and she pulls up in front of his house a short while later.

Suzanne gets out of the car and walks around to the curb side. She notices the cracks in the concrete sidewalk where the roots of the tall, wide trees have partially lifted it. The property has been around for a while, but the house itself looks in pretty good shape. Although stark white, narrow and fairly non-descript, it does have a lovely, in Suzanne's opinion, small veranda—occupied only by two white rocking chairs. She doesn't know why, but she's always been a sucker for any house with a veranda, and she likes the house immediately. The irony of Joe now owning a house with the front porch she's always wanted saddens her.

She walks along the narrow driveway and up the short flight of brick stairs. About to knock, she looks towards her right, sees the rocking chairs up close and, spur of the moment, heads towards them. She sits in the one closest to the stairs, rocking back slightly as she sits down. It's on an angle with the other chair, perfect for an intimate conversation, except Suzanne expects that these seats, this veranda, have gone totally unused. She can't imagine Mr. Anti-Social Joe ever using them with a guest, ever taking a "shooting-the-breeze" moment with a friend. She chuckles to herself.

And then her chuckling stops. Suzanne hears—what is that—piano music? Coming from Joe's house? She's never heard Joe listening to classical music before. How odd.

As she listens a little more, rocking as she does, she realizes the music seems a little stilted. That can't be a professional recording. She turns her head slightly towards the house, peers through the white sheers and sees a couple on a bench in front of an old upright. The man and woman crowd together, sitting with touching thighs. He plays while she watches intently, her hand resting on his thigh—an intimate moment made even more personal when he seems to make a mistake and they both laugh simultaneously.

The scene seems so foreign to Suzanne that, even though she knows this is Joe's home, it takes a moment before she realizes the piano-playing, laughing man sitting so comfortably next to the touching woman is indeed Joe. Her Joe.

Used to be her Joe.

Father of her children.

Decades her sexual partner.

The man she woke up next to year after year.

Sitting on a piano bench, touching a woman other than herself in an extraordinarily familiar way, laughing in an extraordinarily uncharacteristic way.

Suzanne would like nothing more than to leave, immediately, and—all thoughts of her daughter and her reason for being here gone from her head—she stands up, prepared to do just that, except, as she stands, the purse on her lap falls onto the floor, giving her secret audience away. The music stops, and the happy couple turn around, one with perfect recognition.

Joe quickly walks to his front door and opens it as Suzanne stands frozen on the veranda she always wanted but never achieved. He steps partially out the door and looks at her for a moment. "I'm sorry," he says, which, she immediately understands, means there's something to feel sorry about.

"Sorry for what?" asks the other woman who now stands to the left of Joe.

As nausea fights to overcome Suzanne, she summons all her superhuman powers. She looks straight at her ex-husband, which causes him to look down. "You don't need to explain. You have the right," are the words she uses.

If the woman hears these words, she ignores them. "Hi," she says, insinuating herself into this private moment. Of course, Suzanne has just insinuated herself into this stranger's private moment.

Suzanne responds with a smile, of sorts.

"Um, this is, Jessie. She's... uh... she's my piano teacher."

"Really? You're taking piano lessons? So early on a Saturday morning?"

Joe does not respond, but Jessie happily does. "He's

picking it up so quickly. You know, his musical background. I usually teach kids, so this is," she puts her hand on Joe's shoulder, "a pleasant change."

Joe allows the hand to rest where it fell. "You're here for Hannah's book, I guess. Didn't expect you until later."

Obviously.

Suzanne does her best to sound normal. "Long drive."

Joe takes a step back, retreating into the living room. Jessie's hand finally drops off his shoulder. "Did you want to come in?" he asks unconvincingly.

Suzanne doesn't budge. "No, I've got to get going. The girls expect me soon."

Joe returns to the door and proffers the book.

"Thanks," Suzanne says and, without further ado, turns and walks to her car.

* * *

A couple of hours later, Suzanne stops at Hannah's townhouse at the back of the campus, parking her car just steps from where David had kissed her. When she knocks on the door, she finds Hannah with her coat on, ready to go. Hannah had thought to cook but quickly realized she had no real provisions to manage anything other than some pb&j sandwiches, and, knowing peanut butter is the one thing her sister would never even smell, let alone eat, she suggests they pick up Abby and head to the dining center. Suzanne makes a counter offer to eat off campus, and Hannah happily agrees, saying, "I just didn't want to make you spend your money." At this point, though, Suzanne would pay whatever she needs to make sure she spends as little time on campus as possible. She definitely does not feel up to her strange worlds colliding—today or any day.

They stop at Josselyn to get Abby and head out the nearby gate, parking a little ways up the street, just outside the White Birch Grill on Collegeview Avenue. When they inquire inside, the hostess promises a table will open up soon. They walk back outside, preferring to wait in the brisk air rather than at the crowded bar.

As they wait, Abby questions her mom, "How come you didn't just park in the back of Josselyn? We could have walked here in, like, two minutes."

Not about to discuss her deep desire to avoid campus, Suzanne evades with, "Since when do you like exercising of any kind?"

Abby doesn't get a chance to retort, because just then the hostess pops her head out the door. "All set," she says with a smile. They follow her inside and walk a few steps to a table pushed against the wall opposite the bar, a space exactly for three. Suzanne approaches the seat facing the front of the restaurant. The hostess waits as all three hang their coats on the back of their seats and sit down, then she hands them their menus, wishes them a good meal and returns to her post by the door.

Despite the bright day, the restaurant seems dark. Suzanne doesn't let on she's having a hard time reading the menu in the dim light and slowly positions it further away from her face until it comes into focus, hoping her teasing children don't notice.

As they continue to look over the lunch menu, Abby inadvertently bumps knees with her mother. "Sorry," she says, and then adds, "Good thing Dad's not here. He hates small tables like this."

"Well, your father is *not* here," says the mother with a little more vehemence than intended.

Hannah takes it personally. "I'm sorry, Mom. I guess it wasn't a good time for you to come up. I *should* have asked Dad."

Suzanne softens at Hannah's sincerity. "No, sweetie,

it's fine. And I'm happy I'm here. It's a treat to have lunch with my girls." She smiles what she intends to be a soothing and sincere mother's gesture.

The waitress comes to take their order. When she leaves, the girls start up a conversation about their classes, and soon their appetizer— fresh mozzarella on crostini with tomato, fresh basil, balsamic and some "evoo," as Rachael Ray would say—makes its way to the table. "Delish," as Ms. Ray would say as well. It's kind of late for lunch, so the mozzarella disappears in a matter of minutes.

"Nice to have a break from the Deece," says Abby as she finishes her last bite of the crostini.

"Mm-hmm," her mother agrees emphatically, thinking with her stomach instead of her brain.

Abby laughs. "Like *you* have to eat cafeteria food."

Suzanne takes a drink of her ice water so she doesn't have to speak right away. Even in this off-campus setting, she still messed up. Having gained a moment to think, she answers, "I'm just feeling your pain, sweetheart. I've been at college, too."

"You remember back then?" asks Hannah, thinking she's being a smart ass.

"Like it was yesterday, my dear. Just like yesterday."

The main courses arrive. Suzanne has a baby spinach salad with goat cheese, pecans, tart apples, balsamic vinaigrette on the side, and for some extra protein, the suggested added sliced tenderloin. The girls both chose the same fancy sandwich: chicken, arugula and smoked gouda on an English muffin. Hannah ordered hers accompanied by a small salad, to counteract the cheese, as she puts it. Abby asked for hers with well-done French fries, which she eats as soon as the waitress sets the plate in front of her.

"I can't believe you, Mom," says Abby, half-eaten fry

in her mouth. Suzanne momentarily panics, thinking they're back to the cafeteria food discussion. "You, eating a salad for lunch. I think that's a first."

Hannah comes to her mother's defense. "Mom's been working out, can't you see? Why wouldn't she be eating right if she's going to all that effort?"

"I'm trying."

"And you're succeeding."

Suzanne smiles, drizzles a small amount of dressing on her salad and digs in with relish. She's a couple of bites in when she feels a cold breeze from the opening front door and looks up mechanically. A woman who seems vaguely familiar walks through the door, followed closely by someone who looks incredibly familiar. David.

Suzanne's fork hangs mid-air. Her mouth, jaw dropped to accept her food, remains open in shock.

The door has closed, and the two look at the hostess. Suzanne can read David's lips. "Two, please." The restaurant has thinned out, and the hostess turns to lead them to a table, just a few steps from where they stand, on the opposite side of the restaurant from where Suzanne and her daughters sit. They turn towards the trio as they make their way through the narrow passage between the tables. As David looks up, he stops suddenly. Suzanne could swear he's looking directly at her when he does—it seems almost as if he recognizes her. Her heart pounds as if it's looking for a way out, but David starts moving again, and she quickly reins both herself and her heart in. Of course David does not know her. He knows Shoshanna, not Suzanne. He's on a date, rejecting Shoshanna, not herself.

"Mom, what's the matter?" asks Abby. "You don't look too hot."

Suzanne forces herself to look towards the kids. "No, I'm fine," she says, sounding anything but. She can't help herself, and she turns her attention once more to David. He's sitting at his table with his back to her. The woman he's with—another faculty member from the music department, she's pretty sure—sits in her direct line of vision. A working lunch, Suzanne wonders? As if in response to her thoughts, David brings his hand up to the table and places it on the woman's. She looks up, seemingly surprised, but smiles and leaves her hand where it rests, under his.

A wave of nausea hits Suzanne just as it did this morning when she faced Joe and his "piano teacher." But she knows she has no right to feel this way. She and David had one kiss, and he's moved on. His right. One kiss. With Joe they had children together, shared years of life. But with David? One lousy little...

"A little young for you, don't you think, Mom?" asks Hannah, thankfully pulling Suzanne out of her private reverie.

"Huh?" questions Abby.

"Mom's looking at that hot new music professor. You know, the one who walked you home the other night."

"Don't give Mom the wrong impression," Abby complains then turns to her mother. "There was someone else with us. Some other student. They were passing by. Except it kind of looked like something was going on between them, if you want to know the truth."

"I guess not, since he's very obviously with Ms. Paere."

The two girls turn to look at once. David's hand still visibly covers Ms. Paere's.

"Player," says Abby. "Hmm. He seemed so nice. Old fashioned, too. I'm surprised."

"You're surprised?" argues Hannah. "Look at him. He's way too cute *not* to be a player."

"Enough," says Suzanne, since she *has* had enough.

"I'm here for lunch with you two, not some music teacher who can't keep his fly zipped."

"Mom!" both girls exclaim at once.

"Eat," says their mother, and she attempts to do the same.

Chapter 30

I WON'T GIVE UP

ONCE AGAIN, SUZANNE PULLS OFF the New York State Thruway, tears streaming, unable to finish the drive from Poughkeepsie to home. But this time, as soon as she comes to a stop, the tears start to dry up on their own and anger takes over, or at least tries to take over. She would love to feel anger towards Joe, but how can she? Just because he seemed happy with someone else? And David? She has no claim on him, none whatsoever. The real anger, truth be told, is directed at herself—her pathetic, brooding, *rejected by two men in one day* self.

*   *   *

It's a locker room, but which one? I think I'm in NYC. Let me get a look in the mirror, make sure who I am. Okay, yup, that's the old Shoshanna. Well, certainly not old, but not college age, either. The slightly older version of the young woman. So, I guess I *am* back in the city. It's been a while. I'm looking better than ever, though. Look at that shape! Look at that definition in my arms, my legs. Amazing.

Hmm, wasn't I just crying in my car? And here I am,

a second later, admiring the results of my weightlifting efforts. Well, isn't that much better than moping? The hell with them, if they don't want me. Look what they're missing!

A good workout, that's what I need. Concentrate on the weights so I don't think about *them*. Better to exercise, to look in the mirror while I'm exercising and see what they can't have. Well, can't have, don't want, let's not quibble.

I think maybe I'm jabbering away to myself so I don't think about him. Which him? Them. What's his face and what's his name. Shit, I'm doing it again. Get me out of this locker room and into the gym.

See? Better already. I love this place. The sounds of the clanging weights punctuated by the groans of physical effort. The smells of mingled colognes and shower gels tainted by sweat. The swarms of bodies appreciating the thousand-fold views of themselves and others in the mirrors strategically placed for maximum exposure and reflection.

Well, not really swarms. It's kind of empty, actually. Must be late. But it's still open for now, and I'm going to get a workout in. Start with a warm up. Maybe ten minutes on the treadmill. Right. This one's good—a good view of the weight room. That'll keep me entertained while I walk. It's too short a time to bother turning on the television.

Okay, I'll choose a manual setting. Push this, then that and... I'm off. I look up into the weight room and see only a few people, two men and one woman, and no one with the signature training shirt. Okay, so I wouldn't expect Rami to be here anyway at this time. He's worked a whole day probably. He should be home, in bed.

Wonder who he's in bed *with*? Okay, really not my

business. Except it could be my business, couldn't it? From the last time he worked me out? Standing so close. His huge muscles... more... up against me. The only time I felt anything so fucking hot, yeah, that was Rafael. And Rami's even stronger than Rafael, I think. Hmm... Was he serious then? Rami? Was he really saying he wanted me? No, he probably does that with all the girls. He uses the attraction, feeds their egos, to get them to sign up for more sessions—and then goes home to some other woman, I bet. I think a woman, but maybe not. You never know, but what a fucking shame if he actually *is* gay.

"I thought you didn't like me no more."

I'm so lost in my thoughts I don't realize the subject of my musing stands right before me, speaking his almost good English with the Israeli accent.

"Hmm," I chortle. "I still like you."

He smiles, chin down, eyes peering up through a lock of dark hair covering his forehead. I love that look—the short hair in the back but the longer tuft in front. I realize now he'd been in the weight room when I was watching, except at a distance and without the trainer shirt, I hadn't recognized him.

"Good. Why haven't you been here? But you look good. You cheating on me?"

His tone may be playful, but my thoughts go immediately to David, and my heart pounds, faster than is warranted by my slow treadmill pace.

"You been working out somewhere else, some other trainer?"

Oh, that's what he means. "Only you," I assure him and try to smile back.

"Again, good. Come on," he says, reaching up to the treadmill's control panel and slowing the speed. "The gym's closing soon. Come work out with me." He pushes the stop button and then turns towards the weight room, obviously expecting me to follow.

And obviously I do. "You're going to charge me?" I ask, only half joking. The boy's a hard worker, after all.

"Something like that," he says, but doesn't turn around.

Something like *what*?

He leads the way to the lat pulldowns, inserts the metal piece to set the weight, grabs hold of the bar and sits, tucking his legs under the thigh pads. He pulls the weight all the way down and stays like that for a little too long, his biceps at maximum flex. It's way too obvious he's giving me a little show, but I have to say, it *is* a damn good one, with arms as thick as Popeye's. No, that's not fair, because this body's proportions are anything but cartoonish.

Although he does each rep with measured determination, all too quickly he finishes the set. He gets up and gestures for me to take his place, moving the metal rod way up the stack of weights. I may be strong but nowhere in his league, so I don't take offense at his lack of confidence. I would never be able to budge the weight he just handled with ease.

I reach up, grab the bar already warmed from his hands, and start the pulldown. He touches my back softly when I get to full contraction.

"Hold it a few seconds."

I do as I'm told and look up, catching him watching me in the mirror, gazing at my front from his position behind me.

"I did good work," he says admiringly.

I slowly release the hold, allowing my arms to stretch all the way up before I start the next pull. In the mirror I see Rami's intent gaze. Wait, further back, way behind Rami, who is that? Oh, shit! It's him. That weirdo, the dark blond guy who seems to like to watch me. He's doing it again. And where did he come from, anyway? He wasn't here before.

He looks away, as if to hide his stares.

A sing-song bell sounds and a woman's voice comes over the audio system. "The gym will be closing in five minutes and will reopen tomorrow at five a.m. Have a good evening."

"That was quick," I say, disappointed. "Not much of a workout."

"I'll take care of it," Rami assures. "You finish your set." He walks away toward the front desk.

I look up expecting to see the strange man still staring at me, but, thankfully, he's nowhere around. I guess he took off, taking a hint from the announcement. I do as instructed and do more reps, finishing my set, idly wondering what Rami meant by taking care of it. Taking care of what?

In a few minutes, Rami returns. "They're locking up, but we will stay." He winks at me.

Right on cue, we hear a male and a female voice from the front of the gym call in unison, "Night, Rami," and a door closes and locks.

"Alone at last," I think to myself, cliché attempting to fight the sudden panic. But I'm not alone. I'm with Rami who, right at this moment, looks very little like a boy, and very much like a man. A hungry man. A hungry, hunky, Adonis of a man walking towards me and, oh no oh no oh no, taking off his shirt. He looks just like a photo of a magazine model—perfectly sculpted, hairless. I hope I'm not staring. I hope I don't have a stupid look on my face. I don't know if I want to throw up or come just looking at him. Holy, shit, he's practically my older daughter's age. But, of course, so am I. It's not wrong, right?

Wait—why is David suddenly popping into my head? And now Joe? You're a fucking idiot, Suzanne. Shoshanna. Goodbye, get out of my head. Look at what's in front of me. He's taking my hand and leading me someplace. The shoulder press bench? Are we still working out? I can't possibly have these signals wrong, can I? He's got his shirt off, for goodness sake! Okay, okay, you don't need to be forceful. I'll sit. Oh, I get it. He pushes me back into the angled seat so he has room to sit with me, facing me, our legs open wide against each other. Knees... touching. He's taking hold of my hands and lifting them. He wants me to take hold of the bar, above my head.

"Don't move," he says, almost under his breath.

I couldn't if I wanted to, and, believe me, I do not want to.

But *he* moves. He puts his hands on my hips and runs them slowly down, controlled pressure over my leggings, making his way from my thighs to my calves. He takes in a deep breath and closes his eyes. He says something, in Hebrew I guess, and I don't understand the words, but his body language definitely says he likes what he feels. I like this, too.

He opens his eyes and takes his hands off my legs, lifting them up to my shoulders. He puts his hands over my thin-strapped workout tank. "You're mine now," he whispers. I feel his large hands, rough from repeated contact with the weights and the other equipment, touching my exposed skin. Even more slowly, he brings his hands down my torso, along the sides of my breasts. I can't help but let out a sigh.

Rami sighs, too. "So beautiful," he murmurs as he leans in.

Reflexively, I lean back and close my eyes, waiting for his kiss.

"Don't."

I feel Rami suddenly pull away from me. Something's wrong. I open my eyes and see Rami looking off to the side.

What the fuck? It's that dirty blond intruding gawker! What the hell is he doing here?!

He's talking, that's what he's doing. "Don't. Please. Please don't do this."

* * *

What the hell is going on? Why are the lights so much brighter? Where's Rami? Where's that fucking annoying I'd-like-to-rip-him-apart man? Wait, I'm still in the gym. No, I'm not. I mean, yes, I am in *a* gym, but not the same one. I'm back at Vassar, I think. The Vassar athletic building.

I'm so angry, I can feel the heat in my whole body. Okay, maybe it's not from anger, since I'm sitting on a weight bench. I seem to be doing bicep curls. There I am, in the mirror. Right. The younger Shoshanna, back at Vassar for sure.

I put the dumbbells down. My head's not into this, and I don't want to hurt myself trying. I need to get out of here. This is not a place I can think in right now. And I need to think. Or maybe not think.

I get up and head towards the exit, looking down as I start taking off my weight lifting gloves. As I approach the glass door, I can hear it open, and I peek up so that I don't bump into the newcomer. Okay, now you've just got to be fucking kidding me! David? The person I want to see least in this—or any—world, except for maybe that sandy-haired interfering son of a bitch!

"Hi," he has the gall to say.

"I'm leaving," I have the gall to answer.

He follows me back out through the door of the weight room.

"Come for a walk with me."

Are you kidding me? Like I want to be anywhere *near* him? Besides, "It's freezing outside."

"The indoor track." He nods to the left, towards a room I've never been in.

I can't help myself, and I look at his face. He seems so sad. Hell, he always seems sad. He patented that look, but I'm not going to fall for it. I open my mouth to say an emphatic no. "Okay." Shit. Wuss.

I follow, like a little puppy, up the staircase to the elevated track that circles an area obviously used for various ball play. Right now some students play a friendly game of basketball. Maybe not so friendly. "Try not to cheat," I hear one of them say to another.

Yeah, that would be good advice for the man leading me onto the track as well.

Okay, that's a little harsh. I know I saw him with another woman, but, like I've said a thousand times, considering I'm not really a woman of his, I can't see that any cheating has taken place. That's not saying he's not an ass, of course, for the way he treated me after our kiss. You don't kiss someone and then ignore them.

A few other people use the track, but they're up about a half a lap ahead. David starts walking. He looks back to me, and I step onto the track and catch up to him. And we walk, not a peep, until, at almost the end of the lap, he turns to me. Okay, what's he got to say?

"Do you run?" he asks.

That's unexpected, although, duh, we *are* on a track. "Not well," I answer.

"Me neither. Let's try."

He takes off, and, like a continued jerk, I follow. It feels completely not like the treadmill, and, anyway, I only walk on the treadmill. I struggle to keep up. As we finish this lap, I look towards the staircase, wondering if I should make my escape.

David slows, and I follow suit, breathing way too hard for my liking. I'm happy to see sweat already forming on his brow. Good, I'm not the only one working hard. He picks up the bottom of his tee shirt and pulls it up to wipe his face, exposing his abs. Okay, so that's a shocker. Maybe not quite as hard and molded as Rami's, but, wow, I was not expecting that.

With his shirt down, he continues on the path we've taken, circling the track, walking this time, thankfully.

"Sorry," he says as I pull up next to him. "Just needed to work out a little... frustration."

He's frustrated. *He's* frustrated? What's he frustrated about? Women throwing themselves at him at every turn? Good thing he's not getting a view into *my* mind. Rami-interrupted, six-pack abs staring at me from all over the place. *That's* frustration!

"And I'm sorry, you know, for, um, for... "

Spit it out, buster. What are you sorry for?

"You know, it wasn't nice of me, not to... after we... I didn't mean to... "

Is he apologizing for not even acknowledging that we kissed? Or for immediately turning to another woman? No, I'm not supposed to know that, as far as he knows.

We've walked another lap, and I've had enough. I pull off to the side, ready to take the stairs down.

He's right next to me. "Anyway, I'm sorry. And I don't want you to... please don't... "

Again with the "Please don't?" What the hell does *this* one not want me to do?

"Listen, I have an idea. Why don't we do something fun. Together. Go out to dinner or something. Please?"

He's asking me out? Yes, he's asking me out, and he seems so sincere. Well, I have to say, "please do" sounds so much better than "please don't."

But I shouldn't. I really, really shouldn't... "Okay." Damn.

He smiles. Such a sweet, appreciative smile. "Really? You will?"

Okay, so how can I not, with him acting this way. "Yes, I will."

"Great. Okay, tonight then. Tonight?"

I nod.

He continues, "Can you meet me at my apartment? I'm just a couple of blocks off campus. Wouldn't look so good if I picked you up at the dorm... " he says, his voice fading.

I nod once again. He tells me the address, and I repeat it to myself several times, the only way to make sure I'll remember, but, truth be told, Shoshanna's college age neurons work much better in this regard than Suzanne's middle age brain.

We say our good-byes. Good-bye for now.

*　　*　　*

We say hello. It's evening, and I'm standing on the doorstep of his apartment—the top floor of a two-story home. He gestures me in, and I follow him through a small entranceway and into a living room cluttered with mismatched furniture, a couple of guitars on stands and shelves of music and books, exactly what you would expect to see in a young—unattached—music professor's home. Despite the off-white, bare walls, the place feels cozy and comfortable. Well, maybe that's not so much because of the look of things. Could be the smells. What is that? Smells really, really good.

"Do you mind," David asks, "if we stay in? I mean, I was thinking to go out, but, I don't know, I thought maybe a nice home cooked dinner. I don't usually cook, as you know from my visits to the dining hall."

And he's experimenting on me? "Well, that sounds very... appetizing."

He laughs. Hmm, I guess he gets my humor. "We'll be fine. I tasted it. Surprised myself, actually. And it's simple food. Hard to screw up steaks with sautéed mushrooms and onions."

Wow. That's one of my favorites.

"And sweet potato fries. From a bag, heated up, so can't really screw that up either. Unless I burn them," he says, running to the kitchen to check. I hear him open and close the oven quickly, so I guess they're not burned.

Funny, I love sweet potato fries. If he's got brussel sprouts, too, then it'll be a really freaky, mind-reading thing.

"I was going to make a vegetable, but I figured this was enough to handle for me, so just some salad with it."

Not a mind-reader, then. Just a coincidence. A nice coincidence. "Sounds great," I say, because it does.

"Good. Ready to eat? Oh, maybe that's rude? 'Hi, how are you, let's eat?' But fifteen minutes from now, it won't taste as good."

"It's perfect. I'm hungry." And besides, that solves the awkward before-dinner talk.

I follow David into the small, eat-in kitchen and see the tiny table set for two with plain white ceramic square plates and simple silverware. Two small matching white bowls already filled with greens occupy the spaces next to the dinner plates, and a bottle of wine sits between the two settings. No wine glasses, though, just glass tumblers.

"Not really space for a dining room in this apartment," he apologizes. "I probably should be thankful I've got a full bath and a bedroom."

David quickly busies himself, picking up the empty plates from the table and turning to the oven. "Please, have a seat," he says, his back to me.

It strikes me suddenly how odd this is, how odd I should feel. Strangers kissed, he ignored the moment, ignored the girl, the girl almost fucks some other guy in a gym after hours, and yet, here sits the girl, me, feeling... comfortable, at ease. Happy.

I think maybe either I'm a little screwed up or I've gone off the deep end.

Hell, I've been traveling through worlds, simultaneously twenty and fifty years old—I think I've been screwed up for a while.

David places my plate back in front of me, now with a strip of tenderloin covered with sautéed onions and mushrooms down one side and the other side full of well-done sweet potato fries—just like I like them. He puts his own plate down across from me.

"Oh, almost forgot," he says, heading towards the refrigerator. He returns with a small, white dish, like a creamer, which he places in front of me. "A little maple syrup, for the sweet potato."

I'm taken by surprise and can't help exclaiming, "Oh, that's my favorite way to eat them, sweet potato fries."

"Good. It, um... it said it on the, um, package, you know. To serve it that way. I, um, I hope you like it. And the rest of, you know, the dinner."

Why's he sound so nervous all of a sudden? I guess since he's not much of a cook? Is he really that worried about what I think?

David sits back down across from me and picks up his fork and knife. "Oh, sorry, no steak knives. Just the bare essentials, I guess."

"The life of a professor," I say. I try to cut the steak, and it goes through the meat easily. I spear the cut off piece of steak with my fork and show it to David as evidence, and he smiles. "Passed the first test," I say, smiling, too. I add some more onions to the bite and then put it in my mouth. It tastes buttery, tender, with just a hint of sweetness from the caramelized onions. "Wow, this is... delicious."

David beams. He tries a bite for himself. "It really *is* good. Who knew I could cook? Always left that for the wife."

Wife.

And clearly, by his expression, he hadn't meant for it to slip out.

Not sure what to say, I pretend the glaring word was unheard.

"And, you know, you heat up fries really well." I dip a particularly long and crispy one into the maple syrup, take a bite and then offer the small syrup dish to David.

He shakes his head. "Not much of a sweet and savory type of guy," he says, now over his informational slip, at least enough to continue the conversation.

I hesitate but then plunge ahead. "Neither was my boyfriend." Hey, he had a wife, I had a husband who will be known as a boyfriend, since Shoshanna's a little young to have an ex-husband.

David doesn't acknowledge the intelligence I've shared. He keeps his head down and takes a few more bites.

I take a bite of salad to give myself something to do. Balsamic vinaigrette. He's hitting a hundred today, with the food, anyway. Not quite with the conversation. I liked it better without the awkwardness. "Do you like teaching?" I ask to get us going again.

He picks up his head, thinking about the question. "I do, actually. It's... satisfying, in a way I haven't had before. Not sure about long-term, but, you know, it's a pretty good gig for now." He smiles at his little—very little—joke. "Get it? 'Gig' for a music teacher?"

Damn, he's cute. "Ha, ha," I say. "Cooking and a quick wit. What else could a girl want?"

"Oh, I forgot. Some dinner music, right? If we went to a restaurant, there'd be music." He gets up from the table and goes into the living room. In a moment I hear a quiet tune, not something I recognize but nice background music. David reenters the kitchen and, before he sits, he picks up the wine bottle from the middle of the table. "Forgot this, too."

He pours some wine into my glass.

"Oh, you don't want to card me?" I ask, then immediately regret it. Idiot! Why am I reminding him of my age? Of our age difference?

He stops pouring and begins to blush again. "Oh, I... I assumed... "

I lift my glass. "I'm just joking. Bad joke. I'm legal, believe me." He continues to pour but only about a quarter of a glass. Okay, that'll do for now. I take a sip. "Mm. That's good."

He takes a tentative sip as well. "Yeah, it is. That's lucky, because I picked it for the picture of the dancing bull." He points to the bottle and laughs again. Good, we're back on track. And, I have to say, picking a bottle of wine because of a funny picture on the label—I like that. Certainly not a man putting on airs.

We finish our food in silence, but this time the quiet has returned to the comfort zone. I eat until I'm bursting. It's been mostly lean frozen foods or the cafeteria fare for me lately, and this familiar meal, this touch of home—my home, when I cooked for my family—goes down really easily.

David gets up to do the clearing and washing, and I join him. I'm a little surprised he doesn't object to my help, but I'm happy he does not. It's a nice feeling, working together on this small chore. A surprising feeling.

Once we've cleared everything except the bottle of wine and our glasses, David goes to the table, pours a little more wine into the glasses, hands one of them to me then leads the way into the living room. He sits on the couch, and I sit next to him, but not too close, sipping my drink.

I hear the soft rolling tones of a melancholy song playing from his docked iPod. I recognize it instantly as Adele's *Someone Like You*. She's bemoaning the fact that her man found someone else. Ouch, that's a little too close to home.

He takes an unusually long swig and looks up directly into my eyes. "Did you love him? Your... boyfriend?"

Okay, was not expecting *that*.

Adele continues. Did I fail, like the woman in the song, to give what my husband needed? Ouch again.

David waits for me to answer. "Yes, I did. At the beginning. Very much." Well, that's a truth I haven't faced in a really long time.

David's odd response of relief continues to take me by surprise. He leans back into the couch. "I loved my wife, too," he confides. "Very much." His eyes have become a little red around the edges, although he doesn't cry. He does take another sip of his wine.

"Did she... " I have to ask "die?"

"Oh, no. No, no, no. Not that. She," he looks again straight into my eyes, "she didn't want me anymore. She told me we were done, and that was it. We were done."

"But you still loved her?"

"Yes. Still. I still do."

Wow. He still loves his wife. "Then why didn't you

fight for her?" And why is he here with me?

"Because I don't think she..." the pain is palpable in his eyes, "she didn't want me to."

This time I take another swig. This is hitting way too close to home. I asked Joe for the divorce. He didn't fight it. "I'm sorry."

"I think," he says. "I think I didn't make her happy."

We're quiet for a moment as the song continues.

After a few more moments, I find I have to make a confession. "I don't think I made my... boyfriend happy either. I mean, I thought I had, but, you know, then I saw him recently. With another woman. Smiling. Laughing. He didn't act that way with me." Now it's my turn for the red eyes. Don't cry. Don't cry!

"It's hard to feel rejected," David says quietly, head down, but then he looks up at me. "I'm sorry. I'm so, so sorry."

What exactly is he apologizing for? His sad mood? Or remembering back to kissing me and how he rejected me after? The mood's definitely taken a turn south. Maybe I should leave? I should...

I look up and see his guitar in the corner of the room. "Will you play something for me?"

He seems to think about it, then gets up and stops the iPod, moving over to his guitar. He takes it off its stand and brings it back to the couch. He looks so natural with it, the way he holds it, sits with it. He plays so naturally, too, as though the music and the guitar are a part of him. I don't recognize the piece—a classical Spanish song—but I connect to it, to him playing it, immediately.

His joy in making music so apparent, before the song has finished, both of our moods have reset back to the lighthearted start of the evening. He finishes with an exaggerated flourish, and I can't help but giggle.

"You have a cute laugh," he comments.

"Well, I'm a cute girl," I counter.

"That you are. Okay, it's your turn."

A little student panic sets in. "I am so not going to play the guitar for you." In the practice room, in a lesson, yes. But here?

He grins. "Not asking you to. I'll play. You sing. I love to hear you sing."

I'm about to refuse but then think why not? And, anyway, he doesn't give me much of an option. He starts to play without my response, a gentle picking and strumming of the strings.

"Do you know this, *I Won't Give Up*? Jason Mraz's song?"

Indeed I do. I love this song and start to sing, accompanying his playing rather than the other way around.

As I sing, I watch him. He looks down, concentrating only on his guitar. What does he think as he plays? Why does he always seem so sad? Because of his wife? Or is it more?

Suddenly, David joins in, singing harmony. What a beautiful voice—a little rough, a touch raspy, but a genuine, heartfelt sweet sound. And the lyrics... I have to remind myself he's just singing a song. It *feels* like he's talking to me, telling me he won't give up no matter what, but it's definitely too soon for words like that.

I stop singing, but he continues to the end of the song, the last few words not more than a whisper. He puts his guitar down on the couch and walks over to his iPod in the docking station. In a moment, I hear the song again, but this time Jason Mraz sings it. David walks back over to me and extends his left hand. "I wanted to take you dancing tonight."

I put my right hand in his, and he gently pulls me to

standing. In one more slow, deliberate move, he pulls me closer, but not too close, his left hand encircling my back. I rest my left on his shoulder, and we begin to move in time with the beat. I never realized before—this song is a waltz.

Maybe there's not so much room in this cozy apartment, but when we move, it feels like an entire dance floor has opened up. He leads with fluid movements, swaying, turning, one, two, three, one, two, three. He doesn't stop looking into my eyes, and I can't stop looking into his. And with his strong but tender arms around me, even though I'm dancing in the arms of an almost-stranger, in an apartment I've stepped into for the first time, in a world that's not my own, I feel... at home.

A final twirl and the music stops, too soon. David lets go of me, but, before I can protest, he brings his hands to my face, holding me lovingly. He bends and our lips meet.

A tender kiss. A loving kiss, with lips so soft and sweet, so full. I close my eyes and melt into him, and I feel his hands move from my face to my back, never losing contact with me. The kiss deepens, and I feel his longing, his need, and they match my own. He picks me up, and I wrap my legs around him. He carries me with ease through an open door and into his bedroom.

I hardly see the room, but I feel him place me on the bed. I look up. He doesn't touch me now, but gazes at me with an aching, profound desire. I feel my skin burning and my own desire pulsing. He sighs and says something under his breath. What, what was that? Anyway, I can't think now. My body's pleas have taken over. He begins to unbutton my blouse from the top down, too slowly, too damn slowly. Is he doing it on purpose? I reach down and help, unbuttoning from the bottom. He smiles and goes faster. He stops only for a fraction of a moment, when he sees my necklace and touches it pensively. I groan—involuntarily—with impatience, and he picks back up where he left off...

* * *

He's sleeping, I think. I'm definitely not. He's lying on his side, away from me. I see his bare shoulders and a little of his back. To be honest, I'm surprised it's not scratched up—from the heat of the moment, as they say.

It's morning, and I'm pretty sure I didn't sleep at all. Of course, we didn't even *try* to sleep until well into the night, and then I couldn't. Was it my fault for wanting to replay it in my mind over and over? What right-minded woman wouldn't? I think what made it so incredibly sexy and passionate was his unbelievable need for me. And, I have to admit, my need for him. More than physical.

Holy crap! I hardly know this man. Why am I having these feelings? Is it possible? What is *wrong* with me?

It was just great sex.

Wasn't it?

I don't want to move. I don't want to wake him, because, well to sound like the sappy school girl I kind of am, I don't want this magical night to be over. But, to be honest, I've had to pee for about an hour now. How come I don't have the bladder of a school girl, too? Maybe it was the wine? Oh, shit. Was the "magic" the wine, too? No, it couldn't be. I probably only had a glass, if that. The drinking got interrupted by the singing, the dancing, the...

Okay, I'm getting up. If I wake him, I wake him, but it's better than an accident in his bed.

I sit up as quietly as I can and look around the room. I didn't get to see it last night. We entered so quickly, in the dark, and I certainly didn't pay attention to my surroundings. A small room with the bare necessities: bed, night table, dresser. Three doors, and one of them must be the bathroom, because I didn't see one off the living room. One door is open, but it's the door we came through, so I figure the other two lead to a bathroom and a closet. A fifty-fifty chance of picking the correct door. I tiptoe over to the closest one and open it slowly. Of course, it's the closet. Not much in there, though. Doesn't he own more clothing than this? He really is the lost professor type.

I quietly make my way to the other door, which, thankfully, opens to the bathroom. It may be small and terribly out of date, but it works.

In a moment, I'm back in the bedroom. I thought I had been so quiet, but he's sitting up, watching me from the bed. He doesn't look lost now and not sad, either. He looks hot, and possibly horny, which to me at this moment feels like the perfect combination. I smile at him.

"Hold that thought," he grins at me, then hops off the bed, quickly puts on a pair of boxer shorts and darts into the bathroom. I forgot I'm almost naked, too. Just wearing his shirt. So clichéd but so much fun.

I get back onto the bed and cover myself, more because the room feels cold than because of any modesty.

Before I know it, David returns from the bathroom, but in those few moments, his mood seems to have changed.

"I have to tell you something," he says as he gets into bed next to me, sharing the covers.

Oh, no. That was a great night, a near perfect night. Please don't ruin it.

He's about to, though. I can tell from that pained look in his eyes. Just keep it to yourself, buddy, whatever it is.

"I slept with another woman."

What? Huh?

"Um, you did tell me you were married. Kind of didn't think you were a virgin."

"No, not... I, um, I had sex with another woman *recently*."

And I almost fucked a hot-shot muscle man on a weight lifting bench in the middle of a wide-open gym, but you don't see me confessing to that, do you?

"But we were over. You have to know that. Long over," he says, not making any sense whatsoever.

I get a sinking feeling in my stomach. It comes on suddenly, in a huge wave. You see? This is exactly why you should not fall into bed with someone too quickly. It takes a long time to get to know their crazies. Shit.

"I think I'd better go." I start to get up from the bed. He grabs my arm, and I turn to try to get out of his hold. As I do, I see some framed photos on the bedside table. I do a double take. Oh, shit! Fuck, shit, holy hell! Why does he have pictures of *my kids*? Recent photos of *my children*. Candid shots, like they had no idea they were being photographed! I'm going to throw up. Literally, I'm about to throw up.

I've got to get out of here. And maybe call the police. He's stalking my children... what have I gotten into? What the fuck have I gotten into? Why *my* children? And he doesn't know they're mine. He couldn't possibly know!

He sees me looking at the photos. He sees the horror in my face and rushes around the bed, coming towards me.

"You don't understand," he says.

"Stay away from me."

But he doesn't stop. I hastily lean down to the floor

and scoop up my clothing then turn to the night table and pick up the two framed photographs. I can't leave them here.

Now he's right next to me, grabbing my arms. Where's my cell phone? I need to call the police. Please, just let me go.

"Stop," he pleads.

I don't stop.

"Suze, please."

What?

What did he call me?

Suze?

I look at this stranger, holding me against my will and, suddenly, he changes, his face melting Dali-like, and he morphs into... holy shit! The creepy stranger from the gym? What the hell is happening? Did David drug me last night? Am I seeing things? I have to be seeing things, hearing things. What's going on?

The man holding me morphs again, now back into himself, but no sooner is he David again when he changes once more, and his whole body seems to darken. He comes into focus again, and the first thing I see is that he's fully dressed. All dressed up in a tux. I look up to his face. Joe? But not Joe, not the one I know now. The one I knew then, a young Joe. I turn my head and see us in the mirror over his dresser, the young Joe in a tux and a young Suzanne—me—in my wedding gown.

Forget the police. I need the hospital. What the hell did he slip into my wine?

We change again. We're still Joe and Suzanne, but now I'm me, my current age, and "Joe" looks like he did when I saw him sitting next to his music teacher.

I know I should try to run, but I can't keep myself from looking, first into the mirror, then at the morphing man in front of me.

Another moment and we change back again into the people we're supposed to be.

David still holds one of my arms, that is, Shoshanna's arm, but with the other he reaches into the drawer of the nightstand and pulls out... my necklace? How did that get in there? Did he steal it while I slept? I instinctively reach up to my neck, expecting to feel smooth skin where the necklace should be. Huh? I don't understand! The necklace! But if I'm still wearing it, then what's that in his hand?

He's holding it up and speaking to me. I have to concentrate so I can hear what he's saying. "Suzanne, she gave one to me, too."

"What?" is all I can squeak out.

"Cybil. She gave me a pomegranate necklace, just like yours."

Chapter 31

REALLY TRULY

"ARE YOU BETTER?" DAVID ASKS me. Okay, so he's Joe, not David, but right now he *looks* like David.

I'm so confused. I push myself further back into the couch, legs crossed, and lower my head, eyes covered by my hands.

"You look better, anyway. Not so green." Even more odd to hear his voice when I can't see him, sounding exactly like it's David sitting next to me.

"Well, now that I know some sicko's not after my kids."

"Sorry. I guess that was weird."

I raise my head out of my hands. "Weird? Weird?! Take a look at us, Joe. David. Joe."

He laughs the David laugh with the David smile.

"Well—Shoshanna, Suzanne, Shoshanna—at least you know I wasn't really *planning* on having sex with you. I mean, I sure as hell wouldn't have had those pictures by my bed if it was premeditated, right?"

I guess he has a point.

"I was just too damn hot. You couldn't resist me," I say flippantly.

He's anything but flippant as he inches closer to me and pulls on my arm, straightening it and running his hand from my shoulder down to my palm. Then he places that same hand on my upper thigh. I unfold my leg as he caresses down past my knee, finally resting on my calf. "You have no idea," he answers, seriously.

His touch feels... incredible. Okay, maybe a little freaky, but so... no, stop. This is not the time to be listening to my body. This is the time for talk. But the touching feels so... I should start with something easy. "Where'd you learn to dance like that?"

"You liked that, huh? Women love a man who can dance."

Honey, you don't know the half of it.

"It was one of the places I went to. I took classes."

"Wow. That's... fascinating."

"Are you being sarcastic?"

"No. Really, truly, I'm not."

"Do you want me to show you some more moves," he leers.

"No, I do not."

"Really truly?"

"Now you're making fun of *me*."

"Sorry."

"And, yes, maybe I do want to dance with you, but right now I want to talk more. Can we?"

"I don't know if I *do* want to. I might not like what you want to talk about."

"Was it true, what you said?"

"What I said?"

"Your confession. You had sex recently."

"And there you have it, exactly what I don't want to talk about."

"We need to, Joe."

He sighs. "I know." But he stays quiet.

I prod him. "You were willing to talk before. Insisting, actually."

"But you weren't you. I mean, I knew you were you, but you didn't *know* I knew."

"You know, you sound a little bit crazy."

"What's not crazy these days?"

What, indeed? But no turning back now. "Was it your date? The one at the movie theater?"

He shakes his head.

"Why not? She was hot." No denying it.

He gets up and walks towards his guitar. "And vacuous. No, I didn't sleep with her."

I feel weirdly disappointed, but I guess I know why. It wouldn't seem so bad if it were her, a little fling. Because if it wasn't her... "The music teacher, then?" I ask reluctantly.

He stops, his hand on the neck of the guitar.

And there goes Silence speaking way louder than I want her to.

Why did I need to know? I feel the tears forming in my eyes. I think fleetingly of Rafael and realize I'm an incredible hypocrite, except I never shared a piano bench with Rafael, never sat laughing so intimately with him.

Suddenly, Joe seems to have the need to talk—just when I'm thinking I would like him to shut up. "But I waited... a long time. We didn't... nothing happened... until after we—Shoshanna and David, I mean—after they, we, kissed."

"So, you kissed me and you said to yourself, 'Wow, this is so good, I think I'll go and fuck someone else?'" Is this him trying to make me feel better? "And, by the way, *that* was sarcasm."

"Really? Because I couldn't tell." I never realized how infectious cynicism could be, but he looks remorseful immediately. "It's because... because I felt that, if you could kiss David with such incredible passion, then you really didn't want Joe, want *me* anymore. You moved on." Okay, so the sarcasm's gone, all gone. "I figured I should finally move on, too."

He looks down, touching the scroll of the guitar.

"But then I saw you in the gym with that prick. The first time, with him touching you that way, you were doing the squats—what the hell was he whispering to you anyway?—only I didn't know it was you. But this time? How the hell could you let that kid touch you? He was going to..." He clenches and then unclenches his fist.

"Yes, he was. Until you interrupted. Oh, you brought me back to Vassar, didn't you? I couldn't figure out how I got there so suddenly."

"I guess I did. Still not sure exactly how it works. I don't think I can control it. Can you?"

I shake my head.

"Well, anyway, it worked that time. I mean, I got you away from him." He looks at me. That expression of guilt, that's not one I've ever seen on Joe's face before. "Sorry." A guilty apology, yes, but somehow he doesn't really seem very sorry.

"You sounded pretty much like a madman, you know, at the gym, yesterday. But, I guess it all makes sense now. You're fucking Joe."

"Yes. Yes, I am. And you're Suzanne."

We're quiet for a few moments.

And it strikes me. "How did I not figure this all out? *You* did. Am I such an idiot?"

"It's not your fault. I had an advantage. You looked the same—here and at that other gym. Maybe a teeny bit older, but the same." He says "other gym" with such disdain that it's almost funny. "But it still took me a while, after I saw you there, so who's the idiot?"

"Okay. Then when *did* you figure it out?"

He hesitates. "When we walked Abby home. Remember? I dropped the book. You bent to pick it up, and I saw the necklace. And even then it took a while to put it all together. Why you were showing up in two of my... places. Why you acted so weirdly around Abby. Why you were so different from the other students, so mature."

Confusion after the kiss. Confusion, not rejection. Odd how it makes me feel better, even after I have the whole picture. It makes me more relaxed. "I guess you like the maturity, huh? Not so much all the hot co-eds throwing themselves at you?" I tease.

"What is it with you and 'hot?' And, no, I didn't go for any of them." He smiles. "Although, let me tell you, I could have had my pick. Life's tough for a guy who looks like this." He fans his hand down his body.

"You like that body, huh?"

"I believe, judging by last night, that *you* like this body, too."

"Cool it, tiger. I mean, it's not like we've never had sex before."

"Sex like that?"

Let's not go there right now. "That's nice you have the photos of the girls. I mean, I didn't think so this morning, but, now that I know... it's nice," I comment, deftly changing the subject.

A credit to him, because he goes with the flow, even laughs. "I'm glad no one saw me taking the pictures. I was trying hard to pretend I was shooting some buildings, flowers, anything but them. I didn't want to get fired, and I certainly don't think the school wants a peeping Tom."

"Doubtful. And, by the way, you had to wait until we

got a divorce to start cooking?"

"In my defense, I never had to. And this was my first chance, anyway, to cook for a twenty-something, body building co-ed. Couldn't pass that one up."

I can tell he means it light-heartedly, but now it's my turn to feel guilt. I waited until after the divorce to get in shape.

He joins me on the couch once again and brushes his hand on my cheek. "Hey, I didn't mean it like that."

I don't know what brings it on—maybe his touch—but suddenly I remember clearly the words I couldn't understand last night, the ones he said under his breath right before we made love. *"I think I've always loved you more than you've loved me."* That's what he said. Why could I not understand it last night? And the other words, about his wife, that he hadn't made her happy—I remember those words, too.

It was Joe speaking, not David. Joe speaking about our life together. Joe giving me the divorce that I wanted, giving me up because he hadn't made me happy.

I try to fight back the tears, but they creep down my cheeks, and I can't brush them away fast enough to escape Joe's detection.

"I'm sorry," is all I can think to say as he looks into my eyes.

"I'm sorry, too," he says as he takes my hands in his.

I don't want to ask the next question, only because I'm not sure what I want the answer to be, but it's kind of unavoidable. "So, where do we go from here?"

"From here?" he repeats as he lifts my hands to his mouth and places a gentle kiss on my clenched fingers. "From here we do something we've never really done so much, before now, anyway. We continue to talk."

I'm not sure he can hear my little sigh of relief, but I

smile, and he can plainly see that.

"Okay. But can we take a short break? I'm kind of hungry."

Now it's his turn to smile. "Sure."

"I'll cook this time."

"Sure, again," he says, but he stops me as I'm about to get up off the couch. "I love you, you know."

The words startle me. Do I know? Did I ever know? And me who? Suzanne? Shoshanna? I can't help asking. "Which me?"

He looks surprised by my question. "All of you, put together. That's who you are. Just like I'm all of me put together. We've just been forgetting parts of ourselves."

I look at him in awe. "You've gotten wise in your old—young—age."

He laughs. "I guess that's what being a professor does for you." He stands up, bringing me to standing with him, then taps me on the butt. "Now, go cook some breakfast, Woman."

I don't move.

He changes his tune, but still playful. "Please? I did okay last night, but twice in a row? That's pushing it."

"Okay, I'm going." I say, but as I head for the kitchen, he pulls my hand one more time, twirling me and bringing me close to him.

"Really gotten good at this dancing thing," I comment.

"Thanks."

Then I can't help asking, "So, you were never a Cuban superstar on a prime time dancing show, were you?"

"Huh?"

"Never mind. Let's have breakfast."

Chapter 32

CUPID AND PSYCHE

I STEP OUTSIDE MY CAR and close the door. I distract myself as I walk up to the front door of the building by thinking about these last few months. It's taken a while to get things in order, but I can finally get this done, and this certainly will be one of the easier things I've had to do lately.

What's been the most difficult?

Talking things through with Joe? No. Surprisingly, that seemed pretty natural, well, after we got going, anyway. I guess after all we've been through, maybe it's not so surprising.

The fact that I stopped "traveling" to other places? Yeah, I have to say I miss that, but not as much as I would have thought. Maybe because we're making new adventures now. Wow, do I sound corny. Okay, doesn't matter, because it's true. Dance lessons. The band. I mean, who the hell starts a band at fifty? Well, why not? And who cares if it's just to entertain ourselves and our friends? Maybe we'll even get a small gig or two. Who knows?

Should we give the necklaces back to Cybil? They no

longer work, at least they don't seem to. But she hasn't asked for them back, even when we visited to say thank you.

Not telling the girls, especially when they were home over winter break? Yeah, that was a bitch. But we had to work things through. Couldn't tell them, "Oh, your father and I are trying to get back together," and then not have it happen, right?

So, keeping everything from the kids while they were home was pretty difficult, but not any more so than the daily horror of going to work. Five days a week stepping into a place I hate—what a waste of a short life.

Well, that's about to change right now, isn't it? Only sorry it took these months to set things up, get enrolled in the local college. Can you imagine me back at school? I know I've done it recently, but that was in a totally different body, a different world. Would be nice, of course, if I knew what I wanted to study exactly. Even nicer to know what I'll do after, but, hell, I'll figure it out quickly. I'm wiser now, at least I think I am.

I'm at the front door. I take a deep breath of the warm spring air, pull the handle and walk through. "Morning," I say to the receptionist as I head down the hall, straight to my boss's office.

"Do you have a minute," I ask when I find him there, but I don't really care what he answers. "I quit," I say matter-of-factly. "I'll give you two weeks, if you want them, but just know that I think you're a complete ass, a nasty individual, and I despise how both you and the company have treated me."

I have to say, the shock and panic in his face feels quite satisfying. I turn to leave his office. "Think about it," I say over my shoulder as I head to my desk to start straightening things up.

Yes, quite satisfying.

What a weird feeling, being back on the Vassar campus. Even stranger to be holding Joe's hand. No one can say it's inappropriate now, though, two parents holding hands, strolling through campus. Lots of parents are here, anyway, for graduation. Hannah's college graduation. She's finishing, I'm starting back up with the summer semester...

Joe and I had agreed we would wait until we were all together to tell the girls their father has moved back in. A little graduation gift for Hannah and an end-of-the-year surprise for Abby. Well, in truth, we didn't want to field all the inevitable questions, didn't want to jump too far ahead, and, I think, we selfishly didn't want to share this time with them.

But today it feels right, and I'm more than eager to spring the news. I guess Joe is too, and we got to campus a little early, earlier than the girls expected us. We kill time by heading to the library.

As we walk on this campus, where so much took place, I can't help but ask a question that's been on my mind for a while. "Do you miss her?"

"Who?" asks Joe. "The girls? Of course I miss them."

"Not 'them.' 'Her.' Shoshanna. She was prettier. Firmer. Maybe more fun?"

He stops walking and turns me to him. "You're pretty damn firm, you know." He kisses me. "And fun. Anyway, I have what I want, thank you very much." He kisses me again. "I have what I want."

I smile, and we continue on our way.

In a couple of minutes, we reach the library. As always, it takes my breath away, and that's just the outside. As soon as we walk inside, we see a group standing ahead of us, just up the stairs in the "tower" room. A tour group. Funny to have our girl graduating while others have just begun to search, but that's life, isn't it?

The group as a whole looks up at the ancient tapestries hung high above the ground. The tour guide is another student, but not the same one who had illuminated the story of Cupid and Psyche the last time I heard it.

"Some think," the young woman explains, "their story is only about romance and the fight for a happy marriage, but others realize it's much more than that. Psyche is put through incredible challenges to win Cupid, and I think that's what the story is really all about—about jumping through hoops, suffering and fighting all the challenges, the difficulties of life in order to, ultimately, achieve happiness." The young woman turns her eyes from the tower back to her audience. "Sorry, can't help it. The English major in me." The group laughs. "Moving on..."

And Joe and I, still holding hands, move on by ourselves, a slow private tour through this magnificent library, sections visited many times before and, yes, some places as yet unexplored.

The End

*   *   *

Reading Group Guide for

The Pomegranate Blooms

1. What do you feel best describes the theme of this novel? A love story? A magical voyage? A sexual awakening? A journey of self-discovery? The struggles of realizing a happy life?

2. Some people say the worst time to decide on divorce is during your hormonal, mid-life, menopausal years. Do you think Suzanne made the right initial decision to divorce Joe?

3. Who and what exactly is Cybil? Is she magical? Crazy? An ordinary woman with some extraordinary gifts?

4. Have you ever had a dream about having sex with a stranger? Did you feel guilty afterwards? If you've never had such a dream, do you think you would feel guilty? And do you think your reaction would be any different if that stranger happened to be a famous and gorgeous star?

5. What are your thoughts about Rafael? Was he good for Suzanne? Was he good *to* Suzanne? And what about Rami?

6. Joe gives Suzanne an exquisite pair of earrings for her fiftieth birthday—a gift she can never use since she no longer has pierced ears. Why do you think

Suzanne keeps quiet about this? Would you have said something to Joe?

7. What do you think of Suzanne's jealous reactions to seeing her ex-husband with other women—at the movie theater, the intimate moment she interrupts at his house? Does she have the right to her jealousy? How would you react?

8. We don't see much about Joe until the end of the novel, and anything we do see is through Suzanne's eyes. Is that fair to Joe? Or does that fairness matter in this book?

9. What are your thoughts on Suzanne reconciling with Joe? Did she make the right decision? Would you have made that decision?

10. Did you know David's true identity before it was revealed? At what point did you figure it out and what clues led you to that conclusion?

11. Although the story is told from Suzanne/Shoshanna's point of view, we see David/Joe's behavior changes frequently, from friendly to distant, from smiling to sad. What do you think David/Joe is going through? What are some of his thought processes?

12. The decision of what point of view to write from is a major one for an author. Authors have been known to write an entire novel in one point of view only to rewrite it later in a completely different one. This author made the decision to use two different points

of view in the book, one for the non-"dream" world and the other for the "dream" world. What are those two points of view? How do they affect how you feel while reading? Why do you think the author chose to write in this way?

13. Recalling the conversation Suzanne and Lori have in the car at the gym—the one where they debate how Suzanne has mysteriously become so physically fit— what are your thoughts on aliens and alternate realities? Do you believe in them? Do you feel, as Suzanne suggests, that it's not logical *not* to believe in them?

14. Why do you think Cybil chose Suzanne as the recipient of the necklace? Do you feel Cybil chose wisely? Why or why not? Do you think others— besides Joe—have received this gift as well?

15. All through her time in college, Suzanne/Shoshanna debates whether she should be following her physical desires or her brain. Which path do you think she should follow? Which path have you followed?

16. And the biggest question of all: thongs or big cotton whities?

If your book club has graciously chosen to read *The Pomegranate Blooms* and would like to have Cindy Katri call or Skype during your discussion, please contact her via www.cindykatri.com.

CINDY L. KATRI, born Cindy Lenorowitz in Queens, New York, was raised in Commack on the north shore of Long Island. She graduated from Vassar College with a degree in English and broke into magazine publishing—on the business end—soon after. A number of business careers and numerous works of creative writing later, she now finds herself living in northern New Jersey with her husband and two teenage daughters.

www.cindykatri.com

www.facebook.com/cindylkatri

COVER ART by Josh Nelson

http://nelsonarts.tumblr.com

Made in the USA
Lexington, KY
02 March 2014